THE BONE WEAVER

THE BONE WEAVER

A novel by
Victoria Zackheim

ELTON-WOLF PUBLISHING

Designed and typeset by Gopa Design
Front cover insert photo by Damien Eastwood

ISBN: 1-58619-021-0
Library of Congress Card Catalogue Number: 00-109695

Second Printing
Revised Copy October 2001
Printed in Canada

Published by Elton-Wolf Publishing
www.elton-wolf.com
206.748.0345
Seattle, Washington

ELTON-WOLF PUBLISHING

For my mother, Elizabeth
And my children, Matthew and Alisa

DUKE TO CESARIO:

Mark it, Cesario; it is old and plain.
The spinsters and the knitters in the sun
And the free maids that weave their thread with bones
Do use to chant it: it is silly sooth,
And dallies with the innocence of love,
Like the old age.

William Shakespeare
Twelfth Night

ACKNOWLEDGMENTS

WRITING THIS NOVEL has been a long and wonderful adventure; it is my good fortune to have had loving and dedicated fellow travelers along the way.

First of all, my heartfelt thanks to Aviva Layton, friend and editor, for believing in this story—and then taking me by the hand and guiding me through the final leg of this extraordinary journey.

My thanks and gratitude to Susan Sosnick Sabes, Michele Zackheim and Nancy Palmer Jones for astute proofreading and compassionate editing.

For moral support, love and encouragement, I thank my children, Matthew Sosnick and Alisa and Eugene Law.

If it were not for Lois Pendleton and Hazel Cox of Elton-Wolf, I would still be standing in the dark. Thank you for your patience and gentle tutelage.

As the journey progressed, this novel lived many lives. I would be remiss not to thank those who stood by me, inspired and motivated me through each rebirth. My thanks to Roy and Evelyn Jones, Richard and Dorothy Koerner, Shar Sosh, Robin Gammell, Rosemarie Mac-Dowell, Lee Chamberlin, Penny Fuller, Cynthia Benson, Aza and Richard McKenzie, Sharon Childress, Kathleen Archambeau, Barbara Wichmann of Artémia Communications, Charles Ramsburg, Kathy Latta, Letty Herndon, Carol Porter, Dale Rose, Barbara Heller, Daniel Banks, Barbara Fryer, BJ Bartlett, Ruth Ann Barrett, Tara O'Leary, Ellen and Mel Rosen, Ruth Cohen, Susan Fox, Rebecca Alger, and Carla Singer. In Europe, my thanks to Caroline Corre, of the *Centre Artistique de Verderonne*; Susan Langenkamp, Frank Dabba Smith,

Susana and Guillaume Franck, Monique Novodorsqui and the Deniau family; Frieda Menco; the late Lina Nahmias and Jose Kiestra. Friends all, and I thank you.

My gratitude to Elizabeth Zackheim, whose encouragement helped me fulfill the dream of living and writing abroad.

And to Damien Eastwood, you have earned (and earned again) my most loving thanks for reading the manuscript . . . and putting up with me through a long and sometimes exhausting process. Your faith in me has been more inspiring than you will ever know.

THE BONE WEAVER

CHAPTER ONE

✣ Topanga Canyon, Spring 1984

MIMI TRIED ON every suit in the closet before settling on the blue wool gabardine. A passion purchase, Sarah had called it, but the blue always reminded Mimi of the gentians that refused to bloom for her in the parched southern California climate. A bitter aftertaste of coffee rose in her throat; patches of perspiration were already staining her silk blouse. She pulled on the skirt. Its under-slip became snagged in the zipper and she made a little sound. A cry of alarm, she called it, but Sarah had always insisted it was more a bleat.

Sarah. How would she live without her most loving friend? The question caused her eyes to burn. Ordering herself to be calm, she examined the zipper, made one abrupt manipulation, rotated the skirt back into place, snatched up its matching jacket and rushed from the house.

Plowing through the traffic with tight-jawed determination, Mimi achieved the forty-minute drive between Topanga and her mother's apartment in less than thirty, numbed by the realization that she had made this journey with no recollection of having driven here. But then, surviving on the Ventura Freeway in a state of mental paralysis was child's play compared to what awaited her upstairs.

Just keep calm, she told herself. And for God's sake, try to be nice. It was a mantra Mimi had been chanting to herself for years and it was no coincidence that she was most often parked in this very spot when chanting it.

It took some energy to climb from the car, follow the line of junipers leading to the foyer, and then take the stairs to the second floor. Pausing on the landing, Mimi considered how much the building reminded her of an aging woman trying desperately to retain a semblance of youth. Not so unlike myself, she reflected. Stepping into the hallway, she was immediately hit with the odors of *pollo con arroz* and enchiladas. Once upon a time it had been blintzes, knishes, and *mandel broite*, but that was more than twenty-five years ago, when she had lived with her parents in their two-bedroom apartment on the third floor. It was a time when daughters lived at home until they were married, passing their time and learning those necessary household functions that, once mastered, identified them as a serious matrimonial prospect. By the age of twenty-six, however, Mimi figured she had waited long enough and one fine day, accompanied by two suitcases of clothing, fourteen cartons of books, and one leather-bound doctoral thesis, she moved to her own apartment in West Los Angeles. She had prayed mightily for a peaceful exodus, but Sarah's analysis had proven correct: That as long as Rivka Zilber lived, her daughter might be allowed to fold her tent, but she would never be able to steal silently away.

"Mama," called out Mimi, letting herself in. "Are you nearly ready?" When she saw her mother emerge from the kitchen, wearing robe and slippers, she nearly exploded. "You're not dressed. You haven't even started!"

Shuffling toward the bedroom, Rivka patted her only child on the arm. "Miriam," she responded. "I'll be ready when I'm ready."

Mimi felt the headache begin. "I specifically said I wanted to get there early."

"Early, a little after," came the voice from the bedroom. "We'll get there."

Mimi rubbed the space between her eyebrows. When she spoke, her voice was so calm it was nearly flat. "If you are not ready in five minutes, I will leave without you." No way in hell was her mother going to make her late. Entering the bedroom, she found the elderly woman standing before the opened closet, arthritic fingers sliding one plastic hanger after another along the rail. She'll choose the black wool, thought Mimi glumly.

Rivka came to the black wool, nodded decisively, and removed it from the closet. It was the outfit she always wore to funerals. Simple, austere, appropriately funereal. "Why not have a cup of tea?" she asked, laying the suit out on the bed.

"I don't want a cup of tea," Mimi grumbled. Any other time she might have chastised herself for this tone of voice, but not today. Today she was angry, dejected. How else could she feel, with Sarah being buried in less than an hour and her mother not yet dressed and wanting her to sit down for a damned cup of tea!

"Darling," Rivka informed her, traces of the Russian accent still lingering in the elongated first syllable, the clipped "ink" sound of the second. "Have a little patience for your old mother."

The flopping of bedroom slippers across carpet caused Mimi to grind her teeth. Any chagrin she might have felt was eclipsed by the clatter of water flowing into the tub. Rivka Zilber's baths were legend. "Longer than the Peloponnesian War, which went on forever," her father liked to tease. Today, it was not so funny. Working to bite back the anger, Mimi followed her mother into the bathroom. "How would you feel," she challenged, "if I were the one who died and it were Sarah and her mother coming late to *my* funeral?"

Rivka was sitting on the edge of the tub. Her right foot already submerged in water, she was laboring to drag her left leg over the side. How many times had Mimi begged her mother to confine herself to showers, the gymnastics required to climb in and out of the tub far too dangerous for a woman of her age? Filial duty again winning out, she offered a steadying hand.

"That's something you say to a mother?" scolded the old woman, lowering herself into the steaming water. "God forbid something should happen to you, my only . . ."

"Mama," interrupted Mimi, eyes squeezed closed, jaws clenched. "Nothing is going to happen to me, I promise."

"*Gott kholilie,*" came the automatic response. "From your mouth to God's ears!"

Before her mother had finished talking, an unsettling and long-held fantasy flashed through Mimi's head: She was picking up her bronzed tap-dancing shoes mounted on a block of polished oak; she was hefting that block high over her head; she was bringing it down onto her mother's skull with a blow so savage it sprayed her brains against the wall and left a swath of bloody tissue along the carpet. Anger, frustration and disappointment, she felt suffocated by them all. "Take your fucking bath," she seethed under her breath, jaws clenched to hold back the rage. Fearful that she might actually strike out, she fled, leaving her mother in the tub. The echo of a slamming door rewarded her with brief satisfaction. Climbing into the car, she heard Sarah's voice. "Got you again, did she?"

It was not until she arrived at the cemetery's wrought-iron gates that Mimi felt the full impact of what awaited her inside. Vertigo jolted her, caused her stomach to lurch and her bowels to churn. One deep stabilizing breath and she followed the arrows directing her to the parking area closest to the burial site. Locking the car, she stepped around the grave-studded labyrinth and joined Sarah's family.

Joanna, Sarah's only child, was seated in the first row of folding chairs. On her right sat her husband and their two children; on her left, the frail and ancient Mrs. Lehmann.

Mimi slipped into the seat directly behind Sarah's mother and rested a hand on her brittle shoulder. The woman acknowledged Mimi's presence by brushing a parchment-dry cheek against her hand. Mimi felt the dampness of tears and thought, children are not supposed to die.

Within minutes every chair was taken. The rabbi—a young man who, despite receding hairline and tortoise-rimmed Armani eyeglasses, looked like someone's kid brother—cleared his throat and began reciting the first prayer. A nice enough voice, thought Mimi, but she would hold off final judgment until the eulogy. When it came time, he went on and on, somehow managing to omit practically every one of Sarah's attributes. Nothing about the exquisite nature of her laugh, or her absolute dedication as a lifelong friend. To Mimi, it was the same old blah-blah from a man who had known this remarkable woman . . . without ever having known her at all.

When the eulogy was finally over, the rabbi slipped his notes into his bible, closed it with a slap that caused Mimi to flinch and then, with a gesture toward the gaping hole that was to be Sarah's place of rest, invited everyone to shift in that direction.

One after another they advanced, stepping around a green plastic tarp that moments earlier had been stretched across the maw of the rectangular trench. In the springtime freshness of this California morning, the mound of newly dug earth next to the tarp seemed better suited to the cultivation of orange trees than the interring of a casket.

Sarah's mother was the first to approach, both age and grief rendering her incapable of walking without support. She tried to use her cane, but its rubber tip sank into the soft earth and made the journey perilous. She was about to fling it angrily to the ground when Myron, Sarah's older brother, took it from her and hung it over his forearm. When he grasped his mother by the arm, she nearly staggered against him.

Mimi recalled Sarah's concerns for this old woman and a brother who had never quite managed the demands of adult life. How natural it had been to assume that one day *she* would be burying *them*.

A sudden wind blew across the gathering and lifted the rigid mass of Myron's hair. Mimi looked to the side, expecting to see Sarah giggling beside her. Poor Myron, unable to accept his balding gracefully, had grown it long and then combed it into a cluster over his glossy pate. The superhold hair spray worked well, except when a breeze passed by. When this happened, he had the appearance of a bird soaring in lopsided flight. Another gust caused Mimi to avert her eyes. Between the man's absurd hair and the memory of Sarah's describing it, she was afraid of laughing aloud.

Joanna brushed past Mimi to be closer to her grandmother, but stopped short when the groundskeeper rushed forward, his finger wagging as if to say, You want the earth to give way and make you tumble right down on top of your mommy's casket? Joanna gaped at him, stared into the grave, and then backed away from the edge.

Mimi allowed her eyes to drift from face to face. Some of these people had been known to her for a lifetime, others were nameless associates and acquaintances whose presence was more a sign of respect than intimacy. The pucker in Mimi's forehead softened when she recognized the man in the brown cashmere jacket. He stood on the far side of the trench, at the foot of the casket, head bowed and eyes closed, his lips moving in silent benediction. Bending his head even lower, he crossed himself.

How long has it been? Mimi wondered, watching David Gomez step aside so that another mourner could move closer. The question prompted an image of Davey Gomez and Mimi hiding behind his parents' La Toluca Market, the boy sweating as he groped under her crisp middy blouse for one more handful of copious breast. She suppressed a giggle and, turning away, nearly bumped into Daniel Kirsch. He was studying the casket and seemed oblivious to everyone around him. His face was creased by sorrows both past and present. They had been a teenage threesome—Daniel, Mimi, Sarah—and this was his second funeral in two years. Mimi could never forget the many hours she and Sarah had spent with Daniel during his wife's illness, the suffering they shared after her death. So many who have buried a spouse would use grief as an excuse to stay away, but not Daniel. He remained that nice kid from the Heights, the one who had walked Mimi to school nearly every day from third grade on.

When he turned away, stepped gingerly to avoid the mound of earth piled alongside, he looked back and saw his footprint in the dirt. As if fearful of defacing Sarah's grave, he dragged the sole of his shoe across the dirt and erased the mark.

The rabbi released a little cough and the air around the grave became instantly still. When he had everyone's attention, the lull was filled by another prayer, this one accompanied by screeching brakes and horn blasts arriving from the roadway just beyond the cemetery wall. Knowing what came next, a blanket of discomfort fluttered over the gathering and Mimi felt her muscles twitching with the urge to run.

The rabbi took a shovel and passed it to Myron, the loving brother and dutiful son. With his help, his mother scooped a shovelful of earth from the mound and dropped it onto the coffin. The shovel was then passed to Joanna, who flicked a few small clods into the trench. When she held the handle out for Mimi, there was a brief pause of indecision. Take it, said Joanna's eyes, and Mimi did as she was told. With hands and legs trembling, she pushed the wide blade into the mound, came up with a heap of earth and then, turning, dumped it onto the casket. Still clutching the shovel's handle, she fought a powerful urge to vomit.

Within minutes, Sarah Lehmann Arcario's final resting place

resembled a garden waiting to be planted. The rabbi stilled all movement with one sweeping glance and began reciting the Kaddish.
"*Yishgadahl, v'yishkadash sh'mei raba,*" he chanted, and those who
knew the mourner's prayer followed along, either mouthing words or
murmuring softly this prayer that came as second nature.

Mimi wanted to cry out, Tell them to stop! Tell them to go home!
Instead, she pressed her fingers against her lips until the prayer was
completed and the mourners began to move away: the pull holding
her there more powerful than the urge to flee. How she wanted to
drag that damned box out of its hole and announce that it had all
been a bad joke! If only their communal pain could coalesce and gen-
erate a force powerful enough to reverse the atrocity of Sarah's death.
The rabbi had just discussed life, and how everyone must entrust
their problems to the same benevolent power that was used as
justification for every holy war in history. What was so benevolent
about leaving behind a daughter, an elderly mother, two grandchildren and a devastated friend? Lowering herself with effort onto one of
the folding chairs, she closed her eyes.

"Are you okay?" Joanna was bending over her, her expression one
of concern. She took Mimi's hand, held it between her own, rubbing
it as if trying to warm it, and this gesture of kindness reminded Mimi
that she was not okay, not at all. "The two of you," murmured Joanna,
"you were really something." Looking away, she added, "You'll call,
won't you . . . whenever?"

Mimi made a humming sound in her throat. Standing with effort,
she pressed her cheek against the woman's and squeezed her hand.

Joanna pushed her fingers through thick auburn hair. It was
Sarah's gesture, Sarah's hair. What Sarah used to call her unruly
Semitic hair.

A boreal gust lifted a corner of the tarp and sent a fine sandy spray
around their feet and across the ground, settling it on the adjacent
grave where Joanna's father was buried. Two people Mimi loved; two
loving souls taken away decades before their time.

Mimi pulled the collar of her jacket close, kissed Joanna and edged
away. She was grateful that Sarah's daughter, concerned about her
grandmother's health, had decided to forego the expected reception
after the service.

The moment Mimi stepped into the parking lot she spotted the funeral sticker on the windshield of her car. Crushing it into a wad, she dropped it onto the gravel and climbed into her car. Before she could close the door, a face appeared at the window. Daniel Kirsch leaned so far into the Volvo that Mimi could smell the wool of his jacket.

"Will you be all right?" he asked.

Avoiding his gaze, she fished about in her purse for sunglasses. "Do I have a choice?"

He pushed himself upright and stared out over the roof of the car. "No," he murmured, "I guess you don't."

Mimi peered up and saw his vacant stare. When Daniel's wife was buried in this cemetery, the weather had been crisp and cool, with a light rain falling during the closing prayers. Daniel had expressed his concerns to Mimi that it had been too dreary a finale, but she had assured him that rain was cleansing, renewing. How could he stand on this same ground without reliving the pain? Mimi wanted to kick herself for indulging her grief.

As if sensing her anger and trying to smooth over the brief lapse, Daniel asked, "So how's work?" Her dazed look was answered with a sheepish grin and two hands raised in surrender. "Just promise you'll call if you need me," he said, touching her arm.

Mimi felt her resistance, as if she were backing away without actually having moved. She was tempted to ask why everyone assumed she needed their support, but knew how ungrateful it would sound.

"It takes time," reminded Daniel.

She studied her friend's face. His features taken separately were nothing special—medium-brown eyes, with crow's feet adding a touch of humor; flyaway eyebrows; a nose with no discernible features that would set it apart. And yet Daniel's was an interesting face, one suggesting character, sensitivity, wit. While his build was quite athletic, Mimi knew that his physical prowess was limited to leisurely hikes through the canyons and strolling the local beaches. Most touching, however, was the look in Daniel's eyes: it told her that he would always be there. And he had never let her down. Like the day after Sarah's death when he so patiently explained how Mimi had no control over her grief, that grief would continue to play havoc with her heart, toy with her soul, until it was finished with her and tossed her unceremoniously aside.

As if she needed to be reminded. Mimi understood too well how grief functioned independent of reason, that it could arrive in strange, unexpected forms and shake her to the marrow. Just the night before, it had attacked like a terrible virus. She had tried to ignore it, had even managed to evade it by attributing the distress to hunger. And then standing at the sink, eating directly from an out-dated carton of yogurt, she had begun to weep.

Sitting here in her car, only yards from Sarah's grave, she admitted to herself yet again that no one who lived in the world could be spared the pangs of mourning. Bile rose in her throat; her chest constricted so she could hardly breathe.

Daniel crouched beside the Volvo until his eyes were level with hers. "I'll be there when you need to talk. When," he repeated, "not if."

She forced down a sob with a hard swallow. "Talking," she grumbled. "What a waste of time." And then she laughed. "My God," she nearly gasped. "Will you please shoot me? I sound just like my mother!"

Daniel's eyes crinkled as his friend came to life. "And speaking of your mother . . ." Mimi grimaced and he shrugged. "I couldn't help noticing, could I? So is she ill . . . or what?"

Or what, she was tempted to respond. Which means sitting in that mothball-smelling apartment, stewing over her daughter's ruthless behavior and collecting fodder for the next confrontation. "Not ill," she said testily, "just nasty." Accepting a brotherly kiss on the forehead, she put the car into gear and drove off.

The ride home was orchestrated in a fog. Did her mother honestly think she could get away with making her late to Sarah's funeral? Mimi pressed a fist into her aching chest. She was reminded of those hackneyed songs about broken hearts, about being so lonely you could die. Until this moment, and the prospect of a life without her friend, she had considered these songs as little more than clichés. Tears were blurring her vision as she turned onto her road. By the time she pulled into her driveway, the tears became uncontrollable sobs.

❧Nowy Życie, Spring, 1887

Malka Gershon leaned into the doorway and squinted the length of the road in hopes of catching sight of her husband. Drying her hands absentmindedly in the apron's folds, she turned to discover the neighbor's horse ambling toward her vegetables. "Shoo!" she hissed, flapping the apron toward the mare. The beast turned her slow gaze in Malka's direction, took a leisurely nibble of greens, as if settling any question regarding proprietorship and clip-clopped away.

Malka knew how Grischa savored his walk home, how he used this time for reflection, for throwing off the day's tension. "If for no other reason," he insisted, "than to save my family from my bad humor." And in the latter part of the nineteenth century, with czarist policies stifling Jews throughout eastern Europe, there was bad humor to go around.

"Bad humor?" their daughter, Fredl, had responded. "Papa, you're the least ill-humored man I've ever known!" At sixteen, she had known very few.

Malka swatted at a fly buzzing near her face. Their children were due for lunch, so where was he? Meandering alongside that silly field, no doubt. What was it he had announced the last time she had accompanied him back to the store? That he could smell not only the fragrance of the vegetation, but their shapes and colors as well! Malka could barely suppress a scoffing retort.

Rubbing absentmindedly at a painful cuticle protruding from her thumb, she stomped back into the kitchen. "Foolish man," she mumbled, and then her face softened. Foolish, perhaps, but it had been his trusting nature—his belief that everything and everyone bad could be changed for the good—and his love for family and community that had convinced her parents what a good match he would be. A healthy balance, was how her mother had described it. Even a girl of seventeen understood this to be a not-so-oblique reference to her own unyielding nature.

Malka slipped the bread dough into the oven and checked on the simmering beets, the memory of that last walk lingering with her. "And can you tell me, my dear wife," Grischa had concluded, waving an arm toward his beloved countryside. "Who enjoys better fortune than a simple man living in the heart of such beauty?"

"I dare you to repeat that after the next pogrom," she'd nearly declared. But before she could speak, a colorful mass of birds rose from the field and flapped skyward, like a handful of pebbles cast by a farmer clearing his land. The joyful expression on Grischa's face had silenced her for the remainder of their walk.

Malka retrieved the earthenware jug from the porch and carried it down two steps, to the dirt path alongside the house. Grischa had begged her to get one of the girls to help, but his wife would hear nothing of it. She wasn't that old yet! Hoisting the jug onto the hook Grischa had fashioned for her, she pumped the handle until the vessel was near to overflowing. Hauling it with difficulty to the kitchen, Malka set about preparing a stock for the soup. It had occurred to her more than once that the calm her husband gleaned from that simple field was the same calm she enjoyed while cooking. She forced herself to focus on the herbs and spices, adding just enough to camouflage the too-lean chicken. Stirring, she slowly let go of her concerns about the stifling new laws limiting ownership of land, her worries about the deterioration of their daily lives. And the pogroms? The only real question was when, not if. Her escape was to cook, make everything around her seem lighter, more positive. A home could be replaced and their children could even leave Nowy Życie. As for the business: it provided the basics.

Of the several dry goods stores in Nowy Życie, theirs was the most successful. "If you don't find it at Gershon's," people said, "then you'll have to wait until your next trip to Warsaw." Such exclusivity should have diminished Malka's concerns, but it didn't, because something as simple as a neighbor owing a few kopecks and requesting an extension of credit could make her stomach roil. Grischa's lack of concern amazed her. "But why should I worry," he often teased, "when you do it for me?" And if her concerns more often than not fell on deaf ears, so, too, did her husband's attempts to assuage them. She had lived long enough to see the dangers in poverty. As for corruption, watching a fortune in currency pass from shtetl pocket to the greedy hand of some official had taught Malka that it took more than honest work to achieve results. Try as she did, she never could understand Grischa's humor. Was there anything funny about insufferable taxes that induced neighbors to pack their meager belongings and flee? Of course, they could stay and refuse to pay, but the few stalwarts making this choice had been driven to their knees. The problem was that with taxes and pressure growing, Malka saw no option short of raising prices. She and Grischa had argued the point that very morning.

"And force our friends and neighbors to absorb the burden?" was Grischa's response, understanding very well that to hold prices steady meant taking the blow. He saw the flash of anger tighten Malka's mouth and his tone softened. "As long as we can remain in business," he reassured her, "we will survive. None of us will starve." His wife took it no further, knowing that even if the discussion continued beyond his limit of forbearance, the man would refuse to budge.

Malka stirred millet into the bubbling stock until it was thoroughly absorbed. They would be fourteen for lunch, so she was careful to add enough water to stretch it out without turning it bland on the tongue. Fredl and her younger sister, Hannah, had already prepared the table, fitting the length of timber onto the three sawhorse supports. After that, they had rushed out to collect all the necessary plates and cutlery from their brothers' wives.

Tossing in the last handful of herbs, Malka wiped a forearm across a sweating brow. It was pure luck that her entire family was so close. With Warsaw less than thirty kilometers to the southwest, the big city had lured away many with its promise of wealth and excitement. Why stay in the backwoods, was the common argument, when culture and prosperity were so near?

Warsaw was tempting, no doubt about it, but there was another factor that played a major role: geography. Nowy Życie had sprouted up at the intersection of the Vistula, Narev, and Boug Rivers. It was the Vistula that served as the natural conduit to that other world, its shipping routes crossing the Baltic Sea and providing the Gershon business with its steady influx of supplies and the young men of Nowy Życie their avenue of escape. That Malka's boys had obliged their parents by marrying local girls and building their homes within eyeshot of their parents delighted her; that to this day they remained close friends was icing on a well-baked cake.

Malka shifted hot coals away from the center of the pot and prodded them into a circle to maintain a low simmer. A roll of thunder carried her to the window, but still there was no sign of Grischa. "Ridiculous man," she mumbled, closing the shutters against the sudden downpour. If that last storm, the one catching him in its icy squall and leaving him coughing for weeks, had taught him nothing, then he was beyond teaching. And that was after tending to him, forcing upon him an ocean of hot tea and applying such foul-smelling poultices that his skin reeked for days. "This," she had remonstrated each time she slapped the fetid mass of cloth, herbs, and meal onto his chest, "is the price you pay for acting like a stubborn child."

The pinch of Malka's mouth gave way to the memory of poor Grischa weighted down by that stinking mass. With an affectionate shrug she returned to the bubbling stock. Fredl found her there when she entered the kitchen to invite her mother to examine the table. The board was solidly fixed and each setting boasted carefully fashioned plates, utensils, and glass, the design made lovelier due to four vases filled with sprays of wildflowers, their vibrant colors set off by pale sprigs of wheat. Malka studied the space, allowed her senses to be filled with the beautiful tableau, and reminded herself that there was hope for her girls. "Lovely!" she announced. Fredl and Hannah rushed out, their faces flushed from the commendation.

Malka rotated a plate here, shifted a glass there. It was becoming more difficult to appreciate what they had without agonizing at the same time over what they might lose. Snatches of gossip overheard that morning at the baker's rushed back.

Did you hear that the military base is going to be closed?

But the suppliers will become impoverished!

Ah, yes, and what a coincidence, don't you agree, that nearly every one of them is a Jew from Nowy Życie or Zakroczym?

Malka slipped the pot of boiling stock partially off the fire and began to clean the vegetables.

The rain stopped as abruptly as it had begun. Shoving open the shutters, she saw Grischa rushing down the road, pulling the lapels of his heavy coat against a rising wind. He knows about the base, she thought, just as he knew about those girls from Wyszogrod. Violated and murdered, yet he said nothing. As if she would never hear about it from someone else. The thought prompted a hasty prayer for the protection of their daughters. Malka was not deeply religious like

Grischa but she was convinced of a higher power. Not once in her life had she doubted it, although difficult times had prodded her to question its beneficence. She considered herself a good Jew, but also a shtetl mother, meaning she instructed her girls on Hasidic lore, taught them to be on the alert for omens, and prepared them in the ways of warding off all suspicions of an evil spirit.

Malka remained at the window to follow Grischa's progress, squinting as he neared, hoping to discern his expression. "Why bother?" she mumbled, wiping her hands on her apron and moving away from the window. The old fool will do as he's always done: walk through that door acting as if this house and his wrinkled, white-haired old wife were heaven on earth!

ℰ Topanga Canyon, Spring 1984

A hot spring Sunday in the coastal canyons of northwest Los Angeles was not the best time for building a fire. True, the oak and madrone remains of last winter's cord were neatly stacked against the backside of the carport, aged to near perfection and begging for winter's arrival, but a fire in tinder-dry May? The earliest sign of smoke curling from the chimney would summon every fire truck in the area, not to mention some EPA representative levying a hefty fine against this scofflaw air polluter. And yet the comfort of a blazing fire was exactly what she longed to have.

Mimi closed her eyes and leaned heavily into the suede-soft headrest of the old desk chair. The problem with giving free rein to one's thoughts was their insistence on galloping toward the unpleasant. At the moment, they were grazing on a comment made by her mother that same morning. "In my family, in those days," Rivka had complained, "we pulled ourselves together and moved on. We did not give in." Mimi understood that "those days" referred to her mother's life in Nowy Życie, the "we" to those stalwart ancestors of a woman who, at this particular moment, was feeling anything but stalwart.

Remembering the heap of term papers waiting to be corrected, Mimi released such a deep moan she nearly smiled. Compared to how she was feeling, those "good old days"—a time of shtetls and pogroms—sounded like an improvement. There was something so appealing about living in a village, about knowing all of your neighbors and having everyone you love within reach. It took little effort for her to imagine Nowy Życie and the field running between her great-grandfather's dry goods store and the family home; to picture the morning mist hovering just above the many-colored grasses thrusting themselves through the hard crust of earth.

These thoughts floated about Mimi Zilber as she sat at her desk in the tranquil wood-shingled house overlooking her enclave of Topanga Canyon wilderness, her only distraction a neighbor's tin roof winking its deflected rays of sunlight against the assorted objets d'art surrounding her. Staring through the trees, her musings were far from tranquil. Her Great-grandmother Malka had been considered resolute, irrefutable, but had anyone ever thought of Mimi like that? True, she was a tenured professor of modern European history about to advance to the top of the academic heap, but disquiet and confusion assailed her.

Mimi had always known she would have liked her great-grandmother, would have respected and valued her in a way she did not her own mother, much as she tried. Ignoring the intimidating pile of papers, she tried yet again to recall the last time either she or her mother had expressed appreciation, much less true affection, for the other, but the effort caused a familiar headache to threaten. Pressing her fingertips into both eyelids, she rubbed slowly, as much to ease the pain as to stem the tears she was too tired to shed. "Get on with it," she sighed, reaching for the topmost paper.

It was somewhere into the third page of a treatise on the tactics employed by Pétain during the Champagne offensive of the First World War that Mimi heard the sickening thud of bird striking glass. Without having to look, she reached behind her, grabbed the shoe box from the shelf, and rushed outside. The Intensive Care Unit, Sarah had called it, this cotton batting-lined box that served as every wounded bird's stretcher while being taken by ambulance—Mimi's 1982 Volvo—to the SPCA shelter several miles down the canyon. Depending on the season, it was a run she sometimes made twice a week.

She searched under the shrubs, around terra-cotta planters overflowing with a profusion of gardenias and phlox, but the deck was clear of anything feathered, mangled, and fighting for its life.

Mimi spotted a delicate gray feather adhering to the windowpane. She stared for a moment at the wispy gray object, gave the deck and its environs one final scan, tucked the box under her arm and returned inside. Seated at her desk, Mimi wondered if, like her shtetl family, she had the courage to rebound from hardship.

The thought pulled her eyes toward the photograph on the desk. It had been taken several years earlier during a weekend up the Big Sur coast. There she was, standing on the sand, the baggy white sweater failing to hide her zoftig body, one arm draped loosely over Sarah's shoulder, the two women laughing. Mimi recalled how delighted they had been that a passing stranger had offered to take their photo and that, while he struggled with the focus, they were murmuring behind fixed smiles that he was probably going to steal the camera the moment the shot was taken. The background revealed a beach imprinted with footprints and bird tracks, mounds of sea-weed and assorted lengths of driftwood, an expanse of sand broken by a massive rock formation rising dramatically from the surf. Mimi smiled to herself. Not only had the man returned the camera, he had taken one of the few photographs she considered better than pass-able. Sitting in its simple pine frame, it held the undisputed place of honor on the desk.

Mimi touched the glass and warned herself against becoming maudlin. There was no need to count the days: it had been ten since Sarah's death, a full week since they had buried the woman who had been like a sister to her since they were fourteen; the same woman who had laughed with her about what a great couple they would have made, if only one of them had been born male. They were wonderful together, Sarah and Mimi, and now she was struggling with an emptiness that clawed at her insides.

Every day since Sarah's death, Mimi had been plagued by doubt. Why was it was so difficult to express appreciation to living friends when appreciation flowed so effortlessly to the dead? And had Sarah truly understood how important she was? How was she to survive without her confidante, without her chief supporter and rooting section?

Mimi sharpened a handful of red pencils, placed them in an

orderly row next to the keyboard, and then did her best to focus on the term paper. But all she saw was a garbled presentation, an unsatisfactory research effort failing to support flimsy assumptions.

She loosened her bra and sighed contentedly. Sarah, damn her, had never worn a bra, never knew the torture of straps cutting angry tracks into shoulders. They must have been nearly twenty that time when Sarah spread her hands against her flat chest and asked, "So how come you got the brains *and* the boobs?"

Mimi stared at the term paper, fought the urge to make one red diagonal slash across the page and write INADEQUATE or BANAL at the top. How is it, she wondered, that two such dissimilar women shared the same spirit? For the moment, she felt as if she were living with half a spirit. She imagined herself making that revelation to her mother and immediately saw her face looming, ever alert, Rivka's mouth a thin line of disapproval which had developed over more than eight decades of cynicism and distrust. If mothers were such precious gifts, then why did hers always yield disillusionment? And not just disillusionment, but vexation. Sarah had urged Mimi to challenge her mother, if for no other reason than to reassure herself that she had some control, but Mimi could never see the purpose. "So I can be subjected to bitter reproaches?" she had demanded. "I'm better off dragging my fingernail along a blackboard!"

But nothing dissuaded Sarah from her ridicule. "How can a mature and successful woman like you harbor even the smallest hope that your cantankerous old mother will ever become a compassionate woman?" Before Mimi could come up with a pithy comeback, Sarah added, "Like it or not, kiddo, if we're not careful we might become those very same women who raised us!"

Mimi knew that would never happen. For one thing, she was no child of the shtetl. And for another, her mother's generation defined success as marrying well and having bright and well-mannered children. Mimi had long ago accepted this definition, had understood that, in her mother's eyes, the daughter had fallen short. And now, middle-aged, it was no longer an option.

The memory of these conversations caused more grief to rise up into Mimi's throat. Why was it always Sarah who pointed out the obvious? No big mystery there! The obvious was something Mimi preferred not to see. And now, without Sarah to remind her, she was having trouble recalling what the "obvious" had been. What she did recognize was that she gave her mother as much as she could and the woman was invariably disappointed.

Mimi raked her hair away from her eyes and mulled over the curiosity that the French word for disappointment was *déception*. Deceived. Like Sarah's ruby ring: a gift from her grandmother that she had worn for nearly forty years before discovering it was glass. When Mimi heard the news she felt deceived on Sarah's behalf, but not her friend. For Sarah, the pleasure of the gift was diminished not at all. Just like her, she thought, a wistful smile briefly touching her face.

Sarah and Mimi had loved one another with the passion of sisters sharing a history of trust and dependency. From the onset of their friendship they knew, understood without having to explain, that nothing, no one, would separate them. They wore the same clothes, laughed the same laugh; they even bled on the same days. Everything was shared until the day Sarah married and Mimi opted for academia; even then Sarah's husband understood that their home would always be open to Mimi, their marriage more often an arrangement involving three. And after the birth of Joanna, it was a family of four.

Mimi had lived in a series of apartments over the past twenty-five years, each one more comfortable than the last, until she had finally purchased this home. But during those moves the issue was less the elegance of the place, or the distance to her office at the university, than it was the time it took to reach Sarah's home. Ten minutes was acceptable, fifteen pushing the limit. With such love and acceptance readily at hand, Mimi had found little reason to seek it elsewhere. So the years slipped by, the occasional lover arriving to send a rush of pleasure through Mimi's otherwise academic life, and Sarah always there to provide the safe haven when the affair was over.

With Sarah gone, Mimi felt as if her own youth had been buried as well and her mother—the octogenarian whose notion of maternal love was more guile than tenderness—still remained. This was not the Natural Order as Mimi knew it, anticipated it.

She retrieved the essay and read without comprehending. Her mind was too busy imagining herself old and feeble, sharing a room with her mother in the Jewish Home for the Aged, Mimi resting lethargically in some overstuffed chair while an alert Rivka Zilber wiped spittle from her daughter's whiskered chin.

It was courage Mimi needed. Unlike her shtetl family, however, she felt anything but courageous. All of them—parents, children, grand-children, including her own mother—were rumored to have been fighters and survivors. And me, she thought, I can barely gather the energy, much less the courage, to drag myself out of this black hole and take a walk. Besides, Sarah was a fighter and did she survive? When she was at the graveside, she had wanted to berate Sarah for failing to come out the victor, for leaving her friend behind to fend for herself in a world where she felt neither accepted nor secure. Ten days had passed and she was beginning to wonder how long it took to transcend anger, to shake off this feeling that she was grieving more for her own loss than the premature death of her friend. Was it selfish, she wondered, shameful? Perhaps what really mattered was: this is how she felt.

Mimi shifted to settle into the contours of the chair, but nothing felt comfortable, nothing fit. If only she had her mother's knack of turning both deaf ear and cold shoulder to anything unpleasant. But she was not her mother, nor was she her great-grandmother Malka.

Rivka's stories about Malka Gershon invariably brought pride to the woman's eyes, the kind of pride Mimi had always hoped to produce but never had. Her mother's grandmother had been practical, a decisive woman who had left politics and daylong discussions of Torah to the men. Women of that time were expected to dedicate themselves to preparing meals pursuant to the dietary laws of kashrut and observing the daily Hasidic practices. Great-grandmother Malka had attacked her duties with a confident hand, but she was also tough and opinionated, a woman capable of studying any difficulty and then solving it. The school needed repairs? Malka headed the com-mittee. A home was leveled by fire? She organized both the crew and the supplies required for the reconstruction. So dogged was Malka Gershon's resolve to do what must be done that she inspired the townspeople to believe that, standing together, they could protect their beloved Nowy Życie against most harm.

How, then, had Malka Gershon produced a granddaughter whose opinions were rarely based on reason? Or a perturbed great-granddaughter for whom decisiveness was more a risk than a virtue?

As for her great-grandfather, Mimi imagined him not as a rigid figure like his wife, but fluid, bending. She could picture Grischa Gershon walking the road bordering his field six days a week, two round-trips each day. "It was a rare afternoon," insisted her mother with pride, "when my grandfather did not take his noonday meal at home with his family." Mimi had heard all about Grischa, this hardworking man who was as devout as he was sensitive, someone whose honesty and decency had earned him the respect and trust of his community.

That Rivka Zilber had survived pogroms and hardship, that she had sat more shivot for the dead than her only child could ever imagine sitting, this was something Mimi accepted because her own life had been relatively easy and secure, tainted by surprisingly few tragedies. And yet, in her heart, Sarah's death outweighed all of Rivka's tragedies combined. Mimi replayed this thought and felt ashamed. Her mother had lost everyone. Everyone. And Mimi? Her father had died, true, and after they buried him the two women had spent several days putting his things in order. What they discovered was that the space Harold Zilber's departure had created in their lives was measurable by half a closet and a few drawers, all of which were quickly filled. Sarah, on the other hand, had taken up significant space: hers was a tangible presence, the sweet fragrance of gardenia that lingers for days even after it has died.

Unlike Harold Zilber, Sarah had requested there be no shtetl ritual of shiva to honor her memory, only a gathering at the cemetery in one year's time for the unveiling of the headstone. Mimi accepted this, felt that the very act of inhaling and exhaling, of surviving, would be ritual enough. She fingered the corner of the essay. Why bother with a memorial? she asked herself. Every minute of life that passes, every hour that ticks away in Sarah's absence, these were her memorial.

Since the funeral, Mimi had felt so fragile: going to work, answering the phone, everything required a strength she doubted she had. Was it because her parents had failed to give her the courage she needed? Did a bitter shtetl life render one incapable of instilling in a child confidence and valor?

"The hell with it," Mimi mumbled, fighting the temptation to drop all the essays into the wastebasket. Remaining at her desk, hunching and releasing her shoulders, she finally shoved the entire stack to one side and stared at her reflection in the computer monitor. Can something take place within a family a decade, a half-century, even a full century past, she wondered, and leave its scar on future generations? She leaned back in her chair and stared through the glass doors and out onto the gardened deck.

It struck her that so many situations happening in one's home, village, or country could have shattering consequences on the lives of people, even simple people like the Gershons of Nowy Życie. As a history professor she taught about royal families and how they were affected by the events of the time. So why not shtetl families? They had offspring, who in turn had offspring. It made perfect sense that every person, and every segment of history lived by that person, would become part of a tapestry.

Tea was what she required. Irish, with one cube of sugar and some milk. Placing the teapot on the burner, Mimi thought of tapestries and how as a student she had loved studying them at Versailles and the Prado, magnificent weavings depicting beheaded kings and daily life. Perhaps she needed to create a kind of tapestry of her own family. Creating such an object would surely give her a clearer idea of how Malka, Fredl, and Rivka evolved—of how she came to be who she was.

Mimi passed through the French doors, stepping onto the weatherworn surface just as a cluster of dried leaves was blown across her feet. Settling into a bright green canvas butterfly chair, she hugged the steamy mug against her chest and leaned back. The sounds of birds, the rustling of oak branches, even the far-off drone of a single-engine plane crossing the canyon, everything comforted in this place. She adored this spot, loved its privacy and serenity. Throughout the years in her home, this was the one space that never disappointed her.

The phone was ringing inside; she ignored it. There were scraggly hydrangeas to think about, pruning to be planned before summer planting. And her family tapestry. Bones, thought Mimi. A tapestry woven with the flesh and bones and heart and soul of everyone who came before me; everyone who lived, suffered, rejoiced long before I was born.

She shifted her weight in the chair and slipped off one shoe. The wood was warm against her foot, friendly. And what about the thread

representing her, Mimi, daughter of Rivka and Harold, granddaughter of Fredl and Szulen Rabinoff, great-granddaughter of Malka and
Grischa Gershon? Hers felt like such a solitary thread.

And why not? she asked herself. My mother has suffered griev-
ously throughout her life, and her grandmother long before that. Perhaps then it was logical, inevitable, that my own thread, the one
created from their anguish and their losses, would be constructed of
filaments woven together to produce yet another thread of suffering.

In her case, loneliness.

Mimi rose with difficulty from the low-slung chair, crossed the
deck, and entered the study. As she closed the doors, she fought the
urge to walk away from her thoughts and get on with her grading. It
was less demanding and certainly less intimidating. She could hear her
mother's voice inveigling her to "stop this nonsense and put the past
behind you." If only she could! But how to ignore this gnawing urge to
reveal and expose, to tear away the scabs. Mimi touched the photograph taken at the beach. With the exception of Sarah, those transient
workaday interactions that took place over several decades of teaching, a series of inconsequential lovers and an occasional suitor, she
had been alone for much of her life. Perhaps it was going to take
Sarah's absence to force her to understand this expanse of solitude
stretching out before her. Okay, so she hadn't fulfilled her mother's
dreams of the prince and the white horse, but so what? She was a top-
notch scholar, respected and quoted. If marriage and family were all
her mother could see in the success column, that was *her* problem!

That was the crux of it, wasn't it? That she had settled into this isolation like a comfortable chair, had managed to avoid commitments
and love. She fingered the term papers she knew had to be read and
then shoved them aside. She was going for a walk.

Spring 1887, Nowy Życie

Grischa turned through the gate and plodded up the front
steps. The patient tolerance on Malka's face, accompanied by the
flutelike laughter of his daughters, lifted him from his rain-soaked
woes. Before he could cross the threshold Fredl and Hannah were

there to greet him and help him off with his coat. Fredl began bab-
bling about something she had just read, while Hannah was perfectly content to remain against her father's chest, book clutched
tightly, and feel his flowing beard brush her forehead.

Grischa had long ago accepted his daughters' need to read and
was delighted when both girls jotted their private thoughts in the little books they had crafted at the kitchen table. In his youth girls had
rarely read, their time being fully occupied with their mother's skills:
cooking, cleaning, childrearing. Unlike many shtetl fathers, Grischa
had proved himself open to change. "What harm can it do?" he'd ask
the naysayers. "When my girls come to the store they always help.
And Fredl—why, she manages that ledger better than her papa!"

The boisterous family meal finished and the grandchildren carried home for their afternoon nap, Malka left the cleanup to her
daughters and returned to the store with Grischa. Her task was to
organize the new bolts of cloth and note any shortages, while
Grischa sold, tallied, and wrapped. They were preparing for Friday's
morning delivery to the military base at Modlin when a local farmer
entered wearing threadbare trousers and a hungry look. When he
hesitated over the sack of feed, Grischa came rushing to his side.
"Take what you need," insisted the affable shopkeeper, but the offer
made the farmer uncomfortable. "Don't worry, Yitzchak, you'll pay
when you can!" The back of Grischa's neck prickled from Malka's
penetrating eyes. "With no feed," he went on, "how can your chickens thrive? And without chickens there can be no eggs. And with no
eggs," he concluded, one finger raised as if quoting Torah, "your
children will not grow to be strong like their papa." Having said his
piece, he glanced in his wife's direction, his eyes nearly twinkling
with humor.

Malka bit her tongue as Yitzchak carted off a sack of feed twice
the volume he had expected. The moment the door closed behind
him she crossed the room, hands clenched and a tightness around
her mouth: she was itching for the very confrontation she had
promised herself she would avoid. But before she could speak, she
was silenced by Grischa's raised hands.

"I know, I know," he acquiesced, "you think we should be less
charitable."

Malka screwed up her face. Was he suggesting that she was not? "That is not what I meant!" she argued, both of them knowing full well that it was precisely what she had meant. "But we can't give to everyone in need." Righteousness brightened her eyes. "And I am not suggesting that *we* be any less charitable, only that you be more cautious."

"But my dear . . ." he protested, crossing the room. Her eyes followed his movement. Sure enough, it was that damned ledger! Grischa opened it, flipping backward with studied formality to the first page. "You see," he declared innocently, gesturing toward the writing. "The Bad Debts column carried over from last year, and it's practically blank!"

Malka knew it was true: no matter how great the risk always seemed to her, nearly everyone who owed money to Grischa had paid the debt.

Their discussion was interrupted by the arrival of the rabbi's assistant. There was no need to look Grischa's way to know what he was thinking: my reprieve from the firing squad!

"Thursday already?" he asked, the smile still playing across his mouth. "And let me guess," he went on. "It is somewhere in the vicinity of 4:15."

Boris the Rabbi's Assistant had been buying Shabbos candles for the shul every Thursday at 4:15 for more than forty years. He had held this post for so long that no one in Nowy Życie knew him by any name other than Boris the Rabbi's Assistant.

Normally a cordial man, it was evident that he was in no mood for banter. Recognizing this, Grischa reached behind and took down the candles. "My friend has a lot on his mind," he prompted with kindness.

Malka, busying herself with wrapping the candles, had not noticed the old man's reticence. She folded the corners with precision and wound a length of string around the bundle, all the while humming to herself a delicate Schumann composition, one of the tunes her middle boy, Yehiel, had played as a child. It was not until glancing up that she noticed the change. Shifting her gaze toward Grischa, they exchanged worried glances.

Boris had become thin, bone-thin, no longer the gangly young man from their youth. His hands trembled as they reached behind wire spectacles to rub tired, watery eyes in a slow circular motion. Malka and Grischa registered the feeble gesture. "Two years," murmured the old man, jowls shaking as he gripped the counter with veined hands, "five at the most, and then phttt! No more Nowy Życie."

"We must have faith," Grischa soothed, but at the same time closed the ledger, gripping it so firmly it arched in his hands. Having decided that silence was best served, Malka viewed Grischa with a wary eye. And what would she say, that every family has a dreamer and a cynic?

They escorted Boris down the wooden steps and onto the road. As he walked off, each hesitant step raising a puff of dust, Grischa took Malka's hand and kissed it. There was tenderness in his eyes that ran through her like charged heat. Who else but Grischa understood that something molten remained at the core! It had stunned him on their wedding night and it had continued to surprise him in so many situations since. Passion, intellect, kindness: Malka was capable of them all, and so much was reserved for his eyes only.

"The man is terrified," she finally said, gently reclaiming her hand and turning back into the store.

Grischa followed close behind. "If we live in fear," he said, "we give these bastards complete power over our lives."

Malka returned to the tasks she needed to complete before locking up. Despite her husband's comment, it was not fear she felt, but outrage. She cared only that her family was safe. If the girls arrived home even one minute after sundown, they knew too well what awaited them. Malka was not the kind of mother who would gather them in her arms after they ran in front of the wagon, and then weep for joy because they were unhurt. No, she was the mother who gathered them in her arms after they ran in front of that wagon—and then spanked them for causing her such a fright. Who was to say which kind of mother loved her child more?

The next afternoon, while Grischa was sweeping the front steps of the store, uniformed men appeared on horseback. His first instinct was to warn the neighbors, but he realized that an alarm had already gone out. Farther down the road he saw a flurry of apprehension— doors and windows slamming against anticipated violence, followed by abrupt silence. Who else but Cossacks? said the hush. What else but a pogrom? He also knew that behind these closed doors a variety of arms were being taken up, wives and daughters hidden. Grischa remained there, paralyzed, broom in hand, as one of the soldiers led his horse directly onto the porch and stopped within inches of the shopkeeper. The prickly heat emanating from the beast's flank made him want to scratch his face, but he dared not. The moment the soldier reached into the pouch hanging from his saddle, Grischa's lips began moving in silent prayer. In one fluid motion the man pulled out a sheet of paper and nailed it to the wall. Just as gracefully, he leaned down and took Grischa firmly by the beard. "Not this time, Jew," he said, and released the shopkeeper with a sharp tug. He joined his comrades and the men laughed as they cantered away.

Within minutes a crowd was clustered on the porch, Malka pushing her way to the front. Satisfied that her husband was unharmed, she strained to see the text. For the benefit of the illiterate women who enveloped her, she read it aloud. There was another business tax, an assessment on livestock, an even stricter quota on Jewish workers holding government positions.

"If they can't kill us with pogroms," declared the postal clerk, "they'll do it with taxes. Who can stand the burden?"

It occurred to Grischa that while taxes were for obstructing, pogroms were for eradicating, but he said nothing.

"This is beyond a burden," complained Natan the dairyman, sifting through the barrels as if nothing were amiss. "When a man cannot feed his children, it's a crime." He stomped to the counter, spread out his purchases, and checked each item off his list. Crossing to the larger barrels, he began shoveling grain into a heavy sack, every so often giving it a swift kick to settle the seed. Grischa came over and began filling the second sack. "Make no mistake," said the dairyman, giving it another boot, "it will only get worse."

Grischa glanced reflexively toward Malka, the scoop in his hand arrested midair. Worse? said her eyes. What could be worse than rape, murder, and oppression? The dairyman's omen circled over their heads like a death sentence, the hush so menacing that no one in the store dared eye contact. As townspeople filtered out, Grischa called for Saul, his oldest son, to help with the sacks. Natan hoisted one onto his shoulder and followed the younger man to the wagon, while

Grischa remained inside to tally the bill. "And add it right this time!" the dairyman called out. "Yes, yes," mumbled Grischa, checking the invoice. After a lifetime in this place, he was inured to his friend's ribbing. "It's all here: two sacks of feed, fourteen dowels, one bag of nails. Satisfied?"

Natan stomped back into the store. "Seeing as how I took three bags, how could I complain?" He clapped Grischa on the back with a laugh. "How you stay in business amazes me!"

Malka looked up from her work. The smile she managed was devoid of humor.

The two men walked outside, their footsteps echoing off the porch. Grischa steadied the horse while Natan hauled himself into the wagon and took up the reins. When the latter looked down, his face was unexpectedly grave. "Watch yourself," he warned, leaning closer to his friend. "And for the love of God, Grischa, keep a vulture's watch on your girls." They locked eyes, not a vestige of playful humor remaining. Grischa slapped his hand against the side panel of the wagon and set the mare into motion. Back inside the store, he forced himself to focus on the ledger, soon becoming so lost in thought he was unaware of Malka calling for him to close the store and go home.

It was nearly eleven before the bedtime rituals were completed — the candles snuffed, each wick rechecked by Malka; the embers on stove and hearth examined by Grischa, and then once again by his wife.

"My fire inspector," Grischa teased.

"And has there ever been a fire?" she shot back, an eyebrow raised inquisitively.

Malka and Grischa settled into bed, this too being a ritual, one that had begun on their wedding night more than forty years earlier. Since then, not a night had passed when Malka did not move as close to her husband as possible; when Grischa did not wrap an arm around her and hold her to him. In all those years he had learned to read the nature of her thoughts by the tension in her muscles, and what he read this night was not sexual. "We can't stop living," he murmured into her hair, and she nestled even closer. Interpreting this as an invitation, he slipped a hand under her nightdress. When the stroking evoked only a disquieting sigh, he removed his hand. There was no need to see her face to know that her forehead was wrinkled like crumpled paper, that her mouth was compressed into an unyielding line. He kissed the back of her neck and tried to take her hand, but she pulled it away.

Topanga Canyon, Spring 1984

Mimi had grown up believing that her mother's history was a bad dream comprising death, destruction, pogroms and escape. None of it was actually discussed, but the intimation was there: narrowed eyes, dismissive gestures, tight-lipped disapprobation and dramatic silences. What else could explain such behavior, but a monstrous youth? If her scholarly training had taught her anything, it was to question every element smacking of historical interpretation. Which explains why Rivka Zilber's autobiographical bombs were often met with doubt. After years of challenging stories to ascertain their accuracy, Mimi had come to the conclusion that, all dramatic interpretation aside, her mother actually concealed more than she divulged. "Mama's life was not merely a bad dream," she had told Sarah, "it was a fucking nightmare."

Settled into the corner of the couch that was pushed close to the vaulted stone fireplace, Mimi pulled the corners of the cashmere lap robe around her shoulders. It was too early in the season for a fire, but she was sorely tempted. Leaning into the cushions, she tried not to think of work, nor to linger on Sarah or Rivka. Most of all, she tried not to look at the envelope leaning against the lamp. The return address told her it was from the dean of her department. Months earlier she had been interviewed as one of the six candidates for department head. The results were in that letter. It could wait. She stretched against the stiffness in her back and noted with pleasure that her blue jeans were looser; her thighs were definitely thinner, her tummy flatter. So there really was a positive by-product of grief. Great, she thought. For the first time in twenty years I'm going to get down to my perfect weight, and Sarah's not even here to take me shopping. She imagined the pleasure of announcing, "Guess what, Mama? I've lost more than twenty pounds and they're about to offer me the chairmanship of the history department . . . at nearly double the salary!" And then she reminded herself of how Rivka would respond and she laughed. "Twenty pounds!" her mother would say, as if the promotion had never been mentioned. "Darling, twenty pounds!"

Fuck spring, thought Mimi, contemplating once again moving from the sofa to build that fire. Of course, she could always open the letter. No, she was too comfortably ensconced: it would take more than the promise of warmth or promotion to budge her. She fished in her pocket for a mint. The funeral was two weeks ago, yet not an hour before she had spoken to her mother for the first time. And now, the usual aftermath: attempting to control the tic in her cheek; struggling to quell the matricidal notions that, if ever acted upon, would undoubtedly lead to a very long stay in some tacky women's prison. The tic would soon leave, but it would take a miracle of science to eliminate the metallic taste from her mouth. She popped in another mint and warned herself about the dangers of middle-aged women carrying on lengthy inner dialogues.

It was not that she had expected an out-and-out apology for missing Sarah's funeral: after a lifetime with her mother, she knew better than to expect that. Neither had she been prepared for the casual manner in which her mother had sloughed off the issue. "I still can't see why you're so upset," the woman had said. "She was *your* friend, I hardly ever saw her."

Mimi's eyes fell on one of the few existing photographs of the Gershon family of Nowy Życie, indicated by the photographer's embossed stamp in the lower corner. She had come across its filigree frame at a garage sale, the design striking her as appropriate to that era. Picking up the photo, she studied the expressions on the assembly of faces: Malka, Grischa, their five children. Sad-faced, Sarah had called them, but Mimi disagreed. They might appear stern at first glance, but their eyes shone with pride. From somewhere over her shoulder she heard Sarah's scornful riposte and the memory caused her to smile. Okay, so maybe their bearing was a little austere and just a wee bit antithetical to the lively and attractive people her mother recalled, but she would have loved to have known them, to have lived in that family and been a part of that time. After all, these were reputed to be the people who saved her mother's life.

Mimi held the photo closer to the light, the lampshade at her elbow throwing a luminous circle across the faces, but her attention was dragged back to that envelope. She was certain it was the offer, felt it down to her marrow, yet was aware of that nagging fear that it was not, that they had passed her over for someone less capable, more personable. All those years of teaching, research, writing and publishing, how could they not give the post to her? Of course they had! She forced her eyes away. They had . . . hadn't they?

Mimi turned her attention back to the photograph. Father and mother, three boys and two girls ranging in age from ten to thirty, all posed together in a cramped space. The sofa on which Malka and Grischa sat was nearly invisible, buried behind flowing skirts and stiff-standing offspring. The envelope be damned.

She carried the photograph into the study and placed it on the desk next to the Big Sur photo. And then she reached for the one book that rarely left her desk. It was the *yishkor* for Nowy Życie, the commemorative book created by the children of its scant Holocaust survivors.

> Although this book has been written in Yiddish — the language of Nowy Życie — we have added an English foreword, a condensed history of the *shtetl*, for the children who came after. Nine thousand Jews lived in Nowy Życie in 1941, fewer than four hundred were alive in May of 1945. The first dated photographs were from 1918, although most came from those ten years prior to that spring day in 1944, when the Germans, with the willing assistance of Polish townspeople, liberated Nowy Życie of its Jews. Nowy Życie is Polish for "new life," but it is a name that mocks its history.

Mimi knew its history all too well. The majority of the residents were shipped in boxcars to the Warsaw Ghetto, and then on to Oswiecim, the Polish name for Auschwitz. Among them were Grischa and Malka's two surviving children, Hannah and Yehiel; Hannah's husband; three Gershon daughters-in-law, nineteen grandchildren, and fourteen great-grandchildren. Everyone, absolutely everyone. With the exception of her mother.

She was enchanted by the pictures of schoolchildren with large eyes and eager faces staring innocently into the camera. She was fascinated by the strolling townspeople, by the group photographs of professional societies and crafts guilds. She studied the houses and commercial buildings, and the narrow dirt roads separating them. Her mother remembered those roads well.

"There was such dust!" Rivka insisted. "So many horses and wagons going back and forth. In the summer, the dust was so thick it stuck to the inside of my throat. Every year, from May to September, I had a hacking cough. And in winter? Mud and ice. Impossible for those poor peddlers selling from their wagons, and for the men who depended on the military base in Modlin." Here she shivered for emphasis.

Mimi turned to the image of four women standing together on a wooden stoop, all of them squinting into a bright sun. They wore heavy skirts with layer upon layer of material drooping to the ground. Their blouses were modest, the wrist-length sleeves covering nearly every inch of flesh, necklines covering every inch of neck. On their heads they wore *sheytls*, the cumbersome wigs worn by Hasidic women. Not visible in the photo were their thick woolen stockings and high-topped leather shoes.

One page in this *yishkor* was stained from years of fingering. It was the photograph of Malka Gershon and her two daughters, taken on the porch of their home. Hannah, barely ten, already had the face of a wise and serious child. Fredl, nearly sixteen and taller than her mother by inches, smiled into the camera boldly, rather mischievously. She was prettier than her sister, with thick ringlets pulled away from an eager face by a wide ribbon. The round dark eyes, straight eyebrows, and high forehead added to the intelligent look. Mimi touched Fredl's hair, fascinated as always by this lively, clear-eyed girl who would one day become Rivka's mother and Mimi's own grandmother.

Thumbing through the pages, she stopped at one of the photographs showing a cluster of houses. Most of them were wood-framed, with foundations constructed directly upon the earth which, as her mother had explained to her, had made them as difficult to navigate in rainy weather as the roads outside. The Gershon home had three bedrooms and a sitting room. "And real wood floors," Rivka never failed to add, "raised above the ground to keep out the cold and mud." Most of their neighbors were forced to stuff rags into the walls to seal off the bitter Russian cold; some even used clumps of rotting straw between the rafters to keep out rain and snow. "Our home," declared Rivka, "was properly constructed."

"So you never had to use rags and straw?" Mimi had probed, knowing full well that her mother would pull back her shoulders and sniff the air with flared nostrils. "In our house," she insisted, "such filth was never permitted." When Mimi asked about the farm animals photographed in front of some of the houses, her mother was quick to point out that no chickens or goats dared approach their home. "The only people who lived like that," she added, "were the peasants."

Mimi pulled herself away from the book with a rebuke. There was work to be done, no matter where her memories were taking her. She turned her focus to the lecture she was to deliver in an hour's time.

When Mimi arrived home after class she found five messages on her machine. There was an invitation from Daniel offering dinner, a walk, whatever made her feel better. Joanna called to remind her that she was needed on Saturday to help sort through Sarah's personal possessions, one of those "if you think you can't handle it I'll understand" kind of messages. Mimi heard the plea and knew that of course she'd be there.

There were two abrupt communications from her mother. The first demanded that Mimi come at once to take her shopping; the second had to do with a controversial recycling project nullified that afternoon by the Los Angeles Board of Supervisors. "As if we haven't been doing it for centuries," scoffed Rivka. "Do they think we squandered anything in the shtetl? No! Clothing was handed down to the younger children, and food — my darling, every seed we could save from a fruit or a vegetable we dried and labeled for planting. And if we couldn't plant it, it got fed to the animals." The old woman's voice grated. It was the arrogance, that intonation implying social status several notches above royalty.

The last message was an urgent plea from the department head's secretary that her boss was awaiting Mimi's response to the letter and that even though the dean understood the terrible strain Mimi was under considering the death of her friend, there was an urgent need for Mimi to get in touch . . . now.

"Terrible strain, my ass," she muttered, and then declared, "Fuck it!" and stomped into the living room. Grabbing the envelope, she ripped it open. After an extensive search and careful consideration, they were pleased to announce that the position was hers. She read the letter twice, and then once again. Her instinct was to reach for the phone, yet she knew, felt with a pang, that this was one accomplishment she'd have to enjoy without Sarah.

Mimi returned to the study and tossed the letter onto the desk. No doubt she should call her mother, but she was too weary to expend the energy. The blinking light of the answering machine reminded her that the one voice missing from the tape was Sarah, the woman who had soothed and comforted her for the better part of their lives. In a flash of anger, she hit the button and erased all the messages.

CHAPTER TWO

&*Nowy Życie, Autumn, 1887*

THE VILLAGE OF NOWY ŻYCIE awakened each morning to
the smell of freshly baked bread and a silent prayer that
this day, please God, be the one that brings relief to a people too
weary of conflict. In one of its most prosperous homes, Grischa Gershon was spurred awake by hopefulness and the promise of a new
day. As for Malka, there was barely time for a quick supplication
before she was struck yet again by those harsh reminders of shtetl life.
And how could she not be when outside her window passed such
poverty and oppression, conditions that could be neither ignored nor
remedied.

The girls slept as their parents shared an early-morning breakfast.
It was after Malka's third audible sigh that Grischa rested his elbows
on the table and leaned toward his wife. "It is not so easy, this living
in the heart of Mother Russia."

Malka's eyes met his. Don't you mean the bowels of Mother Russia? she was tempted to ask, but resisted. Why point out a truth, she
asked herself, that he understands too well?

It was a game they played, and had been playing for several years.
Grischa knew of the peril and downplayed it to protect his wife;
Malka pretended that his concern softened her fear for their family, as
well as her anger toward him for his annoyingly persistent optimism.
All the while, they both understood that the Pale of Settlement had
been created to confine the Jews, not the Russians. In a czarist state,
you could never be both.

Once Grischa was off to the store, Malka awakened the girls, fed them, and set them to their tasks. At mid-morning, when Malka was in the garden preparing for spring planting, a neighbor raced past the house and lobbed a verbal grenade — the czar's key emissary in Warsaw had been murdered. Not fifteen minutes later, Grischa rushed home with the news and found his wife packing their belongings. "Where do you propose we go?" he asked, taking the folded dress from Malka's trembling hands.

She stared at him, eyebrows drawn together. "You know who will be blamed."

Grischa fingered the garment, folded it, placed it on the dresser and pressed it flat with both hands. When he finally turned to faced Malka, he was pale. How much should I reveal? said his face. If only a part, she will retrieve the rest from one of her many sources. And yet if I tell all, that is more than she can bear. He inhaled deeply, his breath escaping with more force than intended.

"What?" she demanded. "What!"

"The pogroms, Malka, they've already begun. Widespread, from what I hear. But not close to us, I promise."

"How close is 'not close'?"

He reached for her. "Days, perhaps a week. If we're lucky, not at all." She pulled away; any sign of hope disappeared from his face. He had said the same thing after the czar's death, and look how they had suffered! Did she have to tick them off on each finger? There were the May Laws, forcing many of those Jews living in larger cities within the Pale to be herded into shtetls. And then later, after they were lulled into the belief that nothing more could befall them, they were abruptly prohibited from owning rural land and participating in a list of respectable professions. This was accompanied by a quota placed on the number of Jewish children permitted to continue higher education. For this, there was a sense of communal rage. That rage quickly turned to sadness when the Gershons were visited by Szulen Rabinoff, one of Fredl's lifelong friends. The boy had just been accepted into the Gymnasium of Science in Warsaw — the first step toward the medical program at the university. This new edict, however, put an end to his magnificent future. "Will it be so terrible to work with your papa?" Grischa had asked, his heart aching to see such talent restrained. Szulen, nearly as tall as Grischa and even lankier, had struggled to keep his tears in check. Fredl had remained at his side, ready to offer sympathetic support when needed, yet unsure of what served Szulen best. After all, she, too, had wanted to storm against the injustice. When her father added something about living as best they could and praying that life improved, she avoided her mother's eyes. Could her father be so naïve as to honestly believe there would be an end to this suffering?

Now here they were, only a few years later, once again holding their collective breaths and preparing for the onslaught. And once again Grischa was proving to be surprisingly accurate: while the number of massacres within the Pale were unimaginable, they had not reached Nowy Życie. Malka accepted the accuracy of his forecast with skepticism, drawing her opinions from her experiences and not, like her husband, from hope. "It's bad enough we have to fear our government," she complained. "Now there's the Russian Orthodox Church to worry about."

The solid front presented by this meeting of church and state terrified all of Nowy Życie's Jews. Between stepped-up pogroms and the church's assistance in enforcing the laws, it seemed inevitable that the Jewish population would either die out, emigrate, or convert. Be anything you want, was the message all of them heard, as long as it's not Jewish.

&*Topanga Canyon, Spring 1984*

Mimi turned on the desk lamp. Reading the translation in the *yishkor* once again, she thought of how little she had learned from her mother about the pogroms and how most of the information had been gleaned from her studies. She recalled the embarrassment when, well into her first postgraduate thesis, she realized for the first time that the May Laws, and their effect on Jews who later carried out the Revolution, had anything to do with her family. Several years later, faced with having to choose the subject for her doctoral thesis, she had balked at pursuing this research.

"But it'll practically write itself," Sarah had insisted.

"You're probably right, but I can't imagine dedicating two years of my life to comparing, contrasting and defending data on a bunch of tyrannical czars bent on the systematic destruction of my family." Not long after, while standing before a lecture hall filled with first-year students who believed that it was Hitler who first inspired the concept of *judenrein*, she was so vexed by their ignorance that she began to regret her choice. But how much did she know at their age? And then she recalled the sixties and sitting around a popular coffeehouse with other graduate students debating whether or not any of them could have withstood such adversity. Korea was behind them, Vietnam was someone else's war, and there they were, unscathed.

We were so arrogant, thought Mimi, turning the page in the *yishkor* to that chilling column of statistics. Could we have been more full of ourselves, more positive about our bright and glorious futures? And how easy it was to take all the right political stands! We cared less about whose name would be drawn in the lottery than whether or not we'd get laid on Saturday night. More often than not, we would.

As to the often-asked question, "Why are you majoring in history?" Mimi had a standard response. She was good at memorizing dates, the study of history came easily to her, and earning her living at something she enjoyed appealed to her. And she was her father's daughter, meaning she loved the way events clustered around a specific date, as if that date were the hot center of a starburst of occurrences.

"Stop stalling," she mumbled to herself, closing the book and forcing her attention back to the pile of essays. When the overabundance of information began to blur and she could no longer differentiate between 1938 and 1389, Mimi accepted the fact that she needed a break. Time to go to bed, she thought, then nearly laughed. Perhaps six-thirty was a bit early to consider bedtime, no matter how tired she felt. And then came the memory of last night, of slumber cut short by a vividly disconcerting nightmare, and the moment caused her to shudder.

In her dream she was sitting in her office arranging teaching schedules for the following semester. Suddenly, there was a scratching sound that drew her eyes toward the hallway outside the massive oak door. Peering over the edge of her desk, she saw dates being slipped under the door, dozens of four-digit numbers at a time, until the room began to fill. The pile increased, Mimi and her desk were lifted from the floor higher and higher, until in one terrifying moment her face was pressed against the ceiling and she was suffocating, the digits nearest her face gouging her skin, drawing blood as each numeral penetrated her flesh. And every date was the same: 1945.

Shaking off the morbid recollection, Mimi began preparations for the next morning's work. Not even a determined focus could hold back the thought that, in 1887, her Nowy Życie family lived with the daily fear of extermination while their descendent, this professor living her cushy California existence and driving her upscale car, was ill-prepared to survive even the most minor inconveniences of life. During graduate school days, she might have considered the question of survival purely academic. But now, facing it on this balmy spring evening and worn down from fatigue and sadness, she was no longer sure.

Mimi gazed out over the deck. She looked beyond the laurel sumac shrubs whose delicate clusters of white flowers were in sharp contrast to the long-stemmed buckwheat planted to slow soil erosion in a terrain never intended to sustain bulldozers and multilevel homes; beyond the row of sycamores, their branches gracefully twisting, their leaves having not yet attained the vibrant yellow-green of summer; even beyond the uppermost branches of the Douglas firs, their sweet fragrance reminiscent of festivities and the exchange of gifts. It never failed to astonish Mimi that all of this belonged to her, was paid for in full by the tenure she had so tenaciously sought. A few more manzanitas along the front drive, she thought, and paradise will be achieved.

No fatigue, however, no enjoyment of her garden expanse, could stem her recollections and push away the sense of dread. If the sixties meant invasion, resistance, a country at war, then the fifties were her parents reeling from news of Hitler's devastation, speaking Yiddish in public, being overtly and intentionally Jewish. And this despite a daughter who insisted she be allowed to straighten her hair, refused to answer to Miriam, and did everything she could to pass herself off as Gentile.

A wan smile stretched across Mimi's face as she organized the last corner of the desk. How could I have been so insufferable? she wondered, and the thought invited her mother's voice reminding her that Great-grandmother Malka was the real survivor in the family. Mimi swiveled her chair toward the photograph. Malka Gershon had lived to her late seventies despite the violent times, whereas Mimi's greatest challenge to date had been battling the head of her department over curriculum issues. "We're separated by a hell of a lot more than history," she said to the face in the photo. Malka Gershon knew how to cope; her great-granddaughter was hardly coping at all.

The sound of a ringing telephone came as a welcomed interruption to one more round of self-recrimination. It was Daniel inviting her to a film. "A remake of *Roman Holiday*," he said. "It's funny, and there's no violence."

"Does anyone die?"

"No," he assured her, "no one dies." So she agreed to meet him at the box office.

Daniel had been truthful: no one died. And yet sitting in the theater, listening to bursts of laughter, Mimi felt like crying. The lengthy credits rolling at the end of the film allowed her to pull herself together.

"Hungry?" asked Daniel, holding back the swinging door. "We could grab something, a late snack."

Mimi begged off with a stream of excuses: too much work, an early meeting, the desire to drop into bed.

"I could help you with that one," he suggested, his smile as much a tease as an invitation. He shrugged dejectedly when she gave him a quick kiss on the cheek and rushed off.

Mimi drove home, took a bath, wrapped herself in the robe laundered so many times its original print no longer existed and then consumed what remained of yesterday's meat loaf. Climbing into bed, she craved sleep, yet knew it would not come. She was exhausted, to be sure, but fatigue was not the issue: she needed calm, the tranquility of having passed a full and productive day. This process of probing into her family history, while at the same time struggling to uncover hidden data, seemed suddenly more daunting than she had imagined. Perhaps even threatening. And the emotions arising from this tapestry she was endeavoring to unravel were confusing. She closed her eyes and willed herself to sleep. That six-essay exam she was planning to administer in the morning required that she be rested. Instead, her mind became a highway with thoughts rushing headlong in every direction. She thought of Malka, Fredl, Rivka, indomitable spirits. And then Mimi, fourth in line, the coward. Those women worried about Cossacks riding into town and raping the women; she agonized over meeting Joanna at Sarah's house to sort through her things. Sleep? It seemed to her it would never come. Perhaps she should have accepted Daniel's offer! A nice cuddle, comfortable sex with a man who loved her — hell, it couldn't hurt. Grabbing her robe, she headed down the hall to the study. There had been no restful nights since Sarah's death, so why should she expect tonight to be different?

&Nowy Życie, Winter, 1888

The storm was biting hard and it took a blast of gossip whipping from house to house to induce the locals to leave the comparative warmth of their hearths and congregate at Gershon's store. Standing together, they read the paper tacked up only hours earlier by Bogdan the postal clerk. It felt warm and safe inside. Outside, the roads were filled with people dragging themselves from village to village, poor souls buried under bags of clothing and kitchen utensils as they headed for Austria, Turkey, any border open to them. This fear of death was working its way into tissue and muscle, festering like the cut made from a ragged-edged shard. Their only hope was to put distance between themselves and the abominations they had witnessed. The increasing number of glassy-eyed survivors passing through only confirmed what the residents of Nowy Życie had been dreading: that the shtetls under attack bore familiar names and the horror was drawing nearer.

Malka stood at the front of the throng and once again read aloud this new order of conscription commanding that even ill-bodied Jewish men and boys must serve. The sighs behind her seemed to rise and become one with the moaning wind outside. As she repeated the sentence, the other women in the shop pressed close. "It's not enough they take our souls," mumbled the rabbi's wife, "but must they take our flesh as well?"

Grischa joined the women. "Since when has an edict stopped us from living?" He recognized the anger on Malka's face and looked away.

"You know very well that this one is different," Malka insisted. The buzz of support from the other mothers encouraged her boldness. "We're not talking another tax, Grischa, or the confiscation of our business. This deals with our children!"

"Thank heaven my husband is too old," sighed one woman.

"Can he walk?" asked Malka.

"Of course he can walk! What a question!"

"Then they'll insist he can fight."

"But my son," piped up the dairyman's wife. "He's only fourteen." And she murmured a quick prayer of thanks.

"My sister's boy was taken last month," came a reply from the rear, "and he wasn't even twelve."

Malka stretched up and ripped the paper from the wall. "If we don't know," she announced, "then there's nothing we can do."

A large man pushed himself to the front. "I'm sure the czar's soldiers will find your logic very convincing," he sneered. "Before anyone comes to drag us away, I say we consider our options."

"Options?" asked the women, looking around for the answer. "Other than leaving, what options do we have?"

"Amputation," he stated, his voice matter-of-fact, and then added with a touch of sarcasm, "as if you didn't know." It took several moments for the neighbors to make eye contact with one another. They all knew the procedure, were even familiar with people who had practiced it. What army, after all, would accept a man with missing fingers or a blinded eye?

Malka was outspoken in her disagreement. "You would even think of cutting off a son's finger? Poking out a husband's eye?" Her expression left no doubt that she found these thoughts repugnant.

Grischa moved into this circle of anxiety and placed a hand on his wife's shoulder. He could not help but notice how the lines in her face were deepening, how the muscle along her jaw twitched and pulsed. "What we must hold onto," he announced, "is hope."

"Hope!" Malka spat out. "No hope this time, and no miracles. And if any of you is waiting for another Rabbi Nahman of Bratslav, some pious soul who will spin his fantastic tales and lead us, his dear little lambs, toward all that is righteous and good, you're wasting your time." She turned toward the others, her eyes blazing with indignation. "The only place we'll be led is to slaughter!"

There was no need for Malka Gershon to examine her neighbors' faces to know she had hit her mark.

✑ Topanga Canyon, Spring 1984

Mimi was distracted by the clutter: papers and files, stacks of essays spread across the old oak rolltop desk. She needed to read each one, grade it and move swiftly to the next. On top of the slowly diminishing heap was an analysis of the effects of the Vichy government on leftist French literature. She picked it up, glanced over it. The student's attempt was brave but fragmented, as though he had taken several recognizable theses, formed a few loosely held opinions and then somehow managed to weave them together into what his professor might believe was a coherent whole.

Mimi made a few notations on the essay. Funny, she mused, how this paper and I are both being held together by the most fragile threads.

She gazed across the redwood deck, a weather-beaten expanse that began at the threshold of the study, ran past the kitchen, and continued until it terminated abruptly, its edge a drop of no more than three feet. She had recently noticed how, with each advancing year, this drop loomed more and more as a dangerous precipice. Not so long ago she would have hopped off that step; now she stepped gingerly, arms extended like wings, as if hoping to catch the wind to ease herself down.

A pair of young rabbits popped up from the earthen holes leading to the tunneled warren under the deck. Oh yes, she reminded herself, it must be spring. For eight years she had lived there, above the perennial smog of Los Angeles, eight seasons watching new generations of cottontails replenish a family already considered too large and bothersome by a handful of neighbors. It pleased her that after all that time she was still able to put aside her work and watch them, delight in their freedom, even wonder at their innocence. They seemed oblivious to the cruelties awaiting them in trees, behind rocks, in houses.

It was at this time every year—when baby rabbits emerged into what felt and smelled like a wonderful yet frightening world—that Mimi regretted never having married and borne children.   Expecting her neighbors to call any moment and complain about the rabbits, she was tempted to disconnect the phone. The woman living just up the canyon, for example, called quite regularly. "Your rabbits are depleting my garden," she accused.

"What am I to do?" Mimi had asked.

"I don't know, poison them, gas them, anything."

What she had done was drive down the mountain to the local nursery and ask for the flowers and vegetables that rabbits love.

"You mean that rabbits hate," corrected the owner's son.

"No," Mimi had responded patiently, "that they love. I intend to keep them well-fed and close to home."

He formed a little "oh" with his lips and nodded, as if humoring a dotty woman.

She forced her attention back to the papers. "Where do these students dig up their data?" she mumbled, and was brought up short by the next question popping into her head: And where do I dig up mine? What she needed was to buckle down and address the issue. Herself, her mother, her isolation, her anger. Above all, her anger. Like when she had mentioned to her mother that Daniel had inquired about her health and Rivka had dismissed the comment with, "Oh, him." In that simple statement Mimi had heard a familiar door slam shut: someone else not good enough for little Miriam. The mother of a middle-aged spinster ought to be grateful that such a nice man even inquired! And this was not simply a nice man, but the one and only man who had ever proposed marriage. And not once, but three times. The first time was when she was sixteen. A silly joke, she had told Sarah. Who gets married at sixteen? "People who don't want to live in sin," her friend had explained. This stunned Mimi, since she had never thought of Daniel like that! The second proposal came days before her eighteenth birthday, when she was preparing for university and the possibility of marriage had no place in her plans (especially with someone who felt more like a brother). Daniel cared about her, but was quick to admit that, just perhaps, there were ulterior motives: law students were being pulled from their secure little nests and shipped off to the Gulf of Tonkin. The last proposal came when Mimi was twenty-two. It was during a three-week interval when she was lonely and had let down her guard. She considered it a delightful fling, whereas Daniel had taken this as a prelude to commitment.

When Sarah had tried to give Mimi a push in Daniel's direction, she had balked. "I look into his eyes, Sarah, and I see forever. He looks into mine and sees six months, tops." A persistent pang of conscience finally put a stop to the affair.

As one of the cottontails dashed across the deck and disappeared into the warren, Mimi caught sight of the neighbor's cat crouching behind the hydrangea. To that rabbit, she thought, everything is foe. And then she sighed so loudly that the other rabbit made a quick turn, shot across the deck and joined its sibling in hiding. It was far more interesting studying the behavior of animals than her own. And a hell of a lot less threatening.

My students would accuse me of lacking courage, she told herself, and to that I say, Amen.

CHAPTER THREE

&*Topanga Canyon, Spring 1984*

IT WAS MORE than a month after the funeral and Mimi was still letting the answering machine pick up her messages. A ringing telephone had once signaled a welcomed break, an intermission from the ordinary—lunch with a friend, a weekend invitation to Idyllwild, Palm Springs, Santa Barbara—but no longer. Now it jarred, generated anxiety, and Mimi was tempted to let each call go unanswered. On occasion that red light would blink a full day before she could find the energy to hit the replay button, and even then she would only half listen, her gaze drifting around the room and her mind wandering to points far afield. When this happened, she would have to replay the message, reminding herself to focus on the voice. Commiserating friends wore her out and her mother's demands set her stomach churning. As for Daniel, his enticements to drop everything and escape were touching, but she couldn't find the heart to burden him with what she perceived to be extreme emotional need. It all came down to one brutal reality: no matter how many times that phone rang, it would never be Sarah on the other end. So when the phone rang late one afternoon and she heard Daniel's voice coming through the machine, she ignored it.

"I'm worried about you," he was saying. "I've been leaving messages and I only want to know that . . ."

Mimi snatched up the receiver. "I'm here," she said.

"Oh, hi. Well, just checking. Need anything?"

Mimi shrugged, as if he were in the room. "I'm pretty well

stocked," she finally answered. "You know me, Daniel, always pre-pared for the storm, or that unexpected nuclear attack."

"You mean there's actually a way to prepare for one?"

She wanted to laugh with him, but could not find the humor. "I wish I could move," she said. "You know, budge, but I can't seem to do it. I'm glued to the floor." After a pause, she added, "That must sound odd."

"Actually," he responded, "I remember the sensation all too well." When Mimi said nothing, he suggested they go for a drive.

It was a nice invitation, innocent, yet the word *trespassing* popped into her head. Was that how it would be, always looking askew at kindness and seeing interference? Mimi sensed that, in her present state, she was incapable of making the distinction. She nearly said, "I don't need a nursemaid," but stopped herself. It wasn't Daniel's fault that Sarah was dead, or that he cared about her well-being. "It's a lovely offer," she said. "Really, it is, but I'm not in great shape." Was that too curt, she wondered, or had she perhaps managed to interject a bit of gratitude in her voice? The lengthy silence on the other end answered the question.

"Mimi," Daniel finally said, "I have no desire to be a nuisance."

Although the statement was made with remarkable kindness, she half expected a hand to reach through the receiver and slap her face. "I'm sorry," she mumbled.

"Mimi, there's no need to apologize," he responded.

Damn him! The kinder he was, the greater her remorse. "It's just that, well, you know me: I resist anything that smacks of therapy." Having said this, and then hearing Daniel's laughter, Mimi felt sud-denly lighter, lightened.

"I've got an idea," he said. "How about I come by and we walk down the hill for some coffee." Before she could respond, he added, "Something stronger, if you prefer."

Waiting for Daniel, she stared into the open space above the deck and thought about the world of people out there, individuals and families living normal, scheduled lives. Would she ever be able to do that again? The sound of Daniel coming up the drive shook her from the reverie and she rushed outside. "I've changed my mind," she said, climbing in. "If we hurry, we can make it to the beach before sunset."

Without a word, Daniel reversed the car and headed down the drive. When they hit the main road leading down to the coast, he deftly maneuvered the perilous curves. Mimi enjoyed the scenery, while praying for a clear shot, meaning no ambulances hoisting careless cyclists from one of the ravines. With twenty minutes left before sundown and the traffic gods on their side, there was a good chance they'd make it. When they reached the coast route, they headed north past the secured gates of Malibu Colony and its resident movie stars cloistered inside.

They continued in silence, but it was that comfortable silence existing between old friends, two people who had no need to talk for their thoughts to be shared. Daniel concentrated on the road and Mimi tried to stay focused on the vista: sea-green swells topped with white frothy ocean kicking up under an early evening sky. Running through her head were assorted rationales for leaving her job and moving to another state, which meant abandoning this quest and giving up for lost this absurd idea of digging and musing and searching. She had barely begun, and already it was draining her.

Daniel pulled into a roadside parking area. Within minutes they had their shoes removed and were trudging toward the water. The process of digging her feet into the sand proved to be exactly what Mimi needed. For too many months she had been living in a stupor, shifting between the bedside of a dying friend, the demands of a trying mother and several hundred students. She was bone-tired; never in her life had she been so weary. The warm sand between her toes, the magnificent orange-tinted horizon, the comfort of being with Daniel, a trusted friend—everything soothed.

After watching the last breathtaking vestige of sundown, Mimi and Daniel strolled up the beach. When they reached the impassable point jutting out from the shore—the only visible break in an otherwise continuous motif of water and white caps—they paused. Facing the sea, their backs to the North American continent, Mimi found herself thinking not of Sarah, but of her father. He had been cremated, scattered at sea, and was now floating out there among fish and algae. Normally she would dedicate a few moments to the memory of Harold Zilber, but today she could give him little more than quick consideration. She had barely the energy to breathe, much less reflect.

Mimi and Daniel sat on the beach and watched as the sun repeated its daily phenomenon of hovering inches above a vast horizon and then plummeting stonelike from view, leaving behind a glorious aura heralding the arrival of night.

They returned to the car. With both doors open and legs dangling over the pavement, they sat back-to-back, shaking sand from their clothing and digging it out from between their toes. Daniel finished first and came around to Mimi's side. "Take off your sweater," he said, holding out a hand. As he shook sand from the cardigan, Mimi felt like a little girl being cared for by an attentive big brother. She said nothing, but was acutely aware of how loved it made her feel. Loved and, in turn, alarmed. Which is how any man's attention made her feel. Because always, just over her shoulder, was her mother's voice. "He'll take advantage," is what it said. "He'll want something in return."

Daniel helped her on with the sweater. "I was remembering…"

Mimi said nothing, but knew where this was going.

"I can't be around you without thinking of when we were teenagers." He gave a little laugh and added, "Bad timing, I guess."

Mimi turned to face him and her expression left no doubt that he was entering unfriendly territory.

The grimace caused him to smile. "You'd think I was still searching for an explanation."

"Daniel . . ."

"With Vietnam in full swing, who had time to think about marriage, right?" He shook his head and chuckled at himself. "Funny, but in those days it made perfect sense." There was a sadness in Mimi's eyes that turned him instantly somber. He brushed the last of the sand from his pants, mumbled something about ancient history and helped her into the car.

As they were backing out of the parking area, Mimi was struck by an image so vivid she nearly reached out to touch it. She was a child, no more than four or five, and she was leaning across the kitchen table to touch the red cut-glass bowl. Inside were wrapped candies, hard ones filled with sweet jellies. As a child, she was always reaching for food. It's what nurtured and sustained me, she thought. And then she realized that, for the first time since Sarah's death, she was actually hungry. When she mentioned it to Daniel, he laughed aloud. As if this were his greatest achievement.

They agreed on a local diner and headed down the coast toward Santa Monica. Oncoming headlights shot jet streams of light against their faces. "The one love I shared with my father was the beach," murmured Mimi. "I can't be here without thinking of him."

"And my clearest memory of him is being subjected to his history lessons."

Mimi's dramatic groan made them giggle like children.

"No, really!" insisted Daniel. "He collared me one Saturday and I became another of Harold Zilber's history hostages. By the time he let me go, I knew more about the siege of Leningrad than my teachers."

Mimi closed her eyes and nodded. "It was his passion. Imagine what he could have done with an education."

"A passion?" challenged Daniel. "I would've said it was his escape." He glanced quickly toward Mimi and saw the frown. "I'm imposing, sorry."

Mimi shifted her gaze to the scenery passing outside, aware of how angry she was that Daniel would judge her father. She nearly accused him of involving himself where he wasn't welcome, where he hadn't been invited. Instead, she rebuked herself for overreacting and imagined them walking along the water's edge. She felt so safe there, as if each wave breaking against the shore could carry away all this pain. She was much too tired, too confused, to even begin to sort out what Daniel was saying. And yet try as she did, the process of summoning up the memory of her father's face, his mannerisms and gestures, was proving more difficult than she would have imagined. Perhaps it was the fatigue, but Harold Zilber appeared as a vague outline barely visible behind the barriers he had erected between himself and his family. Whether it was a raised newspaper or a closed door, Mimi had never found him truly approachable. She could speak to him, certainly, and he would respond, but there was always that curtain of culture and language that hung suspended between them. Even now, at her age, Mimi had never admitted to anyone but Sarah how his behavior — and this included his indiscretions — was actually an escape from a difficult, indifferent wife. What else could he have been avoiding? Mimi sighed louder than she intended. As always, sifting through these vague and muddled memories was tantamount to peering into a fog.

When it came to recollections of her mother, however, the image was clearer, more immediate. A woman lifting a child onto the kitchen chair; a woman handing the child a spoon covered with cake batter. Mimi felt her mother's hands on her face, dishwashing-dry hands smelling of onions pushing away strands of thick unruly hair. She could see the top of her mother's head as she bent over to rub a shine into new patent-leather shoes that gave off flashes of reflected light when Mimi swung her legs back and forth.

"Daniel," she suddenly said, "do you mind? I'd really like to go home."

He moved as if to touch her hand and then pulled back.

"It's not you," she said. "It's just that I feel so . . . so flat, you know? Empty. Maybe it's too soon to be social."

"Having dinner with me isn't exactly socializing."

Mimi did not respond. In truth, she had barely heard the words, occupied as she was with a voice filling her head. It was her mother's voice, but it wasn't Rivka Zilber at eighty; it was someone young, yet far from youthful. And Mimi was there, a little girl running through rooms and into a space flooded with steam and dampness. Rivka was lifting the child, plopping her into the bathtub. The child squirmed as her mother leaned over the tub and began rubbing her with tar soap, digging the washcloth into her back and chest as if excavating for dirt. You will be clean if I have to scrub all day, said the relentless scrubbing. Decades later and Mimi still felt the harshness of that washcloth, saw tight-lipped determination on her mother's face, and she was mesmerized by the image.

Somewhere on the edge of this recollection sat Daniel, steering deftly through traffic and allowing her the silence she required.

I was supposed to be the most special little girl in the world, she thought. The world's most wanted child. She pressed her fingertips against her eyes.

"Headache?"

She nodded. How does one silence such thoughts? Squeezing her eyes shut against a surge of anger, she could not shut out that little girl, head covered with ringlets held together by red ribbons washed and ironed nearly every day by a woman who considered herself a devoted mother.

Daniel slipped into the left lane, preparing to make the turn into the canyon, and Mimi caught one last glimpse of the water, streaks of silver shimmering in the moonlight. There was something deeply satisfying about the way the ocean's waves rolled in and slammed with jackhammer force against the rocks. Never once did she walk on the sand or drive along the coast without wishing that southern California offered fewer beaches and more rocky coastline. Like Big Sur, she thought, where waves hit with such force that it seemed they had bulldozers behind them.

Daniel slammed on the brakes and swerved to control the car. An earthmover had lumbered out from a side road, heedless of the oncoming traffic. There was a screeching sound as other cars attempted to stop, and then that welcome moment of silence when the realization came that there would be no impact.

Mimi was jolted from her reverie. She watched as the massive machine rolled up the road for several hundred feet before it pulled to the right and allowed them to pass. She imagined her mother standing in front of the machine, hand raised as if daring it to come any closer.

"Are you okay?" asked Daniel.

Mimi turned toward him and forced a smile. "It's a relief to know that bad things can sometimes be avoided."

Daniel started to respond and then changed his mind. Some things, he wanted to say, are better confronted head-on.

When they reached the house, Mimi leaned over and gave him a quick kiss on the cheek. "It was lovely," she told him, reaching for the door's handle.

"At least allow me to walk you to the door," he protested.

Mimi placed a hand on his arm. "Don't bother," she said. "It was exactly what I needed. And thank you, really." Before he could respond, she added, "You know, I actually believe I'll be able to sleep!" Gratitude brought a wistful pleasure to her eyes. She climbed out of the car and walked toward the front door. It pleased her that Daniel remained until she was safely inside. Sarah had always done that, even in daylight and it made her feel cared for, protected.

A sliced apple, half a bagel, and then sleep. Slipping between the sheets, Mimi believed she would sleep for hours. Within minutes, however, it was clear that neither a walk on the beach nor having her lungs filled with the freshest air was going to help. And no amount of tossing and turning was going to make a difference: sleep would not come. Lying in the dark, she told herself that insomnia was a natural by-product of Sarah's death, but a second more insistent voice debated that. Clarify your feelings, it told her, sort them out and put them into columns. Column A will be about Sarah and the myriad emotions you feel, and will continue to feel, without her. Column B will be about your mother. Mimi became aware of an acute gnawing in her stomach. Perhaps I'm better off not making neat little lists, she told herself. It's too easy, too academic. And then the question — Why must it always come down to my mother? She's done her damage, but is blaming her really the answer. Mama's not the issue. The issue is how has a woman who has attained this respectable age managed to avoid relationships or, for that matter, most forms of intimacy, for so long? Mimi jolted upright and turned on the bedside lamp. Her use of third person, that detached and impersonal noun, was so damned safe.

Mimi felt a sudden draft, like a breath from the grave and she imagined Sarah chiding her for being so self-indulgent. Perhaps the question had nothing to do with how she found herself alone, but why? And yet, she wasn't so terribly alone! She had her work, a large number of casual friends, Daniel. And then she heard Sarah retort, "Oh, but you are, my love, you are absolutely alone, and it's got nothing to do with my dying!" Mimi pulled the blankets so close that her head nearly disappeared underneath.

She commanded herself to sleep, but it was no use. "Damn it to hell," she muttered, throwing back the blankets. She should have accepted her mother's offer of those tranquilizers. But no, not Mimi, she was too proud to admit the necessity, the damned exigency.

Over the next few days she managed to correct all of the term papers, a good part of the work accompanied by a light rain and the pleasure of observing one little rabbit's tentative excursions into a new world. Despite this surge of energy and renewed efficiency, she felt heavy, lugubrious. Daniel called twice to suggest they take another drive, but she declined. "I'm not easy to be with," she explained, giving silent thanks when he acquiesced. One night she broke three plates and understood that it was part rage, part love: Sarah had hated them. The fact that this little drama had been preceded by a dinner out with her mother was no surprise.

"You look pale, dear," Rivka had commented after their orders had been taken.

Mimi tried to explain that she was having difficulty sleeping and that Sarah's death had left a painful void.

The old woman made a sympathetic clicking sound. "You'll get over it."

Like a case of the measles, thought Mimi, and ordered a second glass of wine.

Driving home, she felt light, unsubstantial, as if all that remained of her was a shell. It's the wine, she told herself, and then brushed away the idea. For the time being, she was a shell, with a bit of connective tissue and a brain. She wondered what would happen if some loving man arrived from nowhere and offered to soothe her pain. *Like Daniel?* came the immediate question. Who takes your arm when you're walking and sees you safely inside? Mimi thought about this for a moment and decided that Daniel's attentiveness was more disconcerting. Perhaps it was the comprehension she recognized in his eyes that made her uncomfortable. He knew her so well. After having worked so hard to camouflage her needy side, she'd be damned if she'd let Daniel, or anyone else, expose her. *Sarah understood me better than anyone,* she thought, and then grimaced. *Perhaps that's why she was always after me to see a therapist. But who had the time? And for what? To learn that I'm neurotic? To be told that I'm afraid to enter relationships or make commitments? Or that I have destroyed the former with some very eligible men because I feared the latter? I already know that, so why go to the trouble?*

By the time Mimi arrived home, the loneliness was overwhelming. She had once mentioned feeling lonely to her mother, but Rivka had looked away, mumbling something about it being "in the family." Mimi had pushed her to explain, but instead the woman spoke in generalizations about all the women in her family being lonely. "Ah," Mimi had responded sarcastically, "then it's genetic." Her mother had refused to bite. Instead, she had pressed her lips together and fallen silent.

And now it was this very silence that was pushing Mimi forward, urging her to uncover and comprehend all those things her mother refused to tell.

Four generations of women, she thought, and I am the last. Malka, Fredl, Rivka and me. And not the last to date, but the last ever. An only child, a woman with no children; the end of the line. Malka, Fredl, Rivka, Mimi. Period. Fin. If only she could understand why it ended here.

CHAPTER FOUR

&*Topanga Canyon, Spring 1984*

MIMI CARRIED HER COFFEE out to the deck and settled into the butterfly chair. Without the ministrations of a loving hand, the garden had run amok. All that remained of the Dutch irises were stringy stalks devoid of flowers; her Iceland poppies had deteriorated to two-dozen evenly spaced, unrecognizable brown clumps. When Sarah was still living and Mimi was passing every spare minute of free time at her bedside, she had neither thought nor concern for such trivial pursuits as deadheading a bed of poppies. And that clay pot containing three-dozen loose gladioli bulbs — *nanus* variety, white with startling hot-pink centers — that had been awaiting her for months? Now sunbaked and standing in a shallow pool of rainwater, they were beyond salvation.

Mimi pushed away the guilt associated with her neglected garden and thoughts of Daniel rushed into the abandoned space. Why do I feel this need to hold his acts of kindness at such a distance, she wondered. Maybe for the same reason you do with everyone else, came the reply. The brutal directness of the response surprised her, accustomed as she was to her own comfortably detached assessments. Everything at a safe distance, that was her creed.

Daniel had been calling more frequently since the funeral, dropping by and making himself available. His presence was triggering old memories, those marriage proposals among them. Why had she said no? Was it that she had never loved him? Perhaps, as she now feared, she had known nothing of love.

Warming her hands on the mug resting in her lap, she examined the probability of having evolved from a marital disaster. Even as a teenager she had recognized that her parents did not have the marriage she wanted. The union had rung so hollow, with her mother making all the decisions and her father remaining silent behind his daily paper.

Mimi took a cautious sip and was surprised to find the coffee nearly cold. It was so tempting to blame her parents for her avoidance of marriage. Yet she could not fault her mother for not trying! Rivka had made sporadic efforts to introduce her only child to some neighbor's son, a brother-in-law or favored nephew of someone's sister's second cousin. "Miriam," she would announce, face pinched as she confronted her daughter. "He's perfect for you: well educated and from a good family." These attempts always made Mimi feel like an object her mother couldn't give away at a rummage sale.

All these years and nothing had changed. Two days earlier Rivka had called to announce that Mrs. Singer's oldest boy was getting a divorce. "They separated last week," she explained, her voice filled with hope. "Such a shame!" What did her mother expect her to say when informed that another Jewish male had been released to, loosed upon, society? "Mama, Mrs. Singer's oldest boy has been married three times." She girded herself for the comeback. There was a lengthy pause, after which the old woman replied, "We learn by our mistakes."

❧ Nowy Życie, Fall 1887

When the Jews were expelled from Moscow as a measure of ethnic purification, entire neighborhoods were forced to relocate, igniting revolutionary stirrings that simmered for decades. Zionist groups formed in St. Petersburg, Moscow, and Kiev; eager young Jews heeded the call of eminent philanthropists such as Baron Edmond de Rothschild and volunteered to participate in the resettlement of Palestine. In the swamps of the Middle East arose malaria-infested villages like Petah Tikvah—Gate of Hope—places that seemed like the promised land to idealistic young pioneers. The majority of Jews, however, remained in Russia, settling either just outside Moscow or responding to the invitation of their families and moving into the countryside, to the shtetls. Some even came to Nowy Życie.

The Rabinoff family was known and admired by the citizens of Nowy Życie. Benjamin Rabinoff was considered the town's legal expert, called upon both by citizens and their rabbinic council to settle local disputes. His wife, Leah, was the daughter of Rabbi Kamin, one of the great Hasidic scholars of the century. The expulsion of Moscow's Jews increased by four the size of the Rabinoff family. Jacob Kamin, Leah's older brother, his wife and two children moved into the Rabinoff home. With them came more books than even Fredl Gershon thought possible.

"Is it true, Papa, what they say about Jacob Kamin?" she asked.

"And what might that be?" responded her father.

"That he was Dostoyevsky's ghostwriter. Szulen's mother says it's not so, but still . . ."

Grischa looked at Fredl over his reading glasses. "If she says no, then it must not be true."

Fredl seemed torn between believing the word of a good and respectable woman and exciting neighborhood gossip. "To be so learned," she sighed, looking off in the direction of Szulen's house. "And to work with someone as great as Dostoyevsky—" Her voice trailed off in unmasked admiration.

Grischa removed the glasses. "Great, perhaps, but known by many to be an anti-Semite."

"Perhaps this is why Mrs. Rabinoff denies it." Fredl released a disappointed sigh, kissed her father's forehead, and excused herself. In a few days she would turn eighteen and there were many things to do in preparation for her birthday party. She spent hours imagining all the wonderful possibilities awaiting a girl about to become an adult.

Malka had other thoughts to occupy her mind, considerations going far beyond birthday plans. When she finally had Grischa alone in their bedroom, she confessed her concerns. "Fredl," she declared, "is almost eighteen." The words were saturated with intention.

"She's a child," Grischa reminded her. "A wonderful child."

"And it's so wonderful when our daughter announces she won't marry until she's thirty? Thirty! Or that she intends to leave home and become a journalist in Warsaw? A Jewish girl a journalist in

Warsaw? What nonsense!" Malka made a gesture with her hand as if to brush away her daughter's dreams, but then her face suddenly softened. "She may be intelligent, but she has no idea, none." When Grischa shrugged, his wife took this to be reluctant agreement. "Have you ever considered that she has perhaps too much energy?" she asked. "Too great a sense of independence?" When she saw the displeasure in his eyes, she dropped the subject.

On the night of the party, Fredl felt like the princess in a fairy tale. Placed before her was one delightful gift after another. She opened each one and declared her absolute delight, while her parents sat on either side sharing her pleasure. Whenever their eyes met it was with the same thought: So much fear and pain outside, thank God we can take one evening to enjoy what we have.

The party surpassed everyone's expectations. Not only had Fredl been regaled by every member of her thriving family — one niece and two nephews had been added in the last year alone — but friends and neighbors who dropped by during the evening to wish her well. She received hair ribbons, a lovely red scarf knitted by her oldest brother's wife, and books. So many that, after the festivities, she had nearly a dozen stacked beside her bed.

"I guess this means you'll have to build another shelf," she teased her father. When he pretended to be overwhelmed, she put her arms around him and planted a loud kiss on his bearded cheek.

Fredl was the one member of the Gershon family who displayed whatever she was feeling. She was the kind of girl who would sing while working in a miserably hot kitchen, who composed poetry while sewing a hem. Fredl at age eighteen viewed life as a wonderful adventure filled with limitless possibilities. Some called her irrepressible, although Malka occasionally accused her of being pigheaded and stubborn. Despite this conflict, she fought for the girl's right to explore her world. While other girls of Nowy Życie were kept busy baking cakes and cleaning house, Fredl was permitted to rush through her chores and get on to her real work: reading whatever book awaited her; jotting down notations to determine her next project; composing yet another letter in her ongoing conflict with the Warsaw library. Other girls might get annoyed over mud tracked onto newly washed floors; what irritated Fredl most was some foolish librarian who stymied her request for dramatic texts.

"We have a fine library right here," reminded her mother.

"Fine for anything about Torah," replied Fredl. "But William Shakespeare is another matter."

Having encouraged the girl's quest for knowledge, what could Malka do but nod and sigh?

Even the townspeople had come to expect something different from Fredl. When they heard she was preparing a production of Shakespeare, the response was not the expected, "Shakespeare? Why, that's amazing!" but "Didn't she do Shakespeare last season? Ah, too bad, I was hoping for something more contemporary." And when her father asked, "And is there anything wrong with Yiddish theater?" she usually responded by tweaking his chin.

Fredl had a wonderful gift of adjusting to whatever life delivered. When her oldest brother's wife insisted she accompany them to shul every Friday night, she did so graciously. That she had several pages of her novel hidden in the folds of the siddur, the prayer book her mother had given her when she turned thirteen, remained her secret. Which was not to say she lacked interest. All girls were excluded from attending cheder, but this had never stopped her. From the age of six, she had pulled a stool down the road almost daily and planted herself below the school's window, within earshot of the teacher.

All in all, Fredl found life more than satisfactory.

Malka and Grischa admired their daughter's tenacity and had often shared a laugh over that night when the eleven-year-old had stood at the dinner table, demanded everyone's attention, and then, with slender neck stretched in a regal fashion and those dark eyes flashing, had announced, "From this day forward, I shall be known as Alexandria."

"You mean," asked her little sister, "as in Egypt?"

Fredl had shot Hannah a warning look and set her jaw in that very determined Malka Gershon way, which had caused poor Hannah to sink her head into her shoulders and sulk.

"Alexandria," ruminated Grischa, allowing the name to roll around in his mouth as he nodded contemplatively. Picking up a slab of brown bread, he balanced it in the palm of his hand. "Yes, I see your point. It is lovely, Alexandria." Light sparkled in Fredl's dark eyes. Grischa spread a dollop of fresh butter across the bread. "And may I add," he continued, "how very much our Czar Alexander will appreciate this warm tribute." He took a large bite and began to chew. "And has there ever been a more appropriate name for a Jewish girl than Alexandria?" He winked at Fredl and continued eating.

The girl mumbled about one having nothing to do with the other, but her confidence had clearly wobbled. There was a brief silence and then she asked, "Do you know what it's like, having a name like Fredl-Fredl-spin-my-dredl?"

Malka shot a glance at Hannah, who had begun to giggle, and then, with obvious effort, set her face into a maternal glare. When the very same glare was returned by her elder daughter, she was taken aback. A creative streak was one thing, but insolence quite another. God only knows, thought Malka, what awaits us with the arrival of adolescence!

And now their Fredl had turned eighteen. Once the guests had left for home and the glasses and plates were washed, dried, and returned to the cupboard, Grischa moved from room to room performing his nightly tasks: to guarantee that the gas lamps were fully extinguished, doors secured, and no residual ashes remained smoldering in the stove. As he slowly poured water over the last embers, he could hear Malka's voice in his head.

"It only takes one gust of wind," she would warn. "One gust sweeping off the fields to ignite floorboards and walls, and then burn down our house."

Grischa smiled to himself. So much to worry about and she must focus on sparks and conflagration. Perhaps it's better, he told himself. What good does it do to agonize over these new atrocities when we can do so little to stop them? One spark popping out, igniting floorboards—now *that* we can fix.

Satisfied by the low hissing sound of dying embers, Grischa filled the enamel washbasin with the remaining hot water. Once again, he thought, we have been saved from the fiery jaws of death. He carried the sloshing basin into the bedroom and put it on the stand.

Malka was too exhausted from the evening's efforts to follow her husband around and perform her usual backup fire inspection. Before washing her face and preparing for bed, she joined him in their daughter's bedroom for the ritual good-night kiss.

Fredl hugged them both. "It was a perfect night," she said.

"Is this what you would like for your eighteenth birthday?" Grischa asked Hannah.

Hannah chewed on her lower lip. Fidgeting with the corner of the quilt, she drew her fine eyebrows together.

"Don't worry so," he laughed. "You have many years to decide."

Despite the playfulness filling the room, neither Grischa nor Malka could push away the nightmare that was still unfolding. Three boys from Nowy Życie had vanished without a trace and a citizen's group, led by Grischa, had confronted authorities on several occasions before learning the boys had been conscripted. When the aide to the region's superintendent suggested that they should be proud to have sons supporting czarist efforts, the disconsolate little group disbanded in defeat. Grischa had suggested to Malka that perhaps this was not the best time for a celebration. "One must go on living," she had bristled, and her husband could not disagree.

After the good-nights, Malka led her husband into their room, where he collapsed onto the bed. Pulling off his shoes, he began to rub the heel of his foot. "It was a wonderful party," he said, but was quickly silenced by Malka's upraised hand. She cocked an ear toward the room across the hall, heard laughter, and closed the door.

Grischa slipped the yarmulke from his head, placed it on the nightstand, and pressed both palms against his eyes. "Now what?"

Malka made an impatient gesture and set about removing her heavy skirt. She hung it in the armoire her husband had built for her and began working on the tiny buttons that ran down the front of her blouse. "You realize that our Fredl is eighteen." Grischa did not respond. "And what kind of a future does she have?"

He beckoned her to move closer. "She's eighteen," he said, helping with the buttons. "Not exactly an old maid." He looked up at his wife. "Must we worry about her future tonight?" When Malka frowned, he added, "Just look at her, my dear," waving a hand as though the girl were standing before them. "Our world is falling apart, yet somehow she retains her wonderful energy."

Malka moved to the basin and set about scrubbing her face. "Ah yes," she said, eyes squeezed shut, "that wonderful energy." She pulled the little towel from its hook and patted her face.

Grischa was too tired to rehash the subject. Sliding into bed, he pulled the comforter up to his chin, reached under and slipped out his flowing beard. When it settled, it resembled a fine white fan.

The ensuing silence led Malka to believe that her husband had fallen asleep. Watching herself in the mirror, she brushed her hair.

"Her energy reminds me every day," Grischa mumbled sleepily, "that there is hope."

The grimace on Malka's face was obscured as she bent over to brush the full-length of her hair. According to *you*, she told herself. Settling into the feather mattress, she leaned into Grischa and willed fatigue to carry her away, but it did not, would not. Fredl's future was like a needle that probed her. She gripped the comforter, twisted and pulled, tugging until the fringe at the corners began to unravel. If Fredl was already eighteen and not yet married, what would become of her?

Grischa reached out and found her hand. "Don't worry so," he murmured, "she'll be fine."

Her response was not at all the accepting sigh he had hoped for, but a moaning sound. Mustering more energy than he believed possible, he hoisted himself onto one elbow. "Malka, there are too many big problems, serious ones."

No response.

"Must we lose a night of sleep over Fredl's future?"

Her refusal to respond nettled him. Understanding his wife's stubborn streak, however, he settled back into the mattress and fell asleep.

Malka remained wide awake. Perhaps she could do nothing about conscription, but she had every intention of doing something about her daughter's marriage prospects. And she knew exactly who would make the best candidate. Szulen Rabinoff, she thought, shifting her feet against the warmth of her husband. No one will do but Szulen. Fredl is a headstrong girl, but does that mean she must be condemned to a life that excludes a good marriage? Szulen is from a fine family, and I've seen the way he watches her, amused by her wit, her quickness. What other boy can keep up with her? No, it must be Szulen.

The only question is: how do I make it happen? While it was true that most of her friends used one of Nowy Życie's several matchmakers, Malka had always thought this an intrusion upon a family's privacy. Perhaps it was time to reconsider. But what if the Rabinoffs refused? Everyone in town would soon learn of the rejection! Poor Fredl would be humiliated, she thought, and as for me . . .

The wheels turned on and on until, only a few hours before the first gray light appeared through the bedroom curtains, Malka fell asleep.

Topanga Canyon, Summer 1984

Mimi sat at the kitchen table clutching a large glass of iced tea, her best antidote to a heat wave already in its fourth day. She felt sapped of energy, wished that someone would walk through the door and hand her a week's worth of lectures. Better yet, take over this task of self-appraisal and do her thinking for her! At the moment, her mind was locked onto a thought that had been poking at her all morning. Had she been so enamored by the love stories of her shtetl ancestors that she had measured every relationship against theirs? If so, it was no wonder that no man had ever measured up. Mulling this over, she recalled her mother's dire warnings: "If you sneak sweets and get fat, who will want you?" and "If you don't hold back those opinions, who will respect you?" No matter what the admonition, it always translated as nice girls get the prince, difficult girls do not.

Sarah and Mimi had taken Rivka Zilber's warnings and turned them into sport. "Touch that pimple again," warned Sarah in her best Rivka accent, "and the prince will never come! What decent man would marry a girl with scars? You understand, my little Miriam, that you're going to have to settle for the toad."

Was it any surprise that the idea of marriage never appealed to her? The question prompted a recollection of her mother extolling the virtues of marriage and a teenage Mimi judging what was being said as false. "Do you mean . . . like yours?" she had responded. The expression that had moved slowly across Rivka's face had made the girl feel ashamed.

Years after Sarah and Diego Arcario were married, he put an arm around Mimi and asked, "Found Mr. Frog yet?" What he could not know was that she had already given up trying. Looking back, Mimi could not help but cringe. Diego's comment was taken as amusing, but in fact it was not. How funny was it to imply her inadequacy at finding happiness, much less her unworthiness of winning the prince?

She wandered into the kitchen and heated a pot of water. Waiting for it to boil, she poured a little milk into the cup. If it was inadequacy and unworthiness she felt, was it any wonder she had never given credence to Daniel's proposals? He loved her, so why couldn't she love him back? How do you dare to love, came the response, if you feel undeserving of love? Mimi dropped the carton of milk onto the counter with a thud.

&*Nowy Życie, Spring 1888*

Malka awoke with a sense of purpose. Dressing quickly, she set about her morning duties with renewed energy. My Fredl is kind and caring, she told herself, sometimes wise beyond her years. Yes, the girl can be headstrong, but she will make a good wife, a wonderful mother. Before Grischa could join her for breakfast, the list of assets had become quite long.

When she informed Grischa of her decision to visit the matchmaker, he could not suppress the urge to tease. "But you must first accept the harsh fact," he muttered, "that all the kings and czars are taken."

After he had departed for the store and the girls were fed and organized, Malka ran a comb through her hair and marched straight to the home of Sada the Matchmaker.

"Your daughter," stated the woman, "could be a difficult match."

"I admit she's lively, but I would not say difficult."

"My dear Mrs. Gershon, your daughter is an opinionated young woman and everyone knows it. Some tea?"

Malka accepted with a curt nod. Narrowing her eyes, she brought the cup to her lips and examined this maker of dreams through the pungent trail of steam.

Sada, uncomfortable with such scrutiny, readjusted her ill-fitting wig. Her comment had caused displeasure, but it was nothing a nice cup of tea wouldn't calm. "Sugar?"

Malka fixed a little smile across her mouth. Let's stop with the preliminaries, she thought, slipping a second spoonful of sugar into her cup, and get down to business. "My Fredl will be a fine wife, a loving mother."

Sada shifted her gaze away, as if reflecting on how lovely it was outside, how beautifully the flowers bloomed, how freely the birds took flight. In truth, she was reminding herself that she desperately needed to make this match. She fingered a silver spoon, one of the few objects of value left by the tax man following her husband's death. Sada my girl, she thought, stirring her tea, you must move prudently, with attention to detail. And never forget: a second Gershon daughter is not far behind. She met the gaze of her client. "I'll take good care of your Fredl."

Malka squared herself by placing her hands palm down on the shabby ecru lace tablecloth. "Excellent," she stated, "now let's talk specifics."

"Ah yes," responded Sada, head tipped in acknowledgment. "By all means, specifics." Reaching behind her, she took a plate of sweet biscuits from the counter. "Some *mandel broite?*"

Malka ignored the offer. "My husband and I believe that the only possibility is Szulen Rabinoff."

Sada nodded, lips pursed, as if trying to impress on this client her ability to think things through, to reason out the possibilities and consider all the angles before responding. Distracted for just a moment by the pattern of tea leaves in the bottom of her teacup, Sada forced her attention back to Malka and saw that the woman was becoming restless. "A good choice," she said, "and such a fine family," while simultaneously thinking, How can I marry off such an independent girl? A furrow appeared in her brow.

A light rain had begun, its gentle tapping against the tin roof accompanied by the irregular cadence of wagon wheels bumping along the rutted road. Malka leaned forward, stretching both arms across the tabletop until her fingertips were only inches from the elbows of the matchmaker. "So let's get down to it." Her lips parted in anticipation.

Sada became alert. Malka Gershon's eyes dancing with such anticipation meant only one thing: a fine fee would be collected from this one. "I will approach the Rabinoffs at once and see what can be arranged."

As Malka stood and began pulling on her gloves, Sada looked around her shabby kitchen. The promise of a fee made it appear suddenly brighter. Some fresh paint will do nicely, she thought, perhaps a new curtain over the sink.

The match was several days in the making. When Sada finally arrived at the doorstep of the Gershon home and announced that arrangements had been successfully completed, a normally composed Malka gushed her thanks and ran inside to fetch her coat.

Crossing the road toward home, Sada thought of the next challenge coming from the Gershon household. Where will I ever find someone able to live with that one? she wondered, seeing Hannah's sullen face. Perhaps an older man.

Pulling her coat around her, Malka rushed out of the house and hurried toward the store. Bursting through the door, she hooked her arm through Grischa's and dragged him into the storage room. "It's done!" she announced.

Grischa closed his eyes and nodded.

"You aren't happy?"

Grischa kissed Malka on both cheeks. "Of course I'm happy, my dear. Szulen is a wonderful boy."

"Well then?"

"I'm just wondering which of us is to have the honor of breaking this wonderful news to our daughter?"

For a long moment, Malka said nothing. When she spoke, her voice was tinged with uncertainty. "Yes, I see your point."

That night, after several cups of tea braced with a few shots of whiskey, Grischa announced that it was time to approach their daughter. Malka had been sorting through some new fabric samples and had found one she considered perfect for the mother of the bride. Clutching the material in her hand, she followed her husband.

They found Fredl in her room, curled up on her bed with a book. Grischa shifted his weight a bit and then lowered himself carefully onto the corner of the bed. "Fredeleh," he began, and then immedi-

ately regretted using the endearing form of her name. Fredl hadn't
been addressed like this for years; she closed her book very slowly,
placed it beside her on the bed and regarded her parents with suspicion.

"Your mother and I would like a word with you."

Fredl leaned back and waited. What can they be hiding behind
those ridiculous smiles? she wondered. Awaiting her father's explanation, she began imagining the possible scenarios. Perhaps with all this
violence we're moving away, she thought. No, Mama seems too
pleased for that. And then she caught her breath. Mama's pregnant!

"Grischa," crooned the woman, "isn't there something you'd like to
tell Fredl?"

Yes, thought Fredl, that's definitely it. But she's a grandmother!
And then it hit her. She rose slowly from the bed. The book slid to the
floor with a thud, but no one moved to retrieve it. She saw concern on
her parents' faces, but the only sound she heard was a voice in her
head shouting, No! Seeking reassurance, she looked from one parent
to the other. Tell me that no decision has been made, she wanted to
say, but clearly it had. "I am to be married." There was no trace of
emotion in her voice. "That's it, isn't it? You went behind my back and
made a match and now. . . ." She continued in a whisper. "Now I am
to be given away in marriage like some piece of property."

Malka was alarmed. She had expected resistance, certainly, but
never an accusation of betrayal. "Darling," she said, the word lacking
the joy so recently felt.

Fredl took a step backward and looked at her mother with
unmasked hostility. This is not my mother, said her expression, this is
some meddling, imposing stranger.

Malka was visibly shaken. "You must believe me," she said. "This is
a wonderful thing. He's a fine boy, Fredl, a pious boy from a wonderful family. Your father and I are certain that the two of you will be
happy and . . ."

"Your mother's right," interrupted Grischa. "He is a wonderful
young man." He reached out to put his arm around Fredl's shoulder,
but the girl shrugged it off.

Fredl squared her shoulders and faced her parents. "So tell me, my
dear mother and father who are so certain that I will be the happiest

girl in the world: which of you has the decency to inform me just who it is you've chosen?" She tried to step back even farther but had reached the wall. Pressed hard against it, she spoke again, only this time her voice broke into an angry sob. "Who is this wonderful person with whom I am to spend the rest of my life? Or," she continued, arms folded protectively across her chest, "am I not to know his identity until my wedding day?"

Grischa was furious with himself. She feels betrayed, he thought; perhaps she has every right. We made a life-changing decision without discussing it with her. He wanted to tell her that it was for her happiness, her future, but all he could do was stumble pathetically over the words. It was Malka who finally pushed him aside.

"It's Szulen Rabinoff," she said.

The little room fell silent. Malka and Grischa stood there, watching and waiting.

Fredl blinked once, and then again. Her brown eyes shifted from one flushed face to the other, and then her cheeks reddened for a moment and paled.

Malka stepped forward, a sense of anxiety building in her chest. Looking down, she realized she was still clutching the swatch of fabric. Staring first at the material and then at her daughter, her hands began to tremble. What if she actually refuses? she thought, fingering it nervously.

Fredl stared at the fabric, saw how it was growing moist in her mother's hand. And then something akin to amusement crossed her face. She took several steps toward the door, her gaze fixed on that piece of cloth.

Malka looked down and saw that the dye had turned her fingers a strange shade of green. She slipped both hands into the heavy folds of her skirt. "I promise you," she said, "that your father and I have selected your husband with the greatest care, with your happiness in mind."

Fredl swallowed hard and continued inching sideways toward the door. My husband, she repeated to herself. And then, without saying a word, without the slightest hint of the displeasure shown only minutes earlier—or the pleasure she was suddenly feeling—she smiled shyly, turned, and rushed from the room.

⅋ Topanga Canyon, Summer 1984

Mimi had listened to the story of Sada the Matchmaker and her grandparents' loving marriage all her life. It practically headed the list of family lore. Despite its wonderful drama, however, its satisfying result, she could never give an inch when Rivka suggested this route for her. "In the 1880s," Mimi argued, "I can understand, but the sixties?"

"And who's to say you wouldn't be happy?" challenged Rivka.

But happiness was never the issue for Mimi. Instead, it was the thought of being so pathetic, so terribly desperate, that she had no choice but to marry by arrangement. The fact that doing so would give her mother great pleasure was another deterrent: pleasure was something Mimi often withheld. When Sarah had suggested that, by doing this, Mimi withheld pleasure from herself as well, she had refused to respond. But now it was nearly twenty years after the fact and she racked her brain to recall the last time she had actually seen her mother's eyes dance with pleasure. The effort brought back a memory that caused her to laugh aloud.

When she and Sarah were perhaps thirteen or fourteen, they loved to play this game where they would stay up very late during a sleep-over and imagine the kind of man their mothers would choose for them if they could make a *shiddach*, a marriage match.

"Wealthy," Sarah had announced. "In fact, stinking rich."

"And don't forget 'a nice disposition,'" mocked Mimi.

Sarah had made a face and had grumbled, "Ugh, I hate that term. What does it mean, 'nice disposition'?"

"I don't know. I guess that he pays the rent on time and doesn't run around with other women."

"No," argued Sarah, shaking her head. "It means he'd treat our parents well in their old age." And then she'd open her eyes wide in pretended surprise and add, "Did I mention that he has to be Jewish?"

"And all this time," responded Mimi, "I was sure your mom would be happy to have a Gentile son-in-law." The giggling was kept under control until Mimi added, "He'd better not be, or else she'll be standing on a chair with a noose around her neck before the poor guy sets foot in the house."

"At least my mom would only kill herself," howled Sarah. "Yours would make it one of those murder-suicide things!"

Looking back, Mimi was no longer certain Rivka would have reacted so negatively, having turned her back on all forms of religion long before coming to America; nor could she imagine a positive reaction. Not even if it were Daniel.

When Mimi had confided to her mother about Daniel's first proposal, the response was not so much a sneer as an expression of contempt: she did not consider Daniel Kirsch deserving of her child. And Rivka certainly had no inkling that her daughter considered herself undeserving of him. For this woman who preferred not to see her daughter's suffering, such a thought would have been unthinkable.

Something nagging at Mimi took her back to that proposal scene. After rethinking the dialogue—moving nearly forgotten gestures and words through her mind until a clear image took hold—she seized upon the truth: She had never intended to accept. She was a child about to launch herself into the adult world. University awaited her and, although she would be forced by financial constraints to live at home, there was symbolic liberation in the process of boarding the crosstown bus and changing to the Westwood line. But if she understood, then why bother to tell her mother? To irritate her, came the quick response. What could please a teenage girl more than getting the upper hand on her controlling mother!

Mimi stood at the bathroom mirror and applied color to her pale skin. Perhaps arranged marriages weren't such a foolish practice after all. At least you were marrying someone who had your parents' approval. True, replied the voice, but what about free choice and romantic love? Mimi stared into her own eyes. Yeah, what about it? It saddened her to know that her mother had never enjoyed them with her father. Whenever Rivka retold the Fredl-Szulen matchmaker story, it was her way of living someone else's romantic fantasy. Perhaps, in her heart, she had even saved one of those fantasies for her own daughter.

Nowy Życie, Spring 1888

The moment Fredl was outside the house she broke into a run. Rounding the corner of the barn, she threw herself upon a pile of hay, hugging its prickly cushion and burying her face in its sweet smell. Her pounding heart set her ears to ringing; the tightness in her chest made her think she might never again take a full breath. Szulen, she thought, I am to marry Szulen. She rolled onto her back and stared up into the underside of the barn's eaves. How wonderful, she thought, that it will be Szulen. The one boy who never teased her for being smart; the only one who ever listened to her opinion. She had always cared for him.

"I saw your play," he had told her only a few weeks earlier. "I thought it was very good."

Fredl had studied his face, searching for signs of ridicule, but there was none.

"And your symbols of evil were subtle, yet powerful."

Again she searched and saw only sincerity. What a relief to have her work understood and appreciated. "Our neighbors think I'm strange."

Szulen had smiled, almost shyly, and then broke into a laugh. "Of course they do!" he had responded. When he saw the confusion on Fredl's face, he became sober once again. "What matters is how you feel," he stated. "No one has the right to tell you what is right and wrong. And if you love what you're doing. . . ." He had shrugged then, as if to discount anyone who criticized.

Gazing up into the sky, the air sent a chill across her skin. Fredl had never made time for boys, at least not like the other girls of Nowy Życic. There were always more important things to do, more pressing involvements: theater, studies, housework. She had never been one to primp and take special care whenever a boy approached. In truth, Fredl had reached the age of eighteen without ever having seriously considered having a boyfriend, much less a husband. But Szulen had such a gentle nature, such a nice sense of humor. And he respects who I am, she thought.

Wrapping her arms around herself she felt almost giddy, and then muttered, "This is ridiculous," and jumped to her feet. Brushing herself off, she was surprised to find her clothing damp. She stood there and scratched absentmindedly at the places where hay and sweat had come together. It was growing quite dark. Despite her father's admonitions, she turned toward the woods and plunged into the heavy brush. Her eyes moved from tree to tree, each one as familiar to her as her own face in a mirror. Feeling her way through the thicket, she moved even farther into the undergrowth. "Out of everyone," she mumbled, breaking off a dry twig dangling from the branch above her. "Out of everyone in the world." Fredl smiled. Out of every possible young man, how is it they had chosen the best?

Fredl found herself standing before the fort her brothers had built long before her birth. She climbed onto the first platform and sat down. The place comforted her, helped to soften the sharp edges of doubt. Sitting there, a name suddenly entered her thoughts: Rahel. She squeezed her eyes shut and pressed her fists against them to keep the thought away.

This is absurd, she told herself, lowering both hands onto her lap. That's only one instance, rare. Of course there are bad matches, she told herself, terrible possibilities. And then there it was again: Rahel.

Rahel Blum was Fredl's cousin, the daughter of Malka's first cousin on her father's side. Born months apart, Rahel and Fredl had been friends and confidantes since they were old enough to speak. Until stricken by illness, Rahel's father had been a respected craftsman in Nowy Życie, but the high fever and delirium of influenza had left him with a heart so weakened he was incapable of working. And then came depression exacerbated by his wife being forced to take in laundry from those same townspeople who had previously paid for his expertise. Confronted by the full extent of his disability, Blum's frustration soon transformed itself into anger, which in turn evolved into a debilitating bitterness.

Fredl experienced this decline firsthand: she had seen Rahel slapped for leaving a window open during the rain; had felt rage when Blum smashed the girl's hand mirror, avowing that vanity was sinful. On those rare occasions when Fredl entered Rahel's home, she girded herself for the caustic jabs and cynical remarks about her own family. And then one day, an announcement emerged from the maelstrom of his rage. His daughter was of no use to him and must be married off. By the time Rahel came to Fredl with this news, the deed was done.

"But what's he like?" Fredl had demanded, as stunned as she was angry.

The girl shrugged. "Papa says he's a decent man."

"But what about you, what do you say?"

Rahel pulled her shoulders back and threw Fredl a challenging look. "I haven't met him."

"You haven't met him?"

She turned away and stared into the distance. "Do you think I was given a choice?" Color rose in Fredl's face, but if the girl noticed her cousin's discomfort, she gave nothing away. "You know how poor we've become," she said, her voice devoid of emotion. When she spoke again, it was more heartfelt. "Most of all, I'm worried about leaving Mama."

On the day the vows were spoken, Fredl had her first glimpse of Rahel's husband. She watched every gesture, listened to every intonation, and decided that perhaps he wasn't so bad, that he might actually make Rahel happy. Barely one month later she was proven decisively wrong.

When Rahel arrived for a visit — their first opportunity to be alone since the wedding — Fredl dragged her out to the garden, squeezed her hand and urged, "Well? Is he wonderful? Is it? The truth, is it?"

Rahel extricated her hand and looked away. "No, it's not."

Fredl pushed her for more information, but the girl resisted. Finally she released a heavy sign and said, "If I tell you, you must promise not to tell your parents. Promise?"

"I promise."

Rahel began slowly, eyes turned away from Fredl, her voice a whisper as she described in the most general terms some of the things her husband was forcing her to do. By the time Rahel joined her mother and left the house, Fredl was distraught with confusion and fear. Perhaps these weren't acts of violence, but they certainly sounded like indecencies to the girl.

That night, in the throes of willing herself to sleep, she was stirred by a noise outside her window. Vaulting from the bed, she made out first the dark shadow of a figure, and then a face. It was Rahel. Not even the dullness of a clouded night could hide the young woman's terror. Fredl threw open the window and, helping her cousin inside, was surprised by the strength of Rahel's grip on her arm.

"I don't care how angry my father will be," she cried. "If he forces me to stay, I'll kill myself, I swear I will!"

Fredl pressed a hand over Rahel's mouth. In all her life she had never heard such a threat. "If you're so miserable, tell your parents. Surely they would never expect you to suffer." she insisted, but the words rang untrue. Fredl felt confused, distressed by her inability to restore her friend to the trusting, innocent girl she had once been.

After several aborted attempts to speak, Rahel finally whispered, "He's a monster."

Fredl had not expected this. "A monster . . . how?"

Rahel took a fistful of Fredl's nightgown. "I lied to you, Fredl. He does much more than what I said. He hurts me." She squeezed her eyes shut, as if expecting to be struck. "And he enjoys it. I thought it was me, that I had done something wrong." She turned and looked at Fredl, her expression changing from fear to cynicism. "Why am I telling you this? There's no way you could understand."

Fredl squirmed under the grip of her own innocence. She wished nothing more than to refute this charge, dismiss this cynical woman and regain her beloved friend. But when Rahel leaned closer and began to speak, Fredl knew at once that little in her life had prepared her for such a confession and that nothing would ever be the same. She listened, head bent close and face turning ashen. "You don't mean it," she said, throat so dry she could hardly speak. "You can't." She stared into the dark. "Are you . . . are you telling me he's a sadist?" Such people existed only in literature, in plays she had read, in books she felt compelled to hide from Hannah. A writer's imagination was one thing, but this was Rahel, what was being done to her was brutal and degrading. Stroking her cousin's arm, she fought against the urge to be sick.

Rahel pulled herself upright and gripped Fredl's arm. "You must never tell. Promise me."

Again Fredl took Rahel in her arms and they remained there, unmoving. "Now you see," murmured Rahel, "why I'd rather be dead."

Fredl struggled with a sense of shame. How could she not reveal what she knew? And yet she had promised. But this was Rahel and she was in danger! Later, she would recall very little: the color draining from her mother's face as she fumbled for the back of a chair; her father urging the horse toward the Blum house, Rahel sitting beside her in the buggy and refusing to speak. Fredl convincing herself that breaking her word had been necessary. Despite knowing Rahel's father and what a loathsome man he could be, no one was prepared for his reaction.

They arrived without formality, without apology. Gathered in the little room, Grischa coughed several times and then began to speak. Mincing no words, he made it painfully and graphically clear that Rahel was being brutalized.

Rahel's mother gasped and was forced to sit. Her father turned to look at his daughter and then shifted his gaze back to Grischa, eyes narrowed. Pushing Grischa out of the way, he threw open the door and stood at the threshold. "My daughter is a married woman and we have signed a contract. She will return to her husband and you will leave my home." The man took a menacing step toward Grischa, elbows tight against his ribs, his fists balled. Grischa's arm shot up protectively and Blum flinched. Like the others, he was stunned by this show of rage.

Grischa stared at his upraised hand as if it belonged to someone else, fingers trembling as he fought the instinct to strike. Had he ever in his life raised a hand against another man?

For several moments Malka was unable to speak. When the words came, they were thrust at the loathsome man. "When did you become such a beast?"

Blum's menacing expression gave Fredl cause to lean protectively toward her mother.

Grischa struggled to stem his anger. Offering a hand to Rahel, he said, "Come, my dear, it's time to go home." There was relief all around when Blum did nothing to stop them.

Grischa drove the buggy home in silence, all the while rolling and twisting the leather reins in those big hands, squeezing and wrenching the straps until his knuckles were strained white.

It took one short day for word of this *shandeh*, this shameful episode, to reach Nowy Życie. Blum's daughter had done the unspeakable, had broken her marriage contract, and her poor husband was so bereft he was announcing to everyone that Rahel could come home without repercussions. After three months of remaining sequestered in the Gershon home, Rahel announced that it was time to leave. All protests were lovingly acknowledged, but she was determined to begin a new life. And since her husband refused to give her a *get*, a Jewish divorce that could be conferred only with the husband's approval, she would remain in the eyes of her community a married woman. What other hope was there but to leave, seek a new life and a new name? In time, this is precisely what she did.

And now it was Fredl's turn to marry, but she was certain that this story—her life, her future, her very happiness—would be much different. Because the man who was to share all of this was Szulen Rabinoff, the gentle young man she had secretly loved for years.

CHAPTER FIVE

&Los Angeles, Summer 1984

"WE'LL GO OVER THE EXAM on Thursday," announced Mimi, collecting the last of the papers. As her students filed out, their postures reflecting everything from elation to defeat, a young man approached her desk. He was clutching his exam as if it were a death warrant. Fear of authority was so evident that Mimi nearly took his arm.

"Dr. Zilber, I can't be here Thursday," he said, a dry mouth making the words stick together.

This one was definitely afraid. Modulating her voice to sound less than authoritarian, Mimi replied, "I'm sorry, but attendance in my class is mandatory."

His face was a study in misery. He looked about the room, as if hoping to find someone who could rescue him or, at the least, give him courage. "My dad just left my mom," he said, and then paused long enough to swallow hard. "She's falling apart and Dad thinks I should come home for a few days. My flight leaves at four."

Mimi felt the last vestige of professorial stiffness drop from her face. "Check my office hours on Monday and sign up for a thirty-minute slot." She pried the paper from his hand and committed his name to memory. "We'll go over your exam together."

"I'm sure I failed," he told her. "I'm sure. And if I don't pass this class . . ."

"Go home, okay? If you failed, we can schedule a makeup." She looked into his face and recognized doubt. "Which I will personally

administer," she added, her compassionate smile eliciting pure gratitude in the boy's eyes. So much gratitude, in fact, that she had to look
away.

Mimi walked back to her office with the student's plight tossing
about in her mind. She had hardly noticed him in the classroom, yet
she now had a profound sense of his distress. Even when she settled in
behind the desk and faced yet another stack of exams, she could not
shake off his sadness. Going off to university was an adjustment; leaving behind your parents' deteriorating marriage must be sheer tor-
ment. It caused Mimi to wonder when it was that she had first
become aware of the conflict in her own home. Certainly, from the
earliest age, she had understood that her parents were not friends,
sensed that something hung heavily between them—disappointment, failure, neglect. Whatever it was, she had never felt it with
Sarah's parents. Their marriage had always struck her as a partner-
ship, a give-and-take. Whatever that weighty entity was, it spilled like
a viscous fluid over into her relationship with her parents, poisoned
her feelings about them, how she approached them. What she dared
to expect from them. And where she had struggled valiantly to win
her father's attention, she had fought with equal valor to push her
mother away.

There was nothing easy about living in an apartment filled with
sniping. Long past midnight, when her father's key slipped surrepti-
tiously into the lock and her mother's footsteps pounded across the
floor as she rushed to confront him, the result was always the same:
angry voices vibrating through the walls, muffled and urgent, painful
sounds to the ears of a confused little girl. Mimi could still recall lying
stiffly in her bed, arms pressed against her sides as she willed her parents to fall silent. In her mind, everyone else in the neighborhood—
meaning, to a child, the entire world—seemed perfectly content. The
Sterns, married for nearly fifty years, took a walk together every
evening. Mimi often waited for them at the window and waved down
to them as they passed. Her parents never walked. Joey Wilder's parents were so playful with one another, sometimes even kissing in front
of the boy and his friends, that his face turned red with embarrassment. If these married couples were so happy and in love, why not
her parents?

Mimi picked up the student's exam. Glancing over it, she recognized at once that he knew his material, but had failed to apply it properly. Disorganized thoughts and angry cross-outs only magnified his frustration. She put a notation in the upper corner and placed it aside. No matter how hard-nosed she was supposed to be, she would not punish him for what was happening at home.

Her mind drifted to Mrs. Rothman, a young woman in the neighborhood who had lost her husband when she was only twenty-four. Despite her grief, she had always managed a big smile for Mimi. Sometimes she even invited the child to walk with her. On those occasions, Mimi felt as if she were participating in a neighborhood event, because whenever the Widow Rothman walked down the sidewalk, she drove her body like a plow pushing through snow after a blizzard, those tulip-shaped hips cutting a swath the full width of the concrete. And to add to the drama, she wore four-inch stiletto heels that landed like jackhammers against the concrete sidewalks of Boyle Heights. Skipping alongside, Mimi believed that those pedestrians stepping off the sidewalk were making way for her as well. And when the men perched on nearby stoops elbowed each other and let out hoots and whistles, they were sending out the message to a plump little girl that she was a princess. From the age of six, all Mimi ever wanted was to own a pair of shoes just like Sonya Rothman's.

"But who could walk in those things!" her mother had protested, nostrils flaring. "You call those sensible?"

Mimi and her father had responded by gazing down at the woman's brown-laced shoes with arch supports. This marked the first time Mimi understood that "sensible" could also mean ugly and that nothing sensible was meant for her. Even if what she overheard her father say one night was true—that the woman's husband had died because he hadn't been able to handle the excitement—Mimi wanted those shoes.

She gathered the exam papers into a neat stack, slipped them into her bag and left the office. Driving on automatic pilot, she had a vague sense of wondering what in the hell she was going to do with her life. One thing for certain, whatever it was, she'd do it alone.

Pull into the driveway, enter the house, check the answering machine. The pattern had remained unchanged for years—and patterns die hard. But there it was again: that damned sinking feeling that no matter who it was, it would not be Sarah. Blinking messages or not, she told herself, they'll all have to wait.

Mimi wandered onto the deck. It had rained again last night, an event of note for this drought-controlled City of the Angels. The day was nearly over, yet she felt heat rays bouncing off the deck and warming the place where she stood. How odd to be mourning in such beautiful weather. With a resigned sigh, she walked back into the house to listen to her messages. Sarah might not be there, but she could always count on hearing her mother's voice. In fact Rivka usually left three, each one more demanding or doomsaying than the last. To date, the Number One Message on Mimi's list of all-time favorites was: *Darling, could you pick up some whole wheat flour? I thought I'd bake your favorite cake. Only this time I'll use margarine. Butter is pure fat, but then you know that, yes? Good-bye, darling. Oh, did I mention that Anna Hershkowitz's daughter's husband left her for his secretary and she tried to kill herself? Poor Anna found her covered in blood. Being a mother, I can imagine . . . never mind. What's important, the poor woman will be fine. And don't forget, darling, whole wheat.* That message had been left several years earlier. To date, Rivka had not yet topped it, but Mimi figured it was only a matter of time.

As expected, there was the inconsequential message from Rivka asking about weekend plans. There was also a brief message from Daniel. "How about I pick you up at seven?" he asked. "We can try that new sushi place at the bottom of Carbon Canyon. I hear they serve killer raw, dead fish."

Mimi dialed his number, smiling to herself as the phone rang.

"Hello?"

"How could I resist?"

"I know you so well."

"Okay, but who's paying?"

"Who wants to?"

Mimi smiled to herself. "Tell you what, I'll save you the drive up here and I'll meet you there. And to express your gratitude, you can pay. Anyway, you're loaded and I'm a lowly teacher."

"I'll do you one better," he laughed. "I'll drive up there, pick you up, drive you to the restaurant, watch you demolish a side of tuna, and I'll still pay. What d'ya think of that?"

"I think you're too good to me."

"And?"

"Don't push your luck."

"Right. See you in fifteen."

By the time his car came rolling down the driveway, Mimi had managed to change into comfortable clothes, put some color onto her face and push away a good measure of the ennui plaguing her throughout the afternoon. She had no idea where this friendship with Daniel was heading, but there was no arguing with the sense of lightness it sometimes created.

The sound of tires on the gravel drew her to the door. When she opened it, Daniel handed her a rose. Soft pink with white edges. "Let me put this in water," she said over her shoulder as she headed for the kitchen. She filled her mother's cut-glass bud vase and carried it into the study. Placing the vase on her desk, she stepped back and studied its perfection. The flower transformed the room.

When they returned from dinner, Daniel suggested they take a walk. Like the sushi, a walk felt just right. They climbed the canyon road for nearly fifteen minutes, Daniel pacing himself to Mimi's slower gait. When they arrived at the crest and began their descent along the back way, he shifted closer and slipped a hand under her elbow. The gesture at first unsettled her, and then caused her to wonder when it was that anyone had made her feel so protected. They approached the house. "Will you come in and stay for a while?" she asked, and was surprised by her invitation. Was she succumbing to his attention, or was it that she preferred not to be left alone?

Daniel made the gallant gesture of taking the house keys from her and Mimi caught herself just before joking that perhaps he considered her too old to open her own door. Instead, she smiled graciously, stepped inside and told him to make himself comfortable while she fetched the wine. Entering the living room, she found him leafing through the stack of books sitting on the table. The sight of Daniel bent over a page, showing interest in something she loved, sent a palpable feeling of relief running through her. Relief that he was her friend; relief that he was there. The emotion jarred Mimi, and then transported her back to those probing questions about isolation. Why had she opted for it? And had she really been so terribly alone for so much of her life? The answer rose so quickly and hung there, looming, forcing Mimi to swallow back her tears. Squaring her shoulders, she took a deep breath and concentrated on pouring two glasses of wine. "So," she said, making her voice far lighter than she felt. "Tell me about this new case you're trying."

He received the glass with a nod and took a pensive sip. "To be honest, I'd rather talk about us."

She nearly suggested he not spoil a perfectly lovely evening, but the look in his eyes disarmed her. "Daniel, there's been an *us* since we were children." Mimi was afraid that her voice betrayed the agitation rising in her chest. She felt him studying her—it gave her the sense of being exposed, on public display—and tried to read the expression on his face. It was, she believed, somewhere between perplexity and annoyance. Either way, she silently urged him away from the subject.

Daniel smiled. "Yes, there has," he acknowledged and took another sip.

In that smile, Mimi saw the same hopefulness, the same teasing expectation, she had seen in his face so many years ago. Did he really believe that a loving smile and a history of friendship would stoke the fires of an ancient roll in the hay? If he did, it was time to nip it in the bud! "Listen, mister," she warned. "If you're going to ask me to go steady again, forget it!" She nearly cringed when she heard how forced it sounded and was visibly relieved when the declaration prompted a hearty laugh.

In spite of the pleasant evening they were sharing, Mimi was relieved when Daniel finally excused himself and left for home. Carrying her glass onto the deck, she watched dramatic changes moving through the night sky. There was no question that he was being bolder now, for some reason more aggressive in his efforts to win her over. Whether or not she could be won was another thing entirely. Words like *spinster, old maid,* and *too set in her ways* popped into her head. How could anyone seriously consider marriage for the first time at this age? The thought carried her back to her Grandmother Fredl and the arranged marriages so common in the shtetl. And, of course, the story on which she had cut her teeth: Rahel and her escape from the monster husband.

Mimi watched the blinking lights of an airplane and smiled to herself. The saga of Rahel's escape was legendary in the collection of Zilber family folklore. She could remember how, as a child, she had adored those rare moments when her mother let down her guard and recounted family anecdotes. She had clung to every word, every description, and was particularly fascinated by her mother's colorful narratives about her own childhood.

As a youngster, Mimi hadn't really understood Rahel's plight. It wasn't until much later that she caught on, and then she went directly to Sarah with the story. Perhaps that was why, whenever her mother prodded her to date someone's son or nephew, an acquaintance's kid brother or a neighbor's cousin's boy, Mimi's thoughts would shift to Rahel Blum and a sense of dread would set in. Even when Sarah was dating Diego, a gentle and caring man, she kept asking, "Are you sure? I mean, you hardly know him, so how can you be sure?" As if marriage were a bitter pill to be forced down.

Mimi stretched. Where is my Szulen? she wondered, and then realized that family lore had bestowed on him the persona of the ideal man, the man who would love her and protect her, who would be her devoted mate and friend, father to her children. Fredl had known all of that and had lost it, had seen it snatched cruelly away. She was so young when Szulen died, a young woman with three small children, including Rivka, still a baby. Mimi stared out onto the deck. Hardly time to fulfill one's dreams, yet her Grandmother Fredl had forged ahead to make a new life for herself and her children. Mimi found it unsettling that she was well beyond the age of Fredl when Szulen died and what had she done with her life that was even close? Then again, thought Mimi, Fredl was indomitable. Not like me.

Indomitable. The word stayed with her as she walked down the hall to the kitchen. Did I avoid marriage because I feared it? she wondered, choosing an apple from the bowl of fruit. What part did I fear? Its demands and responsibilities, or the possibility that marriage would disappoint or betray, me? Mimi bit hard into the fruit, its tart juice causing the nerves in her teeth to react. But then, she wondered, chewing slowly, is it possible to feel disappointment about something we've never experienced? About something I never even had the courage to try.

She stood at the sink and stared into space. Rahel, Rivka, Daniel. If only Sarah were here to listen, to act as her sounding board.

Mimi had promised herself that her summer holiday would be spent in France, or at the very least driving up the coast of Maine. But without Sarah to accompany her, a vacation was the last thing she wanted. Instead, she had jumped at the offer to teach two summer school courses to doctoral candidates. Better to keep herself busy, not to mention challenged, by a handful of highly motivated history scholars. It was good for the intellect, she reasoned. In her present state, it was also necessary for the soul. So here she was, staring down the barrel at yet another semester, facing yet again another stack of papers and questioning what the rest of her life would bring.

She picked up the sponge and began washing the sink. If only Sarah were here. She wondered about the chances of ever having another friendship that endured nearly without conflict. The formula had seemed so simple: Mimi the academic focused on building her university reputation, sharing with her friend all the excitement and struggles a career engendered; Sarah the wife and mother focused on her family, providing her friend with enough baby stories and photos to satisfy most maternal yearnings. The study was filled with shots of Joanna at birth being held by Aunt Mimi; Joanna blowing out candles at her first birthday party, dutifully assisted by her doting Aunt Mimi; Joanna dressed for her junior prom, clutching the beaded bag loaned to her by her Aunt Mimi. A friendship free of competition was possible because the women were doing what they loved. That they could bestow upon one another that sense of achievement denied to them by time and circumstance only added to the importance of the friendship. There was mutual agreement that Mimi's pleasure at being ersatz mother to Joanna was balanced by Sarah's delight at being the honorary recipient of one undergraduate and two postgraduate degrees.

Mimi squeezed excess water from the sponge. One month since Sarah's death. Leaning against the counter, she recalled a conversation with Daniel the week before. The passage of time had not lessened her remorse.

"Just remember," he had reminded her. "There is no timeline for grief and no gestation period." It was loving advice coming from a trusted friend, yet it had sounded didactic, the expert lecturing the novice.

"Did I ask?" she had responded icily.

There had been a lengthy silence followed by something about not falling into the predictable traps. "When someone we love dies," he had continued, "it's going to hurt; it's got to. The problem is, you don't get to choose the moments, like you do the holidays on your academic calendar. And stop snapping at me. I'm on your side."

Mimi had held her tongue, but she had thought, "If he tells me that time heals all wounds, or that we grieve until we don't, I'll wring his neck." The angry tone of that internal voice had brought her up short. Yes, he was getting under her skin, but at least he cared! So why the annoyance? The grim line across her mouth softened somewhat. The answer was so simple it nearly embarrassed her: Daniel knew her too well. And he was right, she really was following an imaginary timeline, expecting some arbitrary date to arrive and herald the end of her pain. "Okay," she had conceded. "So maybe I am doing that, but it's completely unconscious." She had emphasized that last word, as if to say that being unconscious, existing in a state of unawareness, excused her behavior and, in turn, got her off the hook, justified her behavior.

"Call it what you like," he replied. "It still doesn't change my key point: that grief sticks around for as long as it wants. And while it's here, it eats away at you—until it decides it's had enough. It, Mimi, not you."

She hated to admit it, but she was certain that grief was far from finished with her.

Of everyone in Mimi's circle, Daniel was the only one who seemed to understand her flashes of self-indulgent anger, and how she would suddenly become furious that Sarah's life had been cut short, furious that she had been left alone. She had wanted to discuss her feelings of grief with her mother on several occasions, but could never bring herself to initiate the conversation, fearful of making herself vulnerable.

And yet who knew more about death and suffering than Rivka Zilber? It took no effort on Mimi's part to imagine her mother's face, the quiver of her cheeks, those eyes wistful and watery as Rivka recounted the story of her mother's illness. As for Fredl's death, it was only one of many for Rivka: losing her father when she was a baby, her mother when she was still a little girl, her beloved stepfather when she was an adolescent. But how did any of this compare to the crushing blow when she learned of the extermination of what remained of her Nowy Życie family? Perhaps that was why Harold Zilber's death had seemed almost incidental in the scheme of things. "Just my luck," she had sighed several days after her husband's death. Just her luck that Harold had died and left her grieving, or just her luck that the Angel of Death had once again, and most cruelly, passed her by? The statement had jarred Mimi, sent a jolt through her, yet she dared not ask her mother to explain.

✑ Nowy Życie, Winter 1904

It was Friday evening and Fredl Gershon Rabinoff was seated at the window. Her skin shone alabaster against the darkness, both hands resting in her lap, one over the other, as if shielding something fragile. Her back was so straight she appeared regal. There was a shroud draped over her head, fine black linen tatted into a delicate design. Fredl touched the material and her fingers lingered. Her eyebrows drew together in confusion.

Her clothing was a stark mirror of her grief. The black muslin bodice fit snugly over her slim frame, its row of small buttons beginning several inches below the waist and rising in quarter-inch repetitions to cover every inch of Fredl's throat, all the way to her chin. The skirt fell in heavy folds around her feet, impeding her whenever she shifted her weight in the chair. Behind the drape of the skirt she wore black high-top shoes, their laces pulled into large loops to keep the ends from dragging in the dirt.

Fredl shifted, her dark eyes staring beyond the window's distorted glass, and she absentmindedly rubbed the wedding band against the arm of the chair. Ten years of wear had nearly erased its design. As she sat in the dark room, her mind moved laboriously from one memory to the next. Occasionally, one of those memories would pick up speed and dance through her head, causing her mouth to turn up slightly as, in this dance, it was her beloved Szulen who took the lead. Releasing a lengthy sigh, Fredl gripped the arms of the chair and pushed herself upright. The ball of yarn tucked into the seat tumbled to the floor. She retrieved it, stuffing it into the sewing basket beside the chair, and then, stretching her neck and back against an ever-present stiffness, reached under the linen head cover and pushed the large hairpins back into place.

The window opening onto the street was framed in frost, each pane marked with swirling designs like rings left behind from a wet glass. Cold air crept around the edges of each pane, seeping through the cracks in the doughy substance that held each one in place. In some spots there was no putty at all. Fredl walked over to the window and touched one of the panes, the cold against her fingers almost painful. Who would mix and apply the new putty and make the repairs? Who, she wondered, will stop this chill?

Across the road, someone was lighting the synagogue lamps. "Six-fifteen," she mumbled. Old Boris the Rabbi's Assistant had been lighting those lamps every night at six-fifteen for more than forty years. The day Boris's wife died, Szulen crossed the road to perform the function for him, but before he could strike a match the old man was there. "We die when we stop living," he said, taking the match from the young man's hand.

Fredl studied herself in the window. With all the mirrors draped in cloth, this was the first time since Szulen's death that she had seen herself. How strange that old Boris should still be alive and Szulen is not. And me, not yet thirty, and with three small children who have no father. She had informed herself of these facts many times in the past week and they had yet to ring true. They were empty, mere illusions that dissipated into the air around her.

A movement across the road caught her attention. A man was bending into the wind, his horse struggling to pull away. He leaned against the animal and stroked it calm, leading it to the protected side of the shul. It was Szulen who had always welcomed the visitors. So where is he now? thought Fredl, a shiver running across her shoulders.

Where is that good neighbor who brought strangers into our home, the father who played on the floor with his boys and pulled on the toes of his laughing baby girl? Gone. Shiva was completed three days ago and all the people who sat with her, mourned with her day and night, stayed by her side and recited prayers, comforted her children and prepared enough food to last for weeks: they, too, were gone.

Fredl had a flashing memory of her husband standing near the table, little Rivka on his shoulders and the two boys around his knees, all of them clapping and laughing. Fredl had joined in the laughter as her husband danced through the house, the boys tagging behind and the baby clinging fast to his beard and shrieking in joy as her father approached each doorway and ducked at the last moment, stopping every so often to take the boys by the hand and spin them like tops under outstretched arms. The father who would never again play with his children; the husband who would never again make love to his wife in that gentle and satisfying and passionate way shared between them since that first time, their wedding night.

Fredl pressed her lips together but still could not quell the tears that fell onto her widow's dress and disappeared into the fabric. Fatigue finally getting the upper hand, she crossed the floor and climbed the stairs to her room. The chill prompted her to undress quickly. She pulled on the heavy cotton nightgown and slid into bed, drawing the comforter tight around her shoulders. Stretching her legs, she gave a quick blessing that her eldest son had remembered to put the hot stones at the foot of the bed, and then settled into the eiderdown and dared sleep to come. Fredl counted seconds, minutes, hours, but it was to no avail. She considered lighting her bedside lamp, but she was too tired to read. Willing herself to sleep, she finally did so in fits and starts. And not once during that restless night, nor at any time in the throes of suffering her loss, did she consciously decide to teach her little girl that to love someone could only result in pain. Not once did she consider speaking words of distrust, or conspire to translate her despair into a hopelessness that would be assimilated by the child and passed on to her own daughter more than thirty years later. Fredl never intended these messages to be passed on to the innocent child, but it would happen all the same.

Grief, like a newborn baby, demanded all of Fredl's energy, and it did so with no consideration for her well-being. In fact, it held her in such a grip that Malka and Grischa feared it might never let go. Each morning she rose, sent the boys off to school and returned to bed, abandoning its warmth only when little Rivka's cries turned into wails. And when she did get up, her movements were painstaking: she could have been moving underwater.

It was fortunate for everyone that the boys were by this time quite independent and capable of getting themselves a quick breakfast and off to cheder, where they studied, rarely played and took a short break at midday for a hot meal. It was a ten-hour schedule, six days a week, Sunday morning through Friday afternoon, but it freed them from the concerns of home.

Rivka had no such escape. Having celebrated her second birthday only weeks before her father's death, she was unwittingly made to bear the brunt of her mother's grief. There had been a time when pulling on her mama's skirts would quickly catch her attention; now, even the most heartfelt tug went unheeded. Some days her mother spoke hardly a word, and when she did those words sounded harsh and impatient, so angry the child was left cowering. When this happened, Rivka would search her mother's face, her fine eyebrows drawn together. Where is the woman who was once so calm? said the frown. Where is the woman whose voice was so tender and loving? On rare occasions, a memory would shake Fredl from her lethargy and she would pick up the little girl and hold her close.

It was some eight weeks after the funeral—a day when the weather was particularly harsh and few citizens dared to manage the roads—when Malka arrived with a bundle of provisions. It had been unseasonably cold all week, the rain unrelenting and bone-soaking. Certainly not the kind of weather that would allow a grieving young woman to venture out, and with a baby on her hip at that. What if it snowed and the roads became impassable? Would Fredl know to return home quickly and close the house against the cold? The questions had rankled until Malka had finally given in and done what mothers must do. And yet she knew very well that shopping for her daughter was a risk; the last time she had made a delivery she had run smack into indignation.

"I am not a helpless woman," announced Fredl. "And I am

certainly not one of your charity cases!" Malka had mumbled her apologies while unpacking boxes and filling cupboards. By the time Fredl had completed her defense of herself, the food was stored and a chicken was in the oven.

Days had passed and everything was much the same, the weather just as cold and threatening. Malka climbed from the wagon. Ignoring the mud clinging to her skirts, she picked up two of the string-wrapped bundles, sloshed to the front door, knocked and let herself in. "It's freezing in here," she mumbled, placing the packages on the table. In two more trips everything was unloaded, yet there was still no sign of life. At the bottom of the stairs she called out Fredl's name. "Where is she?" she muttered. Lifting her damp skirts, she climbed the stairs and entered her daughter's room. The young woman was stretched out on the bed, arms draped over her face. On the floor sat Rivka, dressed only in a cotton shirt and a makeshift diaper.

"What on earth!" demanded Malka, picking up her granddaughter. "Why is there no heat in this house?" She carried the baby to the bed. "Fredl, your daughter is cold to the bone! For the love of God, someone could die in this weather!" There was no way Malka could soften the accusation in her voice. "Is this what you want, to freeze to death?"

A painful stillness filled the room. Malka watched her daughter, waited with fear in her throat, but for several moments there was nothing but the rise and fall of Fredl's chest. And then the young woman spoke. "Yes, Mama," she said, "that is exactly what I want."

Balancing the baby on one hip, Malka descended to the kitchen. "This can't go on," she muttered, tears of fear and anger poorly concealed. When she tried to put the baby down, the little girl would not let go. Using her free hand, Malka scooped chunks of coal into the oven. When the coals caught, she carried Rivka upstairs and rummaged through drawers until warm clothing was found. Returning to the kitchen, she filled a pan with water and placed it onto the coals. "You'll be clean in no time," she murmured into Rivka's hair, and then set about mixing a few slices of bread with what appeared to be that morning's cereal. Tasting the concoction, judging it acceptable, she placed this, too, over the coals. While she was stirring, Fredl shuffled into the kitchen. Her face devoid of emotion.

"Have you seen your child?" demanded Malka. "The poor thing's filthy and hungry. When did you last change her?" No response. "Can't you smell her, Fredl? She's been soiled for hours, and look at her, practically blue from the cold." The silence caused a cry to rise in Malka's throat.

The older woman set about bathing and dressing Rivka. Within a half-hour the baby was clean, fed, and sleeping peacefully against her grandmother's breast. Whenever she stirred, Malka stroked her head and made soothing noises until she settled back into sleep. The two women remained silent for some time; it was Malka who finally broke the silence. "You will come home, my dear." Her tone was sure, so resolute even she appeared surprised by its decisiveness. But this was the solution, was it not? "There is no other choice. The children need to be cared for." Her voice began to crack. "And so, my darling, do you." She looked into her daughter's face and saw no clear sign of comprehension. "I'm going to take the baby with me and fetch your father. When we return, we'll pack your things and leave when the boys come home."

Later that day Malka and Grischa, assisted by two men from the village and Fredl's sons, worked against the chill and packed everything they needed. With his family and their belongings squeezed together in the wagon, Grischa clicked the horse into motion. The expression on his face left no doubt that he was painfully aware of the apprehension around him. "I believe this calls for a celebration," he announced. "After all, we'll be living together!" He wanted so desperately to dispel all fears about yet another dramatic change in their young lives. When he turned to offer a reassuring smile, he was surprised to see eagerness in the faces of his grandsons. They were nearly home before he fully grasped that the children were relieved to be going somewhere that promised warmth and hot meals, to live in a home where voices were gentle and affectionate touches no longer the exception. Grischa wanted to cry out "My poor Fredl, what did you ever do to deserve such heartache? And where is that spirited child who once filled our home with energy?" Instead, he reached for Malka's hand and gave it a squeeze. This, too, said the gesture, will one day pass.

❧Topanga Canyon, Summer 1984

Mimi kicked off her blanket at four in the morning with the certainty that nothing was going to allow her sleep. For several days she had been besieged by a question regarding the inevitability of her mother's death: If Sarah could die so young, how much longer could she expect a woman in her eighties to live? And yet Mimi had never truly considered the possibility of Rivka not being there, not making that daily telephone call and, despite decades of limited information, demanding all the intimate details of her daughter's life. She turned on the little fan, hoping to dry off from the damp heat that had been hanging over Los Angeles for nearly a week. Stretched across the bed, she thought back to that conversation Sarah had insisted they have. The drapes had been drawn and a 20-watt lamp illuminated to pro-tect Sarah's eyes from the pain of daylight. Mimi was seated beside her and stroking her arm, hoping to comfort her, knowing there were things they needed to discuss but finding it so difficult to form the words. When Sarah turned her head toward Mimi and smiled, the words suddenly poured from Mimi's heart. "I guess it's time to tell me what I can do for you."

Sarah reached over and touched her leg. "Find someone to come over and give me a good bikini waxing." The smile was wan, but the sparkle in her eyes was still evident.

"You mean in preparation for our trip to the Bahamas? Because if it is, I'll also require full-body liposuction." When she saw the expres-sion on Sarah's face, she sighed. "You know that I'll take care of every-thing."

"The lawyer said . . ."

"It's under control, don't worry. Legal matters, banking issues, the deed to the house, everything."

The ensuing pause made Mimi feel uncomfortable. There was something Sarah wanted to say, but was holding back. Before she could question and probe, however, the answer arrived. And it caught her completely off-guard.

"Sweetheart," asked Sarah. "What are you going to do about your mother?"

"My mother? What's my mother got to do with anything?"

Sarah shifted her head on the pillow until she locked eyes with her friend. "Let's start with the fact that she's still trying to run your life."

Time was so precious and this was not the conversation Mimi wanted to have. "No one runs my life," she responded. "I mean, I live alone, don't I? Work as I please?"

"And every man you meet gets passed through the Rivka Zilber filter. How will you protect yourself from that when I'm gone?" When Mimi looked away, Sarah rolled carefully onto her side and moved closer to her friend. "You're a grown woman. It's time you lived your own life."

There was misery in Mimi's face. "You mean if she'd let me."

"It's not her, Cookie, it's you."

The two women stared at each other for a moment.

"One benefit of dying," said Sarah, "is the freedom to say whatever I want. I don't have to worry that you'll stop talking to me in the future." This time her smile was almost teasing.

Mimi sat there, her discomfort finally dissolving. "So you're suggesting I take a contract out on her life?" The giggle floating up from the bed sounded like music. "We could plan a drive-by shooting."

"No contracts and no shootings," Sarah said. After a pause, she added, "But what about acceptance?" Before Mimi could respond, she had fallen asleep clutching Mimi's hand.

Driving home, Mimi had been hit with a surge of panic. The sensation of being a lost soul had recently been on her mind. With Sarah actually gone, she would be a lost soul not only until that day in the future when the headstone was placed on the grave and the official mourning had come to an end, but for the remainder of her life. Overwhelmed with grief for what was yet to come, she had begun to cry.

&*Nowy Życie, Autumn 1905*

Caring for three young grandchildren came naturally to Malka and Grischa. What challenged them was having to care for an adult child. They knew about people in Fredl's condition, had even heard how such people were sometimes restrained, like wild animals.

But a child of their own? It was nearly unthinkable. So unthinkable that only days after the move Malka gripped her husband's arm and asked, "You don't think she's crazy, do you?" The urgency in that question was reflected by the bruise it left behind. She wanted to know, yet at the same time she was terrified to be told what she most feared.

Grischa pulled his arm away and rubbed the painful spot. "It's a sickness," he told her, and then immediately regretted the gruffness in his voice. "A sickness," he added, his voice softer. "And it will pass, you have my word." He saw how the lines etching his wife's mouth and forehead grew visibly deeper, knew without asking that, perhaps for the first time in their long and satisfying marriage, his word held little, if any, weight.

The weeks ran on and the dedicated parents saw no change. Fredl's meals were carried to her room and on those rare occasions when she agreed to eat, most of the food remained untouched, pushed around on the plate the way a child does when trying to convince her parents that more had been eaten than was actually the case. Hannah, now a woman with small children of her own, made it her business to visit at least once each day, but not even the tender words of a loving sister could cajole Fredl into eating. In the hope that she would react to sunshine and light, Hannah and her mother pushed Fredl's bed closer to the window. They sewed new curtains and crocheted beautiful pillowcases. And as each loving task was completed, the two women turned to her with hopeful expressions, as if to say, "Do you see what we've done for our beloved Fredl, and all because we want you to be happy!" More often than not, their loving efforts were greeted with blank stares. More often than not, Hannah returned to home and family in tears.

Months rolled on and the Gershon family remained steadfast in its dedication to their Fredl's recovery. Loving attention was given without limitation: hours and days, weeks passed, nearly every waking moment with someone at Fredl's side, either recounting the goings-on of the village or reading aloud from her favorite books. The boys, often bedecked in elaborate costumes made from odds and ends, created little skits and performed them for their mother. And while they performed, little Rivka sat silently by and watched.

The perseverance that had proved so tiring to nearly every member of the family finally made its mark. Nearly seven months after Szulen's death, the blank stare was replaced by a timid smile. The moment became cause for great celebration in the Gershon household, became the seed from which renewed hope would flower. Little by little, Fredl took part in conversations. And then she began to ask questions, one day even expressing her desire for the windows to be opened to the fresh air. Each little step brought with it increased optimism until, one day, Malka walked into the bedroom and found Fredl examining objects long boxed away in storage. It was then that she knew they were almost there.

Childhood books, drawings made before adolescence, all were strewn about the room. Malka only watched at first, but a few days into the discovery she found herself perched on Fredl's bed and, together, they pored over little bibelots that conjured up comforting memories. The flower Szulen had given Fredl the night their families finalized the marriage arrangements; the necklace of twigs that ten-year-old Hannah had made for her big sister; a book of poems given to Fredl by her parents on her fourteenth birthday. A history unfolding so that a future could be lived.

"I'd like the children to sit with me while I eat," requested Fredl one evening. Before her mother could respond, she changed her mind. "Even better, I'll sit with you at the table."

Malka could hardly contain her joy and rushed into the other room to share the good news with her grandchildren. "But only if you keep very quiet," she threatened, her heart beating in anticipation of the first real family dinner since Szulen's death. The children nodded, eyes widened by the responsibility.

Despite a controlled elation felt by all, the dinner proved to be one of the more subdued in Malka's memory. When bedtime arrived, she went to her grandchildren and took special care to praise each child, spend a little longer than usual hugging and tucking in. When she extinguished the lamp and walked out of the room, the sigh she released was at last a sigh of hope.

Although the boys adapted quite readily to the changes taking place in the house, little Rivka did not. The child had been too long without her mother's comforting arms, her mother's soothing voice.

She was sullen and withdrawn, pulling away whenever Fredl reached for her. Rivka allowed Grischa to hold her, and yet even with him the trusting moments were too few. Malka found herself watching the child, wondering with a growing concern if perhaps Fredl would emerge from the trauma, while Rivka would not.

It was nearly ten months before Fredl was prepared to accept visitors. Rumor had been circulating throughout Nowy Życie for months that the Gershon's daughter was crazy and the family was forced to keep her restrained and isolated from her children. It was a great relief to Malka when Fredl asked to see Szulen's parents, and when the Rabinoffs were finally able to see for themselves—and, in turn, for the entire town—their daughter-in-law's progress. Seated across from Fredl, they saw a pale young woman, thinner than they remembered, yet her face peaceful and kind. They watched how tentatively her children approached her, reached out to her, and then nearly wept when this beautiful young mother who had suffered so much opened her arms and pulled each child close. In mind and heart, there was no question but that their son's wife had returned.

Soon Fredl was helping her boys with their lessons, bathing little Rivka and reading to her before bed. She began to speak with her children about their father, reminding them of his funny ways, his dreams for each of them. The day finally came when she joined the entire family for all meals and rejected any efforts to keep the house quiet on her behalf. Taking walks with Rivka, stopping at her father's store to chat with his customers, these became her greatest moments of pleasure.

Eleven months to the day after Szulen's death, the Rabinoff and Gershon families came together to place the headstone on Szulen's grave. Later, over tea and cake, there was a sense of communal relief that Fredl, once the spirited and creative girl, had finally recovered from a terrible ordeal.

That night, the period of mourning now officially over, Fredl Gershon Rabinoff disappeared into her room and emerged several minutes later wearing a simple dress, cream-colored with delicate blue flowers on the bodice. The widow's threads were left in a heap on the floor of her closet. She noted how her mother looked up, how her face broke into an expression of joy. She also noted how the aging woman instinctively reached for her husband's hand. This, said Malka's expression, is our Fredl, the daughter we once knew. It was then, at this precise moment, that Fredl understood that all would be well.

Malka patted the chair next to her. When Fredl sat, the woman took her hand and squeezed it, pressed it to her lips. "A new beginning," whispered Malka.

Grischa's face broke into a most satisfied smile. Only half-teasing, he muttered, "From your mouth, to God's ears." As he spoke, something akin to butterfly wings fluttered inside his chest, because this was the joy he had longed for but had feared might never come.

That night, after bedtime ablutions were completed and all fires were doused beyond even the sternest fire marshal's criteria, Grischa and Malka dragged their bodies to bed. Nestling close together under the down comforter, the elderly couple shared an intimacy that had been absent for a very long time. Following their lovemaking, the slumber they shared was deep and most serene.

CHAPTER SIX

&*Nowy Życie, Spring 1906*

SPRING ARRIVED in Nowy Życie. While the chill of winter had thawed, the citizens were not warmed. There was a certainty that pogroms were going to happen, no matter what they did to prevent them, and this certainty precluded the anticipation of warmth.

Grischa arrived home for lunch one afternoon to a bustling center of activity. Malka was adding the last handful of vegetables to a pot of soup and Fredl was bent over an enormous sphere of bread dough, kneading as if it had been invaded by demons that needed squeezing out. The boys, having reclaimed their uncles' fort, were tramping through the kitchen with an assortment of pans and a length of cord. Little Rivka was so focused on setting the table that she hardly noticed her grandfather's presence.

The elderly man managed to kiss his wife's cheek while plunging a finger into the broth. "There's a wagonload of timber coming in before dark," he said, popping the finger into his mouth. "If the quality is what I'm expecting, I can take some and use it to repair the porch." Without having to glance outside, he added, "This time, perhaps the weather will cooperate."

Malka added another pinch of salt. "If you think so," she mumbled, and then exchanged a conspiratorial smile with Fredl. Who could forget the last time?

"I said I'll get it done," he announced, working a bit too hard to sound stern. "And I will." His glance toward Fredl said: After all these years, you'd think she'd believe me!

Fredl laughed, at the same time eyeing the cake to determine how much icing would be required. So much had improved since Szulen's death. Only the month before, Fredl had sat with her parents and suggested, "Perhaps it's time to give you back your privacy, not to mention your house. When the weather permits, I'll pull the covers off the windows, do a thorough cleaning and take my children home." The loud protests triggered by this simple comment had taken her by surprise.

"That house has been boarded up for nearly two years," Malka had argued. "Why, it'll take us a week just to get the windows uncovered and the damage repaired."

"And we'll be so far from the fort!" protested the boys.

When Fredl had turned a quizzical expression to Rivka, the child said nothing.

To the delight of nearly everyone, Fredl laughed and relented.

Grischa watched with pleasure as his daughter worked. She had gained back much of the weight lost during her illness and the color had returned to her face, but she was also quieter now, more reflective. More like a grown woman. And yet the same spirited nature that had once governed her words—and for too long had been absent—now danced in her eyes. Her father ran his fingers absentmindedly through his beard and yawned. "The man delivering the lumber from Berdichev is scheduled to arrive in a few hours. I was thinking, Malka, that perhaps . . ."

"Of course," she interrupted, grabbing his wrist and squeezing playfully. "You mean you haven't already invited him?"

He bowed to her humor. "I have not, my very suspicious wife." Hardly chagrined at all, he added, "But only because he has not yet arrived."

Fredl held out a spoon of sugary icing to her father. "If you like, Papa, I can feed the children early. Three hungry children might be too much for an unsuspecting guest, especially if he's been on the road."

Her father waved away the suggestion. "Sit at my table," he declared, "and you sit with my family."

While Grischa was outside measuring the lumber required for the promised repairs, a wagon carrying that lumber was rolling northward from the Ukraine. Its driver, Shmuel Langer, was fighting the fatigue working up his legs, across his back and shoulders. The idea of a hot bath and clean bed was what urged him forward. And the fact that it was Friday, the Sabbath, meaning that this final delivery had to be made before sundown or it would have to wait until Sunday. "Only a few more hours until Shabbos," he admonished the horse. As if the beast were as observant as his Orthodox master, its pace increased.

Langer arrived late afternoon at Gershon's store. Climbing down with some difficulty, he stretched his legs while one of Grischa's assistants unloaded the wagon. "I'm too old for this," he grumbled to himself. "A man of sixty-three should be at home, sitting before a fire and reading a good book."

As the last plank was removed, Grischa descended the steps to greet his supplier. "A long trip?" he asked, extending a hand of welcome. Langer grunted something about old men and dirt roads. "Of course," announced the proprietor, "you will have Shabbos with my family," and the stranger appeared suddenly refreshed. The two men entered the store. After some quick calculating, Langer passed his figures to Grischa. "This is the price if you pay in cash."

Grischa looked over the numbers. "As opposed to . . ."

"Some of my customers prefer to trade."

Grischa made a wide gesture around the store. "Do you see anything here you need?"

Langer's eyes crinkled into a softer expression. "Thank you, no. But I understand that times are difficult. So if you prefer to give goods instead of cash, I can always find someone willing to buy."

"I see. And then you take the goods and sell them along the way. And what kind of profit . . ."

Langer interrupted with a shake of his head. "I ask only the price of the original trade. It's not my way to profit from hardship."

Grischa held up a hand. "I never meant to suggest that it was, sir, and I'm in total agreement. Nevertheless, your attitude is unusual, especially in these times."

Shmuel Langer looked directly at the shopkeeper. "It is precisely because of these times that we must hold fast to our integrity. Falter even a step," he added, eyes shifting to a place somewhere outside the store, "and the bastards have won."

Grischa paid in cash, thinking that he had just made a new friend.

When the transaction was completed, Shmuel Langer set off to find the shul. A few roads here, a turn there, and he arrived. Standing on its steps, he noticed a house across the road and thought what a shame that such a lovely little home should be boarded up and sitting vacant. Berdichev or Nowy Życie, he told himself, the suffering remains the same.

Langer entered and took a seat. He was genuinely pleased when Grischa appeared at his side. Together they unfolded their tallit, each man reciting the prayer embroidered across the upper border, and then draped the shawls over their heads. Opening their siddurs to the correct page, the new friends began to pray. Lips moving, torsos swaying and bending from the waist in devotional penitence, the voices around them blended into a dissonant song chanted from some inner source, some atavistic connection to a spirit, to an existence every man in that room considered bigger, greater, than could ever be bestowed upon mortal man.

When the service was completed, the men folded away their tallit and Grischa led his guest outside. "My wife is pleased that you're joining us, but I must warn you that Shabbos in our home is very much a family affair."

The stranger smiled. "Which only adds to the pleasure!"

They walked side by side, their appearance almost comical: both of them were tall and exceedingly thin, with beards nearly white and hanging to their chest. Stride for stride, they walked in sync and enjoyed each other's presence. Entering the house, they found the women fully absorbed in preparations. Langer was introduced, warmly welcomed and then graciously invited to go with Grischa and leave the women to their work.

"So what do you think?" Hannah asked Fredl.

Malka dipped a spoon into the broth and tasted. "More salt."

"Not the soup, Mama, the guest!"

Fredl folded the cotton squares and placed one beside each plate. "He strikes me as austere." She glanced toward where the men were chatting. "Maybe it's his height. Being tall and thin can make you seem rigid."

Hannah exchanged a quick glance with her mother. Leave it to

Fredl to give a psychological evaluation, said their eyes.

The meal proved as boisterous as ever and their guest seemed to relish the entire evening. All questions put by Fredl's boys were answered with a lively response, as well as a quick and easy laugh. "Life is much different in the Ukraine," he explained, drawing them a map. Fredl watched and saw that there was nothing austere about this man; one had only look into his eyes to see the depth of his kindness.

The Gershons were watching their guest and Shmuel Langer was making observations of his own. He noted each family member, how spirited they all were and the intimacy they shared. It made no difference to any of them that they were wedged around a little table in a village forty miles from Warsaw; what mattered was that they were together. The scene reminded him of his own family, the primary differences being the numbers—he had only one child, Mottel—and the size of the home. One thing he had not yet mentioned was that he not only sold the lumber, but owned the mill as well.

Fredl watched this lively man who in so many ways was younger than his years. She particularly liked how he listened to her children, made each question important, gave it weight. When near the end of the meal he turned to Fredl and asked "And your husband, Mrs. Rabinoff, is he away on business?" she was momentarily flustered.

"Our Papa?" piped in Nahum, the younger boy. "Why, Papa's dead! Everyone knows that!"

"Perhaps not everyone," Fredl responded, and turned to their guest. "I'm afraid my children believe that the entire world lives in Nowy Życie."

Langer cocked his head toward the pouting boy. "Perhaps it's only that he feels so sure of his world. Your son is not to be forgiven, but envied."

Fredl toyed with her fork. "Sometimes there are more painful affairs than pogroms."

Langer studied her face. "I can't think of any."

Fredl lifted her eyes to meet his. "The death of a mate, the loss of a best friend." Having spoken, she immediately reddened. "I'm sorry," she stammered, her eyes moving around the table. "Of course it's not the same. Nothing can be compared to a pogrom."

Langer leaned forward in his chair, his beard nearly falling into the plate of food. "When my wife died, I often wondered if I could go on. But there was Mottel, my only child. He needed me, and that need was stronger than my desire to run away."

Fredl absorbed what he was saying with her head tilted to one side. Her face suddenly softened. "In a sense, I ran away," she admitted. "Unlike you, I could not go on, despite my children's needs." The glance she directed toward her parents was pure love. "I was fortunate to have a family that helped me through an exceedingly difficult time."

Malka responded to her daughter's loving glance with a tight smile. Such intimate thoughts, said her expression, should not be shared with strangers.

Grischa read his wife, but was too pleased to mind. Here was someone who understood, who had been through the grief and had survived. If ever Fredl were to share her thoughts, this was someone who could listen.

Shmuel Langer finished his business after sundown of the following day and returned to Berdichev. It was six months before he would return to Nowy Życie. This time, however, his intentions had nothing to do with delivering loads of lumber. This time, it was intended to develop his friendship with Fredl. And then there were three more visits, each one separated by a shorter absence, each one deepening his relationship with Fredl and her family. Even more, perhaps, was the opportunity it gave this skeptical lot to familiarize themselves with him.

And then he proposed.

"But you hardly know him!" declared Hannah.

"What more do I need to know?" she asked, clasping her sister's hand. "I know that he is kind, and that he treats my children with love and respect. And," she added, touching Hannah's cheek, "I know that he will be a loving and attentive husband."

Hannah nearly pushed the hand away. "But the Ukraine? That's over four hundred miles! In even the best weather you're talking about a six-day journey! You would go so far from home? From your family?" So far from me, her voice was saying, from me!

"Shmuel assures me that I can visit whenever I wish. He hasn't exactly said so, but I think he must be quite wealthy."

Hannah studied her sister's face, looking for any sign of confusion or uncertainty. Seeing none, she spoke her true thoughts. "How can you consider moving so far away from me, Fredl?" Before her sister could answer, she added, "And why would a beautiful young woman agree to marry a man the age of her father?"

The questions prompted Fredl to touch Hannah's cheek again and then pull her sister toward her for a lengthy embrace. "I've had my love, Hannah, my wonderful passion. Now it's time for something else." When they separated, she refrained from reaching out and stroking that crease in her sister's brow. "Shmuel loves me. More important, he respects me." The smile on Fredl's face was peaceful. "He'll care for me, Hannah. For me and my children."

As Hannah was grappling with Fredl's decision, her mother was fighting her own inner war. Never in her life had she willed herself to exert such self-control over each word that crossed her lips. For days after the announcement she greeted everyone with a manufactured smile, somehow succeeding in trapping each opinion before it could escape. Grischa, for once in full agreement with his wife, also warned himself away from what could be perceived as judging words. From Malka and Hannah's perspective, he was being laughably philosophical. "These things work themselves out," he kept assuring them. "We simply have to trust that whatever happens is for the best."

"I want to strangle him!" admitted Malka to her younger daughter, the complicity they shared making their sadness more bearable.

Almost one year to the day after their first meeting, Fredl and Shmuel were wed. It would be another two weeks before everything was organized, packed, and rearranged.

"But Mr. Langer," persisted Fredl's older boy. "Where is Berdichev?"

"My dear David," responded his exasperated mother. "How many times can you ask the same question? Mr. Langer has drawn you a half-dozen maps. That should be enough!"

But each time Shmuel Langer was asked, he laughed and pulled out his pen. A widower for many years, he was more than happy to comply. Even more, he relished the promise of a home filled with the gaiety and clamor of children's voices. "Allow me to show you one more time," he offered, removing the pen's cap and bending over whatever scrap of paper they could find. "Now, this is the Ukraine, yes? And over here. . . ." Once again the boy watched, all the while attempting to calculate how far he was going from the only home he had ever known.

"And you, Rivka?" asked Langer. "Do you want to see where your new home will be?" The child looked into those friendly eyes, turned on her heels and fled. Sighing, he folded the paper. This one, said his expression, will take some time.

When the big day arrived the children were short-tempered and their grandparents jittery. The wagon was ready, with everything tied down and secured. No last-minute advice or admonitions could change the inevitable: it was time to depart. "All aboard for Berdichev!" announced Shmuel.

"But where is it?" demanded David, climbing into the wagon.

Langer lifted Nahum up onto the seat and laughed. "You'll see soon enough!"

Malka stood to the side. Finally gathering her courage, she sidled over to Fredl, linked an arm through her daughter's and willed herself not to cry. "You promise to write."

"Yes, Mama. And I promise to be a good girl, too." When her mother eyed her suspiciously, Fredl hugged her hard. "Before you know it, old Bogdan will be coming to the door with a sackful of letters from Berdichev."

Malka stroked Fredl's face. "From your mouth to God's ears," she mumbled. It was the image of that difficult old Russian postal clerk hauling his sack of mail, and Jewish mail at that, that finally gave her cause to smile.

When there was nothing more to be said, Malka and Grischa took their positions at the side of the road. Stretched across their faces were broad and unconvincing smiles. Nearby stood all the other members of the Gershon family, each one demanding one last embrace.

Every touch, every tender farewell, was observed quietly and respectfully by Fredl's husband. He offered no words of consolation, made no attempt to diminish the intense pain felt by her loving family. They had nursed her through so much, only to see her leave. The man sat there, reins in hand, fingers slowly rubbing the smooth leather surface, until everything that needed to be said had been satisfactorily expressed. The last to respond was Rivka. When she wrapped her arms around her grandmother's neck, she refused to let go. Malka lifted Rivka from the wagon and held her, nearly crying out in despair. Only Fredl's firm grip could disengage the hysterical child and place her next to her brothers. With the children finally settled, Fredl accepted her father's hand, climbed up to her place and gave her husband a nod. Only then did he shake the leather straps and set the horse in motion.

When Fredl and her children looked back, they saw everyone in the world they had ever loved standing together, arms lifted in unison, one giant arm waving good-bye.

ℰ Topanga Canyon, Summer 1984

The more Mimi learned of her mother's life, the more difficult and painful it was for her to think of the child, of a little girl named Rivka being devastated time and again. That this was the same person Mimi knew as Mother, a woman who had survived the death of her father, the illness of her mother, the move to a strange country . . . these alone would transform anyone's life, leave their mark forever. And there were traumas yet to come. It gave Mimi cause to marvel that her mother had survived at all. It also pushed her closer to seeking out a therapist, someone who could guide her through this journey, but she remained resistant to the idea, determined to go this pilgrimage alone. She had promised herself several times to seek out someone . . . if the terrain got too rough. Each time it seemed impassable, however, she had found her way out.

The more time Mimi devoted to studying the patterns of her own life, the more she understood how her mother's history—perhaps even more than the woman herself—played a role. The drama of Rivka Rabinoff's childhood had become a fulcrum in her family's continuum: on one end weighed her history of grief, struggle, and survival, while on the opposing end dangled Mimi, her only child, and now the end of the family's line. The time Mimi had devoted to this process of reflection and understanding made her keenly aware of the real task at hand: to overcome the imbalance and achieve equilibrium. If she could do this — what felt very much like her life's work — then perhaps she could anticipate, rather than dread, her future.

The sound of firecrackers startled Mimi, and then gave her cause to check the calendar. Only the third of July and some idiot was already setting them off in the canyon. She looked at her watch. It was six o'clock yet it was still hot, Los Angeles hot: sticky and suffocating. As if the heat were not bad enough, she had to contend with the added danger of fireworks, which made everyone in the canyon jittery. How could it not, when it had been hot and dry exactly like this, when a firestorm destroyed hundreds of homes, including several on the ridge directly behind her.

A feeling of edginess insinuated itself into her concentration. This need to keep an eye out on the canyon, to be ever vigilant in the search for the smallest sign of smoke and discover the equilibrium in life, all of it was wearing her out. Relax! she told herself, and then called the local gas station to schedule a lube job for the following morning. When the mechanic asked if she would be needing a ride home, she said yes, thanked him, hung up the phone and burst into tears. Sarah had always provided that ride. "Oh, for God's sake," she muttered. "Pull yourself together!"

The telephone rang and she snatched it up. When she heard Daniel's voice inviting her to dinner, she relaxed. "You keep feeding me like this," she warned, "and I'll get big as a house." The gratitude in her voice belied the joke.

"But this is L.A.," he protested. "Home of the sushi bar and all that is fat-free. Anyway, stop worrying about your weight, you look just fine."

You look just fine. Mimi couldn't remember the last time anyone had said that to her, much less a man. And when was the last time she had looked in a mirror and said it to herself? Suppressing the urge to sabotage his compliment with a caustic allusion to her thighs, she accepted his invitation and ran into the bathroom to brush her hair and put some color onto her face.

They were driving down the canyon road when Daniel reached over and took Mimi's hand. It was a toss-up who was more surprised when she did not pull away. Mimi nearly commented that her mother had warned her that even this simple gesture of affection could ruin a girl's reputation and bring shame upon the family. Untrue to normal form, she said nothing.

Berdichev, Autumn 1911

Rivka yanked open the front door and shielded her eyes against the glare of a late afternoon sun. "It's Papa!" she called out, recognizing the puffs of dust being kicked up by the wagon and its mare. "He's almost here!" Breaking into a run, she rushed through the iron gates and across the clearing, braids flapping like streamers in the wind. When she caught up with the wagon, she slapped its side once and then danced alongside. As soon as Shmuel Langer brought it to a stop, Rivka grabbed the reins from his hands and waited impatiently for him to climb down. Nearly seventy, he did so slowly, gingerly, fingers clutching the wagon's forward brace until both feet were safely on the ground. He watched as the girl, eyebrows drawn together and tongue protruding in concentration, tied the straps to the post as she had been taught. When she finished, she scrutinized the effort. "Okay, Papa, you can look now."

Experience told Shmuel that he must complete this ritual before going inside to see Fredl. Bending with some effort, he inspected the knot, made all the requisite clicks and hums of approval, and nuzzled the girl's cheek. Rivka caught his beard and forced him to bend lower. Leaning back, she peered into his face. "Papa, you have been very bad. You must promise never again to go without me." Pulling him even closer, she took his cheeks in her small hands. "Do you promise?"

The old man pushed a strand of hair from her face. "You know I can't," he murmured, and then pointed to the smoke rising from the mill and hanging cloudlike over the trees. "That one, over there, it looks like a goose."

Rivka tipped her head far back and pointed. "But that one there—no, Papa, there—do you think it's a cat?" Studying the sky, she leaned against him. Her stepfather had taught her to search for figures in the clouds: on windy days she considered it great luck to find a dog or a bird; when there was hardly a breeze, when the smoke lingered and shapes changed slowly, she might discover an entire zoo.

Shmuel sorted through the supplies and came up with a large box. "Since I'm so bad, would you consider accepting this gift with my humble apologies?" He presented it to Rivka with a flourish.

She clapped her hands and laughed, snatched the gift and clutched it against her chest. Shmuel watched with a rush of affection as she began working the knots in the string. It was not so much the intensity with which she attacked each knot that pleased him, but the trust. This was the same child who had arrived several years earlier like a wounded animal, the same child who rarely smiled or showed enthusiasm. And no matter how much Fredl had reassured her new husband, little Rivka would not allow him anywhere near. When the shift finally came, it arrived like a rainbow after a storm.

They were having a rousing family dinner, replete with cheder stories and good-natured banter. Shmuel had been singing songs learned as a child and Fredl was delighting everyone by joining in. In the midst of the enjoyable tumult, little Rivka climbed down from her chair, walked to the other end of the long table, and crawled onto her stepfather's lap. He hardly dared touch her, so fearful of breaking the spell. After several more stories and songs he risked draping an arm over her shoulder; she responded by nestling against his chest. Fredl saw tears in his eyes and worked hard to contain her own. Since that time, the friendship between child and stepfather continued to blossom.

"Slowly, slowly," Langer laughed, watching Rivka shred the wrapping paper. "Whatever awaits you inside that box, I promise it won't grow wings and fly away." He was so engrossed in the frenzied attack that he didn't notice his son coming from the mill. Hearing Mottel's laugh, Shmuel turned and smiled.

"Telling our girl to slow down," laughed Mottel, "is like asking the world to stop turning." The young man threw an arm around his father's shoulder and they stood watching together. "Can you imagine if our mill hands worked with such energy?"

Langer laughed. "Increased production, you can be sure. Tenfold, at the least!" He squeezed his son's arm and thought of that day only six years earlier when a rebellious young Mottel had appeared for breakfast with his face cleanly shaven. For an Hasidic Jew of eastern Europe, this was blasphemy, an unspeakable defilement of Torah.

Some townspeople urged the family to banish Mottel from their home altogether and be treated as if dead. Shmuel Langer listened, weighed the preponderance of advice and then agonized for days in the privacy of his study. There was really no decision to be made. When he finally emerged, he put his arms around Mottel and assured him that he was now, and always would be, a cherished son.

And now they stood together, father and son, two men who loved and respected each other, watching the child who had so completely won their hearts attack her gift with zeal. When the wrapping was finally off and the box opened, Rivka stared openmouthed at its contents. "Does that mean you like it?" asked Shmuel, leaning forward and resting both hands on his knees.

"She's lovely," whispered the child as she removed the doll and cradled it in her arms. Lowering herself onto the wagon's step, she began inspecting every inch: lace cap held in place by a large cream-colored ribbon; curly blonde hair so lifelike Rivka ran strands of it between her fingers to determine if it was actually real. And then she turned her attention to the dress, a blue the color of periwinkles, with a delicate white-laced neckline and hem. Rivka examined the way the legs were attached, marveled at the white wool stockings, the petite black-leather shoes secured with miniature brass buckles. "Oh, Papa," she breathed. "Her hands!" Mesmerized, she caressed the fingers.

Mottel bent down and kissed her cheek. "Perhaps you'd like to show your mama."

Rivka nodded, took a few steps toward the house and then stopped. Her face changed, those fine eyebrows drawing together and the eyes narrowing in suspicion. In that brief moment of consternation, she bore a remarkable resemblance to her Grandmother Malka. "Is she really mine?"

"Yes, my dear, all yours."

"And no one can take her from me?"

Shmuel touched her face. "You have my word." He watched the child hold the treasure against her chest and stride regally toward the house. Turning toward his son, he asked, "And how did you manage in my absence?"

The directness caused Mottel to grin. "There were very few problems, Father."

Langer studied the young man with unmasked pride. He wanted to respond, "Father? When did I stop being Papa?" but held his tongue.

The two men stood together listening to the sounds of the mill. There were workers calling out instructions, an impatient mare snorting to be freed from the wagon. Birds were flapping overhead; hooves were pounded as horses toiled under loads of timber, each clip-clop churning up dust clouds and leaving behind a horseshoe stamped in the road. At one end of the mill road sat two houses, one owned by Shmuel Langer, the other by his older brother, Mendel, and Mendel's wife, Chava. At the other end was the weather-gouged main road, which was the direct route to the railroad storehouse and the only road that was passable in the winter. This was especially vital for carting wood to Odessa's shipbuilders and pulp to the newspapers in Kiev. In the heaviest of winters this road was the lifeline for the region.

The men set off for the house. "The workers are worried about Fastov," said Mottel, and then regretted the abruptness of the announcement. Everyone had heard about the peddler who had reportedly stabbed a Gentile and left him to die in the woods near Fastov. Because it happened only days short of Passover, many were calling it a ritual murder and swearing that the killers were Jewish peddlers who required Christian blood to mix with their matzohs. Despite the peddler's insistence that he had done nothing wrong, the pogroms could not be halted. Less than a week later he was proven innocent, which was no deterrent for a mob swearing revenge. It was exacted when outraged peasants arrived in broad daylight and burned his home to the ground, his wife and children inside.

Shmuel glanced toward his brother's house on the other side of the clearing. "What does Mendel say?"

"What can he say? He's old, Father, and so tired he can hardly make it through the day."

Old? How could Mendel be old? The two brothers were nearly the same age! Shmuel recalled with a smile that day several years earlier when he had approached his brother for advice.

The two men were standing on the edge of the yard, watching two workers deftly cut through a massive cylinder of a newly downed tree.

"I know it's absurd," muttered Shmuel. "Falling in love at my age."

"Do you love her?" Mendel had asked, noting how Shmuel's eyes danced like an adolescent's. "And you say she is how old?"

Shmuel had attempted nonchalance. "Does it matter?"

"It matters. How old?"

He could not bring himself to meet Mendel's gaze. "Thirty, perhaps."

"Thirty," echoed Mendel, stroking his beard philosophically. "Yes, this is good."

An alarm went off in Shmuel's brain. "Why good?"

Mendel continued to stroke his beard, but his eyes twinkled mischievously. "In our culture, that's no longer considered a child." When Shmuel protested, he was silenced at once. "Stop talking nonsense, you old fool! Life is hard, certainly too short: How often does love come your way? Rarely," he answered, not waiting for a reply. "So it must be cherished." He turned and faced his brother squarely. "If you love her, marry her. It's been too long since your house was a home."

And now Mottel was suggesting that they were old men! How old can I be, he wondered, when a beautiful woman of thirty-five is waiting for me inside? "We'll talk later," he said, anxious to wrap his arms around Fredl and tell her about his journey. It was such a beautiful day, and how often was a man of his age about to become a new father!

What a day that had been when a blushing Fredl approached him and placed a hand on his arm. "My dear," she said, "I'm afraid I was introduced into your life to complicate it."

"Please," he had responded, "complicate all you wish. And do you have some particular complication in mind?"

"Would another child do?"

Breaking the news to Mendel was pure joy. The man was speechless. Shmuel finally insisted he say something. "I don't care what: say you're delighted, say you're horrified, just say!"

"Jealous," admitted his brother. "That an old man like you can still make babies makes me jealous." They looked at each other and burst into silly laughter.

As for Rivka, she was enthralled and began hounding her mother, demanding to know what would be expected of her. "Tell me again," she insisted, offering one of her dolls as a model. "Show me exactly how we hold the baby." And each time Fredl took the doll and demonstrated.

"Will I get to bathe the baby?" she asked during her baths.

"We'll do it together," murmured Fredl.

"Will I be able to rock her to sleep?"

"Yes, my dear, you will rock the baby to sleep."

"What if it's a boy?"

"Boys must be rocked as well."

Each question led to another, resulting in several more. As the heaviness of pregnancy settled in, Fredl secretly prayed that each question was the last.

One evening Rivka wedged herself on the couch between her mother and stepfather. "When the baby comes," she asked, "will I still be your little girl?" When her parents professed that her position was forever secure, she slid from the couch and faced them. "Fine," she announced. "Then you may have the baby."

Shmuel pushed open the gate and approached the front door. He loved that child so! She was such a different little girl than when she had first arrived, and now here she was, tethered firmly to her foundation. "My papa died when I was a baby," she had told Shmuel the week before. He had studied her face, kissed that place on her forehead creased with worry. "I intend to live a very long time." Satisfied, she had skipped from the room.

Shmuel entered the house and expected to find Fredl waiting at the door, but there was only Rivka playing near the fireplace. "Where's Mama?"

"I went to show her my dolly but she was too tired to play."

A wave of fear swept over Shmuel, followed at once by a reprimand: Only foolish old men look for problems! He followed the lengthy hallway to the last door and found it closed. Rapping once, he pushed it open and slipped into the room. The drapes were pulled, the room was dark as night. "Are you awake?" he whispered, approaching the bed. A hand reached out from under the covers. "Fredl, are you ill?"

A small voice responded from the bed. "I think I am."

Her fingers were so cold they chilled his own, her forehead hot to the touch. "Are you in pain?" He adjusted the blanket and it shifted, revealing a dark stain. Shmuel pulled the cover back farther and discovered the extent of the bleeding. "My dear," he said, fighting to remain calm," I'm going to leave you for just a moment."

"Please don't."

"One minute, I promise." He touched her face and walked from the room. As soon as he passed through the door he ran outside. "Mottel," he shouted, "Mendel!" His face was gray with fear. His son came running from the barn. "A doctor!" he cried. "For the love of God, fetch the doctor."

It was hours before the hemorrhaging could be controlled. Fredl's face was waxen; her husband would not leave her side. Despite his attempts to be hopeful, to reassure the children that their mother would be fine, he sat down and wrote a letter to her family in Nowy Życie.

The doctor came every day. The most hopeful thing he could offer was that she was young and healthy, that time would tell. And that nothing could be done to save the baby. Shmuel was torn between remaining at her side and soothing the fears of the children. He wanted to stay with her, yet felt keenly his role of father. When the children were busy playing, he left the room only when Mendel, Chava, or Mottel were able to drag him outside for a moment of fresh air. It was nearly two weeks before Malka and Grischa finally arrived, freeing Shmuel to devote every minute to his wife. He carried her tea and coaxed her to eat; he stroked her thin face and murmured loving words. Her condition continued to deteriorate.

"You have made me happy," she murmured early one morning.

"And I will continue to do so," he responded, doing his best to hide his fears.

"You have given us a new life."

"Fredl, my love."

She grasped his hand. "Whatever happens, you must know that never once did I doubt my decision to come here. Never once. And I was right not to doubt."

The children were encouraged to visit, always with the proviso that the room remained calm. The boys were content to kiss their mother's cheek and rush outside to their fort, but Rivka needed to be closer, had even created a nest for herself on the floor, in the corner nearest her mother's head. It was there she took her meals; it was to that spot Mottel came every night to carry her off to bed. She had seen the blood, had watched Chava pull the sheets from the bed and carry them outside. She had smelled the smoke when Mottel burned them in the fire pit. If her mother was to be confined, the least she could do was make sure she was never alone. And so she remained, like a guard dog, on the floor and with her back to the wall, her mouth always set into a frown.

As for Grischa and Malka, they tried to maintain some emotional balance for the sake of the children, but their faces failed to conceal what they feared: that they could lose their Fredl.

Nearly five weeks after the crisis had begun, on a lovely afternoon when the air was so calm and the smoke hanging over the mill so motionless that, had Shmuel and Rivka taken the time to search they would have easily found an entire zoo of animals, Fredl Gershon Langer died.

⬢ *Topanga Canyon, Summer 1984*

Mimi knelt in her garden on knee pads. This little patch of earth just off the deck had always caused her trouble, although she had yet to determine if the culprit was soil acidity or poor drainage. She loved running her fingers through the same leaves she had planted with her bare hands, and smelling the damp earth which gave off that musty odor of growth and decay. Although she bought herself a new pair of gloves every year, they invariably ended up somewhere in the dirt. What was the purpose of being one with the earth if you didn't get it under your nails? The problem was that even after she soaked her mud-caked hands, they remained a broken-nailed, jagged-cuticle badge of honor.

"Hello, my beauties," she murmured to her begonias. Digging through the tool basket she came up with the clippers. A snip here, a snip there, until only healthy flowers and clusters of buds remained. Sometimes this garden felt like her only haven, the one place where she could lose herself and push away all thoughts of this sometimes

exhausting inner journey she had undertaken. At the same time, however, it was while gardening that she felt most comfortable about
reflecting on the progress of this journey. What better place to con-
template why she had made her mother the axis of her emotional life
than right here, in the warmth of day, surrounded by color and fragrance? It took no great introspection to understand that she harbored considerable anger against her mother, but there was more.
Even if Rivka had set the stage, developed the first scene and had then
written the script, it was Mimi who perpetuated the drama. A case of
volition, she told herself, gouging into the soil and going after a tenacious weed. If I didn't bite, she told herself, my mother wouldn't bait.

Her Grandmother Fredl had died more than seventy years ago, yet
her mother still hauled the pain around like a stone. It was more than
a burden for Rivka; it was her bequest to her only child.

"You'd think at my age," muttered Mimi. The thought was left
unfinished. She sat back on her haunches and wiped sweat from her
brow. Why was she surprised? She had taken this burden of discovery
on herself and now she was suffocating under its weight. It made her
wonder about tenderness, about the intimacy and sensitivity her
mother and grandmother had purportedly shared. It was so easy to
tell herself that tenderness was something she had never known, yet
she knew this to be untrue. She had loved Sarah, certainly she felt tenderness toward Daniel. But could a friend provide the intimacy that
is supposed to exist between mother and child? Rivka always insisted
that Fredl had loved her children unconditionally. In Mimi's experience, everything was conditional.

These thoughts churned around in her while she showered,
dressed, and set off for the weekly outing with her mother. There was
a time not so long ago when she dreaded these visits, considered them
a commitment that had to be fulfilled. As she approached the Boyle
Heights apartment, however, she was surprised to find herself humming. Perhaps it was anticipation, looking forward to taking another
step. Mimi always swore to Sarah that the only reason her mother
wanted to spend time with her daughter was to have an opportunity
to complain. She complained about her health, about friends who
were dying, friends who died; she complained about how nice it

would have been if, like every other woman on earth, she had been blessed with grandchildren. And Mimi was expected to grind her teeth, listen sympathetically and give nothing away vis-à-vis her own sense of having failed. But now, with this project of digging up her mother's history and exploring the magnitude of one woman's suffering so that she could understand her own, everything was changing.

The minute she pulled up to the curb, Rivka emerged from the downstairs foyer and marched toward the car. Over one arm was her leather purse, over the other an empty knitting bag with wooden handles. That bag meant only one thing: she had errands to run. This pleased Mimi because it also meant that while chatting and studying shopping lists, there was limited time for confrontation. It also gave her time to formulate her thoughts and conceive new and creative ways to mine information from her unwilling mother's memory. Who knew? Perhaps today would signify that opening Mimi sought for a really good probe!

Leaning across the seat, Mimi opened the door. Rivka climbed in and offered her daughter her cheek. The gesture was accompanied by a whiff of antibacterial soap. Rather than make some comment about the potent odor, which most certainly would have guaranteed instant tension, she smiled and returned the obligatory kiss. "We're certainly eager today!"

Rivka shot her a scornful look and they laughed, the two of them sharing a strong dislike of the collective "we." The older woman reached into her purse and extracted a spiral notebook. "Let's see," she muttered, running a finger down the list. "We'll go to the market first, and then the cleaners, the shoemaker, and the pharmacy." Closing the notebook with a satisfied snap, she dropped it into her purse and waited for her chauffeur to set off.

Mimi put the car into gear. "Have you had lunch?" she asked. It was barely eleven, but the question was reasonable: her mother normally ate dinner at five. "Because if not, there's a new Japanese restaurant in Studio City."

Rivka peered down her nose. "Again you're pushing the raw fish? What about worms? I've read they can grow in your stomach."

Mimi laughed and pulled away from the curb.

After accomplishing the first half of their errands, the subject of lunch came up again. When they agreed on Italian, Mimi headed toward her favorite place. Settling into their booth at Aperto, they gave their order—which had not changed in more than ten years—and Mimi launched into her list of questions about Berdichev.

Rivka studied her daughter's face for some time. "Why this big interest?" she asked. "Whenever we're together, there's always something about home." The woman's tone of voice suggested that, should she divulge anything personal, Mimi might actually use that information against her.

"Don't worry, Mama, I'm not writing an exposé."

Rivka continued to stare, the pucker of her mouth saying, I'm not so sure.

The basket of hot sourdough placed between them broke the tension. But like an old habit that would never die, Rivka nudged it out of her daughter's reach.

And because Mimi cared more about her mother's childhood than she did that delicious bread, she steeled herself and ignored the gesture. This was no great sacrifice, since the smell of the hot sourdough was turning her stomach. It made her wonder how, certainly why, she had gotten herself into this. She pushed aside the cautionary voice and plunged ahead. "I'm not sure how I came to this place in my life, Mama. You know, living alone." Before she could go on, Rivka flipped her hand through the air, as if she understood completely. The dismissive gesture would normally have annoyed Mimi, made her teeth hurt, but today she found it touching and protective. "I'm talking about relationships," she added, nearly cringing when she heard the whine in her voice. "You don't think I'm abnormal because I've never lived with a man?"

Her mother raised an eyebrow. "Do you think it's abnormal?"

Mimi studied her mother's face. It was an honest question, and what she saw in Rivka's eyes was concern. "I'm not sure. For some women, no. For me? Well, I guess I never thought it would happen. I think I always assumed that I'd meet someone and marry."

Rivka pulled her eyebrows together and turned her gaze toward a space over Mimi's shoulder. "I was married to your father for nearly fifty years and it wasn't so wonderful."

"That still doesn't explain it. I mean, why it never happened with me."

"Did anyone ask?"

Mimi felt the bile rising in her throat. "Pardon?"

Rivka seemed suddenly flustered. "To marry him. Mimi, did a man ever ask you to marry him, or live with him? It may sound like a foolish question for a mother to ask her daughter, but you've always kept your personal life such a secret from me."

Mimi wasn't sure which she found more annoying, the question or the accusation. Yes, she had kept her life to herself. And no, a man had never asked. Unless she counted Daniel, which she never did. Apparently her mother didn't either, since she had been told of Daniel's proposal. Thinking about her mother's question, she saw that it was not so unreasonable after all. Except, of course, that it was being asked by her mother. So why did it rankle so? Because of the way it was posed, or because of what she feared was a counterfeit smile on her mother's lips? She saw that same smile when her mother asked such questions as "Darling, are you gaining weight again?" or "Darling, did that nice man ever call you back?" Perhaps she was imagining it. Sitting in the busy restaurant, plates of pasta being delivered to nearby tables, she searched in vain for the best response.

"I see," murmured Rivka.

Exactly what did she see? Mimi was afraid to ask, so she picked up her water glass and studied the ice cubes. When she glanced at her mother, the woman's expression suggested that her daughter was holding back some vital piece of personal data that mothers had a right to know. As always, it was Mimi who blinked first. "Whether or not I've been asked is not the issue." Her calm voice belied a growing panic. "The issue is to understand why I'm still alone." The old despair was creeping up, threatening to grab her by the windpipe. What the hell, she told herself, I may as well go for it. After all, when was the last time I appealed to my mother's sense of motherhood? She took a fortifying sip of wine. "Mama, is there anything you can tell me that would help me sort it out?" There, she had said it, laid it out before her mother, clean and untouched, like a strip of fine white sand on the beach.

A pinched expression crossed Rivka's face, a look so pained that

Mimi had a flash of hope. Bad news was better than no news. But then it disappeared. "Eat your lunch," her mother instructed, picking up her fork and twisting it through her pasta.

"Mama, please." When Rivka gestured toward the food, Mimi's frustration rose. "I don't want to eat my lunch," she nearly hissed through clenched teeth. And then hearing how much like a recalcitrant child she sounded, she nearly laughed.

"When you were fifteen and talked to me like that," said her mother, stabbing the fork in her daughter's direction, "I sent you to your room!"

Mimi felt her smile shifting into a grimace; she made a conscious effort to relax.

"And no matter what you did to deserve it," continued her mother, "it was always my fault."

The comment took Mimi by surprise. Was it true that her anger was always directed toward her mother? Rivka was the one who dangled the fishing rod in front of her daughter's face, but was it Mimi who first baited and then swallowed the hook? She was unhappy when her mother took one last bite of pasta and pushed the rest away. She was still hungry, and yet she knew that every bite taken from this point on would be scrutinized, measured and weighed against her mother's appetite. Oh, she could continue to eat, certainly, but she would be made to feel embarrassed and then guilty, and this always resulted in her attacking her food until not a streak of sauce was left on the plate. A meal consumed in the presence of her mother was guaranteed to end with dyspepsia. She took a few more bites, placed the fork across the plate, and looked up at her mother. Rivka's face seemed suddenly softer. When she announced, "Finish your lunch, darling," Mimi picked up her fork and stared at the food. Having been given permission, she was no longer hungry.

It was during the second cup of coffee that Rivka finally picked up the thread of their conversation. "In my experience, Miriam, looking back can only make you unhappy."

Eyebrows raised, Mimi stared at the woman. Was that it, the great revelation, the most philosophical statement her mother was capable of producing? She needed to take it further. "I think it's okay to be unhappy, Mama, if the results are positive." She saw her mother's skeptical expression and groped for a lifeline. "I mean, if I learn something that makes me sad, but by knowing it I'm led in the right direction—toward being happy, that is—then it's good, right? Anyway, you're the one who insists that I learn everything the hard way." The way Rivka toyed with her napkin, folded and unfolded it, made Mimi believe that she was mulling something over. "Mama, can you honestly say you've never looked back? Never just sat and let your mind drift backward through your life?" Mimi could not recall her mother being incapable of looking her in the eye, but this was clearly such a moment. "Mama?"

Rivka twisted her wedding ring. It had fit snugly once, decades ago, but now it was held in place by an arthritic knuckle. "My life has not been so special."

There it was, plopped onto the table without self-pity. No embellishments, no excuses. Just the simple truth and Mimi was deeply moved by it. She wanted to assure her mother, tell her that, quite the contrary, she believed her life to have been quite exceptional. Nothing ventured, nothing gained. "Mama, you lived through amazing times: czarist Russia, the shtetl, pogroms; the deaths of so many people you loved."

A flash of anger crossed her mother's face, an uplifted hand silenced the litany. "Since when is misery extraordinary?"

They fell into a muzzled truce separated by conflicting universes and two half-eaten servings of pasta. Mimi was torn between wanting to know everything her mother could reveal, while at the same time protecting herself and not causing her mother pain. But hadn't she always done it like this? And wasn't this entire process about pursuing her mother's story for the sole purpose of learning about herself? Mimi had kept her feelings under lock and key for too long; it was time to drop her guard.

CHAPTER SEVEN

&8 *Topanga Canyon, Summer 1984*

MIMI SAT IN HER STUDY, head resting against the chair, watching through heavy eyes as dust particles performed a lively dance on the lone sunbeam that had found its way into the room. The light was muted by late afternoon shadows and she found herself lulled nearly to sleep by the rusts and browns. An occasional stab of light touched upon the room's surfaces, a reminder that light finds its way into even the most sober darkness. It was still so easy to imagine Sarah seated across from her, elbows resting on the armrests, feet propped on the footstool. The posture, the open expression, everything announcing that she was there, available to her friend. Despite the passage of time, Mimi still could not accept the permanence of her absence. As much as the sense of Sarah's presence was unsettling, Mimi dreaded even more that day when it would no longer be so easy to conjure it up.

One image that popped into Mimi's head was an argument the two women had battled in this very room. They had been visiting— nothing unusual there—and Mimi had made a casual comment about the scarcity of available men. When Sarah had raised an eyebrow, Mimi's immediate response was, "Don't give me that look."

"And what look would that be?" Count on Sarah to always know when and what her friend was avoiding.

"The one where you do your bad impersonation of Sigmund Freud."

Sarah had studied Mimi for a long moment before releasing a

snorting sound. "I thought you liked that one? Isn't it your cue to spill your guts out, and then my cue to come up with all the right answers?"

Mimi had been visibly surprised by the force of Sarah's response. "I'll have you know that I find my own answers just fine," she had argued, thinking of the vast collection of self-help books she had purchased covering every inch of the psyche. "Besides, all I said was there aren't any men around. After all those books I've read. . . ." Her voice had trailed off.

Sarah had regarded her friend warily. "Books won't find you a lover."

Mimi had felt something hanging between them. It annoyed her that Sarah appeared so relaxed, so sure of herself that she made little noises as she sucked on the ear piece of her glasses; that her eyes never left Mimi's face. Especially when she felt her own hands fidgeting, her eyes darting away from Sarah's scrutiny. She had willed herself to remain still.

It was Sarah who had broken the silence. "You know what I think? I think you really do believe that reading the right books and talking the right talk will cause some man to magically appear." And then she stared at Mimi with such intense concentration that the latter was obliged to look away. "Sometimes I think that what you're really looking for is someone who'll solve your problems for you. The fairy-tale prince."

Mimi had opened her mouth but had said nothing.

"You're going to hate me for saying this, but I know you, and you honestly believe that you've got it all worked out. The trouble is, there's a world of difference between understanding a problem and acting on it. What good does it do to figure out why you resist or avoid relationships . . . unless you square your shoulders, push aside your fears and take the risk?"

The ridges around Mimi's mouth had left no doubt as to her reaction. After what felt like a good minute of silence, she had spoken. "Are you finished? I mean, have you said your big say?"

Sarah had finally gathered her things and left, leaving Mimi alone in her study wondering what the hell had just happened. It was several hours before it finally struck her: Sarah was determined to put her friend firmly on track while there was still time. Neither woman needed to read the latest test results to know that Sarah was in a losing race against death.

Mimi was surprised to discover that the room had become pitch-black. What she needed was a hot bath, a lot of wine, and a good night's sleep. The first two were no problem; sleep, on the other hand, would not come so easily. A week earlier she had been offended when her mother had tried to push Valium on her. "With two milligrams you'll relax," Rivka had promised. "Five, and you'll sleep like a baby." Mimi had reluctantly accepted and then, looking in the bottle, discovered that the dosage had been meted out and there were only four tablets. "Afraid I'll overdose?" she had snapped, quickly regretting the outburst. Now, with a silent thanks to her mother, she washed one down with a gulp of water. Within a half-hour she was sleeping.

It was nearly ten hours later that a ringing phone broke into her slumber and Mimi was more than grateful for the interruption. If that nightmare about Sarah trying to claw her way out of the grave had persisted any longer she might have finished off the pills altogether.

"The beach is spectacular," declared Daniel. "Twenty minutes?"

Mimi yawned. "Can't. Got a class at ten."

"On Saturday? Now that's what I call dedication."

No way was she going to explain her drugged state. "Oh, right," she murmured, "it is Saturday. Okay, but can you give me thirty?"

The ocean was lovely: waves rolling in and slamming against the rocks; the impact blasting water upward into a wide spray. The spectacle made Mimi think of flamenco dancers and their broad-laced fans. She sat with Daniel on a high mound of boulders, the timeworn crevices forming shimmering tide pools for families of crabs. As the water washed around her, she felt the tension falling away. What could be less stressful than being perched on a rock overlooking the Pacific and awaiting the arrival of the next wave? Mimi rotated her head slowly to ease the last vestige of tightness and then released a contented sigh.

"My sentiments precisely," murmured Daniel.

Mimi smiled and leaned back against the flattened surface of a rock. When Daniel shifted closer she felt suddenly shy, even experienced a desire to invoke Sarah's presence and ask her advice. But then, she knew very well what Sarah would say! Mimi was focused on a mass of seaweed bobbing past and nearly jumped when Daniel took her hand. The anxiety arrived with such a bolt that she inadvertently pulled away.

It was several minutes before he spoke. "Do you mind if I ask what you're thinking?"

She shifted her body just enough to look into his eyes. And then she began to sing a childhood song her parents had forbidden. "The worms crawl in, the worms crawl out, the worms play pinochle on your snout, they wrap you in a big white sheet and then they bury you six feet deep." Her heart was beating so fast she felt faint and the look on Daniel's face brought her up short. "I'm fine, really, I'm fine," she said, knowing full well that she was not. In fact, she was desperately aware that she was waging a battle against hysteria. When the image of Sarah suddenly heaved up and came crashing forward, there was no longer an ocean before her, but the image of a vibrant and healthy Sarah before cancer invaded her, before it took over and occupied her body like a squatter sure of its rights.

Daniel began to speak, as if a lull in this conversation had never existed. "After my wife died," he said, "I wasn't sure that I'd survive. It's funny, I guess, but sometimes I still expect her to walk through the front door. Or I'll come home from the office and be surprised when she's not there."

Mimi could only nod in comprehension. Something caught her eye and she turned to see a woman walking nearby. Her skirt was swinging in the wind and sandals dangled from her hand. The other hand was making a brushing motion across her cheek, as if she were crying. "My God, but we're a world of lonely people," whispered Mimi. This time, when Daniel reached over and took her hand, she did not pull away. "I keep thinking that I could have done more for Sarah, or should have." The grip on her hand tightened.

"I remember how that was," recalled Daniel. "She needed to talk and she had no concept of time, of day or night. I was so afraid of missing one of her lucid moments, they were so few and precious. What if I slept and she needed reassurance? But if I didn't sleep . . ."

"She knew you were there," Mimi interrupted.

"Perhaps."

"She knew." The water was foaming up between the rocks and leaving bubbles when it ebbed. "What is it about the ocean?"

"There's no place to hide here." Daniel tipped his head toward the water, as if that vast expanse were explanation enough.

Tears rushed to Mimi's eyes and she looked away. Damn death, damn loneliness; damn everything! Was there a conspiracy against happiness? No wonder her mother always grimaced. When nearly everyone you have ever loved is dead, how in the hell do you keep going?

&*Berdichev, Autumn 1918*

Rivka leaned against a tree at the edge of the clearing, her legs stretched out on the cool earth. She was so absorbed in her book that she did not notice her Uncle Mendel approaching.

"That must be some story," he teased.

She looked up and smiled.

"I'd join you," he said, "but it could be weeks before I could get up. His eyes twinkled mischievously. "However . . ." From his pocket came an envelope. "For someone named Rivka."

Laughing, she snatched it from his grasp. "It's from Bayla!"

"You think I don't know that? That I'm not the one entrusted with this? Not the one instructed to deliver this as soon as I arrived?" The old man watched her eyes dance from word to word, noted how her mouth twitched as she read and he felt such a surge of love. Just then he caught sight of Shmuel shuffling toward them, the reed-thin body bent like a twig struggling against a persistent wind. Mendel's salutation was drowned out by Rivka's exuberance.

"Please, Papa," she called out, running full speed across the clearing.

"Please, Papa, what?" asked Shmuel.

"Bayla is having a party. A real one! May I go? May I?"

He studied the girl, his fingers running unconsciously through what remained of his beard. Such rare enthusiasm for this normally composed girl!

"I haven't been to Zhitomir for so long, and it's her fifteenth birthday. And you know how much Bayla . . ."

Shmuel immediately thought about the pogroms, about his child's safety, and then weighed all of this against the fact that Bayla was Rahel's daughter, and Rahel had been Fredl's cousin and dearest childhood friend. When he heard Rivka mention something about trains, however, he held up a hand. "No trains," he insisted, and the strength driving his voice stopped the girl cold. "Uncle Mendel passes through Zhitomir next Thursday and you may ride with him. If this meets with his approval, he can bring you back on Sunday."

Rivka turned toward her uncle and held her breath.

Mendel appeared vexed. He rubbed his beard, grimaced, and then mumbled something about inconvenience. When he saw that Rivka could take no more, he shrugged and laughed. "Fine, if I must, I must."

The girl let out a whooping sound, planted a loud kiss on Mendel's cheek and flew toward the house to plan her adventure.

The three days before her departure felt like the longest of Rivka's life. Conversely, the visit itself passed with the speed of light. Seated beside her old uncle in the wagon, the old horse plodding obediently toward home, she said nothing. They were several hours out of Zhitomir before Mendel realized that his niece was crying. He pulled the wagon to a stop, pulled her closer to him and patted her head. "Did you and Bayla argue?"

Rivka dried her eyes on the back of her hand and then accepted Mendel's handkerchief. "It was the best weekend of my life," she said, blowing her nose loudly.

The old man sighed in a wise and knowing way. "Life brings moments of joy, my dear. When they come, we must cherish them."

Rivka folded the handkerchief, pushed it back into his pocket and nuzzled his cheek. Mendel reacted by touching the tip of her nose with a finger and clicking the horse into motion.

They continued at a steady pace through the countryside and several small towns. When they took the last turn onto the mill road and the mare picked up the scent of home, Mendel gave it free rein. As they entered the clearing, Rivka clambered into the back to gather her belongings. They were halfway to the house when she stopped.

"Uncle, what?" He was already urging the mare forward. Several horses were tied to the gate, one of them straining to reach a patch of grass pushing through from the other side of the fence. Mendel made a clicking sound and they covered the last twenty yards at a full trot. Before they reached the fence, Rivka was on the ground and running. Her hand touched the doorknob and she froze. Mendel came up behind her and his quick intake of breath revealed that he, too, heard the sound from within the house. It was a group of mourning voices chanting the Kaddish.

Mendel shouldered Rivka aside, whispering "Dear God, don't let it be Shmuel."

They entered the house and the room fell silent. Cousins, friends, neighbors who lived along the mill road, everyone was there. When Mendel caught sight of Shmuel seated on the couch near the window, the muscles in his face collapsed in relief. Rushing over, he grasped his brother's hand, but there seemed to be no recognition. "Shmuel, what has happened?" Nothing.

To the left of Shmuel was the foreman's wife. Mendel searched the room until he found the woman's husband and motioned him frantically toward the door. Korchav pushed away from the wall and joined his employer. "What is it?" he demanded.

The man's eyes were red and his massive shoulders were hunched. "An incident," he mumbled, lips trembling as he spoke.

"What do you mean, incident?"

Korchav gestured with work-scarred hands. "They're gone."

Mendel noticed when Mrs. Korchav draped an arm over Rivka's shoulder, saw how the girl shook it off and knelt before her stepfather.

"We sent someone on the road to find you," mumbled the foreman.

"Who could believe it would happen here?" said a cousin seated next to Shmuel Langer.

"No, not here," came another voice from somewhere in the room.

Mendel's fear was quickly turning to anger. "You never thought *what* would happen here? What!"

Korchav moaned. "It was a pogrom. Like an army, all these soldiers from other towns, strangers." The big Russian wrung his hands. "You must believe me, Mendel, I've never seen these people. They were not my people, I swear it."

Mendel waved away the disclaimer and hardly noticed when the foreman left the room. Every face around him was struck with grief. He thought yes, a terrible thing, but thank God our people are safe. And then he realized that someone was missing and the realization caused his knees to buckle. As Mendel threw out an arm to stop his fall, one of the workers moved forward quickly to catch him. "Mottel!" he cried out. "For the love of God, where is Mottel?"

Rivka's cry shattered the air.

"There are hundreds dead," said another cousin, a woman from the adjoining village. "In Berdichev alone we've lost twenty-three."

"Yes," said another. "And all Hovevei Zion."

Rivka tried to follow the voices, but her grief was too profound.

"They worked from a list. Methodically, until everyone was eliminated."

"Hovevei Zion?" echoed Mendel, staggering across the room to reach his brother. "Mottel was never one of them, never. He may have agreed, certainly, but a member . . . ?"

"He was visiting one of them."

A bitter sound erupted from Shmuel Langer. "Can you imagine? My son is dead because he was visiting."

Rivka looked from face to face. Hovevei Zion, Zionists: friends. It was too much. She rushed from the room and nearly collided with Mendel's wife, her Aunt Chava. The old woman took Rivka's arm with unexpected strength.

"I want to go outside," sobbed the girl, struggling to pull free.

Chava released her arm. "That's not possible. No one is free to go out, especially the women." She looked hard at the girl, determined to make herself understood. "It's too dangerous, do you understand?"

What Rivka understood was that she was being held prisoner in her own home. It was a sensation she would not easily forget.

Eight weeks after Mottel's death—eight weeks after the young man had been dismembered and his throat cut so deeply that the posterior section of his trachea had been visible through the wound, and his family was still so numb that the gruesome image had not yet been supplanted by recollections of his sweet face and gentle nature

—a stooped and wizened Shmuel Langer gave a quiet rap on Rivka's door, entered, and made a place for himself on the bed. He touched her shoulder several times before the girl awoke with a start.

"What is it, Papa?" Searching the old man's face, she was certain that this sensation churning within her was about to be confirmed as fear. "Another pogrom?" The word was pushed through a constricted throat.

Shmuel sat quietly and then brushed a hand against his daughter's cheek. "Not here, little one, not in Berdichev."

It was so early in the morning that sunbeams were not yet shining through the clump of trees. In searching her stepfather's face, Rivka nearly missed the next words. "What did you say?" she whispered, not allowing herself to believe. Shmuel closed his eyes and repeated himself as if he were praying in shul.

"Papa, no," she begged. "Please, not Zhitomir, not Bayla." The girl fell back onto the bed and buried her face in the pillows, her cries muffled by the eiderdown and the unbearable weight of her stepfather's grief.

❧ Topanga Canyon, Summer 1984

Mimi searched for a pattern in the tide's movement but could discern none. What she saw instead was unpredictability. The similies drawn were so banal that she pushed them angrily away. Besides, she thought, what benefit is there in knowing what comes next when the whole mess eventually floats off anyway? Like Sarah, or her mother having to live with the knowledge that her best friend had been slaughtered as she cowered in her mother's arms. If a woman of my age can't come to grips with the concept of death, thought Mimi, what can I expect of a child of fifteen? In her experiences, fifteen is the age to spurn a mother's affections or defy the wishes of parents; it is certainly not the age for grieving.

Shifting her weight on the uneven rock, she finally settled into a more agreeable position. "God, but I was insufferable," she mumbled, thankful that the ocean's roar was drowning her out. And then she sensed Daniel's scrutiny and held her focus on the water. But it was true: her behavior toward her mother had been hateful, disrespectful. Twenty-five years later, she wanted to forgive herself, perhaps explain it away as a teenager's natural reaction to being suffocated by an overbearing mother. But she could not, because even as a child she had somehow understood her mother's suffering, had heard the stories, had been fascinated that anything so dramatic could have happened to her own mother.

A large wave crashed several hundred feet before the rocks, its surge pushing the water ten feet higher up on the sand. "We're going to get caught if we don't move back," warned Daniel, offering Mimi a hand. Like a good child she allowed him to shepherd her off the rocks and another twenty yards back from the water. "You're in another world today," he remarked, brushing sand from Mimi's shirt. It was one of those automatic gestures, but it soothed her. Plopping down onto the sand, they proceeded to watch a series of waves arrive, saw the seventh one swell larger than the others and then recede.

Mimi envied Daniel his calm and hoped that one day she, too, would reach that place where fears and pain and regrets were either banished or tucked safely away. She forced her thoughts back to her regrets concerning her mother. Certainly she had always known, understood that her mother suffered, yet she had done nothing about it. Except, perhaps, to make her suffering worse. And yet Rivka still called her 'Darling' when she walked through the door and acted as if their time together were precious, dear.

"I think it's time to pack it in," Daniel suggested, popping to his feet. When Mimi offered no resistance, he helped her stand and they set off for the car and Topanga Canyon.

By the time they reached the bottom of Mimi's driveway her head was buzzing with thoughts. This search was taking her far deeper into her mother's life than she had intended, perhaps more than she desired, but now that she was there and viewing the woman from a more detached perspective, she was finding herself less detached than at any other time in her life. Even more important, she could no more objectify her mother's life than she could Sarah's death. They were real and both had seriously and irrevocably altered her life.

Mimi declined Daniel's suggestion that they continue the evening over dinner and gave him a grateful hug when he said he understood.

True to form, she was propelled directly to the answering machine. Nothing, not even a complaint from her mother. She picked up the receiver and dialed Rivka's number.

"Yes?"

"You answer the phone with a question?"

"How should I answer?"

Mimi laughed. "Some people say 'hello.'"

"And all the others?"

She laughed again. "I called to see if you're okay."

"I don't sound okay to you?"

"Mama, you sound just fine!"

"So now you know. And you, darling, are you okay?"

"Fine, yes, I'm fine."

"Good, so we've settled that issue!"

They agreed to speak the following morning and ended their brief conversation.

Mimi realized that she was famished. She popped a frozen curry appetizer into the microwave, leaned into the granite counter and watched the digital display click backward from 8:00. By 7:48 she was lost in thought. As a teenager, she had exhibited all the signs of a well-adjusted girl. She had succeeded in school and had enjoyed her share of friends. Despite those few extra pounds that were a constant source of irritation and challenge, she was pleased that her life was headed in a direction considered successful by parents, teachers, and peers. With everything in place, there was still that distance existing between herself and her parents. It was like a hard edge that impeded intimacy and trust. Certainly every teenage girl resisted a mother's presence, even considered the most noninvasive presence to be overbearing. In Mimi's case, however, invasive it most definitely was. No step could be taken without Rivka observing and commenting. As for her father, his propensity for distancing himself from his family was both a blessing and a curse. If the man was going to be uncommunicative, she had reasoned, let him be uncommunicative somewhere else.

Mimi pulled the food from the microwave and began peeling off the plastic. Perhaps she could have accepted that wedge between herself and her father had there not been an ever more divisive one between her parents. She recalled so clearly her mother asking if there was anything interesting in the paper and her father responding by silently handing over whatever section he had just read. If Rivka asked him "Was it a good week at work?" her question usually evoked a shrug, a mumble, or some brief commentary regarding the struggles of prewar, wartime or postwar economies. Whatever the communication from her father, it was usually delivered from behind a raised newspaper.

Mimi had always known that her father suffered from that chasm between shtetl boy and American-educated daughter. By the time she reached puberty the man was helpless to find a common ground. "Got a boyfriend?" evoked rolling eyes and air blown through puffed cheeks. "School going okay?" was less offensive, yet the response was most often a noncommittal shrug. In those days before self-help and radio psychologists, there was no way to understand the suffering that gnawed away at all of them, creating a deep and hollow place where love could have resided. There was the further irony that when Mimi searched her heart and made an effort to get closer to her mother, it was Rivka who was reticent, who held back.

As for Harold Zilber, he gave what he could, what he thought was expected of him. But a man whose dreams remain unfulfilled finds it difficult to express joy, much less intimacy.

There were boyfriends in Mimi's life. More often than not, however, she was disgusted by the way they rooted around her. "Dogs in heat," she would grouse when she felt another pair of adolescent eyes lingering on her breasts.

"It's those bosoms," Sarah had laughed, making the word sound like "ba-ZOOMS." Having none to speak of, anything larger than flat seemed downright bountiful to her. What Sarah had not understood until many years later was that Mimi loathed the stares; even more, she loathed her body for the attention it attracted.

The kitchen was silent. Mimi checked on the appetizer and was surprised to find it nearly cold. Removing the pieces onto a plate, she spooned a dollop of chutney over it and carried it to the kitchen table. Staring at the curry, she couldn't imagine eating it. The spicy aroma she normally loved was making her ill. "Just eat," she ordered herself, and took a small bite. As she chewed, she recalled her father's first stroke and those days when it seemed he would not recover. She remembered, too, the sensation of standing at his bedside and thinking him a stranger. When he opened his eyes and stared at her, she saw in them an intensity she had never known. When he groped across the bed for her hand, she leaned over and kissed it. It was the most intimate moment they had ever shared.

"I love you," she told him, which brought tears to his eyes. In the course of speaking those words, she realized for the first time in her adult life how much she truly did. Despite her father's reticence, despite the discomfort he showed toward his well-educated and very modern daughter, he had shown her kindness, had been in his own way loving. Mimi took his hand and held it.

When Harold Zilber recovered from that stroke, there was a new tenderness between them.

Mimi pushed the food aside, flicked on the switch controlling the exterior lights, and wandered out to the garden. She might have thought she was searching through forty-plus years of emotional chaos, but it was turning out to be more than a hundred: no search into her own emotions could be done without going back that far, at least as far as her great-grandmother Malka.

Mimi was drawn to the bed of columbines in the neat little patch of earth just off the deck. Their lacy foliage made her think of fairies floating on air, magenta spurs trailing behind them like the tentacles of jellyfish caught in a gentle current. Bending over, she peered into the tight podlike buds about to spring open. When was the last time she had noticed loveliness, had perceived beauty? "You are so jaded," she grumbled, snapping a dead bud off an azalea peeping out from its cloak of ferns.

She returned to the kitchen and caught sight of the little seven-day pill dispenser. It was time to refill her hormone prescription. The last time she had visited her gynecologist the woman asked if she were sexually active. Mimi had responded by rolling her eyes. Now she wondered if that was out of embarrassment. And not because the woman had asked, but because Mimi was not. Only ten years old when she had her first period, she could still recall those nasty sanitary belts with sharp metal hooks, and sanitary pads that felt eight inches thick. And she cringed at the thought of her mother providing the world's briefest, and perhaps least accurate, explanation about her

Monthly Visitor and the importance of washing Down There. Two years later Rivka took her daughter on a bus ride to MacArthur Park, where they had their first chat about sex. Actually, sex had never really come into it; it was more a lecture on reproduction. The poor woman spoke nonstop for nearly an hour and managed not once to get to the point. But it didn't matter, since Mimi was certain she already knew everything there was to know. The afternoon had not been a total loss, however, since it was the first time she had been entrusted with facts from her mother's childhood.

"I was still living with my stepfather," said Rivka. "Being an old man, he had done nothing to prepare me for the blood. When I saw it I could only think of Mama dying in bed. It was Aunt Chava who showed me how to fold the clean rags. If Mama had been alive, I wouldn't have been so frightened."

"We were all frightened," Mimi mumbled, picking up a knife. She began to cut an apple into wedges. "I just never let you see it." Holding the knife in front of her, she had a fantasy about cutting herself. She put the knife down and returned to the patio. As she crossed it, she imagined the damage she could inflict by throwing herself off the south side of the deck into the gully. Or how, driving down the canyon road, she could so easily initiate an accident.

There were so many things she wanted to say and wished fervently that Sarah were there to listen. She would tell her how life sometimes felt so menacing and that she wasn't sure she could face middle age alone. Would she mention the rest? The part about wondering how it would be to stretch out on her bed—curtains drawn against the night—and slip a plastic bag over her head, waiting quietly as her diminishing breath created a thin film of vapor on the inside of the bag?

✢Berdichev, Fall 1918

The deaths of Bayla and Mottel weighed heavily on Rivka, made the sense of isolation even more intense. The garden adjacent to the parlor seemed less a garden now, more like the confined boundary of her prison. She dreamed of packing a valise and running away, but this was no solution. And where would she go? In times like these, it was not even a choice.

She nestled deeper into her place at the end of the sofa and studied how the afternoon sunbeams entered the room in luminous lengths. It was cozy here: the furniture was adorned with her mother's needlepoint pillows and clustered around the fireplace. On the mantle were books, primarily prayer books in Hebrew with Yiddish transliteration. Although it was her favorite room, she hardly noticed it today. "Where is he?" she mumbled. She tried to focus on the book on her lap but frustration intervened. And then she forced herself to read, but soon realized that she comprehended nothing and flung the book onto the sofa. Stomping over to the window, she pressed her nose flat against the pane and studied the garden, how the height of the sheltering wall trapped sunlight and heated the room. Everything was coming into an early bloom: buds tightly closed only days before were bursting into flower; bright new leaves were peeking up through the darker, thicker leaves that had survived the winter. It made her want to cry, because even the lovely garden was off-limits now. Dangerous times, her stepfather had warned, so they barricaded themselves behind doors and windows. Safety before happiness.

"But I have to go out," she had argued that morning.

The concern in the old man's face left no doubt.

"You can't keep me locked up!" For one flashing moment she hated the old man, wished he would leave her be; wished that he would die.

Shmuel Langer had responded by placing a hand on the girl's shoulder and explaining once again the dangers that lurked outside. "Fine," she had mumbled, but they both knew it was not fine, not at all.

Rivka stood at the window and watched her breath leave its misty film on the imperfect glass. "I hate my life," she mumbled, glancing toward the clock. He had promised, sworn, that he would leave the mill early and take her for a walk before dinner, and he was already a half-hour late. Scowling, she plopped onto the couch and picked up her book. "If I don't leave this place soon," she thought, "I'll go crazy." And then she saw his face and the way it clouded over with fear for her safety, and she tried to chide herself. But even this did not stem her anger. For this moment at least, there was no place in her heart for forgiveness.

Rivka squeezed her eyes shut and tried to call up the face of her mother. That she could no longer conjure up her mother's image saddened her. She remembered the dark hair, thick and wonderful to the touch, the white, white teeth, but not the face. Not the face, and not that other thing whose very absence formed a dull pain of suffering in her chest. Because even with eyes shut and nostrils flared, Rivka could not remember the way her mother smelled. And without this, she could not imagine her mother close by, could not recall how it was to have her face buried in her mother's hair and neck. In losing this, she had lost a part of herself.

And now, her freedom as well.

The light told her that the sun was fading. With no afternoon light he would never agree to walk on the road. "Where is he?" she demanded. As if in response, voices arrived. Rivka listened, knew at once they were coming from the mill road. "Finally!" Listening again, she heard an urgency. And then there were shouts and it sent chills down her back. Instantly she thought *pogrom*. Panic gripped her as she searched frantically for a place to hide. Rolling off the sofa onto her knees, she crawled behind the massive piece of furniture. The voices came closer and Rivka trembled. Suddenly, the front door was thrown open and slammed against the wall, footsteps sounding like thunder across a field caused her to cower even farther behind the sofa. Despite her father's attempts to protect her, she had heard descriptions of the heinous crimes committed against young girls and for the first time in a very long time, Rivka prayed. She prayed that she would die quickly and she prayed that they would have the decency to kill her before they raped her.

The footsteps came closer and finally entered the room. "Rivka!" someone cried out. "Are you here? Answer me!"

"They know my name," she thought.

"Go find Mendel!"

"Put him over here."

A sliver of ice shot through her. Scrambling to her feet she saw the mill hands lower Shmuel Langer onto the sofa. The moment she revealed herself they stepped aside. Moving forward, she girded herself for what she had seen in her mother's dying face. But this was not the same. One of the men tried to comfort her; she shrugged them off. Taking a fistful of her stepfather's jacket, she leaned into the material and buried her face in its weave, remaining like that until a savage sound caused her to wheel around. The anguish in Mendel Langer's face would be etched forever in her memory.

"It must have been his heart," explained one of the men. "He was there and then . . ."

"So fast," interrupted another man. "There was no time to go for help."

Rivka touched the lifeless face.

"There was no pain."

"I think losing Mottel was too much."

"No doubt."

"Ah, what a shame."

Mendel kneeled on the floor and touched his brother's face. His tears fell onto Shmuel's beard. "I know this is selfish," he whispered, "but I have often prayed that I would go first." He placed his hands over Shmuel's eyes. "My greatest fear was that you would leave me alone, that you would die first and I would have to live even one day of my life without you." When Mendel removed his hands, his brother's eyes were fully closed. Bending forward, he kissed the man on both cheeks and pressed his lips against the baby-smooth forehead.

It was nearly an hour before Rivka allowed them to move the body. By the time the rabbi arrived there was already sawing and banging coming from the mill. Barely two hours later the doctor and the rabbi supervised the placement of Shmuel Langer's body into his casket.

Rivka could not be comforted. She remained there, face buried in the cushions of the sofa, and inhaled the lingering odors of sawdust, skin and tea absorbed by a body during more than seventy-five years of life. And she was not simply inhaling them, she was inviting them into her lungs and then filing them away in that part of her brain reserved for such memories. This was one she vowed never to lose.

By sundown the following day Shmuel Langer was buried. In the plot to his right, his first wife; to his left, his beloved Fredl. At the foot of their graves lay Mottel. On either side of Mottel, the spaces reserved for the wife and children he would never have. Nearby were two more plots reserved for Mendel and Chava. It made perfect sense to Rivka that there was no place designated specifically for her: she did not belong.

Days passed into weeks and the girl rarely spoke. No one understood what festered in her, how in that moment of anger she had wished her stepfather dead. Added to a profound sense of guilt was an enormous void into which everyone she ever loved had disappeared. It was as if Szulen and Fredl Rabinoff's deaths had poked a tiny aperture into her soul and the murders of Mottel, Bayla, and Rahel had expanded it to the size of a gaping hole. But now this, the loss of her beloved stepfather, and the hole became a chasm so large it felt bottomless, a black hole into which energy, liveliness, and all that remained of Rivka's spirit was plummeting out of control.

Rivka stayed with her aunt and uncle through summer and into fall, remaining closed off and distant, rarely initiating a conversation. She no longer read, and most suggestions of activity were met with stony resistance. There was a hopelessness about her, a limp futility. At the same time, Chava was carrying on an active correspondence with Malka and Grischa Gershon. There was no question in anyone's mind that Rivka needed to go home.

Before the first frost of winter appeared on the trees circling the clearing, Rivka waited with packed bags for the buggy that would take her back to Nowy Życie. She was traveling with everything she possessed, plus a few of her mother's articles: furniture; her favorite samples of needlepoint and embroidery; and a small pouch of jewelry that Chava sewed carefully into Rivka's undergarments. Despite all of this, she felt as if she were leaving empty-handed. There was no Fredl or Shmuel to comfort and encourage, no Bayla to whisper words of encouragement. As for Mendel and Chava, now the most cherished people in her life and the only survivors of her stepfather's family—a family that had loved her without reserve—they were staying behind. It was yet another bead added to her lengthy string of sorrows.

When the wagon pulled away from the clearing, Rivka waved to the old people she would never again see. Gazing briefly into the sky, she never noticed the wonderful animals hiding in the clouds that floated above her head.

✑ Topanga Canyon, Summer 1984

Whenever Mimi listened to her mother's stories she was thrown into a state of confusion. After all, these were not casual family tales, but heart-wrenching accounts coming from the difficult old woman who held everyone, including her own daughter, at a distance. And yet, Mimi wondered, how could she not? When everyone you have ever loved has died, how do you go on trusting, much less risking love? She imagined her mother making that trip back to Nowy Życie, the frightened teenager clutching her bag and wondering if she would ever find a home with people who were not taken from her. Mimi wondered how it was for her mother, sleeping in Fredl's old room, in her old bed, trying to make sense of everything that had happened. Father, mother, stepbrother, best friend, stepfather, all gone. Almost every person she had ever loved, had ever trusted. Is this when she closed her heart? Is this when she finally stopped listening to the voices around her and heeded instead a distant voice that warned her not to trust, perhaps not to love? And was it then that Rivka became so filled with bitterness that her spirit became tainted? Mimi imagined her mother stretched across the bed, staring into the darkness and promising to live out the remainder of her life trusting no one.

A powerful desire swept over her. She snatched up her car keys and raced from the house. Never in her life had she known such a pressing need to go to her mother, to put her arms around the woman and hold her close.

If Rivka Zilber was surprised to see Mimi, or curious about her daughter's motives for this sudden appearance, she gave no sign. A cup of tea and a smattering of chitchat were followed by the decision to dine at Rajapur, their favorite West Indian restaurant not far from Boyle Heights. For dessert, Rivka shared with her daughter a delectable spice-laden yogurt and several new reminiscences of Nowy

Życie. By the time Mimi drove her mother home and was back in Topanga Canyon, she was exhilarated. The pleasure of the evening, the good food and the wonderful stories, had been a shot in the arm. At two o'clock, when she was still wide awake, she decided to clean out her long-neglected desk. Seated there, however, the decision seemed less than stellar. "Tackle the most difficult first," she mumbled, and forced open the bottom drawer. It was her receptacle for nearly everything not pertaining to work. The first item she came across was a rubber angel. When she picked it up and squeezed it, she was assaulted by a flood of memories.

Sarah had been working as a legal secretary and Mimi a full-time undergraduate student. Their only opportunity for exchanging gossip and complaining about their mothers occurred early each evening at the Soto Street bus stop. If the weather was good, they would window-shop, swap complaints about work, school, the paucity of good men, and then go their separate ways. On this particular evening Mimi sensed that something was amiss. Arriving at the corner where they normally said their good-byes, she took Sarah's arm. "Are you okay?"

"Of course!"

"You're acting funny."

Sarah pulled away. "And you're nagging!"

Mimi was stung. "That's not what I intended to do. It's just that you're so . . . distant."

Sarah mumbled something about not having to tell her friend everything.

"Of course you do," replied Mimi, hoping to keep the fear from her voice.

Sarah chewed on the inside of her cheek and Mimi waited. "Come on," Mimi finally said. "Out with it."

Sarah dragged her down the block and stopped across the street from the neighborhood service station. "So what do you think?" she asked.

Mimi followed her finger and saw a man pumping gas. "Cute," she answered, "but old."

"He's only thirty and I'm nearly twenty-one! By my age my mother had been married for three years and had a child."

Mimi stared openmouthed at her friend. "Sarah Lehmann," she accused. "That man is no stranger!" When Sarah blushed, Mimi was stunned.

Sarah admitted that they had only dated a few times but she was sure she was in love. Mimi pressed her twice for his name before she finally blurted it out. "Diego Arcario." And then she narrowed her eyes, as if defying her friend to laugh.

For a moment, Mimi said nothing. And then she scoffed, "I can just hear you now: Mom, Dad, I want you to meet my future husband, Señor Diego Arcario." Unable to control herself, she burst into laughter. "Oh, yes, your mother will definitely be thrilled." When she saw Sarah's shoulders droop and her eyes fill with tears, she became suddenly serious. "Sarah?"

"I don't know what to do."

Mimi looked across the street. "Well, you could always elope. That way, everything will be legal before your mom has a chance to hang herself."

Sarah stomped off, leaving Mimi standing alone and feeling guilty.

Over the following weeks Mimi found herself experiencing overwhelming emptiness. She could see that Sarah was more than smitten and the thought of losing her best friend was terrifying. When she finally met Diego, she discovered that Sarah had found herself a very special man. He was loving and kind, and ambitious enough to convince Mimi that her friend would never go without.

Less than two months later the three of them were huddled together in a chapel on the outskirts of Las Vegas. Before them stood a justice of the peace.

Mimi heard very little of the ceremony. With Sarah married, there would be no more constant companion, a friend always at the ready. She wondered if Diego could ever accept her as the third wheel in this marriage, but not once did she consider the possibility that she, too, might meet someone. That one day they could be a happy foursome.

Mimi was mesmerized by the chapel, and most particularly by the collection of angels scattered about. They were of every size and color, placed wing to wing on every inch of available space. Glass and plastic angels, ceramic angels; angels crafted from folded strips of cardboard; angels pieced together from ersatz stained glass and chocolate angels in various states of moldy decay. She was also fascinated by a family of angels assembled from thousands of colored toothpicks, but what impressed her most was the angel sitting on the shelf directly behind the justice of the peace: it had been fashioned exclusively from miniature white marshmallows.

"My wife's hobby," said the man as Sarah and Diego dug for the rings. "A real romantic." His smile was apologetic. After the ceremony, a woman emerged from the back room, walked over to Sarah and held out a rubber angel. "Squeeze her," she said, making a clutching motion with her hand. "Go on, squeeze." Sarah followed her example and jumped when the angel squeaked.

"Isn't she darling?" the woman asked.

"Yes," they all mumbled, "darling," and then made their escape to the car before exploding into laughter.

Mimi spent the ride home trying to ease Sarah's fears about facing her parents. As they approached Mimi's street she reminded Diego where to turn. He glanced at her in the rearview mirror and smiled. "What, and let you miss all the fun?" Ten minutes later they were leaving the Lehmann house and heading for their new apartment off La Cienega. Diego was squeezing Sarah's hand while Mimi stroked her head. "They just need some time, honey," he said. "A Mexican son-in-law wasn't exactly their dream for you."

Sarah jerked around, took one look at Mimi, and they burst into laughter. Diego's confusion only encouraged them. "This has nothing to do with your being Mexican!" laughed Sarah. She saw her husband's scowl. "Honey, you could have been Clark Gable or Mahatma Gandhi and they would have been just as destroyed. It's not what you are, it's what you're not."

"And what you're not," laughed Mimi, "is Jewish."

Diego thought it over for a long moment. "No kidding," he said. "Gable?"

The boycott against him remained in effect until the day he called Sarah's parents to announce the birth of Joanna.

Mimi squeezed the angel. She had planned to surprise them with it on their fiftieth anniversary. So much was gone now: youth, friendship, the hope of meeting a man with whom she could share her life. Tears filled her eyes and she returned the angel to the drawer. Was she crying for the loss of Sarah, she wondered, or for not having had her own loving family? But then, who did her mother have? Not a loving and supportive marriage, certainly not a loving daughter. For all the affection Mimi gave her mother, the woman would be better off with a cat.

CHAPTER EIGHT

❧Summer 1918, Nowy Życie

MALKA AND GRISCHA planned every waking moment around making Rivka feel welcomed, but no matter what they did, no matter what effort was put forth, the girl did not fit in. It was Malka who spent the most time with her, who took responsibility for the day. And it was Malka who suffered the girl's conduct.

"You're trying too hard," counseled Grischa.

"Arranging tea between our granddaughter and some nice girl is trying too hard?"

Grischa held his tongue. What was the purpose in reminding his wife that every effort ended badly? When he voiced his concerns to Hannah she offered a pat on the hand and a suggestion that he not worry. "Anyway," she added, "Mama is indomitable."

Grischa wondered how indomitable a woman could be who was only a few years short of ninety.

Hannah promised to speak to her mother, but it was weeks before the opportunity arrived. It came on an afternoon when she was helping the elderly woman hem a new dress. Kneeling on the floor to mark the hemline, Hannah felt her mother's tension. "Mama," she mumbled around a mouthful of straight pins. "Everyone knows how hard you're trying. Now stand still."

"Shh! You'll swallow a pin and choke."

Lowering her head to hide the smile, Hannah pressed the gauge against the fabric and marked the spot with a fragment of coal. Erring even a bit could mean a hem fated to be dragged through muddy streets. "I know it's not easy," she said, "but Rivka can make her own friends." She glanced up in time to see her mother's mouth torque in displeasure. Not wanting to pursue a subject that seemed without any possibility of resolution, she turned her focus back to the hem. A moment passed and she felt two hands come to rest upon her head. There was such tenderness in those hands that Hannah was reminded of her youth, of the prayer parents recited over their children:

> May the Lord bless thee and keep thee.
> May the Lord make His face shine upon thee,
> and be gracious unto thee.
> May the Lord lift up his countenance upon thee
> and give thee peace.

At that precise moment, Hannah and her mother were sharing the very same thought: how different it would be, if only Fredl were here.

Hannah sat back on her haunches and stretched against the stiffness. "It takes time to fit in, Mama."

The old woman closed her eyes for a moment, as if controlling her anger. "Fit in, you say? I can understand taking time to fit in with strangers, but we're her family. Do you know . . ." She tried to go on but her voice broke. "Do you know," she tried again, "that your father and I are not permitted to touch her?" Malka's expression became almost wistful. "Imagine, Hannah, we can't even touch her."

"Perhaps in time . . ."

Malka pushed the suggestion away with a quick gesture. "Nonsense! The trouble isn't time, it's attitude. Rivka is cold and distant. At first I thought it was shyness, but it's indifference, plain and simple."

Hannah dared not speak her mind. She was thinking the same thoughts that had plagued her for some time: that Rivka's presence was darkening their lives. Family dinners were no longer celebrations, but brief moments of pleasure connected by long, restless silences. They shared events of the day and Rivka pushed food across her plate. No matter how they tried, she could be neither prodded nor coaxed into conversation. No matter that often it was only Malka, Grischa and Rivka at the table, it was a strain that cast a pall over the entire family.

"Rivka was such a help this morning," Malka announced to Grischa one day at lunch. "Together we put up two-dozen jars of beans and three-dozen tomatoes." She smiled appreciatively at her granddaughter. "I never could have done it alone."

The man turned toward his granddaughter but the girl looked quickly away.

"And then we hung the blankets for airing and scrubbed the kitchen shelves."

"It sounds like a full morning's work," he declared. "Rivka, you're a big help to your grandmother."

Rivka glanced briefly in his direction and shrugged.

"Did you have any visitors today?"

"Oh, yes," bubbled Malka. "Mrs. Feldschpach's grandson came by. Such a nice boy."

Grischa saw her mouth twitching and knew she was trying too hard. "Ah, you mean Abel. A fine young man, yes."

Abel is a fool, thought Rivka. His face is too narrow, his skin is bad, and he always has those little bits of food stuck in the corner of his mouth. Nathan was too short and laughed like a girl; Devorah's mouth had a bad smell. This one was too fat, that one was too stupid: they were all children.

The ordeal was proving too much for Malka and the woman seemed even older than her years. Deepening grooves around her mouth gave her a permanent frown and there was a burst of capillaries beneath the delicate skin that resembled a series of tattoos. Grischa noted with a heavy heart that any bloom of joy that had arrived with their granddaughter was quickly fading.

After lunch the elderly couple sat together in silence. Malka's fingers raced as they guided the crochet needles through a floral pattern emerging from the cloth. Suddenly, her fingers stopped their movement and both hands dropped onto her lap. "Why are we pretending? It's worse than ever!"

Grischa sighed in commiseration. As much as he wanted to reassure his wife, he knew that she was right. Any doubts he may have had were erased after that last experience. In truth, it had upset him so that it still festered in his memory.

It was the Friday before and Malka had coaxed Rivka to help

prepare the Shabbos meal. By early afternoon the house was clean, the table was set and all the ingredients required for the *cholent*—a Sabbath dish of meat and vegetables that could be cooked over a slow fire—were in the pot and ready to be shoved into the oven before sundown. Because no work could be done during the Sabbath, the *cholent* would cook all night and be ready for Saturday's mid-afternoon meal. "And now," Malka announced, closing the oven door, "let's prepare the challah." She began kneading the dough, twisting and pulling, pounding it until the air pockets disappeared. When she gestured toward a second mound of dough, Rivka picked it up and followed her grandmother's lead. She kneaded, rolled, and then slammed the dough onto the counter with a reverberating force.

"No air left in that one!" declared her grandmother.

They divided the dough into halves and partitioned these into five equal sections. After more kneading and twisting, they rolled them into lengths. "Most women use three or four," Malka explained, hair wisping around her face. "But we use five." Rivka watched her grandmother inspect the segments and knead them again, rolling and forming each one with hands toughened from decades of work. "With five," she explained, her breath coming faster and perspiration building on her forehead, "it's much more decorative." She showed Rivka how to sprinkle flour over the pieces and then, wiping her hands on the apron, examined the girl's work. "Good, now watch how we do this." With craftsmanlike skill she grasped the ends of the five portions and began braiding them into a pattern so complex that Rivka was soon lost. "It only looks difficult." Placing her hands over the girl's, she led her through the steps. "Now you do it." Rivka began, and then stopped in confusion. "Take that end," coaxed her grandmother, pointing to the last coil of dough. "Fine, now bring it around to there, and then here, good, perfect. Now pull it through and push very gently and then, yes, like that, so it's securely attached." She guided the smooth young hands through the last movements, looked into the girl's face and saw satisfaction. It took every ounce of restraint not to grab the girl in her arms, murmur words of love and encouragement, promise that she was safe, wanted and cherished. She forced her attention back to the loaf. "Now," she continued with pleasure, "you can make the family challah. You can do what's been done by the women in our family for generations. My mother learned it from her mother and taught it to me. Your mother learned it from me and. . . ." Her voice trailed off for just a moment and she saw the light in Rivka's eyes quickly fade. ". . . and if your mother were here, she would have been proud to see how well you learned." Before Rivka could respond, Malka rushed on. "This tradition has never been broken. Even when there was no daughter, the son's wife carried it to the next generation."

Rivka stared at the loaves. "It's obvious which one is yours."

Malka contemplated them for a moment. "Mine is tighter, but this is your first effort and it's a good one." Her face was aglow with pleasure. "What really matters is that soon you'll be able to pass this tradition on to your own daughter!"

Rivka took a step backward and appeared momentarily stunned. "My daughter?" she finally said. "The last thing I would ever want is to have a child."

Malka blinked, and then blinked again. Not want a child? She had never heard such a thing. What woman does not want a child? Her hands trembled. "I see," she murmured, and before her eyes the girl's face changed from passive to defiant. Malka took a calming breath and pointed to the vegetables. "Could you please take those and . . . oh dear," she muttered, "I forgot to bring in the water. Could you fetch some for me?"

Rivka retrieved the bucket from under the table and walked outside. It was a glorious day, the air filled with sounds of animals freed from the treachery of winter. Chickens ran about; even the old rooster had pushed his way out of the pen. But Rivka did not notice. She walked directly to the pump, filled the bucket and carried it back to the house. Malka proceeded to demonstrate how to moisten strips of cloth and place one over each challah. "What else?" she mumbled to herself, wiping her hands on her apron. "Ah, yes, the fruit. Would you like to help with the candied fruit?" Rivka shrugged and Malka understood that a shrug was the closest she would get to affirmation. She handed Rivka a bowl of peeled fruit. "Start by dicing these." She shifted the coals burning orange-hot in the trough of the stove and nudged them until they were evenly distributed. Placing a pan on the grill, she waited for the water to heat. When bubbles appeared, she added sugar and spices, demonstrating how to stir until the liquid swirling around the spoon turned to syrup. Glancing at her grand-daughter, she saw how much Rivka was beginning to resemble Han-nah more than Fredl. Her skin was fair like her mother's, but the eyes were lighter, wheat-brown like her aunt's. Too bad she had not inher-ited Hannah's disposition as well.

"Grandmama," Rivka suddenly asked. "What are you humming?"

"What am I. . . ."

"You were humming something. What?"

Malka thought for a moment and laughed. "Oh, that! I learned it from my grandmother." She sang a few words. When her grand-daughter's eyes softened, she could not refrain from touching her face. "Your mother loved it. Did she sing it to you?"

Rivka did not move away from her grandmother's touch. "Would you like to learn it?"

She nodded, opened her mouth to accept, and then paused. As if a heavy curtain had dropped, she pressed her lips together. "No," she said, backing away. "Thank you, no."

The door closed with a click and Malka burst into tears.

Rivka yearned to be a part of her family but ached with each lov-ing touch. And the more she ached, the farther away she stepped. Something had wrapped itself around her heart and was strangling her. She had no way of knowing that it was the fear of surviving the loss of one more person she loved. If you never love, said the pain, you will never suffer. But there was something else, something darker and more ominous than the fear of losing a loved one, and it floated just outside of her conscious reach: If everyone she ever loved had died, then being loved by her was to be handed a death sentence.

As time went on her family's concern for Rivka grew. One evening they were all seated together in the parlor and a painful truth revealed itself to Malka: With so many people in this child's life dying, a part of the child had died as well.

❧ Topanga Canyon, Summer 1984

By the time Mimi said good-bye to her mother she was exhausted. How could everything in the apartment malfunction at once? The water pressure in her shower was down. "A piddle that wouldn't bathe a flea," her mother had declared. The light in the hallway was out again. And there was an ongoing problem with the building's new super. "I banged on the water pipes for more heat, but nothing happened." Mimi patiently explained that there was no steam furnace, no basement, and they were called managers. "Heat is heat," said Rivka.

Sarah always swore that Rivka Zilber exhibited more ways to express displeasure than anyone on earth. The thought accompanied Mimi on her drive to campus, through an unsuccessful counseling session with a nervous graduate student contemplating an about-face in her thesis, and during the drive home. Perhaps Sarah had been right. Who else could twist, turn and contort her mouth in such a variety of ways? Who could narrow or roll her eyes in so many directions? List, turn, clench, and torque her chin, hands, shoulders, and torso in quite that manner? "No matter what displeasure, disapproval, or rebuke," Sarah had laughed, "your mother is the undisputed master." Mimi had a clear image of her father accusing his wife of behaving imperially. If he announced that he was going to the ball game and she lifted her chin and looked slightly upward, he would respond, "Ah, I see that our queen does not approve."

Mimi returned to the house. Pouring a bottle of mineral water into a glass, she wandered into the bedroom. The bed was unmade and her clothing strewn, causing her to hear a long-ago refrain, "You are not going anywhere until your room is clean!" She attacked the pile on the chair, sorting and classifying every item. As the room began to take shape, she heard Sarah insisting that it was Rivka Zilber who had invented the evil eye. As young girls, they had done what they believed were clever imitations of Rivka admonishing her sloppy daughter. The memory caused a smile to appear on Mimi's face. The smile disappeared just as quickly. Had her mother become a caricature because she knew of no other way to survive?

Gathering up a pile of dirty clothing, she carried it down the hall to the laundry room. She separated whites from colors, filled the washer with the first load, added detergent and started the machine. The sound of water rushing into the tub was satisfying.

As so often happened after a nonstop work schedule, Mimi needed to acclimate herself to the idea of free time. Daniel had suggested they drive up the coast to Oregon, but her response had been a brooding and uncertain silence. He had not exactly rescinded the offer, nor had he repeated it. Which chafed at Mimi, since the idea was sounding better with each passing hour.

The wash cycle was in full motion. Confident that she would have clean underwear for tomorrow, Mimi retrieved her drink and wandered into the study. Seated at her desk, a feeling crept through her that made her uneasy, a kind of sharpened sensibility to a hard-edge. It seemed never to leave her, like a bruise refusing to heal. Her mother had one, too, this permanent bruise, but she had learned to use her only child as the balm to soothe it, the bandage to protect it. And yet, at the same time, she somehow managed to shield herself from that same daughter and protect her sensitive nerve endings from the woman's absence.

The knowledge that she was there for her mother, that she existed in her mother's eyes as a palpable presence, brought Mimi succor, yet she continued to worry that she was hardly a presence at all. Besides, what about Mimi's nerve endings? Who would look after them? Like Rivka's, they had long ago learned to react as if their only function was to survive a threatening world.

&*Nowy Życie, Winter 1911*

It was nearly four in the morning and Rivka was still awake. Stretched out in the bed once warmed by her mother, emotions of confusion and a sense of being lost in a large and angry world interfered with her will to sleep. Despite the many years since her mother's death, Rivka wanted desperately to call the woman back, learn how she, too, could become that secure and happy woman she had so loved. And if she miraculously appeared, what would she see? That

Fredl at sixteen had been a happy and confident girl; Rivka, at the same age, was lost.

She pushed her face into the pillow and, wishing that morning would never come, did everything in her power to shut out the image of this room. It did no good: even when staring into total darkness she was able to see every inch around her. The tall chest with its four drawers; the desk scarred from years of use, its austere chair softened by a cushion embroidered with flowers and a blue sky; the little table next to the bed. On the table sat a photograph of the Gershon family. Rivka picked it up, turning it so the moonlight could illuminate its image, but the room was far too dark. She climbed from the bed and padded over to the window. Tilting the picture toward the pale light, she made out the outline of her grandparents seated in the middle. Behind them stood their sons, each boy resting a hand on a parent's shoulder. At Malka's knee was little Hannah, no older than six, her brooding face in sharp contrast to the enormous white bows anchoring her long braids. At Grischa's knee was Fredl, a lovely little girl with lively eyes, hair pulled away from her face with a ribbon and then cascading onto her shoulders. Rivka knew the expression on her mother's face, had long ago committed it to memory: Fredl looked as if she were about to burst into laughter.

Rivka touched her mother's face. She had done this so often that the image had turned yellow. And yet no matter how many times she willed herself not to do this, she could not resist. As far as Rivka was concerned, she loved this photo more than any other possession, yet the picture pained her, reminded her of all that she lacked and so desperately wanted: gaiety, the sense of belonging to that large, loving family. In the photo, Hannah and Fredl were leaning slightly toward one another, giving the appearance of an empty space next to Fredl, into which at least one more child could be included. Rivka touched the space, wishing she could magically appear there.

She returned to her bed, stood the photo on the table and stared into the darkness. There was no room for her in that photo. There was no clearing in front of her grandparents' house, no mill road from which wagons could arrive amid dust and noise. No Papa Shmuel, no Uncle Mendel: no place to belong. She climbed under the covers, pulled them around her shoulders and made no attempt to quell the tears. If only Bayla were alive, if only she could see her father, her mother, Papa Shmuel, Mottel. If only there were a way to reunite herself with her family. Tell me, she thought, and I'll do it! And yet she knew that neither accidental death nor suicide would achieve her goal and bring them together, and this knowledge twisted in her, sent a sharp pain through her body and caused her to pull both knees to her chest. "Mama," she cried, "I need you here with me. Bayla, please, just one more letter. Mottel, you were my only real brother; the ones here hardly know me and they don't even like me. Without you to make me laugh, I can't remember how." Weeping alone in this place so far from home, Rivka did not want to die, she wanted only to be someone's beloved child.

⤫ Topanga Canyon, Summer 1984

"If you won't go up the coast with me," suggested Daniel, "will you at least accompany me to this opening?"

"What opening?"

"This one," he grumbled, waving an invitation. When it nearly slipped from his hand and fell into the tandoori chicken, he laughed and slipped it back into his pocket. "An old business friend is hosting a private showing. It's supposed to be a hot new artist, a sculptor. And," he added, eyes twinkling provocatively, "quite the social event." He said this with a very bad Upper East Side accent, which was immediately followed by a sigh of surrender. "If you must know, Mimi, I've never seen the man's work. But it's a colleague, he refers a lot of business to me, and I can't bear the thought of going alone."

Mimi looked around her and took quick count of the number of couples sharing a meal. How could she say no? She had no school to stop her. Then again, she had no social life! And most of all, she reminded herself, she was absolutely out of excuses. "Fine, I'll go." Hearing the edge in her voice, she nearly apologized. "Really," she added, "it sounds like it might be fun."

The problem with having such a long friendship is that it was impossible to hide your true feelings.

When Daniel murmured, "Ever grateful, m'love" and blew her a kiss, what could she do but smile?

Two days later they were heading up Coldwater Canyon. "Are you cold?" Daniel asked, and then turned on the heater before she could respond.

Mimi stared at him for a moment, trying to sort through all the information in her head and find that one connecting piece. And then it came to her that Sarah used to say to her daughter, Joanna, "I'm cold, honey, put on your coat." She nearly mentioned this, but decided that she was enjoying the drive. Bringing up one of her Sarah stories would undoubtedly change the relaxed pleasure of the moment. Here she was, a passenger watching the world from the leather-bound comfort of Daniel's new Mercedes, windows closed against the elements and Bizet playing quietly in the background. No, better to let the comment go by.

Mimi nestled farther into the soft leather and nearly purred. The cozy interior of this car changed dramatically her sense of the space outside. It passed by, trees and flowers and canyons, but it seemed more an image on a theater screen.

They continued higher and then dropped into one of the smaller canyons. Mimi saw at once that it was one of those typical canyon neighborhoods where homes had been designed with little thought to continuity. That is to say, the houses were architecturally varied, as individual as the homeowners who had commissioned their construction. Dotted along the road were houses, cottages, some sitting well below the road and only the roof visible to passing cars. Whatever the size or design, however, it was a mumble-jumble of structures sitting on some of the most expensive real estate in Los Angeles. "I remember some wonderful little cottages that were here," she mumbled.

"Past tense," Daniel complained. "Now they raze them and put up mansions. You wouldn't find a garden along here if you tried." A moment later he muttered *"Ungepatschkt"* and turned up the music, as if this would block out the ungainly sight.

Mimi nearly laughed at his terrible pronunciation. Bad Yiddish or not, however, he was absolutely right: these homes smacked of unnecessary ornamentation and did nothing but interfere with the woodsy setting.

Slowing down, Daniel pulled the invitation from his pocket and flipped it over to study the map. He rotated it several times before he could get his bearings and Mimi found herself fighting an urge to grab it and take control. Before she could offer, he tucked it back into his pocket. "Kills you, doesn't it?" he laughed. She wanted to deny it; instead, she shrugged in surrender and smiled.

When they came upon an almost invisible little private road, Daniel released an exultant shout and headed down the steep grade. They followed the drive for nearly a hundred yards with no building in sight. Mimi was about to question his sense of triumph when they suddenly came upon a parking area filled with cars. Most of them were imported, and a good number of them were far more elegant than Daniel's. He slid the new Mercedes into a space next to a classic Bentley and, as if reading Mimi's mind, said, "We'll only stay a few minutes, I promise."

"Well, you know what they say: You can take the kid out of the shtetl, but you can't . . ." Daniel's dramatic smirk told her there was no need to complete the saying.

Exiting the car, they followed a rocky footpath that took them over a crest. Daniel grasped Mimi's arm as they navigated the stone pathway. She nearly pulled away, aware that she could manage very well on her own, but she did not. Instead, she linked her arm through his and allowed him to guide her around a minefield of rocks and crevices.

The air was brisk, cleansing, and Mimi loved the way it felt in her lungs, was again grateful that she had stopped smoking years before. As they approached the cottage, she murmured, "Quaint, very quaint." How incongruous this was with all those upscale cars parked nearby.

They entered through a front door left ajar and nearly laughed aloud. Before them was a cavernous glassed-in space that extended a full thirty feet before dropping down several steps into an even larger room, now being used as the gallery. Chrome and glass tables were scattered throughout and it struck Mimi that the entire effect would have been austere, were it not for all the colorful pillows, rugs, and throws placed decoratively around the large space. Through the massive windows she could see lush wooded areas, rocky crests, and dramatic canyons. Leaning closer to Daniel, she whispered, "Don't look now, Toto, but I think we've left Kansas."

Daniel guided her across the room, stopping along the way for an introduction here, a handshake there. Mimi smiled, exchanged greetings, but she could not take her eyes from the scene outside. Such delicious isolation, she thought, and what glorious, absolute freedom! Finding herself a chair by the window, she sat down and absorbed the view. There was something about the expanse, a beautiful and liberating expanse, that caused Mimi's mind to drift toward thoughts of her mother.

❧ *Nowy Życie, Spring 1919*

It was several days after Rivka's seventeenth birthday. The war fought against the czar and oppression was finally coming to an end. Countries were being first partitioned and then doled out, piece by piece. The spoils in this case were not limited solely to the victors.

Rivka was reading when she heard a tap on her door. Before she could respond, her grandmother stepped in and crossed the room. Pressing a hand against the bed to ease the stress on an arthritic knee, Malka settled herself onto the bed. It was a long moment before the pain in her face subsided. When she spoke, she did so reluctantly. "I have bad news."

Rivka placed the book down. "Who died this time?"

Malka stared at the girl for a moment, unsure how to respond. She expected no sympathy, that was certain, and long ago she had resigned herself to the girl's passivity, but how had they come to this? Daubing at her eyes with a handkerchief, she said, "Ruth Silverman."

Ruth Silverman was the daughter of Malka's oldest friend. The two families had come together only weeks earlier to celebrate Ruth's fortieth birthday. Rivka recalled the conversation between her grandparents after the party. Grischa commented on what a lovely woman Ruth had become; Malka responded that it was a terrible sadness to Ruth's mother that her daughter had never wed. And having long ago passed that age considered marriageable, any prospects for the future — save the occasional widower — seemed more than bleak. Despite this reality, everyone had been surprised, even amazed, when Ruth had announced her decision.

"But she was leaving for America!" declared Rivka. "She had all her papers!"

Grief marred Malka's face. "I held her the day she was born," she cried. "They say it was her heart." She shook her head at the senselessness of such a thing. "And Ruth their only child."

Rivka surprised them both by resting a hand on Malka's arm. No cry rose from her heart, no grief pressed against her lips, but a voice raced helter-skelter inside her head.

Malka squeezed her granddaughter's hand. "Will you come with me?" she asked. "I want to visit before everyone arrives for shiva."

Rivka nodded, mouth so dry she could barely swallow.

From that moment forward Rivka's life took on new meaning. Each time her grandmother reached for her coat to visit her old friend, the girl was there. When they walked down the road, Malka leaned against Rivka for support. If the old woman was even the least bit suspicious, it did not show.

Before the official period of mourning was over, Rivka's plan was in effect. She waited a few days and then slipped into the gray ankle-length cotton dress her Aunt Hannah had made, pinched her cheeks to achieve the glow of innocence, and set off. Walking along the road, she had to fight the desire to skip and hum. When she arrived at the Silverman's door, she stood there, paused to square her shoulders and calm her anticipation, and then she knocked three short raps. There was no answer. Willing herself to be patient, she made a fist and knocked again, this time so solidly she felt a twinge of guilt.

The door opened a crack and a woman peered around it. Mrs. Silverman's eyes began at the visitor's feet and then moved slowly up to the face. "Oh, it's you, Rivka." She took a step backward and opened the door. "Did your grandmother send you for something?"

Rivka entered, doing her best to present a demure and somber face. She focused on the woman's welcome, while at the same time pushing away the nagging doubt that she could actually carry this off.

Every photograph in the room was shrouded; the mirror adjacent to the door was turned to the wall. Rivka felt the woman's eyes on her, which only made her discomfort grow. "Mrs. Silverman, I just want you to know how sorry I am, and that I understand how it feels to lose someone you love."

The woman's eyes shifted to the draped photograph. "Yes, I know you do," she responded, voice barely above a whisper.

Rivka took a deep breath before continuing. "And if there's anything I can do for you, anything at all, please let me know."

Mrs. Silverman's face softened. "How kind of you, Rivka." After a moment, however, her eyes seemed to narrow. "Have you anything special in mind?"

The girl's hands fluttered in the air. "I don't know, shopping, cooking, things like that. And you should not be alone when you go through your daughter's things."

This time there was no doubt: the woman's eyes narrowed perceptibly. Moving slowly into the little parlor area, she sat down. "Is there something of Ruth's you wish to have?"

When Rivka responded "Absolutely not!" her voice was so convincing that she almost convinced herself. "After Mama died, and then Mottel and Papa Shmuel, the hardest part was going through their belongings. So I thought if you needed help. . . ." She let her voice trail into an expectant silence. The woman stood so abruptly that Rivka believed she was about to be dismissed. Panic set in. "Forgive me if I've upset you," she said. "I only meant that . . ."

The woman waved away the comment. "Your offer's very kind, my dear. And I know that you're right." The inevitability of the awaited, dreaded task, caused her brow to furrow. "All my friends tell me that it's something that must be done." Tears welled in her eyes. "Come back tomorrow, will you?" Having said this, she took Rivka by the elbow and guided her to the door. "With your help, perhaps I can find the courage."

Rivka passed through the garden and knew she was being watched. Even when she rounded the corner and was out of sight, she felt eyes on her back. Nothing, however, could dull the excitement surging through her, an excitement that caused her heart to pound and her mouth to feel dry.

The next twenty-four hours were excruciating. "I must stay calm," she reminded herself over and over. "And serious, but not maudlin."

At the appointed time, Rivka found herself in the bedroom of the recently deceased Ruth Silverman. Everything was in piles, or tucked into corners; it resembled more the room of a teenager than a woman of forty. The old woman began the process by gathering up a stack of dresses and pressing them to her bosom. "What do we do with these?" she asked tearfully.

Rivka took the garments from her. "I'll bring them to the shul and they can give them to the poor."

The woman closed her eyes. "Ruth would have wanted that."

They sorted, folded and packed forty years of a woman's life, and whenever Rivka was offered something—a blouse, a book, a crocheted pillow—she refused politely.

"But this is perfect for you." The woman held up a winter wool coat.

"It will be lovely on Mrs. Helfman."

"And this?"

"Ideal for the Rothstein girl."

And so it continued, Rivka's reputation for generosity growing with each suggestion and each polite refusal. By late afternoon every piece of furniture in the room was emptied, save the desk. Piles of paper filled each nook and Rivka's heart raced at the prospect. "And these papers, Mrs. Silverman? What should we do with them?"

"Put them in the box, dear. Mr. Silverman will sort through them later." The woman excused herself and left the room.

Rivka attacked the pile. Each paper was scanned and then placed in the box. There were letters from friends, newspaper articles announcing deaths, marriages, and births. She had sifted through nearly everything when, near the bottom of the first stack, she came across the envelope. There was no point in opening it, but she could not resist. The paper was heavy, impressive, the stamp affixed in the lower-left corner identical to the one made by the czar's representative that time he had come to her grandfather's store. He had used a contraption resembling a small vise. Slipping paper between metal plates, he had pressed on the handle to create an embossed design. An official seal exactly like this one. Rivka ran her finger over the raised letters and felt each ridge and indentation, felt freedom rush through her skin. She slipped the document into her skirt pocket and continued to work. The sensation of the envelope pressing softly against her leg was more thrilling than threatening.

Time passed, the chores of cleaning and planting came and went.

And then a heavy snowfall made the roads impassable. It was months before Rivka could set her plan into motion. Late one night, perched on her bed, the oversized atlas opened on her lap, there was a knock at her door. Before she could speak, Malka entered, followed closely by Grischa. Rivka was struck by how elderly they now were, like apparitions moving toward her. Crossing to her bed, they gave the appearance of drifting. Their hands were extended, feeling their way, as if tentatively adding balance to each faltering step. Rivka thought of reeds stripped of their foliage.

It was Malka who spoke first, and her voice was so loving that Rivka became immediately wary. "My dear," she began, "we know what you're doing. It took a bit of thinking, but we figured it out."

The atlas slipped onto the bedcover. Rivka gazed at her grandmother, tried to lock stares with her, but the woman would not be challenged. The girl opened her mouth to rebut the statement and was silenced by an upraised hand. "You took those papers, Rivka, and we know why." Rivka knew that the tic in her eye gave her away. "But no one will try to stop you."

Grischa stepped forward on cue and handed his granddaughter an envelope. "It's not much," he apologized. "But it might make things easier." They both kissed the girl and then Grischa led Malka from the room.

Rivka tore open the envelope. Inside was more money than she had ever held at one time. Where had they found it? How had they managed? She counted it once, and then again, knowing it represented more than a month's sales from the store. One month of sales, perhaps a year of profits. She fingered the gift — this unexpected means of escape, this key to her future — and then it hit her. This was a communal gift, something from her entire family. They must have taken a collection. All those people she had so fiercely and truculently spurned had rallied to support her dream. Rivka slid the money back into the envelope and placed it on the desk. From behind the chest of drawers she retrieved the travel documents. From this day forward, she would practice calling herself Ruth Silverman. Standing there, staring at the two envelopes, Rivka allowed herself to acknowledge for the first time in many years that, just perhaps, this family indeed loved her.

Los Angeles, Summer 1984

Mimi was driving home from Boyle Heights after sharing a Thai meal with her mother. It was Rivka's compromise when her daughter arrived hungry for Indian. "Not as spicy," explained the old woman, a hand pressed against her stomach. To Mimi's delight, it had turned into one of those rare dinners when the service was good, the food excellent, and there was little about which Rivka Zilber could complain. As tempted as Mimi had been to point this out, she had decided to remain silent and profit from the rare experience. After escorting her mother to the upstairs apartment and receiving from Rivka an unusually warm embrace, Mimi descended the stairs. Climbing into her car, she could still feel the embrace. All in all, it had been a very pleasant evening.

Following the freeway toward home, she was stunned by the awesome beauty of the sunset. No matter what anyone said about Los Angeles and the San Fernando Valley, there were spectacular moments. With the radio tuned to her favorite classical station, Mimi began thinking of her mother, and the courage it must have taken to steal travel documents from a dead woman's desk. Stretching her back and nestling deeper into the well-padded seat, she took the Mulholland Drive exit and headed up the twisting road. How had the girl done it? Try as she did, it was a challenge to imagine her mother as a teenager, a girl seated on the wood slat in the back of a buggy, being pitched along weather-beaten Ukrainian roads. The logistics alone were daunting. It took Mimi days to plan a simple weekend away, while her mother had somehow organized the logistics of a voyage that would take her halfway around the world, away from the family she would never again see.

Ukraine, Fall 1920

After days of jiggling and bouncing and suffering the conversations of fools, Rivka's face had become so rigid it might as well have been set in stone. Her driver, a jocular fellow, had put great effort into putting her at ease, but he had finally given up. In fact, he made a promise to himself that, no matter what the circumstance, he would say not one more word to this rude girl. As for the others, they quickly learned to ignore her, communicating their shared sentiments with rolling eyes and priggish expressions.

As the wagon entered the northern region of the Ukraine, somewhere between the Nowy Życie Rivka had once perceived as her prison and the vast unknown representing freedom, the rate of her breathing increased. At first she assumed it was fatigue, but the shortness of breath soon became frightening. She dared not complain, since the others had scorned her en masse, yet she found herself vacillating between dizziness and nausea for several days. On the third day out, patches of sweat had formed around her hairline, in every crease of her body. She forced her thoughts back to Nowy Życie but found meager solace: at the very moment that her valise had been lifted into the wagon, she knew she would never return. Perhaps it was that image of her grandparents standing together and waving good-bye that upset her so relentlessly. It was, she knew, the last view of them she would ever have, the last memory of them to be forever imprinted on her brain. In years to come, during those moments when she closed her eyes and struggled against the passage of time to recreate their faces, she would see two old figures disappearing from view, arms raised in farewell.

On the sixth day Rivka felt herself strung between opposing forces, had the sensation that she was being torn from herself. One force pulled her back to that tethered life of relative safety, the other dragged her forward at great speed, into the unknown. The conflict caused her throat to tighten. She focused on birds in flight, clusters of trees, but nothing silenced the voice in her head telling her that she could never go back.

They passed through the heart of the Balkans and arrived at the port of Odessa, a body of water where Rivka felt immense relief knowing that the most difficult segment of the journey was finally over. It was a relief and knowledge she would too soon discover had been wrong, premature.

Early the next morning, Rivka found herself huddled with dozens of travelers in the fetid hold of a freighter of unknown origin, heading in what everybody prayed was a southerly direction across the

Black Sea toward Istanbul. From the moment they boarded the ship, all volition, all sense of pioneering euphoria, had been snatched from them. They had been separated from most of their belongings, except for those few fortunate souls who had loose coins or gems sewn into the hems of their clothing. As for Rivka, the money that Malka had stitched into her garments was comforting, but there was something far more precious. Tucked into the bodice of her dress was her beloved photograph of the Gershon family.

CHAPTER NINE

❧ Topanga Canyon, Summer 1984

THE DAY HAD BEGUN quite nicely: a cup of coffee and a bagel, the newspaper reminding her that the rest of the world was in terrible shape and that, in contrast, her life was far less difficult than most. And then she left for campus, where her arrival triggered a day's roster of nonstop activity. None of this came as a surprise; the planning required before each new term was intense, demanding, and predictably frenetic. The running gag at the university had to do with synchronizing the first planning meeting with a starter's pistol. When the gun went off, department heads were expected to rush headlong across the minefields of academia: Which classes would be taught and who was best to teach them; which egos would need to be assuaged and who would oversee the growing demands of this ever-changing inventory of graduate and undergraduate requirements. Mimi's department was not considered among the nation's top ten for nothing, which explained in part why the battle for the dean's position always included a few good jokes about first-round draft prospects and Nike endorsements.

By the time Mimi returned to Topanga Canyon, the sun was nearly gone and her energy with it. She walked into the foyer, tossed her jacket onto the coat tree and marched directly into the study. Flicking on the light, she dropped the leather attaché case onto the floor next to the desk, snatched up pen and paper and immediately began scribbling down all those ideas that had been racing through her head during the drive home. Only after everything was noted, sorted, and considered did she allow herself to collapse with relief into the chair.

How much time had elapsed, Mimi had absolutely no idea. She wasn't even conscious of staring into the summer sky until her stuporous daze was broken by a flock of birds crossing the northwest quadrant of the window, their movement across the orange-red horizon jolting her into a dulled wakefulness. Capping her pen, she sat there and observed the arrowhead slide effortlessly across the sky, its migrating path taking it toward some remote destination. In sharp contrast to this harmony of movement, low mountain peaks of scrubby brown vegetation jutted across the horizon, appearing even more unsightly when compared to the vibrant sky. The irony of such contrasts did not escape Mimi; when the setting sun delivered such a spectacle of color, its magnificence was because filtered sunlight was piercing through microscopic particles of pollution.

A persistent fly was making click-click sounds against the window as it sought a route of entry. "Not tonight," said Mimi, watching its tenacious efforts. As if comprehending, the insect threw itself against the window one last time and flew away. Mimi smiled to herself and wondered how life would be if everything were so easy.

There were so many parts of the friendship with Sarah that Mimi missed, but perhaps the ease of the friendship, its absence of effort, seemed most poignant. And the calm. Sarah had brought such calm into her life: walking together for an hour without speaking, sunning on the deck, and knowing what the other was thinking. They used to laugh that they were like identical twins using idioglossal speech, making grunts and bilabial noises understood only by them.

With the birds well out of view, Mimi took note of the changing light. The sunset was magnificent, belying a most un-magnificent day. The kind of day when every conscious moment is tainted by the niggling thought that the sooner night fell and you could crawl into bed, the better.

Releasing a very loud and dramatic sigh, Mimi pulled a stack of papers from the bag and forced her attention to the subject. She was in the throes of writing what she hoped would be a convincing justification for a course to be taught jointly by the history and English departments. It would stress European nobility, wars and treaties and their effects on literature. She hadn't even reached the second paragraph when the phone rang. The intensity of the first ring startled her. The second ring, shrill and demanding, causing eardrums to vibrate, warned her that it was most likely her mother. When the third ring arrived as a summons, a call to arms, she relented and picked up the phone with, "Hello, Mama."

"You were so sure it was me?"

Mimi smiled. "You have a very distinguishable ring."

There was a lengthy pause before Rivka spoke, suggesting to Mimi that her mother's sense of humor had not magically evolved since their last talk.

The discussion was pretty much as always: Rivka asking questions about work, friends, life, the next visit and Mimi sidestepping whenever possible. And then her mother surprised her. "Miriam, darling, there's something I've wanted to ask you."

Mimi braced herself. When "Miriam" and "darling" arrived in the same sentence, something was up. Death, divorce, natural disaster, all paled in comparison. This, she knew, was going to be personal. "Yes, what is it, Mama?"

"Darling, I don't want to pry but . . ."

Panic. Rivka's most intimate probing always began with "Darling, I don't want to pry but . . ."

". . . is there something you want to tell me about Daniel?"

Mimi felt her mouth turn down. She had been spending an unusual amount of time with him, true, but how did her mother know? If there was one area where this mother-daughter relationship had never matured, it was in Rivka's need to be privy to her daughter's private life. And not just innermost secrets, but anything and everyone that did not include Rivka.

"I only want you to be happy, dear."

Mimi chewed on the flesh inside her cheek. She saw the warning flag waving and was unsure if she should heed it or not. Her mother wanted her to be happy, no doubt about it, and yet she had never really approved of Daniel. Mimi tried to imagine what the woman would say if she knew the truth. That her daughter's sights had been lowered, now that she was middle-aged and the availability of single men so very limited. Mimi felt herself under siege, although she sensed it was not from her mother, but from her need to keep the woman at an arm's distance from her personal life. "Gotta go, Mama, sorry. It's curriculum week, the committee's meeting in the morning and I'm not ready."

"So you'd rather not discuss it." Rivka's tone suggested wounded feelings rather than petulance.

From Mimi's perspective, petulance was far easier to manage. She murmured something about sleeping dogs and hung up the phone. Catching her reflection in the glass of a photograph, she was brought up short. Sarah used to warn her against frowning, that the lines in her face would only deepen. Mimi leaned over for a closer look. "Right again," she mumbled. Had she not known better, she might have surmised that the woman staring back at her was embittered. Or was that look the price you paid for lying to your mother? she wondered. But it really was curriculum week and the committee really was meeting in the morning. Right, said that nagging inner voice. But you are, as always, more than prepared and another five minutes on the phone with your elderly mother would not have killed you!

Mimi bit into an edge of cuticle and made it bleed. When Sarah was alive, Mimi would get dragged to an occasional manicure. Now her poor nails had gone to shit. "Oh well," she murmured, studying the unsightly wound. "It's just one more gripe that needs to be transmitted to the great beyond."

A thick funk was beginning to settle around her. She pushed herself from the chair and wandered onto the deck. With almost no lingering light in the sky, Mimi decided it was time to eat. Wandering into the kitchen, she reheated a bowl of leftover pasta and tossed a little salad, both of which she consumed while standing at the sink. As she rinsed her dishes, she reproached herself for wolfing down a perfectly respectable meal, without having tasted any part of it.

When Mimi finally climbed into bed, she felt as if she could sleep for two days. And yet, at the same time, thoughts were still spinning around her mind. She glanced at the clock and saw that it was after midnight. How unlike Daniel not to have called. She wondered if it was too late to call him and then dismissed the thought. Restless, she picked up the newest P.D. James mystery and was soon lost in the twists of turns of the whodunit. When she read the last page and closed the book, she glanced toward her clock and was surprised to see that it was nearly four. With a moan, she extinguished the light and willed herself to sleep.

Morning came too fast and Mimi had to drag her body from the bed. If she took a quick shower, put off washing her hair until tomorrow, and settled for nothing but coffee—and, of course, hit traffic just right—she could hang around and sit in the garden for ten minutes before leaving.

Clean, dressed, coffee in hand, she nestled into the butterfly chair, leaned back and closed her eyes. Her only regret with this house was not being able to hear the ocean. It was Sarah who had come up with the positive side to this lament: when the big earthquake hit and the tsunami arrived, she'd be high and dry! Mimi always came back with the same retort: "*Au contraire,* Sarah. When the big one hits, all the houses up here will become valuable beachfront property."

The power of the sea awed Mimi. Tidal waves surging forward and carrying away debris, flotsam, life; the force of a tide eroding the shore one grain at a time, reclaiming itself, taking itself back. How long before buildings would vanish, before the materials holding those buildings together would disintegrate and be carried off? And then after buildings, what? Parking lots, highways, skyscrapers: total destruction; vast and empty, this metaphor for life. Mimi nearly laughed aloud at what sounded like the most melodramatic of all thoughts. Checking her watch, she had two minutes before it was crucial that she leave. Two minutes, and she knew exactly how she wanted to use the time. Rushing into the house, she called Daniel.

"First of all," she said the moment he answered, "I apologize."

"For what?"

"For being self-absorbed. Since Sarah died, everything's been about me. So I'm sorry." It had been four-and-a-half months, certainly adequate time to muster the fragments of her life. "I passed every free moment at Sarah's side, but now it's time."

"Time for what?"

"I don't know," she responded, a bit put out by Daniel's question. And yet it was a perfectly reasonable one. Time to live? Time to move on? But how do you move on when you don't want to let go? She repeated these questions and Daniel made one of those humming sounds. "Meaning?" she challenged.

"Meaning," he responded, "that it's both time to live and time to move on. And no, moving on does not mean forgetting someone you love."

Mimi thought about this for a moment. "So when you're with me, you still think about . . ."

"Sometimes, yes. But not because I'm not enjoying you, Mimi. It's the desire to share a beautiful evening, or a piece of music she would have loved."

When Sarah was dying, Rivka had made her normal demands, acting as if nothing had changed. Daniel, however, had been there to lend support, had understood, had even spelled Mimi on several occasions when she had no choice but to tend to business.

Mimi checked her watch and saw that it was beyond time to leave. "A quick question: Isn't there some magical date when the pain finally goes away?"

"I wish I could say there was, Mimi, but there isn't."

She mumbled something about being grateful for his honesty and then promised she'd call sometime during the day. Driving down the canyon toward the freeway, she considered the possibility that Daniel didn't need her, and being needed is what gave her a sense of being whole, complete. Daniel didn't need her and Rivka kept her on a hook, making her feel responsible for whatever went awry. Mimi heard the condemnation in that thought and immediately wondered, Or does she? What if it were actually the other way around; that in a funny way she depended on her mother to make her feel indispensable. All those outings, those little errands that filled her free time, what were they about? An avoidance of being alone, a need to be needed. "Call it what you like," grumbled Mimi, turning into the east-bound lane. "It's still escape."

Mimi followed the traffic, turned south over the winding pass, and exited into Westwood. Aware of her distracted state, she forced herself to drive slower than usual and thought about the unspoken rules existing in every friendship. It was certainly the case with Daniel, and even with Sarah there was a code that had existed between them. More often than not, the rules were respected. Mimi recalled one situation in which Sarah had crossed the line and the result had been one of their most heated discussions. The subject? Whether or not Rivka had cheated her only child out of her dreams.

"If you honestly believe that your mother did it right," Sarah had demanded, "then where's all this love you've been looking for? Where are the children and grandchildren you longed to have?"

Mimi's skin had burned from these questions and she could find no clever retort.

Sarah was far from finished. "I've watched you with Joanna since the day she was born," she went on. "Are you going to tell me you weren't dying to be a mother? You think your mother didn't have something to do with that?"

"Don't blame my mother for my choices," Mimi had finally responded. She was furious that Sarah would use those particular elements as her definition of happiness. Furious, too, that her friend had crossed that imaginary line and had pricked Mimi in her most tender places.

Mimi pulled into the faculty parking lot. The dark funk was returning and she felt weary. Long ago she had wondered what the forewarning of her death would feel like. Was this the forewarning of her truth? All she knew was that she was irrefutably linked to her mother and her mother's past. She thought of those conversations she had had with Daniel, the ones about how her father, perhaps reacting to Rivka's demanding nature, had held himself at such a distance that he was at times a nonentity in his daughter's evolution. Mimi's defense had been that Harold Zilber had been neither bad nor unloving, but in a house ruled by two strong women, he had felt safer keeping his distance. Until today, it never occurred to Mimi that he, too, had been damaged by his wife's history and the thread of tragedy weaving itself through it.

How uncomplicated it would be to hold her mother at arm's length and simply go through the good-daughter motions. And yet she could not deny that the more she delved into Rivka's long and complicated life, the more her appreciation for the woman grew.

❧ The Black Sea, Fall 1920

Metal walls vibrated with the drone of nearby engines; the space was darker than night. "I understand why they call it the Black Sea," someone said, prompting nervous laughter. But not even light-hearted chatter could alter the reality that the space was closing in on all of them like a tomb. As for Rivka, she was too frightened to laugh. She recognized the voice as belonging to the Polish boy who had boarded at Odessa, the one who had attempted light conversation with her but was silenced by her grim expression. Because we are the same age, said her pinched mouth, and we are trapped in this terrible place, does not mean that I must communicate with you. He had stared at her before walking away.

"We should be there soon," said someone in Russian.

"Not soon enough" came the lamenting Polish reply.

There were moans, sighs, apologies for coughing, bumping, for bodies being jammed hip to thigh. The stagnant air was becoming fetid and there was tension growing among the ragtag assemblage.

From the first day out, when that overhead metal hatch was slammed shut, Rivka had been struggling against a rising panic of claustrophobia. It was the same sensation she had experienced that afternoon so many years ago when she was hiding behind the sofa and mistaking the mill workers for Cossacks. Shut up in this hold day after day, the tightness growing in her chest threatened to close her throat. The dread was sometimes so untenable, the air so stifling, that she found herself gasping like a fish fighting for oxygen in a murky tank. Her only relief was to bury her face in her coat and weep. From the noises around her, she knew that others were weeping as well.

Rivka searched for ways to distract herself from the black surroundings. She repeated over and over her planned itinerary: Odessa, Istanbul, London, America. Odessa, Istanbul, London, America. The repetition was a soothing reminder that this was merely one small step in her journey.

Several days out to sea, Rivka admonished herself to get control and think of survival before all else. With each passing hour her determination grew, the voice in her head became louder, stronger. Either you tolerate the conditions, it warned, or die. If the other passengers chose to fill their time with empty chatter—sounds that grated on her ears—that was their business.

Late one day a man's voice announced that they should be stopping soon.

"But when is soon?" came a woman's query. "And how long have we been out here?"

Mumbling arose from all corners. The voyage, scheduled for ten days, felt like a year. It was Rivka's voice that cut through the noise. "Today is the tenth day," she announced. How could two-dozen people share hunger, unrelenting cold, and suffocating claustrophobia and still come up with such drivel! The whole thing mystified her. "We had this conversation yesterday," she continued. "We agreed it was the ninth day, remember? And since nine plus one adds up to ten, we're safe assuming it's the tenth day." Pushing herself to a standing position, she groped her way through travelers and belongings to the other side of the space.

Ten days with no air. Ten days of living among the stench of unwashed bodies. Rivka remained standing, her back pressed to the wall and the palms of both hands pushed against the metal. Her head fell back, the sound of bone striking steel her only proof that she was still connected to something solid. She squeezed her eyes shut against a rising nausea and wondered if this would ever end.

As if having been miraculously heard, the noise of the engines dropped to a steady hum. It seemed that no one dared to breathe. That eternal sensation of plowing through water suddenly shifted to one of gentle rocking and drifting. And then blissful silence.

Footsteps pounded overhead and the hatch flew open, flooding the room with a blinding light. "Prepare to go ashore!" barked a voice. Rivka pressed the palms of her hands against her eyes as she made her way to her spot. Kneeling, she groped around and gathered her belongings, deaf to the excited laughter that was filling the space. Within minutes, she was following a filthy assemblage of travelers as they inched their way up to the main deck. Topside, Rivka took a moment to turn her face to the sea breeze before clambering down the wobbly gangplank. On the wharf, feet planted solidly after ten days of rocking and pitching, the faintest smile appeared on her lips. Turning to face the quay, she gasped and her eyes grew wide.

They were standing on a dock in the city of Istanbul and they were surrounded by a horde of people, dark-skinned and exotic, most of them peddlers who were speaking faster than Rivka had imagined possible, in a language she had never heard. She instinctively snatched up her bag and held it against her chest, as she marveled at children running everywhere, vendors laughing and gesturing as they lured the new arrivals to gaze upon their wares. Even Rivka was caught up in the festive mood. "If only my grandmother could be here," she told herself, eyes dazzled by the magnificent colorful woven fabrics.

She pulled herself to full height and willed herself to focus on the next move. After arranging temporary storage of her large valise, Rivka hoisted the satchel and made her way through the crowd. Whenever the impulse to stop was overwhelming, she allowed herself a moment to pause, stare unabashedly, and then move on. Everywhere she turned, moved and looked there were vibrant colors and fabrics: hats of red and green, shades and patterns that delighted the eye and pleased the senses. The men wore vests woven with intricate designs; the women bustled about in skirts of radiant patterns, the material flared and pleated, giving them the appearance of floating. The children's head coverings were bright-colored and lovely; some of the girls wore headpieces that were actually braided into hair so black and shining it picked up reflections from the water.

Rivka was as captivated as she was exhausted. She made her way through the labyrinth of bodies without asking herself where she was going. At one point she stopped, glanced up and down a street hardly wide enough for a horse, and considered retracing her steps. After several turns she found herself back at the starting point. Placing the satchel on the road, she stretched against the knot in her shoulder. Suddenly, she was besieged by a crowd of children. They touched her face and arms, prodded and pushed. When she picked up her bag to back away, they encircled her, pressing closer and pushing their hands near her face. She tried to push them away, but they pushed back. Angry, fearful, sleepless, Rivka buried her face into the satchel and burst into tears.

The children backed away at once. An older boy appeared and called out to them, his voice angry. The children laughed at this false show of authority and ran off in a tight cluster of bodies toward the wharf. This one wasn't much fun, said their chatter. She may have cried, but in the end she gave us nothing. The boy touched Rivka's arm and pointed toward a blue door. There was a window cut into an upper section decorated with red and orange hand-painted flowers, a promise of something bright and fresh inside. The sign hanging over the door suggested that it was an inn. Rivka hoisted her satchel and marched resolutely inside, following the boy across a tiled foyer to a desk where a man was seated. The man spoke to the boy, who in turn rushed out.

Rivka glanced nervously about. "I would like a room."

The man smiled.

"Do you have one?"

He continued to smile.

Consumed by fatigue, she held back her tears, repeating the question very slowly, as if more precise pronunciation would make her Yiddish understood.

"English?" inquired the man. Rivka gave him a blank stare. "*Deutsche?*" he continued. "*Español. Français?*" When he asked "*Russki?*" her expression changed. He smiled and left the room.

It rankled her, coming all this way and being forced to speak Russian. But if it meant a hot bath and a clean bed… She allowed the thought to drift away to its wistful conclusion.

The man soon returned with the boy. "Boti," he announced, pointing proudly to his son. Boti beamed. "Boti, da," said the man, pushing the boy forward.

"Rooms?" asked Rivka in Yiddish. Boti's eyes grew wide in confusion. Sighing, she repeated the question in Russian.

"Yes, rooms," he said proudly. "Very clean."

"But expensive, yes?"

He jotted something on a scrap of paper and nudged it toward her. Rivka looked at it and shook her head. The boy snatched the paper back, glanced at it, and laughed at his mistake. He crossed out the numbers, did a quick calculation, and wrote the amount in rubles.

She could afford one night, perhaps two. "Hot bath?" The boy nodded and reached for the satchel. Too tired to argue, she handed it over and mounted the stairs behind him.

Late the next morning Rivka opened her eyes and looked around.

There was no rocking ship, only a bed with fresh sheets and blankets. She had a vague recollection of hot water, steam, and then slipping into a bed that made her think of heaven. She thought she would never get up. As if needing to prove herself right, she wrapped herself in the covers and fell asleep.

Sounds outside the window finally roused her, voices calling from the long string of stalls lining the marketplace just up the road; men and women crying out their wares in what sounded to her ears like music. There was such promise in what she heard that she was finally tempted from the warmth of her bed. She dressed and formed a laundry pile of articles to be washed upon her return. Descending the stairs, she discovered a smiling Boti perched at the bottom. With a quick bow he led her into a dining room and disappeared. Very soon he returned with a basket of hot rolls and a plate of fruit. Before she had split the roll, he was back with a strange little pot that balanced a cone of fresh-ground coffee. He poured hot water through the cone and waited for all the water to drip through, removed the filter and poured the near-black liquid into a small cup. "Good," he announced, gesturing toward the coffee.

Rivka found the aroma tantalizing. She lifted the cup to her lips but then pulled back from what she perceived as bitterness. It was Boti's disappointment that prompted her to try again. The sweetness was a marvel.

Breakfast consumed, Rivka rushed outside. There was no need to glance behind to know who was following. "Come," he said in Russian, "I will be your guide." When she hung back, he laughed. "I know this city," he boasted. "And no cost to you. This is good, yes?" Rivka gestured for him to lead the way and they set off into the labyrinthine streets and alleyways of Istanbul. Her head began spinning the moment she caught sight of the crowds. The lingering odor of exotic foods, the colors and noisy gaiety, everything filled her with a sense of wonder. In the souks she fingered fabrics and wares, chatted with her guide in a language he only marginally understood. What they could not communicate in words was easily conveyed through gesture.

In early afternoon, the sun still quite high, fatigue closed around Rivka and guided her back to the inn. The effort needed to climb the stairs to her room was nearly heroic. When she opened the door she knew at once that something was amiss. Sitting on the bed were all the garments she had put aside for laundering, each piece washed, ironed, and neatly folded. She reached out and touched them. No matter in what form it arrived, Rivka never expected kindness. Placing everything on the chair, she stretched out fully clothed on the bed and closed her eyes. "If I rest just a few minutes," she mumbled to herself, "I'll be ready for dinner." When next she opened her eyes it was noon of the following day.

"I see you are still alive," laughed Boti, when she entered the salon. He rushed from the room and returned with a plate of food. Once again she was seduced by the aroma.

After lunch they sought out Boti's father.

"Poppy says there is a train leaving this afternoon," Boti interpreted. "It will take you as far as Smyrna."

Rivka stared at him.

"On the Aegean."

Smyrna, the Aegean. The words caused her heart to flutter.

It was late afternoon before they reclaimed the heavy valise and transported it from the wharf to the train's quay. Boti made sure that it was safely stored in the overhead rack and that Rivka was settled into her seat. Satisfied that his ward was safe, he allowed himself to be kissed on the cheek before he detrained. Rivka was still waving to him when she heard a voice over her shoulder. Without turning, she recognized the young man from the voyage. She pressed her lips together and stiffened her back, holding the satchel closer to her body as she directed her gaze outside.

"May I join you?" he asked again, his voice betraying little of the annoyance he must have felt at such an obvious slight. When she said nothing, he shrugged and moved on.

It was late the next day before they arrived at the terminus in Smyrna. This time Rivka knew to follow the other passengers as they made their way along the narrow streets leading to the port. Hungry and tired, she listened to their inquiries. It was nearly three hours before they were able to find someone willing to negotiate their passage. Rivka thought the captain gruff and mean-spirited, too quick to take their money. "Yes, yes," he mumbled to all their questions, while at the same time palming their cash.

Rivka was reluctant to hand over her money. How could she be sure that he really was the captain of that unregistered freighter docked at the far end of the wharf? How could she know that, after arguing with Turkish authorities regarding the legality of his ship's registration, he wanted nothing more than to be done with this country? It was two o'clock in the morning before they were aboard ship and heading through the Greek islands. Their cabin was so cramped they needed to sidle between the cots, lined up in a half-dozen rows, six across. Rivka sat on hers and was grateful to have it. It was cramped, to be sure, but what an improvement over the first ship! She had no sense of the time when she was roused from a sound sleep.

"Everybody below!"

Rivka turned her head sluggishly toward the voice.

"Below?" repeated the women in the next cot. "Below what?"

Several muscular men entered the room and positioned themselves near the door. When one of them barked the order to collect belongings and file out, there were no dissenters. As Rivka stepped through the door she saw a collection of people waiting to enter, last-minute passengers who had undoubtedly bribed the purser.

They were herded downward, into the bowels of the ship, to a dark and airless space. Rivka had to press a handkerchief over her nose and mouth to thwart the stench of engine fuel.

"How are we supposed to breathe?" someone demanded.

"And where are the beds we paid for?"

"You can't leave us in the dark!"

This complaint resulted in one of the sailors screwing a bulb into the single socket overhead.

"One bulb and no air? I demand to see the authorities!"

The sailors laughed. "We are the authorities!" Their response to the heated protests was to close the metal door with a deafening clang and throw the lock.

Twice each day scraps of food were passed inside. And like trained dogs, the captives quickly learned that a rap on the door following the second meal was their signal to pass out the communal pot. They devised a hygiene system that offered limited privacy: two volunteers held a blanket in front of the pot while it was being used, while a third unscrewed the single lightbulb and waited until being directed to screw it back in. Rivka found the entire process repugnant and undignified, deciding straightaway that it was better to cease liquid intake altogether and limit solid foods.

"If you don't drink," advised one of the passengers, "your kidneys will fail."

"Let them," she thought, preferring death over having anyone listen to her bodily functions.

On the fourth day everything changed. Not only had they received no food, no one had appeared to take away the stinking pot. What little patience and civility existed were stretched near to breaking.

"Can't you move this mess?" demanded one of the men. Using both feet, he upset a bag of belongings and pushed it away.

Another voice came back taunting, "Why, so you can stretch into my space again?"

Rivka was herself suffocating from a shortage of oxygen, the sickening stench, the interminable misery of those around her. Each morning she awoke and repeated the same routine: checking the satchel to make sure she hadn't been robbed while she slept; reminding herself of the day and date; forcing herself to remain calm and in control. It was sometime in the midst of this ritual that she suddenly realized it was her eighteenth birthday. The realization made her instantly melancholy, which only augmented the sense of isolation. She felt profound despair, thought that if she closed her eyes her entire breathing mechanism would come to a halt and she would die. The sensation stayed with her throughout the day, ending only when she prepared for bed. Curled up in her limited space, she imaged herself seated around the table with her family, gaily wrapped presents piled up before her, Grandmother Malka flitting about to verify that everything was perfect.

Shortly after falling asleep Rivka was awakened by someone pressing against her back. She shifted away, but the body shifted with her, its odor rank and vile. Before she could speak, a hand reached around and began to fondle her breast. With her heart racing, she wrenched away. He tugged at her blouse with one hand, reached under her skirts with the other, somehow managing to touch her despite her efforts to repel him. She thought of Rahel and the husband who brutalized her. Rivka wanted to scream out, but she stifled her cry, too ashamed and fearful to draw attention to her plight. Weeping, she finally managed to battle to her feet and drag her belongings to the farthest corner of the hold, tripping over sleeping bodies as she used her toes to feel her way in the dark. When she came to a clearing on the floor, she dropped down, curled into a fetal position and pressed her satchel against her. Only seconds later, a hand on her shoulder caused her to jump.

"It's only me," whispered one of the women. "Are you all right?"

Rivka wanted to grasp that hand, to be held and rocked and soothed, but that would require trusting a stranger. "I'm fine," she mumbled, embarrassed to hear petulance and ingratitude in her voice. "Thank you," she added, her voice softer. "Thank you."

Morning arrived and the door was finally opened to admit a tray of putrid leftovers. When a few of Rivka's fellow passengers related what the boy had done, the sailors laughed and slammed the hatch. There was enough indignation among the travelers, however, that the boy kept to himself during the remainder of the voyage.

It was twelve days from the time of departure that the rocking and lurching that had become the rhythm of their lives suddenly slowed to a gentle roll. All voices stopped; no one dared to breathe. Within the hour the door clanged open and the filthy band of immigrants was ordered topside. One after another they staggered, pulling and hoisting boxes, valises, sacks, clothing, bodies weary from too little food and air. Some of them had barely the energy to complete the climb and required assistance from the others. None of the sailors would touch them. When they arrived in the fresh air they raised their arms to the sky and rushed to the railing to see for themselves that land was truly in sight. A few of the travelers dropped to their knees and gave thanks for having survived.

Rivka, among the first to disembark, had never imagined that solid ground could feel so welcoming. Eight hours and two trains later she found herself standing at the door of a house on the outskirts of London, a slip of paper clenched in her hand. On it her Aunt Hannah had carefully written the address of a distant cousin. Rivka knocked, knocked again, and a woman opened the door. She was stout, her posture straight, almost rigid. Her hair was ebony black and pulled into a severe bun at the nape of her neck. Without speaking, she gave the travel-worn stranger the once-over.

Rivka was offended by the distaste in this woman's eyes. But then she remembered that weeks without bathing must have left her looking and smelling worse than derelict.

The woman's expression announced, Please, not another relative foisted upon me! Nevertheless, she took the paper being offered and read it. "And what can I do for you?" she asked. When there was no response, she repeated the question in Yiddish. When Rivka explained that she was arriving from Nowy Życie, the woman responded, "So you have, and you're the third one this year."

When formal introductions were completed, Edna Farbstein led Rivka up several flights to a tiny space in the attic. The room was clean and light, the bed barely large enough for one. "I realize it is small," the woman said.

Rivka stroked the pillow. Mustering what little energy remained, she forced a smile. "I apologize for being a nuisance, but is it possible to bathe?"

Mrs. Farbstein excused herself and returned carrying a large towel. Directing her guest to the downstairs bathroom adjacent to the kitchen, she took her leave.

Rivka pulled out everything that needed laundering and made her way down three flights to the bath. With Mrs. Farbstein's help, she lugged three cauldrons of water to the tub. Adding enough cold water to make it tolerable, she climbed in and let out a moan of pleasure. Scrubbing and rinsing until every drop of water pouring from skin and hair ran clean, she emptied the tub, scoured it and filled it once again. The dirty clothing was washed, rinsed and squeezed until, nearly an hour later, everything was hanging to dry in her little room. She donned clean clothing, made sure her hair was in place, and then returned to the bathroom for a final inspection. Satisfied, she followed the wonderful aromas until she came to the kitchen. When she entered, she was pleased to see the surprise on the woman's face. Ah, said the woman's smile. This is no peasant, but a proper young lady.

"Sit there," directed Mrs. Farbstein, using her cutting knife to indicate a chair. "Now tell me all about yourself."

In ten minutes Rivka had related her connection to the Gershons, some of the less dramatic events of her adventure and a brief outline of her plans.

"Ah, yes," sighed the woman, "America. Everyone goes to America."

Rivka was tempted to argue in defense of her choice, but said nothing.

"A bunch of big shots," said Mrs. Farbstein in English, waving a hand in the direction of America. "The land of opportunity." She saw Rivka's confusion, laughed and shifted to Yiddish. "*Ganser knockers,*" she repeated in Yiddish. "Everyone wants to go to America. And for the life of me, I can't understand why. England's so much more civilized, if you know what I mean."

Rivka nodded politely, having no idea whatsoever what this woman meant. And between the overbearing fatigue and her difficulty understanding Yiddish spoken with a British accent, she had little energy to try.

Mrs. Farbstein suddenly laughed. "My dear, will you be able to stay awake until dinner?" Sympathy crossed her face. "No, it's best to feed you now. Introductions with the rest of the family can wait 'til morning."

Rivka thanked her and smiled. It took nearly every remaining bit of energy to force down the food. By the end of the meal, she struggled to simply lift the fork.

"Please," urged her hostess. "Go to bed."

Rivka pulled herself up to the room, undressed and fell into bed. Just a little nap, she thought. In a while, I'll be just fine. She slept for thirty hours.

Within days Rivka had learned her way around London, marveling at its size and grandeur, covering her ears against its clamor. She found it odd that strangers would speak to one another on the street and began to understand that there were large cities where people lived without fear.

Two weeks after her arrival she was taken by her hostess to an agency specializing in finding work for Jewish immigrants. After an hour's wait, a stuffy little man in a shabby jacket gave her a fifteen-minute interview. At the end of that time, he offered her a job.

"I've got something that pays well in Bristol." He rechecked the requirements noted at the bottom of the form. "Can you begin on Monday?" Rivka looked at the roomful of people awaiting their turn, dozens of men and women, most of whom would be thrilled to be made such an offer. Like it or not, she was one of them. She lifted her chin proudly and responded, "Monday will be fine, thank you." The man handed her the paper and she was dismissed.

Early the next morning she was at the train station, satchel hanging over one arm and the large valise resting by her leg.

"I know this is difficult," said Mrs. Farbstein. "But Bristol isn't far and you can visit on your days off." She saw the girl's eyes narrowing, the mouth set into its hard line. "A seamstress is considered respectable in this country, Rivka. You must not be ashamed." When the announcement was made for the train, the woman reached into her purse. "You must be grateful," she mumbled, taking out a package. When she caught the grimace on Rivka's face, she laughed. "But it's true! If you were a man, we'd be on another platform waiting for the train to Wales." She saw the confusion. "That's where the Jewish men are sent, my dear, to the coal mines." She handed over a cake made especially for the voyage and then kissed Rivka on the cheek. "Be sure to write," she murmured, knowing the girl would do no such thing.

Rivka accepted the kiss, even returning it with a little hug and a few heartfelt words of thanks. As the train pulled out of the station, the two women waved good-bye.

For four years Rivka lived a life not so much frugal as penurious: every shilling not spent on food or rent was saved. Not once did she take a meal away from the boardinghouse or buy an article of clothing. And her routine was always the same: six days a week she was up at five and out the door by six; thirty minutes were allotted for lunch (she was paid by the piece, so she frequently took no more than five); and then home by eight, dinner completed by nine, reading in the parlor until ten. Nothing varied, nothing changed. Nothing, that is, until the evening three years into her stay when she returned from work to find a letter from Hannah. She took the chair nearest the gas lamp, her hands shaking with excitement as she opened the envelope. Thanks to Hannah's love of writing, she was kept up to date on family news.

"Last night," wrote Hannah, "your Grandmother Malka died in her sleep." She went on to ask if Rivka could return. Grischa was confused, he seemed so lost. "Perhaps you could help?" Rivka sat with the letter for nearly an hour, the dampness from her fingers smudging the ink. After all she had been through, suffered, but how could she not go? And then she thought to check the postmark: it had been mailed nearly ten weeks earlier. Rushing to her room, she took pen and paper and wrote a lengthy letter. In it, she explained the delay and her need to continue on the journey. In closing, she sent her love and her hopes that Hannah would not be angry.

The death of Malka Gershon in the spring of 1923 was like an earthquake that strikes in one place but reverberates with such force that its aftershocks are felt elsewhere. Rivka wrote to her grandfather, doing her best to describe the depth of her sadness and her need to move on. "I'm going to America," she wrote, "because I think I will be happy there." This was the heart of her explanation, simple and yet weighted with hope. There was little more she could say.

Grischa received the letter. Although his pain was hardly relieved, he understood and encouraged her to go. Two months later, shuffling past the field he so loved, he thought of how difficult life was without his Malka, his lifelong mate. He no longer noticed the morning mist hovering above the flora, how the filtered sunlight played against the profusion of wildflowers. And so suffused was the man with an overwhelming emptiness that he hardly thought of Rivka, what she was doing or where she was going. He was old now, old and tired: imagination of the unknown required too great an effort. He neared the end of the field, his house in sight up the road, and his face suddenly softened. There was a clarity in his eyes that had been absent for too long, and then surprise. A smile appeared on his mouth. Malka was with him: he could feel her. Could feel the warmth of her hand against his own. His fingers curled around hers and for the first time in months his sigh was one of contentment. Gripping his wife's hand, his heart racing with the vigor of a love-struck schoolboy, Grischa fell slowly onto the road.

๙ Topanga Canyon, Summer 1984

After months of hard work, both academically and personally, Mimi decided to give herself a much-needed gift. And Los Angeles was hot, suffering through one of those heat waves that takes a carelessly tossed cigarette and turns it into a conflagration.

"You're going alone?" Her mother responded to the news. "What kind of nonsense is that?

"Mama, some people call it a vacation." She could read her mother's mind, knew with a certainty that Rivka Zilber was searching for some way to get herself invited, without coming right out and asking. That would be too easy.

"Santa Barbara should be lovely," sighed the old woman. "Not stifling like L.A."

Mimi smiled to herself; her mother was just warming up. It was somewhere between a second reference to the heat wave and the soaring crime rate in Los Angeles that she heard the call-waiting tone. "Be right back," she said.

"I just wanted you to know that I'll be gone for a few days," Daniel announced.

"You, too?"

"It's this fucking heat. You know how I hate it. So I've booked a room in Santa Barbara."

"You're kidding."

"Why would I kid?"

"Because I'm on the phone with my mother explaining why I'm going to Santa Barbara."

"You, too?"

"Yeah, but I'm winging it. Last minute decision, you know?"

"Mimi, winging Santa Barbara over Labor Day weekend usually means sleeping in your car."

"Hold on, I'm hanging up on Mama." Mimi clicked back to the other line. "Gotta go, Mama. I'll call you Monday." Before Rivka could protest, Mimi cut her off and reconnected with Daniel. "I lost track," she moaned. "Completely forgot about the holiday. Damn!"

"I'm staying at the Biltmore."

"You rat! It's the most elegant hotel in town!"

There was a heavy pause before Daniel spoke. "You know . . ."

The way he was stringing out the last word, she knew very well. "I can't."

"Why can't you?"

"Because you're my oldest living friend."

"Mimi, it's not as if we're related. I mean, I'm not your brother, for Christ's sake."

Mimi could have sworn she heard Daniel's teeth grinding. "Come on, you know how important you are to me."

"Okay, okay. It was just an idea," he said. "Gotta go. Have a nice holiday."

"You're angry." The silence on the other end confirmed the accusation.

"I'm not," he finally said. "It's just that. . . ."

There was another silence, only this one concerned her.

"I've got to say this, but you're not going to like it." Before she could respond, he rushed ahead. "You've hit your stride at the university, you're published and quoted and admired, but what about us?"

Mimi felt anger rise and warned herself to keep it in check. Us? Could Daniel still presume that, especially after she had kept him at arm's length? She wanted to tell him that there was no us, at least not in the traditional sense.

"Are you still there?"

"Yes, Daniel, I'm still here. I'm just not sure how to respond. What would you like me to say?"

"Not say, explore. I want you to look honestly at your relationship with your mother and then tell me that it hasn't always been in our way."

Mimi took a deep breath and let it out slowly, hoping that Daniel wouldn't hear. "So you want to blame my mother for the fact that we're not together," she said, while thinking, Go on, I dare you.

"That would make it really easy, wouldn't it? Rivka gets in your way, you're helpless to move forward, so you don't. It's a great excuse for doing nothing."

Mimi was not at all pleased with the direction this conversation was taking. "Daniel, did I miss something?"

When he responded, his voice had a what-the-hell-I-may-as-well-just-say-it tone. "I know you'd like to blame your mother for this fear you have of making a commitment, but it's not Rivka's fault. It's your own decision. You use your mom as your scapegoat. And now you can use your new position, and all that it requires, as another justification."

There was just enough truth in Daniel's accusation to contract the muscles in her jaw. Nevertheless, she came back with "You don't really believe that."

"Oh, but I do." The response was direct, unemotional. "Tell me you don't want me around and I'll accept it. But I always feel like you're beating around the bush."

"Fuck you," muttered Mimi and hung up with a slam.

Bristol, England, Winter 1925

Two full years after the death of her grandparents and nearly five since she had left their home, Rivka booked passage to America. She could have left six months earlier, but the extra time allowed her to save the difference between steerage and a cabin on a registered ship.

The day of her departure, she stepped onto the gangplank, hoisting her satchel high on her arm. Her focus was directed upward, to the ship's officer checking the list and assigning quarters. When Rivka turned to look behind her, she found herself nose-to-nose with a bespectacled young man.

He tipped his hat. "May I assist you with your bag?" His English was heavily accented.

Rivka looked him up and down, turned away as if he had never spoken, and continued up the ramp. When it was her turn to be received, the white-uniformed officer offered a crisp bow. "Name, madam?"

"Silverman," said Rivka. "Ruth Silverman." All those years of practice did little to quell the pounding of her heart.

He searched through a sheaf of papers attached to a clipboard, flipping from one to the other with such speed that she feared he would overlook her name. Stopping suddenly, he ran his finger across the page and scribbled a notation. "Two seventy-five," he said, but so quickly that she missed the number. Before she could ask him to repeat it, the man behind her echoed the number in Yiddish.

She gave him a perfunctory nod, shifted the satchel, thanked the officer in her best English and set off in search of her cabin. Not a half-dozen steps later she heard a voice behind her. "Zilber," it said. "Harold Zilber." Turning briefly, Rivka was surprised to see the young man staring at her. She thought him terribly impertinent, shrugged him off and proceeded below deck in search of quarters she prayed were commensurate with four years of eyestraining work. So what if she were several levels below the water line and in a space hardly large enough for one narrow bed? Did it matter that she was sharing a bathroom with two-dozen other passengers? No! What mattered was that the bed was clean and the toilet could be disinfected before each use. Here she would find no bedding on the floor, no chamber pots stinking up the room. And there was no one to lock her in or threaten her virtue. The memory caused an involuntarily shiver. "This time," she told herself, "I'll lock the bastards out!"

The cabin assigned to her was closet-sized and Spartan. Rivka spent some time happily organizing her valise, making neat little piles of clothing, toiletries, and reading materials. By the time the room was to her liking, all thoughts of oppressive crossings and menacing passengers had slipped into that space reserved for vague and distasteful memories.

Unlike Rivka Rabinoff, Harold Zilber did not go below upon receiving his cabin assignment. His motto was: First things first. He made himself current on the placement of every lifeboat, as well as standard procedures for all emergencies. Satisfied that he could survive anything, he hoisted his heavy valise and headed down to his quarters. With each descending level his sense of irony grew. By the time he opened the door to the communal space known as "The Tomb" he was grinning. It may have been in the bowels of the ship, but it was clean and safe.

Harold dropped his valise onto the lower berth and took out his beloved notebook. "Historic day for travel," he wrote, delighted by his good luck. His first day out was the same day Hannibal began crossing the Alps. "A fine day for beginning an adventure." Then he set about stowing his few belongings: one change of clothes, two pair of underwear, several dozen history books, each one wrapped in paper and waterproofed with a layer of wax. Had he known that he would one day be forced to sell his books to pay the rent, he might have treated them with even greater care.

Harold Zilber held the same reverence for newspapers as he did for books. One scant day without submerging himself in a newspaper left him feeling empty. It was more than the infusion of information, more than the simple act of holding the pages between his fingers, feeling the texture of the rag and getting ink on his fingers. In a very special way, the news of the world defined his relationship to life.

As soon as Harold unpacked he went topside, where he nearly bumped into Rivka. The way she was walking, he was sorely tempted to inquire if she had royal ancestry. Tipping his hat, he wandered over to the railing. The sea air was wonderful after three years in the coal mines of Wales and the "hot bed" system: three men sharing the same bed in eight-hour shifts. Harold was feeling nostalgic, clinging to the belief that his family in Vilna would one day join him in America. His voyage represented freedom, but it also symbolized isolation. "Such a little boat," he mumbled, leaning against the rail. "And on such a large sea."

They were only one day out before Harold was running the gamut from euphoria to self-loathing. It had nothing to do with the humble quarters he was forced to occupy, nor the third seating he was forced to endure at each meal. It was this terrible weakness he had for Rivka. He was nettled by it, so embarrassed that he grimaced at his reflection while shaving, chastised himself for acting the adolescent. And yet he could not control the desire to loiter about the deck at all hours awaiting the passing of that aloof young woman. "When will she walk by?" he mumbled to himself, lurking near the metal stairs on the third deck. There was something about her expression—proud and yet vulnerable—that touched him. And she was so small, barely coming to his chin, yet she carried the weight of the world on her shoulders.

Harold had waited for several days before crossing her path, but the best he was able to muster was a bumbling hello accompanied by a slight bow. She had glanced his way, but had given no indication of his presence.

This morning would be different. He would lie in wait, like the leopard about to pounce, and then step directly into her path. How could she avoid him? He was so deep in thought with strategic planning that Rivka walked right past him before he noticed. "Miss Silverman," he called after her, rushing to catch up. "Might I interest you in a cup of tea?" Rivka eyed him suspiciously and then shifted to the other side of the walk. "Please," he beseeched, and felt instantly humiliated.

She held a hand above her eyes and squinted into the sun. "Why should I?"

Harold was not prepared for this question and found himself groping foolishly for an appropriate response. "Well, for one thing, it would be nice to speak my language again." Good one! he thought. She can find no objection to that! "I only want to talk," he quickly added, as if this would dispel all fears.

He seemed harmless enough to Rivka. And despite her dearth of experience with men, she sensed that if she did not accept, she might never be rid of him. With a tip of her head, she gestured for him to lead the way.

In the course of the voyage, Harold and Rivka shared many pots of tea and a good number of cakes. It was only in the context of sipping and chewing that they learned about each other's life. It took Harold a full week to find the courage to ask the big question. "Could you tell me the date of your birth?" Reluctantly Rivka complied, confused when he pulled on his lower lip and looked away.

"Is there a problem?" she asked.

He pressed his lips together in thought. "I'm afraid," he finally admitted, "that nothing of any consequence whatsoever took place on that date." When she appeared relieved, he was utterly bewildered.

Rivka found herself counting on Harold's presence. He was a bit slow for her liking, yet always curious and polite. And she felt safe with him. He was never demanding, he never forced his attentions on her: he was simply there. They shared the thrill of approaching Ellis Island, of standing in line and awaiting entrance into the New World. They were comforted by each other's presence as they nervously awaited clearance from Immigration.

Several days after being released from the quarantine holding area, Rivka took up her valise and satchel and headed toward the pier. Awaiting her was Harold Zilber. "How long have you been waiting?" she asked.

Taking up his own bags, he said, "Not long. Two days." When he saw her expression of disbelief, he smiled. It would be some time before he could admit to Rivka that he had told the truth.

The two immigrants filed past dour-faced officials manning a variety of desks. "Papers!" one of them barked. Rivka handed over the document, perspiration running down her back. There was a thirteen-year difference between herself and Ruth Silverman. What if he noticed? The man scanned the information, looked up and studied her face, the smooth skin of youth long ago invaded by a permanent scowl. With a dramatic flourish he affixed the official stamp and handed the papers back. "Welcome to America," he stated.

Rivka and Harold reunited outside the building and made their jubilant way toward the ferry. This time when he offered to carry her heavy valise, she did not refuse. They clambered aboard and rushed for two spaces nearest the railing. It was here, with America looming before them, that they shared their first real freedom. As the ferry approached the New York harbor, Rivka leaned close to Harold. "There's something you need to know. My name's not Ruth Silverman."

Harold peered down at the woman. "I don't understand," he shouted over the din of engines.

"It's Rivka. Rivka Rabinoff."

Harold removed his hat and pressed its brim between his fingers. "I see," he mused, almost to himself. "So why the story?"

Leaning close, Rivka spoke directly into his ear. "I took my travel documents from a dead woman."

Harold considered this information, eyes never leaving the Manhattan skyline that was drawing nearer. "Does that mean you lied about your birthday?"

"No," she said, almost apologetically. "That part is true." When she saw his sigh, she burst into laughter. It was the first time Rivka had laughed aloud in many, many years.

They shared a common language and a desire for a new life. Other than that, Rivka Rabinoff and Harold Zilber were opposites: she was cool and detached; he was open and friendly; she was considered by some to be thoughtless and selfish; while he was looked upon as generous and kind. Where she preferred the quiet of a room, hands busy with sewing and such things, he delighted in the sounds of voices, opinions, playful banter among friends, the strains of music filling a room, the roar of a soccer match and the liveliness of concerts in the park. Harold and Rivka were hot and cold, summer and winter, putty-soft and rock-hard. Had anyone taken a poll, the consensus would have been that these two had absolutely nothing in common. As it was, there was no one to poll, no friends to advise, no family to judge. Which is why, when the boyish Harold Zilber faced the solemn Rivka Rabinoff several years later and mustered sufficient courage to ask, "So will you marry me?" it seemed perfectly natural for her to respond, "Why not?"

CHAPTER TEN

❧Los Angeles, Summer, 1944

To DELVE into Rivka Zilber's life was to achieve a clearer understanding of the character of the survivor. It explained how someone could survive, even after having fallen into a crevasse of cynicism and gloom. If Harold understood anything of the true nature of his wife, it was that he hoped to protect her, to somehow remove from her this blanket of darkness. To have a child with her, encourage her out into the light where she could flower.

It was nearly eighteen years into their marriage before their daughter was born, eighteen years of adjusting to a new country, to those candid and disarming Americans. For Harold the years were a mixed bag of frustration, excitement and challenge. He had never imagined, for example, that a language could be so complicated! That there could be so many ways to communicate one simple concept was something he found amazing. "Do people sit around and make up these things?" he asked Rivka, then regretted the question. How would she know, this woman who huddled in her kitchen, exchanging only an occasional word with her neighbors, and most often in Yiddish?

For Rivka, those eighteen years were pure hell. She felt alone, wanted desperately to return to the familiarity of Nowy Życie; at the same time, she wanted to give her husband a child. There had been eighteen years of disappointment, of seeing the light of hope that shone in his eyes turn dimmer. Each menstrual cycle became her guilt. If nothing else, Rivka was a dutiful wife who did her best. Several

206 THE BONE WEAVER

times each month she lay passively while Harold penetrated her, each thrust his dogged effort to make the distance between sperm and egg as short as possible. After three miscarriages she was tempted to give up, but not Harold. "Just one healthy baby," he reasoned, "and you'll forget all that other unpleasantness." Rivka wanted to share his optimism, but the emotional strain was taking its toll, and it was exacerbated by her belief that Harold's mission of fatherhood had little to do with his love for her. What he wanted was a child, period.

The first miscarriage happened several months after they had arrived by car in California from New York. Rivka was just regaining her strength after several weeks of morning sickness and they were comfortably seated in their new Boyle Heights apartment, their Philco tuned to the final drama of Sacco and Vanzetti. "It's over, ladies and gentlemen," intoned the announcer. "Sacco and Vanzetti are dead." Within the hour, Rivka began to bleed. "It's probably nothing," said her doctor when Harold placed a frantic call from the grocer's phone. An hour later Rivka was in the hospital being subjected to the minor surgery required to bring closure to a failed pregnancy. Days later Harold draped his arm over her shoulder. "Maybe it's for the best," he told her. Rivka appeared first bewildered and then angry. "Because of Sacco and Vanzetti," he said, as if this were explanation enough. When he saw that it was not, he sighed loudly. "My dear, it was an ominous sign. Can you honestly say that you haven't considered that? A pregnancy that fails on such a terrible day, well, maybe it's a baby who shouldn't be born?"

"But the doctor said . . ."

Like all authoritative statements, Harold waved it away. Stress and fatigue? Some whim of Mother Nature? He knew better. Rivka had no energy to challenge this foolishness, and by the time her strength returned, she had forgotten the specifics.

The second pregnancy was shorter, the miscarriage so brief, Rivka suffered little more than a lingering disappointment. Harold, on the other hand, suffered greatly.

"Don't worry," she reassured the downcast man. "I promise you, you'll be a father."

"But this was so perfect."

Rivka searched his face, eyebrows pulled together. For once, she dared not ask.

Their third loss was the fall of 1929 when attention was riveted to Wall Street and even their immigrant neighborhood was feeling the pinch. Radios everywhere were tuned in for news flashes and market reports. On the streets, in the shops, even at their leftist picnics sponsored by the Workman's Circle, finance was the principal subject. Harold felt grateful to have a job, even though selling bathroom appliances was not his idea of success. The salesmen in his office were riveted to the financial news, speaking of little else, casting out dire warnings of impending disaster. As for Harold, he believed the disaster had already arrived.

"And you know who gets hurt?" he asked rhetorically. "We do, the struggling workers, schmucks like you and me. And you know why? Because the rich borrow and spend, and then they expect us to pay for their greed."

"You want to know who's really to blame?" shot back one of the salesmen.

Harold instinctively moved toward the door, creating distance between himself and the man convinced that the Jews were controlling the media and destroying the banks.

A decade later came war, a tragedy being played out so far from Harold and Rivka, and yet leaving a dark stain on every moment of their lives. Harold had heard nothing from his Vilna family in nearly a year. It was easier for him to imagine them unable to post a letter, or moving from one relative to another, than being caught up in the Nazi horror. As for Rivka, her contact with her brothers and Hannah had slowed to a trickle, an occasional note, so the absence of news was not so much frightening as unsettling. Besides, whenever she voiced her concerns to Harold, he would reassure with "Hitler has no time for shtetl Jews like us." They could only live their daily lives and share an expectation that the monster would be stopped.

The final pregnancy, the good one, came out of the blue. For Rivka, now in her mid-forties, it seemed to last for years. She rode the bus to her doctor's office twice a week to be assured that everything was progressing smoothly. And although the fifth month came and went, and then the sixth and the seventh, she could not shake the fear of impending trouble. Harold's anxiety did little to assuage her concerns. The closer they came to the due date, the greater his frenzy. Every morning he combed through the newspaper in search of some historic event destined to occur on the day of his son's birth.

When the contractions began on the evening of June 5, Rivka called out for Harold from the bedroom. There was no reply. "Harold?" She eased herself from the bed and struggled with a housedress. "Must I do this alone?" she mumbled, making her way into the living room. "Harold, I think we should hurry."

They drove to the hospital in silence. As Rivka was being wheeled into the delivery room, Harold bent down and kissed her forehead. While he fidgeted with the other expectant fathers, his wife fought valiantly against each contraction, as if hell-bent on denying this child its liberation. It was because of her controlling and intractable nature that labor was prolonged by at least an hour. Birth occurred at two minutes past midnight. When they wheeled her into her room, she struggled valiantly against the anesthesia, forced open her eyes and asked, "*Nu?*"

Harold took her hand, stroked her face, feeling tenderness for Rivka, perhaps even love. "A girl," he said.

"A girl," repeated Rivka, squeezing his hand. "You wanted a son."

Harold touched her cheek. "A girl is fine."

Satisfied, Rivka closed her eyes and slipped under the delicious influence of drugs.

When Harold arrived the next morning, he was laden with bouquets.

"Such extravagance!" declared Rivka.

Pulling his chair closer, he took her hand. "Do you realize what you've done?"

Rivka could not suppress the smile. "Women do it all the time."

"You don't understand!" he insisted. "Eisenhower and our boys invaded Normandy! Because you took your own damned time, our baby was born on D-Day!" The love and pride in his voice warmed Rivka, made her proud to be Harold's wife.

"D-Day, Rivka! May the Germans rot in hell, our daughter was born on one of the greatest days in history!"

Rivka shifted onto her side. Wincing, she forced a smile. As if I had any control, she thought, but she said nothing. Knowing Harold, it would only dampen his pride.

Naming the baby was not as easy as Rivka had hoped. When the doctor arrived for morning rounds, Harold pounced on him. "So what do you think of my little girl being born on the same day as the Normandy invasion?"

The doctor turned toward Harold, fountain pen held midair.

"Perhaps he's too busy," suggested Rivka.

"Don't be silly, Rivka. Men love history!"

The doctor smiled. "A great day, yes, to be sure."

"And only months following Eniwetok. That was on, what, February, February. . . ." His voice trailed off as he searched for the day.

The doctor could do nothing but stare blankly.

"Ah, yes," said Harold. "The seventeenth, wasn't it?" He posed the question politely, but his expression gave him away. Just imagine, it said. And this from a man of science.

When the doctor left the room, Rivka reached for Harold's hand. "I'd like to call her Malka."

Harold walked to the window and pressed his palms against the glass.

"My grandmother raised me, Harold, gave me a home when everyone else was gone."

"I understand." Still he remained turned away. "It's just that I was hoping we could call her something that would make her proud, to remind her that she's special, American."

Rivka held her breath.

"How about Lillian Hellman Zilber?"

Rivka blinked very slowly and grabbed the metal railing of the bed. "Lillian Hellman Zilber?" She fell back into the pillows. Glancing over, she saw the muscles around his mouth crimp and she nearly laughed. "If not Malka, how about Miriam? Miriam Lillian Zilber." She saw the tension in his back relax. "Then it's settled."

Rivka held the red-faced infant in trembling arms and was convinced that Miriam Lillian Zilber was the personification of perfection, her one great accomplishment. She also knew that the accomplishment would never be replicated. Perhaps understanding the uniqueness of this achievement contributed to her belief that Miriam had come into this world without flaw. So what if the baby in those early photographs was bruised, blotched and swollen after fighting her way out of the womb? In her mother's eyes, she was the quintessence of perfection.

After the birth Harold found his wife to be gentler—even the sharp corners used to fend off her threatening world were a little rounder. Her voice was sweeter, as if she were finally admitting that the world was not as dangerous or ugly as she had once believed. Harold was pleased, but still skeptical. Can a woman who is lonely and fearful really change? But it was the wrong question. What he should have been asking was, Can a woman who has suffered pain that gouges the heart ever really trust? Little Miriam filled Rivka's heart with love, covered her face with smiles, and yet Harold continued to doubt.

Eleven months after Miriam's birth they received an envelope with a Belgian postmark. Wartime overseas mail was so rare that Rivka placed the letter on the cabinet near the front door and walked away. One thing she knew, it wasn't Hannah's writing.

Each time she passed the letter she stared at it, touched it, and then moved on. It was a dance of fear that continued well into the afternoon, and the fear intensified with each passing hour. When it was nearly time for the baby's nap, Rivka picked up the envelope and carried it into the living room. Miriam was on the carpet, amusing herself with squares of brightly colored material and a pan filled with wooden utensils. If Rivka needed to dredge up more courage than she believed she possessed, she wanted her daughter nearby. She touched the baby's hair and sat down, hands shaking as she removed the single sheet of fine paper.

"My dear Mrs. Zilber" it began, the Yiddish letters so cramped and poorly written that she had to hold the letter to the light to make out the words. "I am Aaron," it continued, "the youngest grandson of Yankl, whom you may remember as the dairyman of Nowy Życie."

The dairyman of Nowy Życie? A fierce pain was building around her eyes. Leaning back into the chair, she read on:

I was among the few to leave Poland. As such, I was asked by several families to take with me addresses of someone — family or friend — living free from the stain of this ugly war. It was from your brother I received your address. Now I have returned to our village, but I am among the few. Yes, I have returned, but it is no longer as it was. Living in our homes are strangers. We Jews were nearly three thousand before the war, but this is no longer so. We are now perhaps twenty souls. There is no other way for me to say this. It is my hope that you hear my grief. Your family did not come back. I have been told by someone who miraculously returned that only the youngest daughter of your Aunt Hannah managed to find her way out of the flames. Do you understand what I am telling you with a heart near breaking and with eyes so flooded with tears that I cannot see? Of your family, only one survived. I will say Kaddish for your aunt and her brothers. I will pray for your uncles and for their children and grandchildren, and for your brothers, their wives and your nieces and nephews. I will pray for them, dear woman, as I will pray for you. And for me. Because I, too, am alone. Of all my six brothers and sisters, their husbands and wives and children, only two (blessed) remain. G-d willing we will meet one day. Perhaps next year . . . in Jerusalem.

Rivka read the letter a second time, and then a third. It was a lie, someone's cruel joke, but her denial rang false and she knew with every part of her being that it was authentic. She folded the paper and slipped it back into its envelope. Placing it on the table, she rose and crossed the room to the little cabinet. From its drawer she removed the yellowed photograph and returned to the chair. Holding it between thumb and forefinger, she willed herself to appear in that space reserved just for her, the one next to Fredl, the girl with the laughing eyes. Rivka stared at her family and did not hear the door open. It was not until she felt a presence that she started and looked up. There was a man there, his face first jubilant and then confused. She wondered who he was, this stranger leaning down, his eyes so filled with concern. The baby looked up and smiled.

Harold bent down and placed a hand over Rivka's. "My dear, I've come to tell you: the war is over. Do you hear me, the war is over."

Rivka searched his face, felt a vein pulsing at her temple, but she did not speak. What was there to say? That for the first time in her life she no longer doubted that in the deep place, the place called the soul, nothing existed? Nothing existed and nothing mattered.

Rivka would never learn the entire truth: the months that her brothers, her Aunt Hannah, all of them were hidden in a crawl space found for them by Yankl the dairyman above a neighbor's livestock pens; how the German soldiers arrived in the middle of the day and went directly to that hiding place. She would never learn how her brothers and their families, led into the light of day, were forced to watch as the farmer and his family members were shot for the crime of hiding Jews. And she never learned that it was the son of old Bogdan, the postal clerk who had served Nowy Życie so well, who had traded knowledge of her family's whereabouts for one week's ration of bread. And most of all there was no way for Rivka to understand that from that day forward—from that day until the very last breath of her life—the distance between her mouth and God's ears would never be bridged.

But what she and so many immigrants did understand, and with a pain that drove through like a lance, was that it was because of this act of flight to the land of opportunity that they were spared the fate of their families. Rivka and Harold, and every Jew who had ever fled czarist Russia, were left to grapple with the knowledge that, by embarking on their adventure, by sailing off to strange and distant lands, they had eluded death. Not even the reality of survival dulled the grief, eased the torturous realization that living life to its natural conclusion was their punishment for having survived.

The shroud cast over the little apartment in Boyle Heights left a shadow on every facet of their lives. The joy of a new baby, the possibilities stretched out before them, everything took on a somber cast. Plodding through each day, welcoming with gratitude nightfall and sleep, Harold began to grasp his wife's philosophy: the gifts of life known as joy, peace and contentment were not gifts at all, but ephemeral pleasures offered to people like them in the form of a temporary loan.

Los Angeles, Summer 1984

"I couldn't have been more than four or five when I began to understand my father."

Mimi and Daniel sat facing each other in a Santa Barbara café. Between them sat the remnants of a Japanese meal: one piece of sushi, a few slices of ginger, and a small mound of wasabi.

"Let me give you an example," she went on, gesturing with her chopsticks. "The more historical events I could accurately recall, the greater his pride."

Had Daniel not known Harold Zilber, he might have doubted the claim. But he had known him, had understood the man's obsession with all things historical, factual. Which is why he responded, "Yes, I remember," and poured them another shot of sake.

"So you understand that the greater his pride, the bigger the ice-cream cone."

Daniel laughed and sipped the hot liquid. He gestured toward the last piece of sushi on the plate. When Mimi refused, he trapped it in the jaws of the chopsticks and popped it into his mouth. The pungent green horseradish caused his eyes to water. "Great for my sinuses," he declared, washing it down with the rice wine.

Mimi emptied her cup as well and held it out for a refill. "So," she went on. "The bigger the feat, the bigger the sweet. And for a kid of four, it was a very simple equation."

They finished off the bottle. Despite the date, Saturday night of Labor Day weekend, the restaurant was surprisingly empty. Earlier, when they had walked in, Daniel had taken Mimi by the elbow and suggested they try another place. "But it looks fine!" she insisted.

"Look around," he had insisted. "Not one Asian face. This is not a good sign."

Mimi had leaned very close. "Daniel, relax. It'll be okay."

The point taken, he had agreed to stay. All in all, it had been a good decision.

Daniel paid the check and they stepped into a mild night. The sidewalk felt warm under their feet. They walked several blocks before Mimi took his arm.

I'm glad you came," he told her.

Mimi smiled, her eyes never leaving the walkway. When she had arrived earlier, she had stumbled upon what the motel owner swore was the last room in town. After emptying her overnight bag, she had called Daniel at his hotel and was a bit disappointed by how quickly he accepted her apology. As far as she was concerned, behavior that reproachful deserved at the least some caustic resistance.

They turned onto the main drag and strolled toward the beach, dodging skateboarders that barreled past them. Daniel paused at several windows, some of them displaying the most tempting desserts, but Mimi managed to propel him forward. When they came to the Double Rainbow parlor, however, all resolve disintegrated. A few minutes later they were holding ice-cream cones, Mimi groaning with pleasure as she ran her tongue slowly up the chocolate-chocolate-chip.

"We were talking about my father," she finally said, wiping ice cream from her fingers. When there was no response, she forged ahead. "There came the time when pleasing him became too difficult. Like that first year in high school. I was, what, fourteen? I couldn't wait for him to come home so I could watch his face while he read my report card: five A's, a B-plus. He arrives, goes directly to our marble-topped table where we put the mail, and picks up the card. I hold my breath, I'm so excited, but he says nothing. Just takes a pencil from the drawer, draws a big circle around the B-plus and hands me the card."

After dropping the sticky paper in a sidewalk receptacle, she rejoined Daniel. "Coping with my father's moods became an art form. It was long before adolescence that I figured out that some things were important to him and everything else was just inconsequential."

Daniel took Mimi's hand and slipped it around his arm. "I'm not defending him," said Daniel, sounding very much as if he were. "But those were hard times: the men were back from Korea; jobs were scarce. Not even the postwar economy was what they'd expected."

Mimi nodded, yet she knew that this had nothing to do with the economy. It was about her father and the fact that he couldn't keep a job. Rivka had accused him of being irresponsible, but even a teenage girl knew better. Harold suffered sleeplessness, shortness of temper and a general malaise that manifested itself in a loss of energy. It certainly didn't take an expert to recognize that the man was severely depressed. And why not? He had sought the land of opportunity and had discovered instead a life of struggle, a life in which his government failed to do what was right and his every paycheck was viewed as a personal affront.

A painful memory pricked at Mimi. She recalled being a little girl adept at pleasing her father, reciting historic events for him and giving him a great big love-me smile. And all the while her stomach had churned with worry.

Daniel guided them through a series of cement pylons and then along the walkway leading onto the pier. "No matter what he said," insisted Daniel, "your father was proud of you. Everyone could see that." The plaintive sigh reaching his ears made him smile. "At least he never said you were stupid."

"Your father did that?"

"Only when I flunked chemistry."

"You didn't!"

"I had to make it up in summer school."

Mimi slapped him on the arm and laughed. "What else didn't you tell me?" When he raised his eyebrows and crossed his eyes, she nearly kissed him.

The moon was throwing a shimmering light across the water, its luminescence broken only by a series of masts rising from the yachts tied to their slips. Mimi was soothed by the gentle rocking, the sound of water slapping against fiberglass hulls. And she loved the names she read out loud: *Leaking Lorelei, Ruthie's Runaway, Al's Annuity.* But her favorite was *I Rhyme With Rich.*

"So where's mine?" Daniel asked. "Where's Danny's Dinghy?" He took Mimi's hand and led her back toward the motel. Walking, she mused about the comfort of being with a friend who understood, who could walk without feeling obliged to speak; a friend who respected her need for contemplation, introspection. Daniel was a breath of invigorating air and she knew that he would never hurt her.

An image came to mind of her parents standing together with a line drawn between them. On her father's side were books and expectations, the quest for knowledge; on her mother's, a pile of fantasies.

When it came to Rivka's fantasies for her only child, they were limit-less: a future so dazzling that the eyes of the world would smart from the light; a life so perfect, a talent so great that her friends would feel cheated for not having been blessed with such a child; a marriage so ideal that parents would look upon their daughters and try to hide their bitterness while praying that their own child might enjoy, please God, a fraction of what Rivka and Harold Zilber's only child would one day possess.

And what about the reality? That Mimi was a lumpy and rather sullen adolescent; that despite the appearance of each new pimple, the next embarrassing pubic hair, an extra two pounds, her mother insisted that she was the equivalent to a teenage goddess. Despite everything, Mimi still feared that she was letting her parents down, in some way failing them.

By the time they arrived at Mimi's motel, she was reeling from confusion. Daniel had invited her to come back with him, to share his room and his bed, but she had declined. "Afraid?" he asked. "Not afraid," she said, "fragile." She needed time to think and, for the moment, her focus was on her mother's dreams and her father's lack of attention. Was it neglect, or something else? She had not decided, yet believed that there was a clear link between his inability to get emotionally close and his love for history. Neither, after all, required emotion or commitment.

After Daniel left, she turned on the television and discovered that Santa Barbara went to bed early. With no movies to watch and noth-ing worthwhile to read, she waited ten minutes and called him.

"You should have stayed with me," he teased. "My Jacuzzi is ter-rific, the cable station offers all kinds of great films and room service continues until midnight. And your place?"

"There's a stain on the carpet next to my bed and a knob's missing from the dresser."

"A big stain?"

"Big enough."

"Like where a body could have been?"

"Thanks. Now I'm going to be up all night wondering if I'm pay-ing eighty bucks to step over the scene of a stabbing."

Daniel whistled. "Eighty bucks, huh?"

"Good-night, John-boy."

"'Night, darlin'. See ya for breakfast." There was a heavy pause and then he added, "Last chance."

Mimi declined his offer, hung up and climbed into bed. When the big semi rolled past the motel at four in the morning and caused the sliding-glass door to vibrate wildly, she nearly reconsidered. But spending the night with Daniel? No, this was not a good idea.

Los Angeles, Winter 1948

Post-war America was getting back on its feet, but Rivka continued to suffer. Harold tried to soothe his wife, reassure her that Truman would do what was right, but her standard reply of "From your mouth to God's ears" affected him like a big gulp of milk gone bad. Mimi had once asked him if the distance could really be measured. "What distance, my dear?"

"The one from your mouth to God's ears."

He had responded by stroking her hair and smiling.

The emotional separation that existed between Harold and Rivka was sometimes even more pronounced because of Mimi. One day the girl rushed into the living room to show her father her new tap shoes. She tried to get his attention but he refused to lower his paper, mumbling something about the Americans exploding the first hydrogen bomb and killing innocent children. Not wanting to displease him, she smiled sweetly and tap-danced out of the room. Within seconds Rivka stormed in and demanded an explanation for what she perceived as a slight against their child. "We have a hydrogen bomb," he said, the paper still hiding his face.

For Harold, detachment was protection. It was easier to keep his family at a distance when he was absorbed by the study of history and its juxtaposition to daily life. That he could find historical significance in guessing the final score of the second game of the World Series and winning the office pool was certainly an indication. When he called from a bar to marvel that the baseball victory corresponded to Kosygin replacing Khrushchev, Rivka shrieked, "I don't care who's in power, just come home!" But when she finally heard his key turning in the lock, it was three-thirty in the morning.

The Korean War thrilled Harold. He turned their kitchen into the local information center, his large map hanging on the wall doubling as a comprehensive plan of troop movements and enemy positions. Mimi loved to hear her father explaining his strategies for winning the war and was proud to see that he was so respected by their neighbors. What she could not understand was why he was mocked by his wife. Nor could she see how this war was driving a stake through the heart of her parents' marriage, nor how the patriotism running through Harold like rich blood struck Rivka as chauvinistic foolishness.

They argued often—at the dinner table, over breakfast—and Mimi would respond by slathering butter on a piece of bread and eating it in her bedroom closet.

It was a chilly afternoon when Harold Zilber tensed, tilted his sparse frame closer to the radio, and listened with rigid concentration, his face expressing first confusion and then disbelief. As if a force were guiding him, he snatched the notebook from its place on the side table, opened to the first blank page, and noted: *January 24, 1965: WC* and then rushed into the kitchen.

Rivka was seated at the table, a cup of tea growing cold before her, the telephone pressed to her ear. She looked up at her husband, annoyed to be interrupted once again by something she would probably consider foolish, and was struck by his appearance: only sixty-three, he looked so much older. She had recently noticed that he had taken to gripping the arms of the chair to steady himself as he sat down.

"Churchill just died," he announced. "Thrombosis."

"It happens," she said with a shrug.

Harold had hoped for more: an expression of grief, a cry of dismay. If Rivka was unmoved by the loss of a great leader, a man of vision, how would she react when he died? The thought settled into that space reserved for the accumulation of more than forty years of marital disappointments and he returned to the living room.

Comfortably seated, he became aware of a strange sensation, like a drape being pulled slowly over his eyes, followed by a gentle flood moving across the underside of his skull and setting off a low tone in his ears. He appeared surprised and then confused. Emitting a soft exhalation, he slipped into a sitting position onto the floor.

Rivka finished her second cup of tea and a rather lengthy telephone conversation with her daughter, during which she had reminded Miriam that, although she was living in a boarding house near campus, was nearly an adult and undoubtedly very busy and probably living a life entirely secret from her mother, the two evenings a week she managed to get home before her parents fell asleep were not sufficient. Considering how much they loved her, needed her, counted on her, she surely could make more of an effort? After rinsing the cup, Rivka walked into the living room and found Harold unconscious on the floor.

By the time Mimi found her mother at L.A. General, her father had been moved to intensive care and hooked up to a series of monitors that alternately beeped, ticked, and blinked. The two women were instructed to wait in the lounge. Neither of them willingly left; there was something about the electronic cacophony that Mimi found reassuring.

"There's no way of knowing," explained the doctor, catching up with them at the nurse's station. He noted how Rivka glanced nervously toward the curtained room. "It takes time to evaluate the extent of CVA damage."

"Talk English," she barked.

His smile was apologetic. "Cerebral vascular accident, Mrs. Zilber. Your husband has had a stroke."

A second doctor arrived, scanned the name on the chart's metal spine and slipped it into the rack. The other doctor introduced her as the head of neurology and then left. "Your husband is still unconscious," she stated, "but this can change at any moment." She stanched the flow of Rivka's questions with an upraised hand. "I know it feels like we're putting you off, but the truth is we just don't know. And I'm afraid we may not for several weeks."

"Weeks?" echoed Mimi.

"It takes time for the swelling around the brain to go down. Until then, we can only guess."

Rivka and Mimi entered the room and positioned themselves on either side of the bed. "I don't understand this swelling nonsense," complained Rivka. "He looks fine, so why isn't he waking up?"

Into the late evening her questions were met with tolerant smiles, sympathetic nods and brief explanations, almost always followed by a reassuring pat on the arm and a kind word. Mimi watched in fascination and thought, "No wonder they call them Angels of Mercy."

Rivka wanted her husband home. After several days of listening to her demands and interrogations, a fair number of hospital employees prayed that she would get her wish. "Imagine having to go home and face rehab with that one," griped one of the nurses. Everyone within earshot sighed in agreement.

Harold Zilber came home one month later and Rivka cared for him, fed him, bathed him and struggled to return him to normal. Mimi thought her mother conscientious to a fault and was not at all surprised when he showed marked improvement within the first few weeks.

"He has no choice," Mimi confided to Sarah. "With Mama in charge, it's rehabilitation through intimidation."

Nearly four years later, Harold Zilber stretched out on the couch for his afternoon nap and didn't wake up. On the day of his death, nothing noteworthy was taking place anywhere in the world. Rivka remained by Harold's side as the attendants lifted him onto the stretcher. She walked outside and stood passively as her husband's body was slipped through the ambulance's gaping doors. It made her think that a huge mouth was preparing to swallow up the body of the man who had been her husband for more than forty years. When the car screeched to a stop behind the ambulance, she turned to face her frantic daughter.

"Miriam, Papa's gone."

Mimi rushed to her mother's side and threw her arms around her.

In her entire life, Mimi could not recall hearing her mother refer to her father as anything other than "your father." And now, a corpse tucked away in an ambulance, he was suddenly Papa.

The big doors were slammed shut and Mimi turned toward her car so that she could follow. Her mother's grip on her arm would not permit this. As the ambulance pulled away, she nearly waved good-bye. For just a moment, Mimi felt like that little girl with ringlets and shiny new tap shoes.

They returned to the apartment, where Mimi straightened the disorder left by the emergency technicians. "While you weren't looking," said a voice in her head, "your window of opportunity slammed shut." And perhaps it was true. Following her father's first stroke, she had taken it upon herself to be there every day. If she felt confined or restricted, she said nothing. But how would it be now? The word that popped into her head was *suffocating*.

Several months later, she confided to Sarah that her life felt like a bad prison movie.

Sarah had shuddered at the thought, had tried to be positive and hopeful, but there were no words that could cheer her friend.

The escape route finally came with the last-minute departure of one of the professors in her department. She agreed to take on two additional and demanding courses, four Masters candidates and two more teaching assistants.

"Aren't there laws against slave labor?" demanded Sarah. "I think they're doing this because you're unmarried and childless."

Sarah's heartfelt defense of her rights caused her to laugh. "But look at it this way," she explained. "The upside is, I'll have an excuse to spend less time with Mama."

Now it was Sarah's turn to laugh. "Put like that, it makes perfect sense."

Two weeks into the new semester and Mimi was regretting the extra load. Even a quick lunch with Sarah was stressful. She did little more than pick at her food. "Full schedule or not, it makes no difference to my mother. I'm still expected to rush home every night and keep her company."

Sarah reached across the table and speared one of Mimi's French fries. "So cut back on your work."

"Great idea. Give me two weeks and I'll be deciding between a razor blade or a noose."

"For her or for you?" Sarah handed the waiter her credit card before a check-snatching war could take place.

In bed that night, exhausted as much from work as from all she had been unable to accomplish, Mimi wondered if the years ahead would feel this empty. A shiver ran through her. What she would give to be free! And then she mumbled into the darkness, "Don't worry,

Mama, I'll take care of you" and the thought had prompted an image of Rivka Zilber rolling her eyes, clasping her hands and moaning "From your mouth to God's ears!"

After all those years, the incantation still rankled. More than rankled: it scratched like a serrated instrument across her brain. Mimi tried to comprehend, wanted to, but could not grasp how a shtetl atheist and lifelong cynic could umbilicate herself to a God she swore did not exist.

CHAPTER ELEVEN

&Los Angeles, Winter 1984

IT WAS MID-NOVEMBER, which always meant one thing: the history department's annual retreat. It was a tradition started shortly after the war, when turnover was high among the faculty and efforts were made to create a sense of community. Trial and error had finally resulted in a November meeting, when new teachers were becoming acclimated to the program and everyone else had been given adequate time and opportunity to pass judgment on them. It was also discovered that scheduling it the weekend before the university's long Thanksgiving weekend built on the momentum of a holiday.

The plans for this retreat had begun nearly six months earlier: it was no easy task housing a full department under one roof. When Charmayne Gibson, one of the newly appointed Assistant Professors, offered her Rancho Mirage home for the retreat, the newly appointed department head, Mimi Zilber, was skeptical.

"We are twelve," Mimi reminded her, imagining herself sharing a bed with several of her coworkers.

"It's no problem," insisted the woman, a published and highly respected academic who specialized in pre-revolutionary France. Her last book had been short-listed for a Pulitzer and there were rumors that the MacArthur people had been sniffing around. When Mimi and her interview committee had first met with applicant Gibson, they had displayed their very best behavior.

Mimi discussed the woman's generous offer with a few of the more senior professors and they agreed to take a chance. After all, was the argument, hadn't they already decided on Palm Springs? And with Rancho Mirage only minutes away. . . .

"I don't suppose this has anything to do with the four hundred dollars those two nights would have cost?" probed Mimi. Economics prevailed and she reluctantly, but graciously, accepted the offer.

Now that the weekend was here, Mimi wasn't sure this private home thing was such a good idea. For one thing, she hated sharing a bathroom. And then there was the question of comfort and privacy, not to mention the freedom to indulge in that delicious pleasure called Room Service. She pushed aside her list of complaints. The decision had been made and it was only a weekend. With the house locked up tight and the porch light timers set, she headed off to meet Daniel for dinner. She had tried to beg off, what with tomorrow morning's break-of-dawn departure, but he had dangled her favorite couscous restaurant before her eyes. Comfort food, she had thought, and had finally relented.

They weren't seated five minutes when the conversation shifted to her emotional journey.

"No matter where you start," observed Daniel, ladling another serving of lamb, grains, and sauce. "It always comes back to your mother."

Mimi felt herself in a slow burn. "Must we?" His ability to rip scabs off wounds was infuriating.

"You brought it up," he returned. "Always talking about negative messages, disapproval and judgment."

"I don't think my mother is quite as nefarious as you make her out to be."

Daniel's face twisted into an uncommon scowl. "As usual, you've managed to misconstrue what I mean."

"After all these years, Daniel, I think I understand exactly what you mean." And I'll have none of it, said the rigid face.

They continued the meal, consumed it in awkward silence, and Mimi felt it turn to stone in her stomach. She wanted to talk to Daniel about her confusion, about this thread of distrust and isolation woven into her cloth by her mother, but if he was going to be difficult, what was the purpose? Besides, it was impossible to discuss anything sensitive when you're on the defensive, and it seemed to her that he was. At the same time, Mimi was itching to explore all those red herrings her father had employed to keep his family at a distance — World War II, Korea, miscellaneous dramas concocted around money issues, social injustice, job insecurity. But now was clearly not the time.

"You're smiling," accused Daniel.

Mimi seemed startled by his accusation and then laughed. "Sorry, but I'm remembering how my dad was in absolute heaven throughout the McCarthy hearings. I can still see him: totally mesmerized, remaining for hours on end with his ear pressed to the radio." The smile faded as she also recalled how, like so many incidents, this one segregated him from his family. Whether it was a radio transmission or a newspaper held before his face, he lived in a world apart.

"My mom was openly resentful," observed Mimi. "Here she was, a woman ravaged by so much loss, and then in a way left abandoned by her husband's detachment." Toying with her fork, she tried to remember any kind of intimacy between her parents. Intimacy? she thought. They were never even friends.

Daniel's voice broke into her thoughts. "I always felt that as much as your dad made a life for himself here, he never really adjusted."

Mimi could not muster the energy to argue. Besides, argue what? Neither of her parents had ever fully adjusted to American life, although they felt very much American. Believing that she had said enough for one evening, she halfheartedly nibbled at her meal.

"You do know that I liked your father," stated Daniel. "Despite the fact that I always considered him a weird duck." Before Mimi could respond, he added, "What I mean is, he lived the way he chose." He popped the corner of a pita triangle into his mouth. "He was a nice guy, Mimi, just not a terrific role model for his daughter."

She looked across the table, recognized that this statement had been made with neither malice nor anger, but with absolute certainty. She mulled over the opinion, thought about the ways a daughter uses her father as a role model. Sarah, for example, whose father provided love and support, had sought and found a husband who offered the same. What if Sarah had had a father like Harold Zilber? Mimi knew the answer, had always known it: we seek what we know.

She was relieved when they made it through dinner without undue turbulence; relieved, too, when Daniel made no effort to extend the evening. Placing a good-night kiss on his cheek, she mumbled about getting an early start. Both of them knew that explanations were not necessary and that this was one of those times when nothing would click. It was better, safer, to separate before fuses were lit.

Early the next morning, with directions scribbled on a piece of scratch paper and taped to the faded dashboard of the Volvo, Mimi left home. Once she pulled onto the Ventura Freeway, she headed east through the San Fernando Valley, past Studio City and Burbank — where conspicuous high-rise glass buildings caused shards of deflected sunlight to hit her windshield. It wasn't until she was snaking through the interchange and traveling alongside Pasadena that she enjoyed her first sign of open road. Her first sense of being liberated from Los Angeles.

To her left, the lush San Gabriel Mountains loomed as one of the last reminders that urban blight and pollution were not mandatory. Testing the speed limit, she reveled in the lengthy stretches of empty highway. As she coasted along, the changing light and rare autumn colors both soothed and excited her senses, and she had to struggle not to allow her mind to shift into automatic pilot. "If you don't pay attention," she mumbled under her breath, "you'll end up in Las Vegas." Serenity turned to enthusiasm when thousands of spinning windmills, each one laboring to provide supplemental energy for Los Angeles, came into view.

Mimi followed the highway as it curled through the pass and found herself suddenly faced with the wonder and magnificence of the San Jacinto Mountains. Before she could fully adjust to the colors and shapes of the geography, to the scrub vegetation of the high desert, she was rolling into Palm Springs. After two cups of coffee at The Watering Hole, a place she and her classmates had frequented during rare college weekend escapes, she got back into the car and headed toward Rancho Mirage, home to the stars, the rich and the powerful.

She checked the directions twice to be sure the address was correct and then rolled to a stop before an iron gate that she estimated to be fifteen feet high. The gate was set into an equally high stucco wall topped by ornate terra-cotta tiles. Looking around for some kind of intercom system, she nearly jumped when a guard stepped up to the car. He waited for her to roll down the window.

"Name, please," he said, clipboard in hand.

"Zilber. Doctor Miriam Zilber." She heard how pretentious that sounded and blushed.

The man scanned the small list and asked for some photo identification. Mimi's first instinct was to protest, but she pushed that aside and produced her driver's license. As he compared photo to face, she flashed a counterfeit smile. Shoving the license into her purse, she mumbled, "Mata Hari never went through this." The gates swung slowly open and she drove forward.

She followed a cypress-lined drive, passed at least two tennis courts and a pool, and then pulled up to what she assumed was the house. Before she could climb out of the car, however, a man carrying a large rake rushed over. "Not here," he said, flashing a row of perfect teeth that were glaringly white against leathered skin. "Up there."

"Who lives here?"

"Staff," he explained. This smile persuaded Mimi that the teeth were new acquisitions.

She looked around approvingly. "So where do I apply for the next opening?" The man was suddenly ill at ease and forced a laughed. Mimi quickly thanked him and continued toward the house.

"Jesus Christ," she muttered, drawing up to the front door. The Volvo was barely out of gear before a young man leaped gazelle-like down the steps, flung open the door and helped Mimi out. In a fashion that would put most five-star hotels to shame, her bag was carried inside and she was taken to the most luxurious bedroom she had ever seen. She would have been perfectly happy to remain here, secluded and pampered, but the young man informed her that the others were waiting. He escorted Mimi down the stairs and into what he called "the family room," but what Mimi thought should have been called "the convention center." The only reason she was able to contain the Rivka Zilber Scowl of Disapproval was the tasteful elegance of the room. It had never occurred to Mimi that anything so cavernous could be intimate. She passed through the door and Charmayne Gibson rushed to meet her.

"You found us!" declared her hostess delightedly.

Mimi had to drag her gaze away from the amazing room. Bestowing on her hostess a warm and grateful smile, she responded, "Well, you're pretty hard to miss."

Charmayne sighed, as if having resigned herself long ago to the bother of unlimited wealth. Linking her arm through Mimi's, she directed them toward a table festooned with assorted pastries, fresh fruit, meats, cheeses, and beverages. "When I married Leland," she said, her voice low and almost conspiratorial, "we were college students on the East Coast. If I had known about this," she said, gesturing in a sweeping motion toward the opulence, "I'm not sure I would have fallen in love with him."

"Just your luck," commiserated Mimi, and then saw that the woman was serious. "You really didn't know?"

"His father paid for his education, but he was not lavish. On our first date, he actually borrowed two dollars! My friends at the dorm warned me that he was a gold digger." She laughed at the memory, her face glowing with delight as she pushed a mass of hair away from her tanned face.

Mimi looked at the woman, studied her for the first time. She was rather pretty, thin with those subtle jowls women have when there's no fat to support the skin. As much as she would have loved to hate her, to resent the affluence and complain to someone about the woman's need to impress, there was no basis: Charmayne Gibson was a knowledgeable scholar, clearly an unpretentious woman able to accept her wealth with grace and aplomb.

Charmayne led Mimi on a guided tour of the house and its environs. As each wonderful room or garden was exposed, Mimi thought of how Sarah would have enjoyed this, how much she wanted to share it with her. "You should've seen it," she imagined herself saying. "Turns out that Charmayne's married to Leland Gibson of Gibson Mining. My entire house would fit in her master-bedroom wing."

Mimi was tempted to ask Charmayne the whereabouts of their 2.3 perfect children, but kept her mouth shut. This was a nice woman, gracious and friendly. Was it her fault she was richer than Midas? When they returned to the living room, the hostess excused herself. Mimi wandered outside and followed a path leading to the pool. A man was walking alongside and dragging a long-handled leaf skimmer through the water. His worn blue jeans, Oxford-cloth shirt with sleeves rolled up to the elbows and deep tan identified him as the pool boy.

"Now that's a cushy job!" she announced, bending over and testing the water with her fingers.

The man smiled broadly and gestured toward a second skimmer leaning against the fence. "Try it," he suggested. "Very therapeutic, Zen-like."

"Really?" she responded, walking around the pool to approach him. "And is Zen your religion or your passion?"

"Oh, there are too many passions in this world to confine myself to one. Don't you agree?"

Mimi studied his face for a moment, tilted her head to one side as she did, and then released a most unladylike laugh. "You're Charmayne's husband, right?"

The man offered a slight bow. "At your service, Madam. And you are . . ."

"Mimi Zilber," she said, completing the circle until she was close enough to offer her hand.

"Oh-oh," he announced, returning the handshake. "The boss, yes? Well, I hope you've made yourself comfortable."

"In your humble home? I've never been more comfortable, thanks." After a quick good-bye, she returned to the house and joined her fellow professors.

The primary purpose of the retreat was social, with only a smattering of school work, which allowed Mimi time to luxuriate in her bedroom, or in the spacious warmth of her marble bathtub. Given the chance, she would have stayed in that tub for hours.

The tranquility of the weekend was invaded on several occasions when her mind wandered back to her childhood and the lives of her parents. Neither of them had ever seen such a home, much less imagined its existence. She wondered how her mother would react. Mimi was also visited by memories of the conversation she and Daniel had failed to have the night before. She pictured his face, saw that expression he always got when he was pushing for a relationship more intimate than what they now shared. It was a look that fell between frustration and hangdog sad. Could she give him more? She didn't know, but every instinct warned her away from further discussions about her family. Perhaps it was time to honor those instincts.

Mimi could not recall the last time she had taken a nap. As mid-afternoon rolled around, however, she felt such penetrating fatigue that a nap was inevitable. Excusing herself, she went up to her room and immediately fell into a deep and delicious sleep. Upon awaken-ing, she was surprised to see that it was nearly six. With great reluc-tance, and feeling as if she were being dragged against her will, she went downstairs. There, she found Charmayne and a handful of pro-fessors having tea in the dining room.

The woman's voice was low and pleasant as she apprised them of dinner. When she saw Mimi her face broke into a wide smile. "Having a nice rest?" she asked. "Because nothing is more relaxing than this desert air."

Mimi returned the smile, reminding herself that loyalty for Sarah did not preclude her from making new friends. They chatted for a few minutes and then she asked if she could use the phone. "I'll use my phone card," she added quickly.

Charmayne pointed toward a door that seemed more than sixty feet away. "No need for a card," she smiled. "It's one of those super-cheap lines. Practically free."

Mimi smiled her thanks and crossed the large room. When she opened the door, she found herself in a beautifully appointed study that managed to be both sumptuous and cozy. Making herself com-fortable in the leather chair pulled up to the burl-veneer desk, she called Daniel.

"I was just thinking of you," he said. "Didn't you go to Palm Springs?"

"Rancho Mirage."

"Well, excuse me," he joked. "Having lunch with the Reagans? Or is today set aside for the Sinatra family?"

"Actually, this place is so sumptuous that even the Sinatras would be jealous. No," she went on, "I just needed to talk." Having said this, nothing more would come. She hoped Daniel would pick up the rope, but his silence suggested that he was willing to let her hang her-self first. "Are you still there?" she asked, feeling more than guilty for making such a nasty assumption.

"I'm just waiting for you to give me some hint about why you called." There was no mockery in his voice, no recognizable sarcasm, yet it grated along Mimi's nerve endings.

Again she imagined a trap and again she warned herself away from it, in one breath admonishing herself for believing Daniel capable of trapping anyone, in the other reminding herself that he was an attorney and setting traps was his specialty. She regretted having made the call and desired only to bring it to a safe and expeditious conclusion. But she had been the one to barge in on Daniel's life; she had been the one to share so much with him, to insist that he listen. Perhaps the poor man had had enough. It was one thing to understand her, it was quite another to read her mind.

"Mimi," he finally said, "it's been a tough five months. You've lost Sarah, you're dealing with lots of issues around your family and where your life is going, so how about taking it easy on yourself for just one weekend?"

The suggestion made sense but she wasn't sure she could comply. "If you want to know the truth," she admitted, "I'm more concerned about taking it easy on you." Recognizing what a declaration of affection that statement was, she nearly hung up. With the words already out of her mouth, however, there was no choice but to forge ahead. "Daniel, I'm afraid that I'm turning into one of those angry women I try so hard to avoid." She heard him sigh and hoped it was out of sympathy rather than boredom or annoyance. She was afraid to ask. "I'll be fine," she added, and then winced at yet another pathetic attempt at bravado. Swiveling in the chair, she caught sight of her leg. Running down her calf was her first varicose vein. "I've really got to go," she mumbled. "The others are waiting. I'm sorry if I upset you."

"Please, don't."

Mimi examined the leg more carefully. So this was it, the beginning of what the French delicately call *entre deux âges*, middle age. She was looking straight down the barrel at another birthday, she had varicose veins, and only months earlier she had noticed those little rolls of fat that appeared each time she strapped on her bra. "God, Daniel, I feel like shit."

"Mimi, I love you."

"I love you too, Daniel, and I'm sorry I'm being so trying. You're a wonderful friend."

"You don't understand, Mimi. I love you." There was a lengthy silence. "Have I offended you?" he finally asked, his voice filled with concern.

Mimi could not answer. Tears obscured her view and she was hopelessly confused. Why was this declaration of love so painful? It was kindness she was hearing, not cruelty. "I'm not offended, of course not." Had she spoken the next thought—that more than anything she wanted Daniel to hold her, soothe her pain—he might have jumped into his car and arrived unannounced. Would that be so bad? She felt herself shrinking into the chair, a woman about to disappear.

When was the last time a man had professed his love? Her eyes were riveted to a place on the wall. When was the last time she felt lovable, much less deserving of love?

As if reading her mind, Daniel murmured her name with such sweetness that she squirmed. She wanted him by her side, yet she was grateful he was not. "I have to admit I don't feel very lovable, at least not at the moment." The admission surprised her, but only because it was so rare for Mimi to reveal her tender underbelly.

"Have you ever considered that your parents contributed to that?" Before she could respond, he quickly added, "Meaning your mother."

"Last night it was my father. Now you've got something against my mother?"

"Not something against her, but it seems that you've been so victimized by everything that's ever happened to her."

"I'm not sure I know what you mean." Mimi imagined Daniel glaring at her. Of course she knew what he meant!

"Fine," he responded. "I won't push." Before she could breathe a word, he added, "Yes, I will."

"This isn't the time."

"You're surrounded by colleagues?" There was a moment of silence. "Apparently not. Fine then. For starters, the way she interferes with your life and tries to alienate you from everyone. If Sarah hadn't loved you so much, your mother might have succeeded there as well. The difference between Sarah and me," he said, "is that she wouldn't stand for it. That's why your mother resisted her so much. Sarah held her ground and won." Mimi's silence bolstered his resolve to continue. "Do I dare mention how she has poisoned you against men, or taught you how unloving relationships can be? And, far be it from me to reveal how she's cheated you."

The words held back for decades were now spilling out of control. Mimi knew that nothing was going to stop Daniel from speaking his mind.

"Can you honestly tell me you've never wondered what your life might have been like if not for your mother and her tragedies?"

The noises in Mimi's ears were like gunshots. Of course she had wondered, but to hear Daniel point this out was too much.

"I loved you, Mimi. When we were kids, I was the one who wanted to be with you, to make a life with you."

She began to shiver. Covering her eyes, she pressed her palms against them. The darkness would not go away. It was as if every emotion she had ever felt, every anxiety and terror were rushing forward to assault her. "Stop, please." The silence in the room was funereal. She placed the phone on its cradle and returned to her room, grateful not to pass anyone in the corridors. Climbing into bed, she pulled the cover over her head, but no safety was to be found. Was being hurt by accident any less painful than being hurt on purpose? Mimi was in no condition to form an opinion.

The pain remained for hours, shifting occasionally into simmering resentment. What right did he have to make the revelation of her life's truths his own personal quest? Words and phrases continued to appear and then fade, like floating scraps of paper. Mimi had a vague recollection of an incident that had occurred more than twenty years before, when her mother had said something to Sarah, an offhanded comment that landed like the insult it was intended to be. When Mimi had tried to apologize, she was stunned by Sarah's response.

"I've had your mother up to here," she had announced, the cutting gesture she made across her throat both swift and clean. The two of them didn't speak for several days.

Mimi extricated herself from the covers and stumbled into the bathroom. As hot water ran into the tub, she stood and watched steam form on the mirror. This melodrama was wearing her out. And now, with Daniel on the attack, she was confused and frightened.

Submerged to her chin, she breathed deeply and experienced momentary relief. The air around her was so still that its silence pushed against her. A wonderful man had just professed his love, so why was she feeling such dread? Nothing he had said was reprehensible or ignoble, and yet there was such pain.

She managed to make it through dinner, primarily by using the old ploy of shifting her attention to whomever was speaking, and then nodding as if she were in agreement. But all the while she was thinking only of Daniel and how his words of love were so neatly juxtaposed with an ability to hurt and stun. Yes, that was it: Daniel had struck her with the blunt instrument of his love and she was stunned. So while the others continued their chatting, Mimi continued to nod, while at the same time commanding herself to remain clinical, analytical and clear-sighted.

As the evening wore on, her focus shifted to staying in control. No matter how powerful those surging emotions were, there was no way in hell she was she going to show her fragile side to these people! And especially when she felt stripped down and exposed to the world.

It was well after midnight before she was safely tucked under the feather-light comforter. With eyes closed, she began to view her life as one lengthy progression of empty spaces that she tried to fill with work, friends, and family. On very rare occasions, sex. But never passion, and certainly never commitment.

Exhausted, she strove to push it all from her mind and sleep. In fact she begged for sleep, threatened what she would do if it refused to come, but nothing helped. It was nearly three in the morning when she rushed into the bathroom, leaned over the toilet and became ill. Staring at the putrid mess, she wondered for just a moment if perhaps she had just eliminated a lifetime of painful memories. "Oh, please," she mumbled under her breath while padding back to bed. "You're in deep enough shit as it is, so cut the melodrama."

By the time sunrise was in its first stages she had managed to consider all viable options: she could take a sabbatical and travel; she could do a *La Strada* exit and disappear into the sea. Also on the list were selling her house and disappearing altogether or running off with Daniel. But how could she leave her mother and pretend that Nowy Życie, Auschwitz, and Sarah's death had never happened? On the edge of these thoughts lurked one disconcerting clarity: contrary to the adage, things really were etched in stone; we can no more revise history than we can be unborn. And while her mother had tried to spare her daughter the family's Auschwitz tragedy, her own tragedies had nevertheless created for Mimi a concentration camp of the spirit.

Dawn crept into the room. If sleep were to be had, it was now or never. Lying in the half-light, Mimi wondered if there would ever be a time in her life when she could walk away from her mother's history, separate herself from it: find the courage to disengage. But like her mother, she, too, had been lonely nearly every waking minute of her life.

Climbing out of bed, she walked to the window and looked out. There was already someone in the narrow garden separating the house from the pool. It was the man with the new teeth and he was planting flats of seedlings at five-thirty in the morning. When a sudden wind kicked leaves onto the nearby lawn, he jammed his hat onto his head and chased them down. His work, this process of eliminating debris from something planned and beautiful, appealed to Mimi. It was straightforward and uncluttered, representing a simplicity that, for the moment, she desperately craved.

She returned to bed and remained there until ten, most of the time spent in restless sleep. When she finally dressed and joined the others, there was no inquiry: they could see from the circles under her eyes how she had slept. And if someone had asked, what would she say? That she had been sleepless because her mother had reared her to a life of solitude? That while Rivka's violent history had shaped her daughter's attitudes about life, love, men, the girl-now-woman had offered no resistance? She knew the people in this room and decided that, like Daniel, few of them would let her off the hook.

She filled a plate with food and joined the others at the table. When she bit into the bagel she thought of Sarah, of bagels and cream cheese and Sunday brunch. Perhaps Sarah had been right after all: perhaps a therapist wouldn't hurt. As soon as the thought was formed, it was under siege. Mimi imagined herself blurting it out to her mother and Rivka responding, "A therapist? Why, do you think you're crazy?"

"Sorry if I'm rousing you from your thoughts," said Charmayne, leaning toward Mimi.

Mimi swallowed the last bite and returned the smile. "Musing," she explained. "The musings of a woman on vacation."

Charmayne accepted a cup of coffee from a colleague and turned her attention back to Mimi. "How would you feel about getting together one day for lunch? Or dinner, if you're available. My husband travels so much, and my evenings can get very lonely."

The eagerness in Charmayne's face instilled in Mimi a wonderful sense of belonging. "I'd like that very much," she responded. "I normally eat alone and I'd love the company."

"So there's no one special in your life at the moment?"

At the moment? Mimi nearly laughed, suppressing the urge to say something about that moment lasting for decades. "No," she admitted, "not at the moment." But there could be, she thought. Yes, there could.

She finished her breakfast in silence, and it was the most comfortable silence she had felt in a long time. She listened to the conversations around her, occasionally looked in the direction of the voices to give the appearance of participating, but all the while she was reveling in this new sensation that perhaps those vultures that had been circling overhead were out there looking for someone new to victimize.

CHAPTER TWELVE

❧Topanga Canyon, Spring 1985

SPRING SEMESTER was only weeks away and Mimi was already accepting accolades from members of her department. Who could recall such an outstanding job, such thorough and creative organization? Her greatest fan, the professor known less than a year earlier for his deep reservations about her appointment as department head, nearly gushed his admiration. Despite the praise, however, Mimi was still visited by a sense of stumbling through life, and that whatever good came her way was attributable more to happenstance than merit.

Charmayne had made good her offer and the two women had enjoyed many shared meals. It was a new experience for Mimi, building a friendship of trust with someone other than Sarah, but she found it nurturing and thoroughly enjoyable. She had told Charmayne about Daniel, about this lifelong and as-good-as-unconsummated affair. When the woman suggested they all get together — Mimi and Daniel, Charmayne and her husband — Mimi could only laugh nervously and declare that it was too soon.

Her mantra of "one more day," which had become the impetus urging her along from dusk to dawn, was becoming less forceful. While she continued to miss Sarah, the loss no longer hung around her like some weight she was required to tow. As for Daniel, they had gone on a few comfortable drives and taken several walks in the months past, and that intensity Mimi had felt had begun to diminish to a level of comfort. More a truce, in fact, but something she could handle. As if finally getting her message, he had backed slowly away. So slowly, in fact, that Mimi had hardly noticed. As for their angry exchange, it too had faded, becoming a fuzzy blur, a photograph out of focus. She was hardly aware that they hadn't spoken in weeks.

And Rivka? There were days when she asked, "Are you all right, dear?" as if sensing her daughter's shifting moods. Mimi's normal response was to force a bright smile, anything not to give herself away, but her mother rarely accepted the performance. Her expression declared "Something's in the air" and she reminded Mimi of a cat sniffing the air for the mouse.

Despite her occasional moments of agitation, Mimi felt herself changing, found herself less apt to lay the blame for everything at her mother's feet. Not that the woman was exonerated from responsibility for her daughter's neuroses, but the concept of "Blaming the Mother" no longer washed. Mimi was fascinated not only by this process of letting her mother off the hook, but by her increased understanding of the woman who had for so long rubbed her like a pair of ill-fitting shoes.

Mimi and Sarah had shared wonderful laughs about motherhood, the latter swearing that mothers fell into two categories. "There's the mother who gazes upon her baby and croons that giving birth was the most joyful experience of her life," Sarah explained. "And then there's the mother who clutches her baby to her breast and whispers that childbirth was agony beyond description but, God, it was worth the pain." On Mimi's fortieth birthday, she called Sarah and announced, "I've got it all figured out. My mother isn't mean, she's just suffering from a very long-term postnatal depression."

Mimi was seated at the desk in her study, last-minute classroom assignments for the summer session spread out before her. The phone rang, but she ignored it. As the message came across the answering machine, she heard Daniel's voice.

"It's been too long, Mimi. How about we go for a ride?"

She was tempted to pick up the phone but decided against it, relieved when he finished his message and hung up.

It had been more than ten months since Sarah's death, a lifetime. Mimi had come to the realization some time ago that this search into her family's history, this unweaving of such a complicated tapestry, was as much for her own survival as it was to keep Sarah's voice alive.

The time between the cancer diagnosis and Sarah's death had been so painfully brief, yet so much changed between the two old friends. Up to the time of that diagnosis, Sarah had given freely of her advice, but always with a certain caution. Being told that her life was nearly over, however, was all the permission she needed to become brutally honest. It was as if every change that needed to take place in Mimi's life needed to happen now, while Sarah was still alive. Because if they waited, there was a good chance the changes never would come.

Mimi leaned back in her chair and stared out over the back garden. More than one year had passed since Sarah had broken the news, one year since they were visiting over coffee and doing what they always did: muse, give each other unwanted advice, swap gossip. Mimi sensed that something was amiss because Sarah kept compressing her lips and rubbing them together, something she did only when trying not to cry. Whatever Mimi was expecting to hear, it had nothing to do with losing her lifelong friend.

But how do you tell a woman who shares your spirit, who's so close that it's sometimes difficult to determine where you begin and she ends, that sometime in the near future she will be left alone? All Mimi could remember was the sensation that, while listening to Sarah's words, her own heart was giving out. As soon as the words *pancreatic cancer* were spoken, the nature of their friendship was altered. One quietly stated diagnosis and the weight of the friendship shifted. It was now Mimi who offered support, who provided strength and the foundation for living day to day. She would be the one to muster her talents, to take those lessons learned from the fleeting experience called life and apply them to the loving task of creating an infrastructure for the remainder of Sarah's life.

Mimi tried to push away her recollections of a dying friend and get back to work. When that failed, she tried to sleep. At two o'clock in the morning she got dressed and drove to her office. The canyon road was deserted, as were all stretches of freeway leading over the hills and along Sunset Boulevard to the campus.

She was fully absorbed in the analysis of a doctoral thesis when she heard a rapping on the outer door. Its persistence made it impossible to ignore. "Who the hell. . . ." she mumbled, getting up from her desk. Pushing away thoughts of invasion and death, she stalked into the main office, turned the lock and yanked the door open wide. "What!" she demanded.

It was the assistant chairman of the department. "Forgot my keys," he apologized, adding, "And what the hell are you doing here?"

Mimi was too tired for a clever comeback. The best she could do was, "Couldn't sleep."

Leonard pressed his lips together and nodded. His wife had died several years earlier. "I do everything possible to avoid home," he admitted.

Mimi studied the face of this scholar, a man not prone to exposing his private life. "It's hard, I know."

He sifted through the letters that were stuffed in his mail cubicle. "To be honest, I go home when I'm ready to drop." He seemed embarrassed by this disclosure.

The moment of intimacy passed quickly and they adjourned to their respective offices. A short time later, he reappeared at Mimi's door. "Got a minute?"

She smiled and cleared away stacks of books, papers, and correspondence from the second chair. Once he was seated, the man could not meet her stare. Instead, he focused laserlike on a few objects sitting on her desk. When he came to the graduation photo of Joanna, he seemed confused.

"My niece," she explained. "The daughter of my dearest friend."

He pulled on his lower lip, nodded, crossed and uncrossed his legs. "I can't seem to adjust to her death," he finally said.

Mimi listened, nodding occasionally, which seemed to soothe him.

"I've decided to take a sabbatical. At least a year," he added. "Perhaps longer, if I need it." Having revealed more than intended, he stood and walked to the door. "And by the way," he added, his hand on the knob. "I might not be coming back."

Mimi watched him leave, heard the click of his office door. She tried to return to her work but told herself that coming here had been a foolish mistake. After several more failed attempts, she packed up her papers and left. Instead of heading home by freeway, she followed Sunset Boulevard out to the beach. What was lovelier than the Pacific Ocean illuminated by the moon? In all the years she had traveled that road, not once had she failed to experience surprise when the boulevard terminated at the water. And once again, in this moon-reflected splendor at four in the morning, she was moved. She pulled off the highway and rolled down the window, thought about how the dull music of waves building and crashing along the coast sounded more beautiful than Mozart.

Returning to the road, she continued north, frustrated by the string of unimaginative houses interfering with her view of the water. When she arrived at the turn for Topanga Canyon, she took the curve too fast and had to swerve to avoid running into a tow truck hauling a mist-green Silver Cloud, its bumper scraping against the asphalt. She was too tired to imagine what a Rolls was doing breaking down at this hour. As she headed up the canyon, she savored the sense of dangerous freedom that comes from taking curves too fast.

By the time Mimi arrived home, there was just enough time to grab a few short hours of sleep, dress and drive back to the campus. She made it through three lectures and several hours of thesis counseling and then headed for home. As if the Volvo had suddenly developed a mind of its own, it changed direction and turned eastward, toward Boyle Heights. Fine, she thought, I'll drop by and see how Mama is doing. Instead, she found herself buying a ticket, a medium box of popcorn and taking a center seat in the same movie theater she and Sarah had frequented during nearly every Saturday afternoon of their youth. By five o'clock the place was still empty, so she munched the popcorn and settled in for the film.

The opening credits began to roll and Mimi burst into laughter. How stupid not to have realized that the film would reflect the changing neighborhood. It was in Spanish.

She sat through both features.

When she arrived home, there were two messages. The first one, from Daniel, sounded very much like a cloaked apology. "You're forgiven," she replied, erasing it and moving on to the second. Again, Daniel's voice. "I know it's been tough," he acknowledged. "And I know that I haven't always been as, uh, responsive as you would like. But that doesn't mean I don't care, or that I don't love you."

A feeling of wariness came over Mimi and she stood perfectly still as he continued.

"So I was thinking about it, about us, and, well, what would you say to our living together? I know it's sudden . . ." he chuckled nervously. "But then, how sudden can it be after loving someone for nearly thirty years? God, I feel so stupid leaving this message! That's what I hate about answering machines. You don't have the option to erase your message! Wait, there is some way to do it. . . .shit! I'll have to find my directions. Listen, here's the deal: you move in with me and then we'll see how that goes and . . . damn! Here I am fumbling and bumbling along like some idiot . . . never mind, fuck it, I'll talk to you later. Call me, promise?"

The message left Mimi with so many emotions. Sadness, confusion, humor, hope, all of it rushed through her. Which one would win out, she had no idea. Despite open windows and a respectable draft, the air around her was stifling. "I should have stayed at school," she mumbled. Then again, did it really matter where she was if she could be so easily found?

Her world was feeling almost surrealistic, spinning and changing form before her eyes. It reminded her of her theory about airplanes: that they actually levitated, hovered at thirty-five thousand feet and waited until the earth underneath rotated to the right airport. When everything was lined up properly, the plane descended with a roar.

Daniel expected an answer.

Mimi tried to imagine how he would react when she declined his offer. Polite resignation, no doubt. Or worse, tolerance. And what would she say to this tolerant man? Simply smile in her most womanly fashion and say, "Thank you, but no." And if she said yes, then what? It wasn't like buying a house or a car; there were no assurances, no paragraphs regarding full disclosure. How could she know if it would work? Sarah always said that love was like a latex diaphragm: you never really knew if it was foolproof until you tried it out. Sarah. If only she were here to lend support. Where could she turn, to her mother? She imagined Rivka's face, those determined eyes.

As if someone else were speaking, Mimi blurted out, "So *that's* why she didn't go to the funeral! God, I am so stupid!" If Sarah could become ill and die, then so could Rivka's only child. Mimi shuddered at her failure to recognize the obvious.

Pouring herself a glass of wine, she wandered into the living room and sat on the sofa. When she looked around, she realized that, despite the fact that she loved this room, she hardly used it. Meals were grabbed in the kitchen, work took place in the study. There was no time for television or fires, and no inclination toward invited guests. Leaning into the sofa, Mimi pulled her thoughts back to her mother and Rivka's refusal to attend the funeral.

Why this memory now? Because Mimi had been searching for a fit, some connecting thread, and there it was. The discovery made her smile. "Priorities," she mumbled. In the case of her father, they rarely included his family. He loved his daughter, was proud of her many accomplishments, but he never expected anything of her. Life, he believed, was just too unpredictable, too damned hard.

As for Rivka, she wanted her daughter to have what had been denied her: education, love, independence. Wanted it so powerfully that she nearly sabotaged it.

Mimi wandered out onto the deck and began inspecting the plants. The agapanthus were snail-infested again. Following the footpath that ran between a gnarled oak and a cluster of manzanitas, she came to the little shoulder-high shed her gardener had convinced her to purchase during the last storm. He was right: the tools were still dry and rust-free. She retrieved the box of snail bait and carried it back to the deck. "Eat up, you little fuckers," she murmured, spilling a neat line at the base of each plant. She replaced the bait and returned to the house. What felt suddenly right was a nice little fire, a good book, and that cozy spot in the corner of the couch.

The oak log was ablaze, Mimi was comfortably ensconced, but there was no way she could concentrate on the book. Daniel's offer had come like a jolt. She considered calling him to decline, but he would expect, and he certainly deserved, an explanation. Fine, she thought. I'll tell him that I don't love him and have no desire to live with him. A voice in her head responded, Well, that's less painful than admitting that you're scared. Or that you feel undeserving.

Mimi tried to push away the voice. She closed her eyes and recalled when she was a child and believed in her heart of hearts that everything taking place in the world was her fault: war, earthquakes and other natural disasters. She could even remember her mother anxiously awaiting the rattle of the mailman in the downstairs foyer. The moment he arrived everyone in the building rushed down to check the mail. They said they were hopeful of finding just one surviving relative, but even then Mimi knew the truth: they rushed to the mailbox because there was an urgency to receive all the bad news and be done with it. It reminded her of the urgency she had felt as a child in school during practice fire drills. The teachers always reminded them that it was only a drill, but as soon as the siren sounded the children were herded out as if the flames were inches behind them and they were all about to die. That experience left Mimi with her heart beating wildly in her chest for hours.

Returning to the kitchen, she brewed a mug of herbal tea. If nothing else, she needed to sleep. After two hours of CNN and a bad film, she commanded herself to bed. Lying in the dark, she understood what it was that she had been trying to get at all along: feelings of panic, the sense of impending danger, powerful emotions that existed at the core of her life. It was the most logical explanation for why she never dared marriage and family. Malka, Fredl, Rivka, Mimi.

She stared into the darkness. Imagine living for more than forty years with the belief that there was no point to marriage and family because one day, like all the women in her family, she would lose everything and be left alone.

CHAPTER THIRTEEN

⅋ Topanga Canyon, Spring, 1985

M IMI DRAGGED HERSELF from the bed into the shower with enormous weights attached to both ankles. There was no mystery as to why she felt so awful: she was one day away from the first anniversary of Sarah's death. In twenty-four hours she would be standing at the grave, confronted with the inscription on the head-stone. The undeniable truth, substance. Physical evidence. The cere-mony was intended as closure, but Mimi was not prepared to close anything.

Adding to this strain was that she and Daniel had not spoken for nearly a month, not since that call when she explained as clearly and unemotionally as possible that she needed time. And not only time, she told him, but breathing space so that she could get through a painful time that she absolutely believed was coming to its conclusion. When Daniel had understood—had gone so far as to wish her well in her quest—her expression of gratitude was heartfelt and tearful.

The shower was hot and biting against her and she considered staying there until the service had been completed. Mimi knew all about water conservation laws, and she certainly had no problem with bricks in the toilets and timers on the sprinklers. But she'd be damned if she'd take dribbling showers! A good, long, hot shower was her constitutional right. As far as she was concerned, it fell clearly under the *pursuit of happiness* clause.

She attacked her skin with the loofah, but not even the biting, stinging pain could deflect her thoughts from what was coming.

Finally resigning to the inevitable, she turned off the water and wrapped herself in her largest towel. Stepping out of the shower, she considered slipping and breaking an arm. Certainly that would preclude her from returning to the cemetery. But then, what if she broke her neck instead, or her back? She would be incapacitated, unable to work or care for herself. Her mother would come to live with her! No, better to simply dress, drive out to that damned place and get it over with.

"It's not until tomorrow," she reminded herself, giving herself a brief glance in the mirror. "It will come and go and be finished, so stop obsessing!"

Despite her efforts to calm herself, Mimi was restless and on edge. She had promised her mother that she'd stop by, but she felt so distracted, so at loose ends. Wrapping herself in a terry robe, she made mental notes regarding her schedule for the day: final exams to be graded; student complaints to be lodged. And then she needed to record every grade and get over to campus to hand over the four-page computerized grading form. If she dropped it off on her way to her mother's, she could be done with it.

She lost the inner argument against breakfast. After fetching the morning paper from the driveway, she marched into the kitchen and prepared a mug of high-octane coffee and a bagel. But no cream cheese, she reminded herself, those last thirteen pounds driving her nuts. Carrying her little breakfast to the table, she settled down. The *Times* spread before her, two rabbits scampered by the French door. A morning sun was forcing its light through various branches and shrubs to create a peaceful, serene setting. In this quiet, Mimi was able to forget for just a moment the service, Daniel and his declaration of love, her mother.

Breakfast dishes in the dishwasher, counter sponged and ready for the next paltry meal, Mimi headed to the bathroom to brush her hair and apply some light makeup. When she opened the medicine cabinet, the contents of an entire shelf tumbled into the sink. "Shit!" she sputtered, staring down at the pharmaceutical debris. Grabbing the wastebasket, she accomplished a quick sort-and-dump, keeping everything usable, tossing away the rest: bandages with torn wrappers; eye drops turned milky yellow; mysterious tubes with sticky emanations; half-opened things. At the bottom of the pile was an unopened box of condoms. "What's the point?" she sighed, tossing them into the basket. The gesture caused her to think of Daniel, but she brusquely pushed that thought away. The effort it took, however, surprised her. Was this a rejection of his offer, a dismissal? Or perhaps she was rejecting the possibility of preserving his friendship as well.

She looked at the contents remaining in the cabinet, considered that she could either clean out the whole thing or leave for her mother's. The decision was an easy one. She emptied out the remainder of the cabinet and washed off the shelves. When everything salvageable was returned to its place, she hunted through the wastebasket and retrieved the condoms. Holding the box, she noticed an expiration date stamped on the flap. The condoms had expired three years ago. Mimi stared at the date, transfixed, unsure how to respond.

Had she finally reached the pinnacle of pathos? She smiled, but it was as much irony as humor. Those condoms meant something, were a reflection of her life. Her unloved, untouched life. No lover to hold, no one to caress. True, she thought, but no one to obstruct my way, either.

She closed the cabinet. Had Sarah been here to witness this folly, what would she have said? That it was sad, pathetic, another indication of how desperately lonely Mimi had become? Mimi considered that for a moment and then laughed aloud. Hell, if Sarah were here, they'd be sharing fits of laughter, bent over in spasmodic, convulsive chortling as they held onto each other and gasped for air! It's not that box of condoms that's so pitiful, thought Mimi. It's that I can't laugh at myself anymore.

Not at herself, not at anything. And she couldn't recall the last time she had.

Mimi wandered into the bedroom and began to dress. What would Sarah say if she were here? Hopefully, she would breathe a sigh of relief that her friend was making progress. If it was true that everything had its season, perhaps Mimi's had finally arrived.

The day was glorious and Mimi almost resented having to spend even one minute in her mother's musty apartment. She considered taking Rivka out for a drive, but she was preoccupied, sorting through so many issues. Besides, if anyone could pick up the scent and expose

Mimi's thoughts, it would be her mother, the one person she wanted most to keep at arm's length.

Mimi drove toward Boyle Heights, her mind so focused on the events of the past week that she accidentally took the exit leading to Griffith Park. The park brought back wonderful memories of family picnics and concerts. She recalled an outing to the Greek Theater, sitting with her parents on hard benches, with deli sandwiches in the picnic basket at their feet. They laughed and ate, joined the audience in one voice singing "Mathilda" with Harry Belafonte. Nestled between her parents, Mimi had felt like a star.

Griffith Park also conjured up memories of Saturday-night interludes, a handful of high school and college boyfriends, some wonderfully passionate moments, and then trying to hide the purple marks on her neck. Her mother had accused her of being bad. But how could something bad feel so good?

Mimi parked near a grove of eucalyptus and wandered into the park. It was as peaceful as she remembered, the groves of trees as inviting as when she was a child. Her mother had been anxious, her daughter wandering like this, fearful of murderers lurking behind trees, evil men jumping out at her, armed with a deadly knife, a gun, a penis.

Mimi found a cushy patch of grass. When she lowered herself onto it, the effort reminded her that she was being ambushed by middle age. She stretched out, the leafy branches overhead filtering the blue sky. Relaxing, dozing, staring into shrubs, across the chimneys of what were once considered the most luxurious homes in Los Angeles, she realized how tired this introspection was making her. Today, however, it felt like a good tired, the kind that comes from a job well done. Her family thread was less knotted now, its course through the intricate Gershon-Rabinoff-Zilber tapestry easier to follow. Whether it was first tainted by Szulen's death and an inconsolable young Fredl, or by events that occurred long before Fredl and her family, there was no way of knowing. What Mimi did know was that into the motif had been woven a thread of pain and loss, a thread of tragedy that permeated all of their lives, including her own. But she was an only child, meaning she was fated to drag that tapestry all alone through a life she now believed had been half-lived.

Mimi rolled onto her stomach and rested her cheek on her forearm. There was a professor in her department, a tough old gal who had lost her adolescence in Auschwitz. She explained to Mimi once that she survived by taking the horrors of her life, placing them in an imaginary box, wrapping that box in silk and carrying it tucked under her arm. It was always there, but it was never permitted to obstruct her life. Her husband, on the other hand, had draped his camp history over his back and dragged it wherever he went. "Who can live with such heavy burdens?" she had asked Mimi. Who, indeed. The woman had divorced the man years earlier.

When the air started turning cold, Mimi gathered herself and walked back to the car. Driving down from the park, she thought of Daniel's offer, of whether or not she could accept someone into her organized and predictable life. She pondered the possibilities, and then questioned why predictability was so damned important. It was about safety, she thought. I need to feel safe, have everything neat and predictable.

Predictable? Then there would be no surprises! She glanced at herself in the rearview mirror. "More like your mother every day," she complained to the woman staring back. "Rivka hates surprises." The peacefulness of her brief respite at the park vanished and in its place came a flood of thoughts and rejoinders, criticisms. Mimi found it difficult to concentrate on driving while being assailed by these revelations.

If you live your life only to be safe, what's the purpose? After all, a life lived in absolute safety is a life barely half-lived. There it was again! This half-lived thing was too prevalent to suit her, yet she could not resist its pull. No one wants to be told that time has been wasted. Wasted time was a wasted life. What did she think, that everything up to now had been air, a void larger than life itself? And that she could choose to begin living, really living, whenever it suited her?

The entire process was making her angry. If she bought into this, believed her own accusations, then she was negating her life. A life she was living as best she could!

Daniel's voice inveigled its way into her thoughts and she remembered something he had said months earlier. Was it true? Had she tried to use Sarah's death as an excuse for a life barely lived? Because that's what Daniel was saying. Not love him because he might be her last chance, but because it could be her beginning.

Mimi was bone-tired and she wondered if fatigue was actually a precursor to surrender.

She arrived in front of her mother's apartment and turned off the engine. Rivka was the last of the original tenants, the survivor. What would life be without her? She climbed out of the car and walked toward the entrance. There was a time when she had been a child of five emulating her beloved mother, and then a girl of ten, the personification of everything good and pure. As a teenager of sixteen, Mimi had been convinced that her mother was Satan in disguise, a woman existing for the sole purpose of embarrassing and humiliating her daughter.

Mimi glanced up to where her mother awaited her, a fragile old woman with gnarled hands and stiff knees; a woman who knew more about loss and suffering than most people could imagine. A woman who was of no solace to her only child. Mimi entered the foyer and began climbing the stairs, vaguely aware of the tears on her face. Was she such great solace to her mother? None at all. She stopped climbing, one foot on the next step, body leaning. No solace. The thought made her back ache, her calves cramp.

And what of the solitude? Mimi knew that she had allowed it to happen, had made the choice to be alone. A floodgate opened and she was forced to sit on the stairs. She knew very well that Rivka had never expected the prince; it was Mimi who had hoped, waited. Emotions caused her to cover her face. She had always considered misery her birthright, and yet how many of her choices had truly been forced on her by her mother? Or by a family history fraught with pain? The questions lifted her from the step and supported her as she climbed to the second floor. It was time to set things straight. As much as she dreaded going inside, she pushed her key into the lock and opened the door. "Mama?" she called out, entering the apartment. It seemed empty.

"Is that you, dear?" came a feeble reply from the bedroom.

Mimi wanted to announce that the prodigal daughter was finally returning after a long absence, but she did not. That would be disagreeable, unkind. Remember the history, she told herself. Remember

the bones. She entered the bedroom and found Rivka in her house-
coat and stretched out on the bed. "Mama, are you ill?"

Rivka lifted her head from the pillow. "No, I'm fine." She lowered
her head with equal effort.

The melodrama was not lost on Mimi. Things are different, she
told herself. New patterns are being established and it will take time.
"I'm glad," she murmured, and bent over the bed to kiss her mother's
cheek.

Rivka reached out and touched her arm. "Will you stay?"

The hopefulness pricked directly into Mimi's guilt. "For a while,"
she murmured, lowering herself onto the bed. "But then I have to go,
I've got plans." She forced a smile.

Rivka raised her head again, this time with little effort. "Plans?"

Yesterday Mimi would have reminded her mother that, despite
what she believed, she still had a life — even if Sarah was dead. "Don't
worry," she said. "I'll prepare you a nice dinner before I leave." She
stood and moved toward the kitchen.

"You'll leave a number where I can reach you."

Mimi returned to the foot of the bed. "I'm a middle-aged woman,
Mama. Do you really think that's necessary?"

Rivka's eyebrows drew together and her eyes became watery. She
looked at her hands, fingered the blanket. "It's for me," she mumbled.
"Not for you."

Mimi heard the fear, reacted to the plaintive tone that tapped
directly into her heart. More guilt, she told herself, and then thought,
No, not guilt. Not anymore. This would be different. Now that she
saw, could push aside the resentment she had harbored for this
woman who had been an intruder into her private life, compassion
was allowed to surface. "It's for me," her mother had said. So many of
her friends were long dead. Who was there for her, if not her daughter?

Mimi picked up the morning paper from the bed and scanned an
article. "You know," she said from behind the paper, "You can always
leave a message on my machine. I check it quite often."

"But what if something happens?"

Safe behind the barrier, newspaper raised and jaw clenched, she
said nothing. And then she thought of her father and dropped the

paper onto the bed. The mother was worried; the daughter needed to assure. She resented having to be accountable because she was an adult, but at the same time she understood that she was the center of this woman's circumscribed universe. When she rested a hand on her mother's leg, it was reed-thin and vulnerable. "Mama," she suddenly said, "there's something I want to tell you." Rivka studied her daughter's eyes and waited, wispy hairs floating about her face, softening the fine wrinkles, the uncompromising mouth. "Daniel has asked me to live with him."

Rivka pushed away the covers and climbed out of bed. Picking up her robe, she covered her frail body. "I hope he wasn't disappointed when you refused." Tying the belt, she stepped into her furry slippers and crossed the room.

The response wounded a place already bruised by guilt. And yet surely her mother had bruises that went even deeper. "I haven't refused, not yet."

Rivka faced her squarely, chin raised in that regal manner which suggested that the offer need not be dignified by a response. At the same time her cheeks quivered and her eyes clouded over. Sadness grew within Mimi as the seconds ticked by, as these two women groped for the wisdom or the kindness to guide them toward a loving place. In that split second she saw herself from a distance, a second Mimi watching how rigid she must appear, defiant and adolescent. She was struck with a truth so painful that she nearly pressed her fingers to her mouth. It was so simple: her mother was afraid of losing her. And not to death, but to love. Grief and compassion flooded over Mimi and she stepped forward, drawing the old woman into her arms. "I'm not your little girl anymore," she murmured. "This is my life, Mama, and however I live it, it will always include you." She felt her mother's body soften, was buoyed by what she interpreted as acquiescence. She kissed her mother's forehead. "I honestly don't know what I'm going to do, but you have to trust me. Can you do that?"

The silence jarred her, made her fear that perhaps she had given her mother the very opening she had hoped to avoid. Forcing the thought away, reminding herself that this was a very old woman, a fragile old woman, she waited. And as she waited, she felt shadowed by anxiety, felts scabs being torn from old wounds.

Mimi sat her mother on the bed and took the chair across from her. This was no trap; it was an old woman struggling with conflict. Mimi sat quietly and waited, telling herself again and again that mothers have a right to know about their daughters' choices.

At the same time, Rivka was looking at her daughter and her expression spoke volumes. Her eyes spoke hope, a mother's wish that her child might find the happiness that had long eluded her. In those eyes Mimi saw kindness, saw *I know that your journey has been a hard one. And if it's Daniel who can bring you home, then so be it.*

When Mimi was certain her mother was comfortable, she went into the kitchen and prepared dinner. With a casserole in the oven, she returned to the bedroom, kissed the old woman and swore to call before bedtime. Rivka offered a dry cheek without protest, but then she held her daughter in a tender embrace.

At three in the morning Mimi was seated at the kitchen table grappling with questions and doubts. She was finding it difficult to dredge up the energy required to forge ahead. Fatigue and aching muscles were becoming the obstacles separating her from logic and clear solutions. At the same time, a part of her questioned whether such solutions actually existed. "You don't unravel a tapestry of that size and complexity without tremendous effort," she reminded herself. "And you certainly don't deconstruct and analyze its components without a fight!" After consuming one more cup of herbal tea and a hefty spoonful of peanut butter, she turned off the lights and headed for bed.

While Mimi was tossing and turning, Rivka was closing her novel and placing it on the bedside table. She was too tired to concentrate on the words, although she had been trying for hours. With hands folded across her chest she tried to relax, but everything about her appearance suggested tension: rigid body, short breaths, expressionless face. She turned her gaze toward the hall and half-expected her Miriam to walk into the room. Hearing the click of a door, she raised her head to greet her child. But it was only Mrs. Rodriguez emptying her trash. Old people don't sleep, thought Rivka. They can't afford to waste the time. And then she heard a car engine and went into the living room to investigate. Pulling back the curtain, she pressed her face against the glass, knobby fingers gripping the wooden sill for support.

Rivka craned to see the street below. She caught sight of a car moving up Soto Street, past houses and apartments once belonging to people she knew, but it was not Mimi. "She'll come back," she murmured, her breath creating a circle of vapor against the pane. At that precise moment Rivka bore a striking resemblance to her mother, to the young Fredl standing in her widow's threads, looking through the window in her little house in Nowy Życie, grieving over the death of her husband.

Rivka watched the car disappear around the corner. Mimi had disappeared just like that, had grown and left, never to return. The only child of Rivka Zilber, the only child of Rivka Rabinoff Langer Zilber; the only daughter of the only daughter had driven away; the only child had thought of herself first. Blinking into the darkness, Rivka pulled a handkerchief from the pocket of her robe and dabbed at eyes so pale they seemed transparent. She shuffled over to Harold's chair and eased herself down. Sitting ramrod straight, she stared into a dim light and had the sensation that someone had bracketed all those years of motherhood and then had erased everything within the brackets. Daniel Kirsch, she thought. Hearing the judgment in her voice, she forced herself to acknowledge that he had been such a nice boy.

Rivka studied the high-school graduation photo perched on the little table next to the chair. "Will you be happy?" she asked, as if the decision were already made. "Will you?" She waited for a response, waited a long time, and then stood with considerable effort and shuffled into the kitchen. "Mimi told me not to worry," she explained, as if someone were nearby. "She says everything will be fine. She says she loves me. Of course she does." She moved across the linoleum floor and fetched the sugar bowl. "What would Bayla think if she were here?" She dropped a teaspoon of sugar into the cup, returned to the stove and lit a match. "Bayla," she called out, her hand hovering over the burner. "Do you think my Mimi will be happy?" That she had not seen her friend for nearly seventy years changed nothing. Sensing heat from the match, she put it to the burner and waited for Bayla's response. Head cocked, listening, a light suddenly appeared on her face. Clasping her hands, she whispered, "Yes, from your mouth to God's ears!"

Rivka felt elation. Filling the teapot, she shifted it onto the burner. "Everything will be fine!" she assured herself, leaning heavily into the counter. "Bayla says everything's fine and Mimi promises we'll be together." She waited for the water to boil, pushing wispy strands of hair away from her face. Her Miriam was smart; she would know exactly what to do. Smart, and from strong stock. From a grandmother who moved her family across Russia, and a mother courageous enough to steal travel documents from a dead woman.

The teapot's whistle caught her attention. Pouring water into the cup, Rivka recalled the joy of riding with Mendel on his business trip to Zhitomir and wondered if such things happened again, perhaps in another life. She checked that the tea bag was fully immersed and stirred slowly, contemplatively, the hot fluid eddying around the spoon. In that moment her mind was free of thought: no analogies drawn; no metaphors created. Seized by tiredness, she crossed to the table, placed the cup and saucer on the shiny surface and lowered herself into the chair. "I shouldn't worry," she said, studying the thin column of rising steam. "Isn't that what Mimi said? That it will be fine?" Taking a cautious sip, she sighed. "I only want her to be happy," she mumbled. "Is that so terrible? Why do children always act like it's so terrible when parents want happiness for them? Wanting my only child to be happy, this is not such a crime."

Rivka sighed again, only this time it was the sound of contentment. She was tired now, perhaps her body would allow her a few hours of needed rest. Setting the cup squarely onto the flowered saucer, her mouth curved into a hopeful little smile. She returned to bed. Within minutes she was fast asleep.

CHAPTER FOURTEEN

&⁊ *Topanga Canyon, Spring 1985*

FIVE O'CLOCK in the morning and Mimi concluded that insomnia was to be a permanent companion. With emotions too poignant, too heartfelt, and arriving in waves that threatened to pull her under, she dared not sleep. Driving away from Boyle Heights, she had foolishly believed herself clear of those emotions, and yet this force was now pulling her along so quickly that she expected to fall. Finally surrendering to wakefulness, she groped her way into the bathroom. The face in the mirror was haggard, belonging to someone far too old to be middle-aged; a woman no man would want. Or so she had thought.

The day before, when she had returned from a visit with her mother, Mimi was surprised to find another Daniel message. "Call me," it had said, the abruptness as startling as it was annoying. She had done as she was told. "It's about time," he chastised. "I left that message what seems like years ago. I thought you were dead."

"No, very much alive." How she felt was another story, but she decided not to elucidate.

In the ensuing silence, she heard judgment, angry judgment.

"You don't want to live with me or share my life, fine. But at least have the decency to respond."

"But I did respond! I told you that I needed time, remember?" When he said nothing, she added, "I've had a lot on my mind."

"And I haven't. You know, Mimi, you don't own the exclusive rights to suffering."

"Meaning?"

"Meaning we've all got problems, tragedies. You live with them, you don't let them control every waking, breathing second of your life."

"Sarah died, in case you forgot."

"Thanks for the reminder." His voice was cutting. "Unlike you, I've never lost someone I really loved. My parents and my wife don't count."

Before Mimi had been able to form a response, decide between shame and indignation, the line had gone dead.

A phone call at five in the morning was not going to make this right.

Emotions churned inside her, yet when she tried to push Daniel out, the image of Sarah slipped quickly in. Stretched out on the sofa with a forearm draped over her eyes, she wondered if she would ever find peace. It had been easier before, when she was oblivious and numb. When you don't feel, you don't suffer.

Like mother, like daughter.

The room was dark, a sliver of light filtering in from the light on the deck. Lying there, she imagined her mother's footsteps, considered the possibility that her mother had been born angry. Angry because Mimi had grown out of her expensive tap shoes too quickly; angry that little Mimi was too fat, too smart; angry that her daughter had never married the prince.

Mimi was jolted by her own acute sense of anger. Perhaps she had made herself the prisoner and her mother, a woman who desired for her daughter the happiness she had never known, was the designated warden. But what had been her crime?

In a strange way, revealing Daniel's offer to her mother had loosened the yoke that had been hanging around her neck. Perhaps now she was free to make decisions with her mother's knowledge and without her mother's approval. Perhaps now she could show the same kindness she had shown a dying friend. Visiting was not enough; her mother needed tenderness and reassurance. Who didn't?

The earliest signs of dawn crept up from below the deck, casting a soft light against the house. But the air was heavy with humidity, thick with moisture and the promise of rain.

It was time to move on.

A shower, a leisurely coffee and toast—both of which settled into her stomach like a twenty-pound lead weight—and it was suddenly morning. The last time she had pulled an all-nighter was in college, but she was younger then, more resilient. Had it been any other day she would have gone back to bed and slept until noon.

Mimi climbed into the car, turned the ignition and cautioned herself to stay alert. Driving down the canyon road was perilous enough; doing it with no sleep was downright half-witted. Tuning into the local all-news station, she drove the distance between Topanga and the Shalom Hills and Valley Jewish Cemetery with almost no recollection of having traveled. Within a few blocks of the main gates, the skies opened to one of those rare tropical storms. The weatherman attributed it to a low-pressure area but Mimi was certain that Sarah was making her presence known.

Rain continued to fall, torrential pelts sending sheets of water so blinding that not even high-speed window wipers could clear them away. Mimi was grateful to be in the car, grateful that she had come so close to the cemetery before the cloudburst. She checked the clock and saw that she had twenty minutes to spare.

"The City of the Angels and its storm drain systems are under siege," said the weatherman. "There are predictions of widespread flooding."

Mimi plowed through puddles that were beginning to resemble raging streams. On the passenger seat was the envelope with the grade sheet she had intended to drop off the day before. Now she had no choice but to return to campus after the service. Between choosing the right outfit, and making her way through commuter freeway traffic, she feared she was running late.

A rush of relief swept over her when the cemetery's imposing gates came into view. Driving through them, she followed the road through a series of turns and then parked. Her hands were clammy as she struggled to open the car door. Fighting a powerful gust of wind, she managed to free herself without coming to any harm. With her head bent against the rain, she fumbled with the umbrella. It popped open with a whoosh.

The short distance to Sarah's grave was accomplished with no small effort. Mimi had to keep her body bent into the wind to stay upright. A sudden gust inverted the umbrella, tearing its metal ribs away from the fabric. "Mary Poppins gone berserk," she mumbled, draping the tattered remnant over her head. By the time she arrived at the gravesite, she was drenched.

The family had already congregated, huddling together under the kind of oversized umbrella used by hotel doormen. Mimi recognized a few friends scattered about, but no Daniel. She could not believe that he would avoid this ceremony because of her. When she snuggled next to Joanna, the woman slipped her arm through Mimi's and squeezed it. Together they watched rainwater splash off the tarp covering Sarah's headstone.

Mimi hardly saw it, yet her eyes were riveted to that tarp. Why you, she thought. Why you and not me? Who gets to choose? When she caught sight of Daniel rushing toward them, holding a drenched newspaper over his head, she felt a palpable ache in her chest.

The service began. Everyone crowded closer, friends and family huddled together under a collection of umbrellas. The tarp collected rainwater; the runoff forced rivulets of dirt to striate the surface. Mimi resented the sullied tarp, yet at the same time feared its removal. Under it was the gravestone bearing Sarah's name.

"Perhaps God's plan is to cleanse," suggested the rabbi. "Rain is a nourishment of earth and spirit." Having said this, he nodded to Joanna, and the woman stepped forward and pulled the cloth from the headstone. Leaving it in a muddy heap near the grave, she returned to Mimi's side.

The rabbi recited the first prayer.

Mimi tried to concentrate on the rabbi's face, tilting her head as if this would help her absorb his words. She studied his mouth and the way his collar was improperly ironed; she stared at everyone and everything. She never once looked at the headstone.

"Lord of spirit and flesh," the rabbi intoned. "We have turned to you for comfort in these days and months of grief." There was a deafening rumble as the sky opened and cast a pelting rain upon the mourners. No umbrella could stop it from running down Mimi's collar and pooling in her shoes. "And now we rise up to face the tasks of life once more." The man had repeated this so often he no longer needed to glance at the page.

To face the tasks of life. Mimi looked toward Daniel but he was no longer there. She heard the rabbi reading from Psalms. "A woman of valor. Seek her out, for she is to be valued above rubies. Give her honor for her work; her life proclaims her praise." Not until Joanna handed her a tissue did Mimi realize that she was crying. A woman of valor.

They recited the Twenty-third Psalm, The Lord is My Shepherd, followed by the closing prayer: Kaddish, the mourner's prayer. It was the same prayer chanted over the graves of Szulen and Fredl, over Mottel, Bayla, Rahel and Shmuel; over Grischa and Malka. But never over the bodies of Hannah and her children, husband, brothers, aunts, uncles, and cousins. Their final resting place had been a mass grave, a crematorium; ashes drifting over shtetls where they had once lived.

It took prodigious courage for Mimi to finally shift her eyes to headstone.

SARAH LEHMANN ARCARIO

1944–1984

ADORED DAUGHTER, WIFE, MOTHER, FRIEND

The words burned into her eyes until she could no longer see. When a hand gripped her elbow, she knew without looking that it was Daniel. Who else but Daniel would buttress her, steady her? Who else but Daniel would be there for her?

His presence gave her the heart to look again at the stone. The name carved on the marble struck her like the clarion call of trumpets, the final declaration of the truth: Sarah was dead. Look, it said, the name is carved in stone. Neither wishing nor dreaming, pleading nor pretending can change that reality. This is how it is and will always be.

After several more minutes, Joanna and the others walked away. Mimi remained with Daniel still by her side, hand gripping her elbow as a reminder of his support. It was not until they reached her car that he finally spoke. "I miss her, too," he said.

Mimi turned and touched his face, the warmth of his skin on her fingers.

"Get in the car," he told her, his voice gruff. "You're already soaked."

Struggling against the wind, she climbed in. Daniel closed the door and then tapped on the window. Mimi lowered it, the rainwater gusting in leaving wet marks across the dashboard.

"Tune your radio to the highway reports, okay? They were about to close the canyons when I got here."

Mimi met his gaze. "I'm on my way to the campus," she explained. "But I'll listen, I promise." When he appeared confused, she patted the envelope on the seat. "Grades."

Rain was running off his chin and dripping into the car. He backed away and then sprinted across the parking lot toward his car. Mimi watched him for a moment, closed the window and drove off.

The Golden State freeway was tediously slow. After several near misses she decided to take Sunset Boulevard, which proved even more harrowing. When she finally turned in at the faculty gate, she breathed a sigh of relief. The fire lane running alongside her building was practically empty, with occasional campus police officers to direct her away from flooded areas. With the place practically deserted, she pulled into the red zone twenty feet from the side door of her office. Pressing the envelope protectively against her, she raced inside, deposited the grades, rushed back out to the car and cranked up the heater. Slipping off her shoes, she rubbed warmth back into her feet and set off.

Wanting to avoid the hazards of the freeway, Mimi decided to take Sunset all the way to the coast and then come up Topanga from the back way. She had traveled nearly half the distance to the coast highway before remembering Daniel's warning. Turning on the radio, she discovered that slides had already closed down several sections of Pacific Coast Highway, and that two of those sections were north of Sunset. "Damn!" she muttered. Turning the car around, she headed back to the freeway. The sky was bucketing and there was no doubt that, with everyone trying to get home, she would be moving in inches. When the traffic advisory warned that all roads leading in and out of Topanga were closed, Mimi decided to ignore it. She drove a Volvo; it could go anywhere!

Passing successfully through several severely flooded areas, she arrived at the bottom of her road.

"This is an emergency broadcast," the voice on the radio was warning, as if speaking directly to her. "This is not a test. High waves are washing over Pacific Coast Highway and flash floods have been reported in the valley. Mud slides are blocking all access to the canyons and motorists are being warned to get off the roads."

Mimi circumvented the first slide and came upon a road crew setting up sawhorse barriers. A solidly built man draped in Day-Glo orange signaled her to turn back. Instead, she inched closer and honked.

"No can do!" he called out, pointing up the road. "The whole area's covered! You're talking twenty feet of debris!"

"What about the back road?"

"Worse yet, lady! Never seen 'em like this!"

He guided Mimi around mounds of rock and branches until she was clear of the debris. With both fists clenched around the steering wheel, she maneuvered the mud-slick turns. It wasn't until she achieved the final harrowing curve leading onto the lower straightaway of Mulholland Drive that she pulled to the side of the road and heaved a sigh of relief.

"Okay," she mumbled. "Let's look at the options." She could attempt an hour's drive to Boyle Heights, or drive over surface streets for perhaps fifteen minutes and go to Daniel's. If there was any debate, it was short and unequivocal.

When Mimi pulled into Daniel's driveway she was welcomed by a warm light casting its glow from the porch. The distance from her car to the front steps was a mere ten feet, but water rushing from the gutters and storm drains made it perilous.

Grabbing her purse and shoes, she hauled herself out of the car and sloshed her way toward the front door. It struck her that, considering everything, she was pretty gutsy arriving without notice, but she reasoned that she had no choice.

The front door swung open and Daniel raced out. Grabbing her arm, he hustled her toward the house. "If I had known you were coming," he called over the rain, "I would've built that ark!"

Safely inside, Mimi stripped off her dripping jacket. Daniel hung it in the downstairs bathroom and fetched a robe and warm socks. While she undressed, he returned to the family room and built a fire. By the time she joined him, the oak was ablaze and warmth was seeking every corner of the room. Her shoes, sitting on the hearth and propped as close to the flames as was safe, were already drying. Mimi picked them up and sighed. "Two hundred bucks," she said. "I wonder if they're covered under my homeowner's policy."

Daniel pushed a few logs around and the fire was transformed into a raging conflagration. Mimi stood as close as possible, turning to warm herself, and felt consoled by the scene. Her contentment was made that much sweeter by an oboe concerto filling the room.

When Daniel offered her a brandy, she curled up on the sofa and accepted. "Nice," she murmured, sipping the warmed liqueur. "Brandy, Haydn and warmth." Closing her eyes, she leaned back into the pillows, hardly aware of Daniel settling into the wingback across from her.

A crack of thunder rolled near the house and they both smiled. "This is how it was meant to be," he said.

Mimi opened her eyes. "Do you think?"

"I know," he replied, and the certainty in his voice left no doubt.

Mimi shifted her gaze outside. Sheets of rain fell onto the Italian pavers. She swished the brandy in its snifter and took a sip. "Crews are out in full force. I tried to get through. They say the slides are twenty feet deep."

Daniel crossed the room and returned with a portable phone. Settling back into the chair, he pushed a button and waited. Before Mimi could comment about a frequently called girlfriend, he held up a hand and listened. A moment later he punched in a code, listened, and then turned off the phone. "All the canyons are closed indefinitely." Mimi raised an eyebrow. "So I guess you'll have to stay."

"Or go to my mother's."

He paused. "Yes, or that."

Mimi felt the heat from the fire, heard the plaintive reedy cry from the oboe. Rain was falling hard against the deck and her mother's was the last place on earth she wanted to be.

Seated in the comfort of this wonderful room, she felt something. At first she could not define it, could not ascertain what it was. But it caused her to close her eyes. "I have to call Mama," she thought. The fire crackled and the thought slipped away as quickly as it had arrived. She glanced toward Daniel and smiled, felt something stirring, spreading throughout her body like the warmth of the brandy she was holding in her hands. It had been so long since she had felt this, had felt anything, for that matter. For one brief moment she was completely exposed, and then fearful that Daniel could see through her and sense her pleasure. The color rose in her face and she resembled a schoolgirl awkwardly confronting her own innocence. Another quick glance in Daniel's direction convinced her that he was relaxed, comfortable in her presence. The way it was meant to be, he had told her.

Daniel returned Mimi's glance and then smiled. Rising from the chair, he crossed to where she was sitting and joined her on the sofa. Mimi leaned into Daniel and allowed him to hold her.

Perhaps he was right. Perhaps this was a decision that had been made a very long time ago. And yes, of course she would stay. If this was where she belonged.